AN INCONVENIENT WAR

DUTY, HONOR, MONEY: THE BEGINNING

AN INCONVENIENT WAR

J. F. CRONIN

AN INCONVENIENT WAR
DUTY, HONOR, MONEY: THE BEGINNING

iUniverse books may be ordered through booksellers or by contacting:

iUniverse
1663 Liberty Drive
Bloomington, IN 47403
www.iuniverse.com
1-800-Authors (1-800-288-4677)

Because of the dynamic nature of the Internet, any web addresses or links contained in this book may have changed since publication and may no longer be valid. The views expressed in this work are solely those of the author and do not necessarily reflect the views of the publisher, and the publisher hereby disclaims any responsibility for them.

Certain stock imagery © Thinkstock.
Any people depicted in stock imagery provided by Thinkstock are models, and such images are being used for illustrative purposes only.

ISBN: 978-1-4917-3640-1 (e)
ISBN: 978-1-4917-3639-5 (sc)
ISBN: 978-1-4917-3641-8 (hc)

Library of Congress Control Number: 2014910833

Credit for the Maps: University of Texas Libraries
Kuwait Map: http://www.lib.utexas.edu/maps/middle_east_and_asia/kuwait_pol96.jpg
Pakistan Map: http://www.lib.utexas.edu/maps/middle_east_and_asia/pakistan_pol_2002.jpg

Printed in the United States of America.

iUniverse rev. date: 7/25/2014

THE GULF WAR

CHAPTER 1

IN THE SAUDI DESERT, FIFTEEN KILOMETERS SOUTHWEST OF QASR, KUWAIT

EARLY IN THE YEAR 1991

If war is hell, the marines on the front lines waiting for the start of the Gulf War were in purgatory. Those living in tents attached to the Saudi desert by double and triple tent pegs, to prevent the winds from creating canvas pennants, felt lucky for their time above the dirt. They all knew that their numbers would be called to man outposts. There, they would hunker down in fighting holes and spend a day looking into the blinding sun and a night that would chill them to their cores. In position to look into Kuwait, they would burrow into the ground, covering themselves with anything they could find that could help them beat the elements. They would look for an enemy that hadn't yet arrived, but whom, they were told, would. A twenty-four-hour shift was all they could handle mentally and physically. At the end of a day's stint, the uppers that had kept them alert wore off, and those who relieved them would pull their comatose bodies out of the dirt and recycle them back to the tents.

No matter in which part of the desert that marines resided, the daily grind entailed becoming familiar with chemical and biological suits. They were called MOPP (military-oriented protective posture) suits in military terminology, but the marines called them MFPS (mother fucking pieces of shit) because of the hardship involved in using them. The gas mask, part of the suit, had to be carried at all

times, and in a climate that was much too hot, the extra weight was
a burden. Drills were conducted to familiarize the marines with the
protective suits because it was expected that they would be exposed
to chemical and biological weapons. The goal was for marines to be
able to suit up in less than a minute. If the timelines were not met,
the drill was repeated. On hot days, the suits were worse than saunas,
and the effort required in getting them on and sitting in the sun was
unbearable. The troops laughed at the clothing drills. They, unlike
their superiors, knew there was no way to fight in the heavy gear.

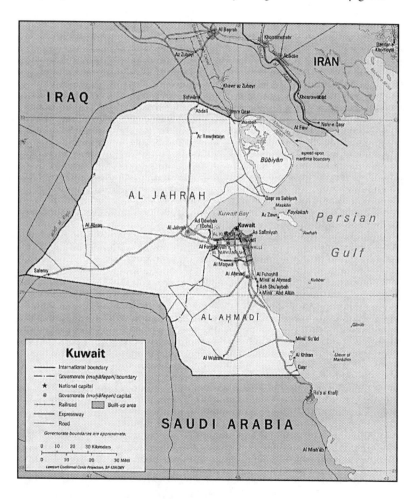

The Third Battalion, Third Marine Regiment, positioned abreast units of the Saudi National Guard, were acknowledged to have the greatest chance of encountering nontraditional methods of warfare. It was felt that the Iraqis would try to defeat the Saudis with chemical and biological weapons, as the Saudis' area of responsibility was between the Persian Gulf and the only north-south road running from Saudi Arabia through Kuwait. The four-lane artery paralleled the shoreline and was fashioned after the American interstate roads. It was the strategic objective in the eastern part of both Saudi Arabia and Kuwait and had to be held, because it was the only road capable of handling the volume of supplies that would follow the allies' assault north.

Lieutenant Colonel Jake Gregg, the battalion commander, had been assigned two missions. His battalion would be the easternmost American force in the ground assault of Kuwait, with the responsibility of anchoring the American line. The Third Battalion also had to secure the road to ensure that the Iraqis didn't use it to roll up the Saudi forces.

The battalion took pride in the fact that they had been given such a pivotal role. They thought that they were the best and had been picked for the job because their commander, Jake Gregg, was on the fast track to making general. He was respected throughout the Marine Corps, and, more importantly, he was respected by those he would lead into combat. The troops' affection for him was evidenced in their wont to define him. Many names floated around the battalion trying to characterize him, but the commonly used nickname was "Colonel Jake." It indicated the marines didn't overlook his rank but were comfortable enough to call him by his first name when he was out of sight.

Jake was a marine recruiter's dream. He was an athletic six foot three, with broad shoulders that tapered into his tight waist. Even in the desert, his uniform looked painted on. He had the uncanny knack of being able to sleep in the sand, awaken, brush off his uniform, and look as if he was ready for a photo shoot. When he smiled, the corners of his eyes tightened into crow's-feet, emitting a mischievous glint that made him seem playful. He had a dimpled square chin and straight white teeth. He would have been considered extraordinarily handsome if it weren't for his nose. It had been broken several times and had a slight twist where it hadn't healed correctly. His arms, exposed under the rolled-up sleeves of his utility uniform, were like hams, the result of a weightlifting training regimen he had adopted. He looked like a fashion model and linebacker in one person. For a man his age, forty-one, there was no evidence that he shaved. Marines had seen him lathered up with a razor in his hands, but there was never evidence of stubble. His close-cropped blond hair was so light that it looked white. Some marines toyed with the idea of calling him the silver fox, a play on the desert fox title given to Rommel in the African desert fifty years earlier.

The naming of the commander was a needed diversion, because the wait to go to war was agonizing. There were so many false alarms that troop leaders had to find ways for the marines to keep their fighting edge. Officers trained the troops and had ample time to repeat the drills. Several iterations through the same exercises, griping started, and nerves became frayed. The marines were in the desert to fight the Iraqis, and prevented from doing so, they sought anyone to fight, even their friends. Brawls were rampant, as amped-up young men took affront at minor transgressions and struck out to release the pressure.

On January 17, the air war started, and ground forces thought that at any moment they would be called upon. Their spirits rose in anticipation, but after watching flocks of planes fly over their position heading north, they were convinced that those running the war had forgotten them.

On the night of January 29, the Iraqis attacked the Saudi National Guard troops protecting the oil fields and oil terminal at Khafji, a port on the Persian Gulf south of the Kuwaiti border. The attack caught the American-led Coalition Forces off guard. After sending aircraft-gun-camera footage and glowing news reports home to the American people with inferences that the air war was going to be all that was needed to drive the Iraqis out of Kuwait, the attack caused panic. It hadn't been expected, and its success was an embarrassment.

Iraqi tanks and infantry, thought decimated by air attacks, crossed the border into Saudi Arabia and seized Khafji. It would have been a masterstroke, but the Iraqis didn't consolidate their position. They had the city and the oil terminal, and instead of driving forward to fortify their gains, they left the tanks and vehicles that hadn't made it to the city strung out in the desert. Exposed, the tanks and heavy equipment were easily targeted by airplanes, and within two days there was no way for the Iraqis to reinforce their lead elements.

Being the closest American unit, the Third Battalion prepared for an attack to relieve the pressure on the Saudis but received instruction to avoid a direct assault. The Saudis wanted to defeat the Iraqis on their own as a matter of national pride. The marines were given the mission of assisting the Saudis and did so by cutting through the Iraqi lines to prevent reinforcement. The Third Battalion wedged itself between advancing and retreating Iraqis.

The Iraqis advancing toward the city from the north were the easiest targets for airplanes, and only a few Iraqi tanks got to the Third Battalion's blocking position. The Iraqis retreating from Khafji were tougher. They were escaping and were frantic. Fighting bravely, they could not withstand the overpowering firepower the Third Battalion had at its disposal. In a war where the Iraqis expected dumb bombs, the weapons that were dropped were smart and could differentiate between a tank turret and the chassis. It confused the Iraqis, and they fought harder to escape the onslaught.

Jake led his troops in a multifaceted battle. Those Iraqis that had been pressed into service were quick dropouts of the fight. The Republican Guard units that were professional soldiers fought bravely and didn't cede ground until they were knocked off it. The trained units tried to change their tactics, thinking that if they engaged the Americans at night, they could overcome the total dominance from the air. They were unaware that targeting systems were night-capable and the shroud of darkness didn't protect them. By the time they engaged the marines most were on foot.

A command decision was made by people far removed from the firefights to call off the air support for the Third Battalion. It was determined that a million-dollar smart bomb was too steep a price to pay for one or two Iraqis retreating through the desert. By default the Third Battalion got the job of mopping up remnants of the retreating army in close-in combat.

A desperate enemy was dangerous, and they hit the marine lines in force in an effort to break through, and in many places the fight deteriorated to hand-to-hand.

Jake was all over the battlefield. If he physically couldn't reach one of his units, he was on the radio offering guidance. He felt that he needed to be in the fight so that he could sense how the ebb and flow was affecting the marines. He was up front to set an example, knowing if he showed he wouldn't waver, the marines wouldn't.

The battalion had been trained to keep attacking and moved north to capture any Iraqis that had slipped through their lines. They were stopped at the Kuwaiti border—not by the enemy but by higher headquarters. The Americans were making the same mistake the Iraqis had. They weren't pushing their advantage. Jake tried to argue the point, but the war was being fought on schedule, and the Coalition Command wasn't ready to barge into Kuwait.

Things changed for the Third Battalion after Khafji. The Iraqis started probing across the border and engaging isolated outposts. Jake asked for permission to run patrols into Kuwait to try to stop the raids, but his requests were denied. He was informed that the battalion could engage the enemy and pursue them to the border, no further.

At 0200, Major Jim Ajo, the battalion executive officer, opened the flap on Jake's tent and entered. His flashlight threw an eerie beam that found Jake's face.

"Skipper, wake up."Ajo shook him.

Jake was instantly alert. "What's up?"

"We have a situation at outpost Sells. It was overrun, and by the time the reaction force got to it, they found four marines dead. They are bringing in the bodies."

"Any indication of which Iraqi forces were involved?"

"The reaction force thinks they are out of Qasr. At least they used the tactics the Qasr units have been using. They sent three units out, willing to sacrifice one or two to our air if we could get it overhead. We couldn't, and the three units joined at the border and came across. Once they took Sells, they retreated and split up to return to Qasr."

Jake thought about the situation at the outposts. "Here's what I want done. Re-man Sells, and beef up all the outposts. I want a quick reaction forces one sand dune away. If the Iraqis come across the border again, I want the reaction forces to follow them back into Kuwait to destroy their vehicles. If they are in contact, I want the Iraqis pursued until they break it off or the marines become too extended. This crap has to be stopped."

The Third Battalion was suffering under policies that made no sense to marines who were losing friends, and Jake thought if he could inflict damage to the Iraqis by engaging them in their safe haven, the across-the-border assaults might stop.

"Jake, we've been ordered not to pursue. You can't do it."

"We all know that we are going to be crossing the border in the near future to fight this war. We can't keep losing marines while we wait for the orders to fight an epic battle. I'll take responsibility for starting early."

Jim Aho had served as Jake's executive officer for almost a year and knew his quirks. Jake was protective of his troops. He was losing marines to an enemy killing and running to safe ground. Ajo knew that irked his boss. He didn't think it would do any good, but he had to caution Jake about disobeying orders.

"We have been specifically prohibited from crossing the border. If you do, even if you defeat the entire Iraqi Army, the powers that be will hang you. You've got too much at stake to risk it." Ajo referred to the upward path of Jake's career.

"When I start worrying about how doing the right thing might negatively affect me, it will be time for me to hang it up. I have an obligation to these kids to look out for their safety, and that is more important than having this war kick off in one grand battle. You've seen the plans. The assault is all about perception. The Combined Command wants the grand coalition to jump into action at one time. It makes for great theater, and the marines dying every night are pawns in the larger game. As their commander, I can't sit by and let more die needlessly."

"You're the boss, and I know how you feel, but I hate to see you piss your career away," Aho consoled.

"Don't worry about it. I was looking for a job before I got this one." Jake smiled, but Ajo was concerned.

The plans for the quick reaction forces to cross the border were set in place for the night of the twenty-fifth of February. The warning order for the ground war arrived the night of the twenty-third. The ground offensive would start the following day.

In the lead-up to the war, aircraft could be seen overhead carrying their deadly ordnance somewhere north into Kuwait. On the day of the assault, the sky was dark with airplanes dropping ordnance in proximity to the front lines, and the marines were afforded a deadly air show. As the planes did their damage and departed an artillery barrage, unlike any the marines had seen or heard in their time in the desert, was unleashed. Observing the killing grounds, it was unimaginable that anyone could have survived the onslaught.

While the marines in the Third Battalion appreciated the beating the desert took, they knew that the Iraqis were in the coastal cities and that they were going to be the closest American unit to them. The beach cities sitting between the Persian Gulf and the road were left untouched in an effort to protect infrastructure that would be needed after the war to get Kuwait up and running.

The problem the battalion faced was that they had to anchor the eastern end of the coalition assault while maintaining contact with the Saudis to their east. They were militaries that fought wars differently. The marines used maneuver warfare, where authority and responsibility were given to small-unit commanders, and they responded to the situations that faced them. In having worked with the Saudis at Khafji, Jake knew their command and control was centralized. Decisions were made at the high command level, where the overriding aim was to mass superior firepower and invest objectives in form of siege warfare. As the marines would be tearing across the desert, the Saudis would be moving methodically. Staying in contact with two militaries that fought wars differently, the Third Battalion had to prevent itself from becoming stretched too thin.

The coalition war plan called for a steady advance, not taking into consideration the problems the Third Battalion would face. Jake's concerns were that in moving north, the Saudis would get through the first city, Qasr, but that the Iraqis would retreat and join forces in the cities farther north, slowing the Saudi advance. Each successive city would become more formidable until the distance between the main American assault and the Saudis would become problematic, leaving his battalion strung out. Although there were no cities on his side of the road, and the Saudis had the job of clearing the coast, he knew the marines were going to have to break out of their area of responsibility and get into the fight for the cities.

Jake discussed various scenarios with his superiors and was told he could do what he felt needed to be done, but he couldn't allow the straight-line offensive to bend. He thought about risking lives to meet an arbitrary goal, a straight line in the sand, and decided he would operate in a way that would minimize the danger to his marines.

Beach cities stretched out before the Saudis like a string of pearls. The desert surrounding them prevented urban sprawl, and each city was an individual objective.

The assault on both sides of the highway kicked off and went as expected. The Saudis kept up the pace of advance until they reached Qasr, the southernmost city. With the marines racing north, attacking targets of opportunity, the Saudis started massing for a siege. As the hours passed, the Third Battalion's lines contorted, and staying in contact on both flanks left them vulnerable to counterattack.

The situation on the ground was untenable, and Jake made the decision at Qasr to support the Saudis. As the Saudis were lining up their tanks and artillery to attack, the Third Battalion crossed over the highway boundary line between units and attacked Qasr from the west, negating the need for a Saudi frontal attack.

The lead element in the marine attack was a company of light armored vehicles. Dismounting from the vehicles, the marines didn't push into the city. With the Saudis' overwhelming numbers to the south, the Iraqis were squeezed between the marines and the sea, and they took the escape route north that was left open. When the city was emptied of Iraqis, the Saudis sped to catch up to the coalition offensive, and almost did until they reached Al Khiran.

The Third Battalion struck at Al Khiran as they had Qsar and watched as some Iraqi troops fled before the Saudis got into an attack position. As the second city fell, those Iraqis remaining did not retreat to augment troops in the cities farther north. They turned west toward the strung-out Third Battalion lines. It was a soft spot any military would have tried to exploit.

The vanguard of the Iraqi force was a Republican Guard battalion spearheaded by three tanks. Trying to exploit the thinness of the marines' lines, they paused to consolidate their forces for an assault that would take them to the rear of the coalition offensive.

Taking the path of least resistance, they followed a dried riverbed that would take them through hastily manned marine positions. As the wadi would have channeled water, it provided a path of least resistance for the Iraqis. The tanks moved easily, but as they did, they broke through the crust of the sandy soil, and the heavy metal treads threw up clouds of dust and dirt that made breathing difficult for the trailing foot soldiers. With the infantry loathe to breathe tank exhaust and dirt, they lagged, and the gap between armor and infantry grew.

Third Battalion's infantry companies were with the main assault moving north, and Jake couldn't recall them to counter the move the Iraqis were making. The manpower available to make a stand consisted of the light armored vehicles used in the attacks on the cities and the marines on the battalion staff. As every marine was trained as a rifleman, Jake took cooks, clerks, truck drivers, and mechanics and hastily organized them into squads that were rushed into positions to face the advancing Iraqis.

The site Jake selected to counter the Iraqi advance was a sharp bend in the dried riverbed. The turn was so acute that the tanks would make the corner and the infantry would be out of sight and out of the protection of the tanks' guns. Selecting a position that was about fifteen feet above the base of the hundred-foot-wide dried water course, the marines waited undetected and watched the enemy advance unfold below them.

The Third Battalion's heavy antitank weapons were with the main assault, and all the marines plugged into action had available were light antitank weapons (LAWs). They would be of no use against heavy main battle tanks, and two of the three tanks moving toward the marines were main battle tanks. With the riverbed restricting the tanks, they could spread no wider than two abreast, but they moved faster than the infantry could walk. As the foot soldiers lagged farther behind the armor, they were easy targets for the marines on the rims above the riverbed.

With the senior officers with the bulk of the battalion, Jake took command of the fight that was brewing.

"Here's how I see this thing going down. I don't think these guys have good comm between units. You can see the tanks' turrets are open and the tankers signaling with flags and light signals. So." He sucked in a deep breath because when he exhaled he was going to tell them how they were going to defeat a much larger and heavily armed enemy.

"Since these guys haven't put out any outriders, they don't know we are here. I think they are going to proceed to the highway and swing north to create havoc in the rear of the main assault. Our job is to stop them." He received many "are you crazy?" looks.

"Once the tanks pass, we are going to have to separate them from the infantry. Are any of you expert shooters?"

The marines shied away from the question, and one raised his hand.

"Are you good or did you just have a good day on the rifle range?"

"I'm good."

"Great. Here's what I need you to do. We are going to be taking on these guys in a couple of minutes. When everyone starts firing at the infantry, I want you to concentrate on the tankers that have their heads sticking out of the turrets. You have to scare them so that they will close their hatches. If we can do that, the tanks and the infantry may not be able to communicate. Think you can do that?"

"Yes, sir."

"Good man." Jake displayed a coolness he didn't feel. "Who's the best driver here?"

"I am, sir." A baby-faced marine spoke.

"Okay, you're my driver. I'm going to need a volunteer to come along with us on a ride that may not end well."

Several marines volunteered.

"You." Jake picked one who looked as if he were too young to shave. "Here's the deal. Once the firing starts, we are going to take a

Humvee over the embankment and into the wadi. My ace driver is going to go as fast as he can at the tanks. We are not going to be able to stop to get a stable shot, but we are going to have to get in close to have a chance of scoring a hit." Jake paused. "You," he spoke to the marine who volunteered. "Have you ever trained with a LAW?"

"No, sir."

Jake had expected as much. The marines he was leading weren't grunts and would not have had the training. "That's okay. This is a LAW." He showed it to the young volunteer. "It is loaded, as are all the LAWs in the Hummer. You flip this switch and this switch, and you get these lights, meaning it is ready to fire. Once I fire, I'm going to chuck the spent LAW tube overboard, and I want a fully ready tube ready to go. Think you can do that?"

"Yes, sir."

"Look at the switches and make sure you can flip them because once we start, there can be no mistakes. Hot Rod," he named the driver. "The tanks have forward-firing machine guns, so we'll make our firing runs from the rear. Don't get ahead of any of them unless they are disabled." As Jake finished, he couldn't believe what he had proposed.

The fight started, and casualties caused the Iraqi foot soldiers to stop while the tanks rolled forward. With the separation opened, Jake had the driver roll over the embankment, and, like a dune buggy going down a dune, they slid and powered their way toward the tanks. They didn't go after the main battle tanks. The driver chased the lighter tank, which could be disabled by the LAW's armor-piercing shells.

The first shot wasn't a success. The Hummer had to swerve to miss a rock, and Jake's shot sailed wide. The second shot was more stable and penetrated the tank's fuel cells, causing them to explode. After three successive misses, two shots hit the heavy tanks, but they remained unharmed. Flitting in and out and swerving to eliminate becoming a target, Jake couldn't get off a shot as the tanks' gun muzzles tracked him. Taking a chance, he had the driver go between the tanks so that if the main guns targeted the hummer, they also had the other tank in their sights. It would cause them to hold their fire.

Once between the tanks, Jake had the driver dart in close. With a hit, a tank spun toward him. Unable to stop, Jake had to get in closer. Firing, the missile hit the tread sprocket and the tread unraveled, but molten metal ricocheted and found his shoulder. It gashed his skin, but the hot metal cauterized the wound as it passed through flesh. The pain made him momentarily dizzy, but he fought the urge to pass out and continued to direct the driver.

Trying to figure out what to do next, Jake witnessed an act of heroism that stunned him. The lead tank climbed out of the riverbed. Sure that it had the marines trapped, it didn't bother to fire its machine gun. It lowered its turret gun to blast the marine position. A young clerk stood and faced down the tank. Rifle in hand, the clerk fired at the tank gun that was aiming at him. Somehow, either the marine or one of his comrades managed to get a slug or several into the gun's muzzle, or the Iraqis had loaded a defective shell, but when it fired to kill all in its path, smoke and fire belched, and the unintended explosion caused the tank's gun to peel back like a half-eaten banana. No one cared, because the tank hatch flew open, and the Iraqis surrendered.

Jake had not expected mass surrenders and little accommodation had been made to handle prisoners of war. As the numbers grew, Jake had to take marines out of the assault to become wardens of fenceless POW camps. Sensing the mood of the troops, he had to prevent young marines who were serving as prisoner guards over an enemy that moments before had been trying to kill them from seeking revenge. Marines couldn't be trying to kill Iraqis one moment and turn into their protectors the next, and Jake didn't want young marines making emotional mistakes. He took officers out of the fight to maintain control and ensure that there were no acts of revenge.

With the Saudis facing light resistance, progress in the battalion's sector was speeded up, and Jake directed the battalion's advance from a mobile command post. He listened to reports of dead and wounded as some Iraqis stood and fought from fortified positions. As the intensity of the fights grew, casualties increased, and Jake guessed that a lot more marines were going to have to sacrifice.

To the chagrin of all those who warned him about staying in line, the Third Battalion had to be stopped at the Kuwait airport. The marines waited while the Saudis caught up and passed through their lines. The Saudis would be the liberators, not the Americans.

The battalion had taken casualties, and Jake was piecing together units, waiting for the order to continue into Iraq. Scuttlebutt swept through the ranks that a cease-fire was being negotiated. Rumor had it that there were politicians who wanted to continue the war. The marines laughed at those wanting a continuance. They hadn't lived in the dirt or had to wear MOPP gear into battle. They hadn't had to carry a dead friend out of the fight.

Jake thought about the letters he would have to write to parents and loved ones telling them of their child's, husband's, father's, brother's valor and selflessness. It was a job he detested, and stopping the war might not make sense to those who hadn't had to fight it, but for those who had lived and died in the sand, it was the right thing to do.

In the aftermath of the battle in the wadi, Jake put seven cooks, a driver, and six clerks in for awards for heroism. Missing from those receiving recognition was Jake himself. He squashed the attempts of anyone trying to get him a medal. He considered the recognition and the respect of his troops reward enough.

CHAPTER 2

MARINE CORPS BASE, CAMP PENDLETON, CALIFORNIA

The ear-shattering roar of artillery fire usually looming over the California Marine Corps base was replaced by a stultifying silence. The majority of the marines and their weapons had deployed to Saudi Arabia. Those few remaining, including prisoners, patients, and women marines, didn't have a lot to do. With stay-behind personnel idling in place, commanders took the old puritan admonishment that "idle hands were the devil's workshop" to heart and invented work. Offices not painted in decades received facelifts, and lawns were mowed and re-mowed to putting green perfection to ensure that there were no idle hands.

When the ground war kicked off, anxiety among the marines at Pendleton was evident. All had friends in the fight, and every television in every office was turned on to follow the war. With the good news coming from the front, commanders were faced with a new set of problems. Young marines who had kept their emotions under wraps were ready to party, and commanders, fearful that their troops would find ways to get into trouble, organized athletic competitions in an effort to burn off pent-up energy.

First Lieutenant Fran Matthews was one of those who hadn't deployed. It wasn't her choice. An intelligence officer with skills that could have been used in the war, she was left behind along with other women marines. It was felt that their uniformed presence might offend Arabic cultural mores, and qualified women marines were shifted to jobs where they waited out the war.

With no training, Fran was assigned to an Air Control Group and was given oversight of air controllers handling airplanes operating in and out of the base. Since most of the base's airplanes were deployed, there wasn't much for air controllers to do. To stay busy, she volunteered to become an investigating officer looking into petty offenses within the command. She had little interest in pursuing minor crimes to judicial ends, but it was something to do where she had to think.

With the war coming to a rapid close, marines gladly loaded buses that would take them to the Del Mar beach for an athletic field day. By noon, the troops were gathered, nets were strung, and teams were picked for a version of beach volleyball.

Fran had played volleyball in college and glided over the sand. Athletic, and with a familiarity for the game, she could set the ball for other players, and if anyone positioned the ball for her, she could get up above the net and spike it.

On a warm day, where everyone wore bathing suits or cutoff shorts, she wore a bikini hidden under an oversized sleeveless T-shirt top. Her uncovered legs were muscular, and her long arms were toned. Moving effortlessly, she went from frontcourt to backcourt more quickly than her teammates, and playing against the men, she was determined to win. Having grown up with four athletic brothers who dragged her into their games, she was used to the rough and tumble of competing against men. She learned at a young age that she had to compete and not be bothered by the taunts of boys who didn't want her involved in their games.

Normally affable, she focused on winning, and her face lost any hint of softness. Her green eyes, set wide and highlighting a small turned-up nose, were expressive and told everyone on both sides of the net that she was playing for keeps. When on duty, she wore her hair close, but on the beach her honey-blonde hair fell to shoulder length and danced over her neck in rhythm with her body.

Fran was too beautiful a presence among gnarly young men not to draw their attention. She could hear their comments, and was embarrassed for those who made them. She had played volleyball at the Naval Academy and was used to playing before crowds in short shorts and figure-revealing tops. She had never bothered to think about her body and the effect it might be having on people who watched her. In listening to young male marines comment on her figure, she regretted that she hadn't dressed differently.

As the games went on, her cheeks flushed, and her smooth skin radiated under a film of sweat. Working hard, her breath shortened, and she gulped in air, causing her chest to heave against the tee top with every inhalation. Her sensual appearance excited young eighteen- and nineteen-year-old men-boys, who became more sexually vocal. Each time she elevated her arms to set the ball, her shirt rose, exposing her flat stomach and hipbones and directing all eyes to the patch of cloth, the bikini bottom, covering her crotch. It was like waving a red flag before a bunch of young bulls. They snorted and pawed and really didn't know what to do, but they wanted to see more.

She was an officer and could have ordered them to stop off-color comments, but no good would come of it. They would stop for a minute and change their positions to hide in a crowd, but the calls would start again. What she couldn't understand was why the male officers didn't stop the behavior that she deemed inappropriate.

Her team won the Commanding Officer's Trophy, a six-pack. It wasn't much, but winning had been fun and Fran stood with the victorious team members sipping a victory beer.

"A group of the officers and their wives are going to go to dinner at the Crab Pot down at the pier this evening. We'd like it if you came," her section leader, Captain Tim Pitt, said in a casual manner. He was six feet, an inch taller than Fran, and was older. He had the paunch of an officer who sat too much. Up until the invitation, he had been unfriendly and had barely spoken to her. He seemed intent on keeping her, an officer on temporary duty in his section, at a distance. Fran thought that after almost ten weeks, it was about time she was welcomed.

Fran had enough time to return to her room, shower, and change. She blew dry her hair so that it looked silkier and combed a strand so that it fell over her left eye. Since Pitt hadn't mentioned what the others would be wearing, and she assumed it was a casual gathering and put on an IZOD knit shirt and a miniskirt. Leaving her apartment, she didn't look like a marine officer; she looked like a Southern California beach girl and younger than her twenty-three years.

The Crab Pot was not what she expected. It was in a great location on a marina, but it didn't fit. In a row of four upscale restaurants, it was the one that didn't belong. The exterior was dimly lit, with most of the light coming from overhead lights in the parking lot. The neon sign identifying the building was not working, so she had to guess she was at the right place. It looked seedy, the type of place where locals hid to avoid the tourists. The tin roof was rusted, but in the semidarkness it was difficult to tell if that was the result of a California designer's attempt to make it look weather-worn or if normal wear and tear hadn't been repaired. Trash was blown up against the sides of the building, and the trash cans outside the entrance were overflowing.

Fran entered reluctantly, and the low impression she formed on the outside carried over. The Crab Pot billed itself as a seafood restaurant, and efforts had been made to make the place look nautical, but the fishing nets strung through the rafters were dirty, and broken spiderwebs dangled from them like stalactites heavy with dust. Overhead recessed lights were dim, making it hard to see across the full length of the room. A U-shaped bar dominated the space.

It was a drinkers' bar, and she couldn't understand why the Control Group officers would take their spouses there for dinner.

She saw Captain Pitt sitting alone in a booth and sensed that something was wrong. She had expected most of the officers to be with him, but in looking at the table he occupied, it had setups for only two people.

He waved her over. "You look great," Pitt complimented her. The way he looked at her was not normal. He didn't focus on her face. Instead, he looked at her breasts and made no attempt to soften his stare.

"Thanks." She brushed aside the compliment. "Where is everyone?"

"They backed out. They said they had already had too much to drink. So it is you and me." He didn't take his eyes off her, and it made Fran uncomfortable.

She didn't want to be alone with him because it smacked of being a date, and that wasn't her intent, causing her to worry that if she backed out it might make her situation at work untenable.

"Sit down." Pitt stood and allowed her to slide into the booth opposite him. When she sat, he didn't return to the seat he had occupied but slid in next to her. She was between Pitt and the wall and didn't like the feeling.

"What would you like to drink?" He waved the waitress over.

'I'll have a Virgin Mary." Fran wasn't going to drink because she didn't like the way the evening was shaping up, wondering what would have caused a dozen officers to back out of a unit function. She could think of no reason. At least one other officer should have been there.

"Would you like another?" the waitress asked Pitt

"Yeah. The usual." He handed over his empty glass. As he did so, the waitress arched her eyebrows and flipped her head. It was a signal Fran picked up. She was sure the waitress was warning her about Pitt.

"I know you drink. I saw you drinking beer at the beach."

"I have to drive, and I don't want anything else."

"Why not? If you get too drunk, I'll drive you home." He patted her hand.

The drinks arrived and Pitt ordered the waitress to bring Fran something with bite.

"What do you want? Order anything, and put it on my tab."

"If it's okay, I'd like to order dinner. I'm starved."

The meal was unbearable. Pitt's company took away her appetite. He continued to drink, and his speech became slurred. After each drink, he pressed in closer until he had Fran pinned against the wall. When she could slide no farther, his hand touched her leg. The first time it happened, she tried to reason with him, but he ignored her requests to move away.

"You're beautiful. I want you," he slobbered.

"Captain, this is inappropriate." She pushed him away.

"Aw. Come on. I'm paying you a compliment." He tried to kiss her, but she was strong enough to stop his advance.

The physical contact excited him, and he reached under her dress, trying to fondle her. With all her strength, she shoved him.

With the rebuff, he grew more excited, and his hands groped for her breasts, clumsily pawing her shirt, ripping open the top button.

With her back against the wall, she swung her legs onto the bench seat and pushed him out of the booth. It aroused him sexually, and he went berserk.

"You fucking bitch. What is it? Are you too good for me?"

There was no reasoning with him. He was angry and tried to punch her. Fran backed away and took the brunt of the blow in her shoulder.

She couldn't get around him and didn't know what to do.

The bartender, seeing what was happening, got between them. "Hey, marine, Tim." He knew Pitt and tried to calm him. "I've warned you about this kind of behavior before. I'm not going to warn you again. This is the last time. You're outta here."

It was all Fran heard. In the space opened by the bartender, she ran. Fearing for her safety, she went to her car and locked herself in. Emotionally shaken, she fumbled with her keys and had difficulty getting them into the ignition. Managing to start her car after several attempts, she sped out of the parking lot before Pitt came out of the bar.

She drove in a haze, trying to comprehend what had happened. Pitt was her boss and a marine officer. There should have been a mutual respect and a distance maintained. Looking in the rearview mirror, she could see scratch marks on her neck where he had torn open her shirt. She didn't have to look at the shoulder he punched. It hurt, and she assumed that it was going to be bruised. Her upper legs had scratch marks, but she hadn't been violated.

With emotions between rage and fear, she drove and didn't bother to return to her room. The bartender's words warning Pitt "again" stuck in her mind. Fran thought about the words and assumed that Pitt had acted that way before. If he attacked her, there had to have been others, perhaps young enlisted female marines. They would have succumbed to him because he was an officer. She was furious. If Pitt was preying on female marines, she had to try to stop him.

Fran called in sick for work the day the Gulf War ended, knowing her absence wouldn't be noted and extended her time off into the weekend in an effort to ferret out her emotions. Unable to escape the thoughts of the events in the bar, she didn't want to talk to friends, and the self-imposed isolation left her prey to the randomness of her imagination. She thought of a thousand different scenarios, things she might do to stop Pitt, whom she had come to see as a serial predator. There were no easy answers. Not knowing if the witnesses in the bar would support her or dismiss her claims as Pitt being just a guy having fun, she didn't know what to do. Taking her issues to civilian authorities was an option, but she and Pitt were marines.

She decided it was an issue that had to be settled within the Marine Corps.

She called the Control Group adjutant and requested "mast," a hearing, with the commanding officer. It was every marine's right to speak to his or her commander to address issues of a personal nature that could be resolved at the command level. On temporary duty, technically she wasn't part of the Control Group, but the commanding officer became hers by default. Fran was surprised after telling the adjutant that the issues she wished to speak to the CO about were personal and urgent, that she was scheduled two weeks in the future.

In the waiting period, she sensed the marines in her office distancing themselves and was sure Pitt had told his version of the events. Since he would be in the unit long after she left, and the marines would have to continue working with him and for him, they seemed to take his side. Fran was ostracized for being a victim and wondered if she was making too big a deal of it. She began to rationalize that she might have had some fault in the encounter by not leaving when she saw that Pitt was alone in the bar, and toyed with the idea of canceling her "mast" and living with the events.

Sitting at her desk, she looked through a pile of correspondence and came upon a white envelope addressed to "Lieutenant Matthews." She didn't know what to expect and thought the worst, thinking that it might be a threat.

Opening it slowly, she read the few words scrawled on a piece of lined yellow legal paper: "Lieutenant Matthews, please stop him." Fran looked up quickly to see if the women marines working around her would give an indication of who might have placed the letter on her desk. All had their heads down. They were too intent. Fran didn't ask any questions, but any thoughts about not going forward with her complaint were dispelled.

She entered the CO's office after working hours on a Friday afternoon wearing camo utilities, the work uniform. She was immediately put on the defensive. Lieutenant Colonel O. J. Hartlet, the CO, had changed uniforms without having informed her, and Fran felt underdressed. He wore his ribbons and badges, giving his tan shirt color. His sandy crew-cut hair was giving way to male pattern baldness, and his flushed skin made him look as if he had high blood pressure. For a man in his early forties, it wasn't a good look.

He didn't bother to stand but sat with his feet propped on his gunmetal-grey desk. His office, with a view of the Pacific Ocean, was bleak. A false ceiling hid fluorescent lighting that hummed to an annoying level. Perfectly square, the boxlike room had gray walls the color of the desk. An attempt had been made to give the office some color by painting the concrete floor red with yellow footprints leading to Hartlet's desk. A leather couch along the wall was sagged and torn and didn't look inviting. Several straight-backed chairs were scattered about, and Hartlet instructed Fran to sit in the one across the desk from him.

"You requested to see me, so I guess you have a problem. What is it?" There was no greeting, no warmth. His attitude indicated that Fran was wasting his time, and on a Friday afternoon he had better things to do.

"Yes sir, and I want to thank you for taking the time to listen to me," she said, hoping to make him think he was doing her a favor, when in fact it was his duty to listen to her.

"Just so that we don't take up too much time, I think I know what this is all about." He let his feet fall to the floor loudly and leaned forward over the desk. "Captain Pitt has already been in to see me, and he told me that things got out of hand between the two of you. He apologized profusely and admitted he may have made a mistake. Now, I don't want this to turn into couples' counseling. And I surely don't want to get between a 'he said, she said' tiff." Hartlet paused. "I think his apology was sincere. Does that solve your problem?"

Fran felt like she had been slapped in the face. She didn't know what Pitt had told Hartlet, or whether they had had a good laugh over it, but an apology given through a second party wasn't going to cut it.

"Sir, did Captain Pitt tell you that he molested me in a public place and had to be pulled away from me physically?"

Hartlet's nonchalance faded, and he sat erect in his chair. Fran's words were the kind that could not be ignored.

"What happened?"

Fran related the story. She couldn't show the scratches on her neck or the bruises she received because time had healed them, but she made a case that she had been sexually assaulted.

"Pitt told me that you both were drinking at the beach."

"Everyone was drinking. I was playing volleyball, and it was hot, and I had a beer."

"But you were drinking."

"Yes, sir."

"Pitt told me that you wore provocative clothes for your date."

She couldn't believe the case Hartlet was making.

"There was no date." She almost shouted. "The captain told me that the other officers and their spouses would be in attendance. They weren't."

"But you had been drinking and were dressed to suggest that you might want to be involved with him?"

"Sir, you're wrong. I have no blame in this. I was sexually assaulted by a senior officer. I came to you for redress within the system, and I can see that isn't going to happen. I have no choice but to go to civilian authorities." She sensed that the "good old boys club" was going to protect one of its own and stood to leave.

"Sit down," Hartlet ordered. "Tim Pitt is a good marine, and if you go forward with this you'll destroy his career. That is your upside. The downside is that if you win this fight, you'll not only destroy his career, you'll put the entire Marine Corps in a bad light, and you'll destroy your career." He looked directly at her and enunciated his words so that she would get the meaning. "The Corps is a small outfit. Given that, you'd never be able to keep the fact that you destroyed a respected marine's career under wraps. When the word got out, and it would, there wouldn't be a male officer who would feel comfortable working with you. If no one will work with you, you will have no career."

"What he did was wrong. It is illegal in this country."

"Legality is not what I'm talking about. I'm talking about your future. If you were my daughter, and this happened to her, I'd tell her to pursue this until she got satisfaction. However, my daughter isn't trying to make a career in the Marine Corps." Hartlet softened. "Listen, what Pitt did was wrong. The question is are you so damaged by this incident that you are willing to sacrifice your future in the Marine Corps?"

Fran was indignant. She was being offered a choice of having a career or trying to right a wrong.

Hartlet broke into her confusion. "If you have a sexual assault case in your record, people are going to see you as trouble, and there won't be a commanding officer who would take a chance on you. It's not fair, but people in the Marine Corps know Tim Pitt, and if he goes down the drain, so will you. It's your choice. I'll write a letter of reprimand or assign the case to an Article 32 investigation, either of which will end his career, but as soon as the word gets out, you will be toast." He paused. "Have you noticed that on a late Friday afternoon, no one has left work? They all know your reason for being here, and you are going to have to decide what you want me to do."

Fran was stunned. She disliked what she heard and had to decide whether she could live with the memory of the assault. The physical scars had healed, and she hoped over time the memory would vanish.

"It appears I have little choice." When she said it, she wanted to crawl away.

"I think you've made a wise choice." The relief on Hartlet's face was evident. He was saved from having to destroy the career of a friend. He didn't care about her. "So that you won't have to work in the same office as Tim, I'm going to have you transferred out of the unit. I'll get you located somewhere on base so that you won't have to worry about him."

CHAPTER 3

THE WHITE HOUSE, WASHINGTON, DC

FEBRUARY 1991

Don Frieze, the undersecretary of defense, rushed across the city to attend a cabinet meeting at the White House. His position in the Defense Department didn't require his inclusion among the principal decision makers in government, but he was a man who exerted more influence than that of an undersecretary. He arrived early, as did the key players scheduled to attend a meeting in the executive conference room off the Oval Office.

A polished teak table surrounded by twenty-four leather chairs was covered with briefing books that contained the latest data on the war. Attendees had a book next to their nameplate, identifying them and their positions in the government. The nameplates were superfluous. The men sitting around the table were friendly and communicated on a daily basis, but they made small talk to avoid getting out ahead of what the president might say.

Like all Washington meetings there was a pecking order. The principals sat at the conference table, and directly behind them, against the walls, were one or two assistants who could feed them answers. An indication of Frieze's influence could be seen in where he sat. He was at the table, wedged between the secretaries of defense and state. The SECDEF considered Frieze his most trusted aide and wanted him close because he agreed with what Frieze might be given a chance to advocate. The SECDEF didn't want to be a proponent. He wanted to lurk in the shadows and let Frieze run interference.

A political insider, Don Frieze had lived off the government. Regardless the political party of the elected administration, he always had a job because he was considered brilliant, a reputation that he carefully nurtured. He was the consummate ideas man, who didn't busy himself with day-to-day problems. He had a clear vision of the world and wanted to solve its problems.

Short and broad-shouldered, he had a natural stoop that caused him to raise his head no matter the height of the person to whom he was speaking. Wearing a perpetually rumpled suit that exaggerated his no-nonsense appearance, he looked like an absentminded professor. That wasn't the case. He was a type A personality that worked prodigious hours. With a full head of black hair flecked with gray at the temples, it made it difficult to pinpoint his age. His face had many distinguishing characteristics, but the compilation didn't exude character. His ears drew attention because they were large and hung like pennants from the sides of his head. They made the back of his head look wide and every other feature was pinched in front of them. A hawk nose dominated his face, and dark brown eyes were feral, darting, seeing no joy or sadness in anything. They accentuated his down-turned mouth in presenting a standoffish appearance. When he spoke, he did so with a slight lisp, and people had to listen to him carefully to try to catch up with his ideas, overlooking the impediment.

Having been part of an administration that reaped the benefits of the ending of the Cold War, he envisioned a robust American foreign policy spearheaded by military adventurism. While many in Washington took a go-slow approach and wanted to withdraw America's tentacles from around the world, he and his cohort of like thinkers wanted America to become more aggressive and interventionist. He saw America at a historic moment in time. It had the wealth and the power to shape the world to its liking. Those who preached American exceptionalism followed Frieze's lead in advocating the use of national power to achieve American ends. They self-described themselves as neoconservatives and dreamed of Pax Americana.

When Iraq occupied Kuwait, and America went on a war footing, Frieze saw it as a laboratory for his ideas. The introduction of American force could change the dynamic in the Middle East. American arms could remove a dictator and make Iraq a client state. He had it all worked out and was giddy with the knowledge that American troops were sweeping through Kuwait. It proved to him that American arms had the ability and would change the world.

He entered the meeting thinking the president was going to seek advice on expanding the war's stated goals. It seemed logical, because he considered the original war aims too narrow.

When the talk started, Frieze was incredulous. He was sitting in on a meeting to halt the war without deposing Saddam Hussein.

"Would you like to add anything to the discussion, Don?" The secretary of defense gave him the opportunity to speak before the president, the secretary of state, the director of the CIA, the NSC adviser, and the chairman of the Joint Chiefs of Staff. The only person in the room without credentials was the president's son.

"Mr. President, gentlemen, never in history has a government been given an opportunity to shape the world. Even Alexander the Great and Caesar had limits to their reach. We have none."

Some at the meeting shook their heads at the imperial references.

"We have the Iraqi army disintegrating ahead of us. We can continue on to Baghdad, capture the city, and depose Saddam Hussein in a matter of days. With him out of the way, we could install a government that would be our surrogate in helping us change the Middle East."

"That isn't our mandate," the secretary of state cautioned. "We formed a coalition of international partners with the agreement that we would drive the Iraqis out of Kuwait. Anything more would cause the alliance to shatter."

"This has been an American enterprise. All the allies do is hinder us and prevent us from becoming a force for good. We could introduce democracy to an area that sorely needs it." Frieze rushed his words, trying to get many ideas aired while he held the floor.

"I've laid my honor on the line with the international community. Besides, we have no one to replace Hussein. If we topple him, we will be the de facto rulers of Iraq, and the situation on the ground may become chaotic. I can't see us getting involved in that kind of mess." The president tested his ideas before the others.

"Sir, I understand that, but no matter what happens to the government of Iraq, even if we have to build a new one, we will have access to Iraqi oil revenues that could pay the cost of keeping our troops there." Frieze argued his way through the difficulties others foresaw.

"Isn't that a bit like exacting tribute from a conquered land?" the secretary of state chided.

"It wouldn't be tribute. It would be reinvestment. Oil money could pay for the rebuilding of the infrastructure destroyed. There are dozens of companies that would jump at the chance, and it wouldn't cost us a dime. American companies would make a fortune, and we could help establish a democracy while they rebuilt the country." Frieze disregarded any downside arguments.

"We don't have the capability to keep troops in this part of the world indefinitely. We've got thousands of reservists making up the forces at war and at home. They can't be kept on active duty much longer. People would raise hell." The chairman of the JCS pointed out a real challenge to Frieze's argument.

"We can't worry about what the people want. We're the decision makers."

"Maybe, you don't have to worry about the people, but I have an election coming up. I have to worry about them," the president joked, hoping to lighten the mood.

"It won't take many troops to control Iraq. With air power

available, we could get by with as few as thirty thousand troops on the ground to maintain order. We could sell that to the public." Not being a politician, Frieze didn't have to worry about building a consensus.

"The Saudis want us out of their country and out of Kuwait. Our presence causes them problems," the secretary of state mentioned.

"We can't let the Saudis prevent us from taking this opportunity. If we topple Iraq, we can change the calculus in that part of the word. A thriving democracy in Iraq would be the seed that would cause neighboring countries to change their governments. If the Middle East becomes democratic, we can have peace between the Israelis and the Arabs and peace throughout the area. It should be our goal, because we are on the threshold of a great turning point in history. We can't let the present difficulties distract us from the future." Frieze took a deep breath, realizing he was getting emotionally invested in his argument. "Those of us in this room have the opportunity to change the world. We can't let it slip through our fingers. We have rolled up the Iraqi forces, and we could walk into Baghdad. We'd be greeted as heroes. The people would throw flowers at us in thanks for overthrowing their oppressor."

"Don," the NSC adviser started slowly, "we are pushing Iraqi forces off Kuwaiti soil, something that they never really owned. Once our troops enter their country, there is every indication that the Iraqis will fight. It won't be a quick and easy fight, as you say, and a lot of people on both sides will die. Right now, we have the American public on our side in this war. We told them when we started what we were there to do. We've accomplished that. If we continue as you suggest, it is going to take a new compact with the American people." The NSC adviser paused to see if his words were having an effect. "Our resolution to enter this war barely got through the Senate. If we go back and ask for a new mission, we are liable to lose any support we have in Congress. They surely will not let more kids be killed, especially after accomplishing the mission we had them buy into. What you want is an open-ended mission, and Congress won't buy into that."

"We can get around Congress. They approved the war and aren't in a position to stop it. Only we, in this room, can determine when the war is over." Frieze could see his idea of bypassing Congress was not well received, so he pivoted his argument. "For the last forty years, the flash point in Mideast relations has been Israel. We can eliminate any threat to Israel if we continue into Iraq. Once it fell, we could roll over Syria."

"What do you mean roll over Syria?" the chairman of the JCS asked. "Are you suggesting that we use force?"

"If need be, yes. We could topple the Syrian regime, and with Syria out of the way, Lebanon would follow. That would eliminate the contiguous threats to Israel. It would bring peace to that part of the world. We could solve the world's most intractable problem."

"Don. I can appreciate that you want to save Israel, but this war isn't being fought to protect an ally. It is being fought to ensure that the world continues to have a steady supply of oil. We can't just change course now and keep our troops in that part of the world. The Saudis would raise hell and all the good attained by neutralizing the enemies on Israel's north would be for naught if the Arabs to the south rose up." The NSC adviser tried to put limits on Frieze's oration.

"That wouldn't happen. The Saudis don't have an army capable of threatening Israel."

"They don't need one. They sit on a tub of oil, oil that we need to keep flowing. I, for one, am not willing to jeopardize the world economy for a wild goose chase through Iraq." The secretary of state was talking realpolitik.

Before Frieze could counter the secretary of state, the CIA director jumped in. "Don, the Sunni religious minority rules Iraq and are the group propping up Saddam Hussein. If we invade, and the Shia majority sides with us, the Sunni would not sit still while their former servants tried to wrest power. Since the Sunnis have all the guns, our presence would provide a motive for them to use them. I don't see, as you do, a walk in the park."

'There would be risks, but to forsake this opportunity would be a historical blunder." Frieze could see his arguments losing the group, who were not interested in the arc of history. They were myopic in wanting to end hostilities.

"Don, we will be dead before histories are written. We have to live in the present, and the situation we face presently is that we have accomplished our mission. I'm satisfied with that, and if there is no further discussion we will end the war." The president made his decision.

"Mr. President, I feel American power has the ability to do good in the new world order that we can create. I feel it will be a mistake if we don't use it to democratize the world." Frieze made one last attempt to sway the group.

"Your concerns are noted, but I think most of us feel our job is done." The president ended further discussion.

A few at the meeting bought into Frieze's arguments; among them was the president's son. He thought his father was making a mistake.

Frieze returned to his office in the Pentagon and buried his head in his hands. He had hoped the president would have seen the clarity of his ideas and wondered if there was anything more he could have said to make his case. He was incensed at the small-mindedness of the men at the meeting. They merely wanted to solve day-to-day problems, and he didn't feel the euphoria that eddied through the Pentagon with the victories being achieved. He was especially harsh in his judgment of the military. They had played a big part in swaying the president with their cautious approach. At every turn in the buildup of troops in Saudi Arabia, and then the war, they dragged their feet. They always needed more troops or more time and were unwilling to take risks. Frieze was convinced that if they had moved more rapidly without bothering the president with time-delaying requests, America would have been on its way to changing the world.

It was rare for the secretary of defense to go to a subordinates' office unannounced, and he surprised Frieze.

"Stay seated," the SECDEF instructed. The secretary was a man of indistinguishable features. He had a round face and wore rimless glasses and could have easily been mistaken for a retired auto-shop teacher. His cold brown eyes never looked at those with whom he spoke, but what set him apart was not his physical appearance but his detached personality. He was a philosophical dualist, seeing things as good or evil. There was no middle ground. If he thought something right, he worked assiduously to attain it, and he used as much energy working against things he considered wrong. He acted on his gut reaction and expected his staff to know what he was thinking. "You got beat up pretty badly today, but I wanted to tell you that I agree with what you were proposing."

"I appreciate that, sir."

"I didn't come to your aid because I read the room and saw that the deck was stacked against you," the secretary confided. "But don't consider this a dead issue. With his poll numbers, the president is sure to be reelected. In his second term we will have opportunities to change the face of the Middle East. When that time comes, we have to be better prepared, much better prepared."

"The president let a monumental opportunity pass." Frieze understood the politics of ending the war but considered it insane in light of what could have been accomplished.

"He's pretty much a captive of the military, as you have seen from their objections to continuing the offensive, and they got their way. That's the first thing that has to change if we are ever going to be able to use American force in organizing the world to our liking."

"Why are the generals so averse to using force? It is what they are paid to do," Frieze commented.

"After Vietnam, the military rigged the system so that the active military couldn't fight another war without calling up the reserves. At its core, the 'Total Force,' where active and reserve forces go to war together, assures that the pain of war touches almost everyone across the spectrum of society. By having war affect many people, the military hoped the politicians would be cautious in deciding to use military force. You can see that it worked. The chairman scared the president from continuing because we have so many reservists called up, and that affects main street America. The 'Total Force' essentially returns the war-making powers to Congress. If we are ever going to get the military to respond to our ideas, that has to be changed."

"How?"

SECDEF didn't answer quickly. "We are going to walk back the 'Total Force' so that we can go to war without using many reservists. Since many of the reserves' wartime functions are transferable to civilian contractors, we have to start privatizing as many of those functions as we can. We will need the military to be trigger pullers and to do the dying, but just about every other function can be outsourced. There will be an outcry over civilianizing the military, but the contractors, who stand to make millions on this type of structural change, have assured me that they will exert their influence so that the outcry such a change is sure to make doesn't distract Congress from doing what we want done. The CIA is just as big a problem. They are unwilling to use intelligence to shape policy. In order to develop the arguments, we will need to get the president to assume a more assertive posture; we have to have intelligence sources and products that can be evaluated along with those that the CIA provides. We have to start contracting out the cyberintelligence requirements to get contractors in the door. Once we get them established in the cyberfield, we can expand their functions so that they can develop other intelligence-gathering products. With differing interpretations of intelligence, it will allow us to shape the political environment." SECDEF paused for an uncomfortably long time. When he continued, he did so to show his subordinate that he had thought out what he was saying.

"While in the process of getting this building and the intelligence community realigned so that they become more willing to go to war, we have to do a better job of propagandizing the need to use force. I want you to establish tighter relationships with the think tanks that see the world as we do. We will need studies that we can cite as substantive research in support of our aims. Their writers have to detail the dangers in the world and develop a body of work that will evoke fear. That will be a lot to do, so set up a war room and staff it with the people you know you can trust. Make sure you have all the parts in place before the election, because after the president is reelected, we have to be able to move quickly." SECDEF paused. "I'll take it upon myself to start culling the ranks of the generals to assure people who are on our team are in the right jobs. If we do this right, we won't miss an opportunity like we missed today. The president will have all the pieces in place so that he can go to war without having to overly impact the voters."

"As a first step, sir, you are going to have to put out a directive that will take talk of the 'Total Force' out of the vocabulary of the building. We should stress the 'All Volunteer Force,' and change the balance of power in the military-industrial complex."

"What are you driving at?"

"Sir, industry has influence in this building in the procurement of weapons systems. If we have them take over some of the military support functions, their influence will grow, but we have to expand their role into operations. As I see it, we have to make it easier to use mercenaries in lieu of the military. It will make going to war easier because we can classify the use of nonmilitary personnel; we can keep Congress in the dark. That will essentially put war-making powers in the president's hands. "

"I was thinking along similar lines, but I haven't found the mechanism to make it happen without having Congress interfere.

Since you are way ahead of me on this, take it on and formulate a plan." SECDEF felt good that preparations for the next war were being started on the heels of an unsatisfying conclusion to the one in which America was engaged.

With SECDEF's approbation and doing things that would allow like thinkers to prepare for another opportunity to change the world, Don Frieze remained bitter. The war was over, and an opportunity had been lost.

As days went by, he could not let go of his antipathy toward the military. He considered the generals the reason he had failed to persuade the president. Their obstructionism was the reason for the loss of a historic opportunity.

When he was called upon to testify before Congress about the war, he was uncharacteristically incautious in telling the Senate panel that America had made a mistake by not driving into Iraq. He was forceful in his testimony, wanting to put distance between himself and the decision to end the war. When histories were written, he didn't want his name associated with those who missed a historic opportunity.

CHAPTER 4

THE PENTAGON, WASHINGTON, DC

JULY 2000

Don Frieze sat out the eight years of the Clinton administration. It wasn't that he hadn't tried to stay on in government in some capacity, but the new administration considered his ideas of American unilateralism unsuited for the world that was evolving. It was the first time his public service had been interrupted, and like all those of the Washington permanent class, he felt he was entitled to live off the government. Unable to hang on and work within the government, he stayed in Washington to trade on his influence, as he lobbied Capitol Hill for various special interests. It was tedious work, and he wanted to tackle big issues, beyond the intellectual grasp of politicians who had dumbed themselves down to get elected.

Offered a position in academia at George Washington University as the dean of the School of International Affairs, he jumped at the chance. In the university setting, his thoughts and his ego flourished. Unfettered by the inhibitors found in the real world, in academia he set out to define America's direction for the next century—as he referred to it, the American Century. His published thesis, defining his ideas for the American future, was received with acclaim, and he used it to educate like-minded people. At the nexus of academia, government, and money, he became the darling of the Washington think-tank business, and he wrote and lectured for them, putting forth his ideas of a hyperactive US foreign policy. Under the umbrella of academic research that the university setting provided, he created arguments that were supported by the skewed data put forth by like-minded people employed by think tanks.

With the contested 2000 election decided, and his former boss in charge of selecting people to fill the upper levels of government, Frieze returned to service as the deputy secretary of defense, DEPSECDEF. He didn't arrive in the Pentagon alone. Those who had left government with him and followed his lead in the private sector were brought back into government to fill important positions in the Defense, State, and Justice Departments. They were embedded throughout the Washington bureaucracy, and Frieze, from his position in the Defense Department, oversaw an unelected shadow government that wanted to rectify what they considered the mistakes of past administrations.

The people he brought back into government had years to think about the changes required in the Defense Department if they were going to be able to make their ideas reality, and the first thing the embeds did was to strike an adversarial relationship with the military. It was the opening shot in changing the military culture. Generals who disagreed with the neoconservatives were nudged toward retirement, and their replacements learned to agree.

A more complex task facing the DEPSECDEF was changing the military structure to fit in with the new secretary's vision. Small shifts in the Pentagon's alignment started at the newly appointed secretary of defense's confirmation hearing, where he exposed his plans to streamline the military. In his testimony, he stressed a smaller, more high-tech force with the civilianization of some military roles and missions to senators, who had been primed to accept his views by defense contractors and their political allies. Armed with erudite studies produced by think tanks that indicated that the use of contractors would save money, politicians ignored the

Pentagon's move toward a mercenary force. Elected officials missed that they were abrogating their constitutional duties by taking little interest in the decisions of how the country went to war. There were discussions about the new alignment creating jobs, overlooking the fact that war wasn't an employment opportunity; people died. With all its flaws, the secretary of defense's testimony was accepted as a new Pentagon paradigm.

One thing that had changed in Frieze's years out of power was the rise of the cable networks. They aired opinions packaged as news and were eager to ally themselves with the new administration. With the embeds planning for a militarized foreign policy, it was important that a link between the administration, the Pentagon, ersatz news outlets, and think tanks be nurtured so that they could speak with one voice. Hints of a dangerous world, substantiated by virtual research, put forth by poser intellectuals, were fed to media outlets. They would carry the ball and create misimpressions to stoke fears that would make the public willing to use force to solve world problems. The misinformation would be spun so that the public would be made aware of a threatening world that only American military might was able to overcome.

Sitting in a conference room without windows, Frieze called a meeting of the threat-assessment working group, an organization found nowhere on the Pentagon's organization charts. All its members were Frieze disciples. The working group's ostensible purpose was to look at threats from around the globe, and the meeting was the second one scheduled that week to discuss threats various intelligence communities were developing and forwarding to the Defense Department. The intelligence discussed would not be new, but the embeds at DOD were looking for things no one else could see.

As the deputy director of operations for the Joint Chiefs of Staff, Brigadier General Jake Gregg was the person assigned as the JCS representative to the working group. Nominated to become the director of operations, Jake's confirmation to the three-star rank required to fill that position was before the Senate for confirmation. Everyone assured him that he was a shoo-in to be confirmed, but until the actual endorsement, he remained the deputy for operations and the representative to the threat-assessment group.

Jake had been the Marine Corps' liaison to the CIA, but as soon as the military saw the people the new administration was selecting to fill the policy positions in the Defense Department, his assignment at the CIA was cut short, and he was brought to the Pentagon. He was a logical choice to become director of operations, because he had personal relationships with many of the civilians put in positions of power. The military hoped that with his friendships, he could work with the embeds, who were pushing the military to the sidelines.

Jake had met many of the newly installed power brokers in a previous assignment. Serving as a White House Fellow, a part of his fellowship entailed completing a year of independent study at George Washington University. In the year spent studying, his faculty adviser was Don Frieze, and through him, Jake got to know many of the men populating the upper echelons of the DOD. Even in the university setting, the embeds operated as a cabal, contextualizing their ideas so that they would have a doctrine and plans in place if an opportunity arose to make their ideas reality. In a circle of friends, ideas spun around until the neoconservatives spoke with one voice.

While a student, Jake had been impressed with the intelligence of the men who attached themselves to Frieze, but he noticed a blind spot among them. As a group, they resented that the Gulf War ended so quickly. In their thinking, they had lost an opportunity to alter history. Just a few more days: Just a few more days was all that it was going to take, and they harbored resentment toward G. H. W. Bush because he had stopped military operations. It was a subject on which argument was not tolerated even in academia.

Jake was happy that the Gulf War had ended quickly, but he was looking at it from a military slant, where people died. At George Washington, in the middle of discussions about America's failure to prolong the Gulf War, the neoconservatives didn't buy into his arguments that the war had been successful. He tried to explain that all the war's aims had been met, but those he tried to persuade weren't buying. They wanted the regime in Iraq overthrown. They hadn't thought out the difficulty of doing that. Theirs was an academic exercise devoid of downside analysis, and from Jake's point of view, devoid of the toll it would take on human life.

The same zealots Jake had argued with in seminars reemerged in Washington. They softened their rhetoric so as not to scare the politicians, but they avidly and quietly developed plans that foresaw American intervention as a staple of foreign policy. Their wont to use force to change governments reminded Jake of people playing war games. They had no knowledge of the meanness of war. None had put on a uniform, but that didn't prevent them from wanting to send others to war as the white mice in their experiment.

As a group, they had an underlying distrust of the military. Men put in positions to ensure that the military remained viable worked to limit its ability to influence future military decisions. Under the guise of streamlining forces, they changed traditional relationships within the Pentagon, and the president showed no interest when the embeds started exerting themselves into foreign policy issues separate from those of the NSC, the State Department, and the intelligence community. The president had more human issues to deal with, and the neoconservatives surrounding him understood the Oedipal conflict and subtly nurtured the president, hoping to provide him with an avenue to surpass his sire.

The secretary of defense, the DEPSECDEF, and the neocons planned for a smaller, highly trained and technical force and silenced anyone who disagreed. A few in the military dissented and tried to show that using highly paid contractors in lieu of sergeants and privates was a cost the military budget could not absorb, but they were moved aside and replaced with team players. The embeds didn't bother themselves with budgets.

To pursue the aggressive foreign policy the embeds envisioned, a smaller force that wouldn't impact many Americans was required. It was repudiation of the lessons learned in previous wars and the undermining of the "Total Force." The military stopped fighting what the SECDEF and the DEPSECDEF wanted done, because opposition was cause for removal, and those officers that held on to their jobs rubber-stamped anything the secretary proposed.

The people embedded in the Pentagon didn't question the validity of their ideas. Dangerously, none acknowledged that what they wanted to do would be difficult. Theirs was pie-in-the-sky planning, not taking into account the problems that any military interventions were sure to generate.

Jake raised objections and tried to stem the tide that was moving the Department of Defense to offense. Friendly embeds listened when they were new to their jobs, but as they settled into office, his advice was ignored and often ridiculed.

In the meetings that the Pentagon was famous for, a change took place. At one time, meetings would have all the services represented. The new arrangement was to have meetings with one military person in attendance. The new formulation allowed contractors and think-tank personnel to sit in, and only the enablers of a militarized foreign policy were given speaking slots.

Going to meetings where he was the only military representative, Jake was usually steamrolled. His objections were inundated with reams of data showing how he was wrong. He worried that the data used to counter his objections was cherry-picked, used to bolster arguments that supported Freize's thesis. Trying to stem the tide of activism by preaching caution, he was ignored. The men who had longed for a few more days of the Gulf War were convinced it was the military's measured approach that was the reason for what they perceived as a failure.

Don Frieze didn't usually chair the threat-assessment working group meetings, and his presence in the windowless conference room indicated that he wanted to interject the latest of his ideas. As the avatar of a preemptive foreign policy, he had formulated answers, and they depicted a best-case scenario. In his mind, all the bullets would be going one way. He was too much of a true believer to think that in the war he wanted anyone would fire back.

If Frieze hadn't slept in his suit, he hadn't bothered to change. He wore thick black-rimmed glasses, not for reading. They helped him avoid looking anyone in the eye. He physically turned away when speaking and readjusted the glasses so that all that could be seen was the side of his face. For someone as tall as Jake, all he ever saw when speaking to Frieze was the top of his head. At slightly over five feet eight inches, Frieze wasn't an imposing figure but got his way by citing that his positions were those preferred by the White House and the secretary of defense.

Calling the meeting to order, DEPSECDEF started by informing the group that Jake's confirmation hearing had been set for the following day and that he would be the new JCS director of operations as no objections had been voiced by the Senate Armed Services Committee. Those in the room that knew Jake congratulated him. A few left their seats to shake his hand. Oddly, the defense contractors in attendance were most happy with Jake's pending promotion. As a three-star general, he would be in a position to let contracts, and they were happy to open their sales cases to him.

When the group settled back into their seats, Frieze cleared the room of nonessential personnel. Jake thought that some of the people who remained should have been asked to leave. He was used to contractors and think tankers sitting in on meetings, but at this meeting foreign nationals remained.

"I've invited Mr. Chalabi and members of the Iraq National Congress (INC) to join us and to listen to the latest threat analysis provided by the CIA. It is felt that they might be able to shed some light on what is being reported."

"Don," Jake interrupted, "we are going to be discussing classified material. Has everyone been cleared?" He referred to the Iraqis.

"For the purposes of this meeting, Mr. Chalabi and the INC have been cleared." Frieze didn't like the interruption.

"By whom?"

"They have been approved by the White House," Frieze fumbled.

"Who?" Jake was tired of vague references. He wanted a name so that if classification laws were broken, everyone in the room could reference that name. Jake was angry because the embeds followed no rules. Clearances were not an impediment to them. They felt that the military used clearances to avoid doing what they wanted done without considering that the military was following US law. The embeds categorized calls for following the rules obstructionism, but for a military officer to sit in on a meeting discussing treat analyses required a full background check, and then they could only sit in on a need-to-know basis. Jake worried that the Iraqis had no need to know.

"I have approved their being here." It hurt Frieze to have to expose himself.

It made no sense to Jake. Chalabi and his group were discredited by many of the world's intelligence agencies. Since the meeting had been called to discuss terrorist threats against the United States, with Chalabi present, Jake felt that Frieze was going to try to make a case for an Iraqi threat that would fit into the neoconservative view of the world.

"Let's get going. I want your inputs before I speak to the national security adviser." It was DEPSECDEF's way of skirting any further objections.

The meeting followed a familiar pattern. The group thumbed through their briefing booklets, and Frieze highlighted the things he wanted discussed. Regardless from which part of the world the threats emanated, he kept working the group until they concurred that the many threats from many places were but one threat, Iraq, and one person, Saddam Hussein. Jake marveled at the fixation and understood that the intelligence was being massaged. A case was being built to make an intervention more easily salable to the American public.

"Osama bin Laden and his crew are tossing out threats, but they are tucked away in Afghanistan and don't have the capability to threaten anyone," Frieze started.

"You can't write them off. They struck the USS *Cole* in Yemen, and that indicates that they have a worldwide reach." Jake wanted to stop the dialog he saw developing.

"Al Qaeda is barely surviving, so I think that we can write them off. The real threat is Iraq. Al Zawahiri has the support of Saddam Hussein and has the capability and money backing to strike the United States. Mr. Chalabi has information that will highlight that link." Frieze turned over the meeting to the Iraqi.

"Thank you, Deputy Secretary," Chalabi started. "Recent defectors from Iraq have indicated that Saddam has given the Al Zawahiri group millions of dollars and has provided training and facilities in an effort to help them export terrorism internationally. We know that Al Zawahiri has teams of men ready to strike at the United States. They are a real threat, and I agree with Mr. Frieze, bin Laden has no capability. He is trapped in a backward country and is a prisoner of his location. Al Zawahiri, on the other hand, can slip cadres into many countries in the Mid East and from there they can move globally. In a few weeks, I will have proof that Al Zawahiri is the primary threat America has to worry about."

"Now when you look at the CIA documents, keep in mind what you have just heard. There is a real and creditable threat to the United States from Iraq. Saddam Hussein is bent on damaging this country." Frieze put a postscript on Chalabi's story.

All in the room nodded in agreement.

Jake knew better, and the people in attendance should have.

"With all due respect to Mr. Chalabi and his group, I think they are overselling the Al Zawahiri-Hussein connection. You know as well as anyone," Jake addressed Frieze, "that after the Gulf War those of you who were dissatisfied that we didn't rush into Baghdad pushed to have the CIA fund indigenous terrorist groups inside Iraq to disrupt the government and overthrow Hussein. Foremost among the funded terrorists was Al Zawahiri. When I left the CIA a couple of months ago, that arrangement was still in place. There is not a chance that Hussein is supporting him. Al Zawahiri is a religious zealot, and he has sworn to bring down Hussein's secular regime; that's why the CIA is paying him." Jake spoke slowly because he was saying things no one wanted to hear. "The case being made is that Hussein is funding a terrorist group that is bent on his destruction. That doesn't pass the sanity check."

"Our sources tell us that they are working in concert and trying to strike a blow at the United States." Chalabi was fighting for his creditability. His words were rapid-fire, but he would not look at the marine.

"The CIA won't buy into your interpretation. They have pretty much discredited the people you are using as sources and the scenario you depict." Jake stood his ground.

"The CIA has it wrong. We have confirmation from other outside sources that Hussein is funding terrorists." One of Frieze's embeds tried to support the Chalibi argument.

Jake felt that he was in a fantasy world. He was arguing with an Iraqi who had a vested interest in having Hussein toppled. Others at the table should have known that, but the more he talked the more he distanced himself from those in the room. "It doesn't make sense. Hussein is a survivalist. He would not fund someone bent on his destruction."

"Do you have any proof of what you are saying?" Frieze was angry. He had brought Chalabi into the meeting to support the position that the neoconservatives were developing and didn't like that one of the lynchpins of his argument was unraveling.

"Only the CIA and common sense."

"Your objections are noted. Let's move on to the next subject."

Jake thought he might have overstepped, but he wasn't there to be a yes man.

"That's it for today." Frieze dismissed everyone. "General Gregg, could I speak to you for a moment."

Nothing was said until the room was cleared.

"I resent your trying to make a fool out of Mr. Chalabi before the other members of the working group. I invited him here to shed light on the threats this country faces. From now on, I would like you to keep your comments to yourself."

"That is not my job. I'm supposed to give you my best advice. Your job is to take it or leave it, but you should listen." Jake wasn't intimidated.

"Mr. Chalabi has human intelligence sources that are better than the electronic intelligence the CIA relies on."

"Don, you guys have been skewing the threat intelligence since you got here, I think I know why, but that is not important. What is important is that you give the president the truth, not what you wish to be the truth, because if you fuck it up, people are going to get hurt."

"The president and the vice president are with us in this. They want the best intelligence that can be attained. We know the CIA doesn't want to touch Chalabi, but he brings intelligence to us that our agencies don't have. We are acting in the best interests of the country."

"The threats to this country are coming in from around the world. Saudi Arabia is a greater threat than Iraq. Why don't you guys make a case against them?"

"Saudi Arabia is one of our staunchest allies."

"That's crap. The Saudi royals are funding terrorist groups

around the world to save their own skins. All the real intelligence indicates that. Why aren't you looking for a fight there?"

"The president and vice president are sure of the Saudis and have vouched for them."

"Iraq is a minor player in the grand scheme of things. You can't focus on a nonexistent threat."

"Iraq is a serious threat and has to be stopped before they attack our interests."

"You guys are fighting the last war, and you've got the president tied up in a Greek tragedy. That is dangerous."

"You'd better stop talking that way." Frieze changed his tone. "Why don't you get on board with us and become a team player?"

"Because the team is wrong."

"Your lack of cooperation indicates that you may not be capable of becoming the director of ops. In fact, I'm having difficulty seeing you serving in that position."

Jake had heard others say if you disagreed with Frieze you'd better be ready to put your stars on the table because you were toast.

"Well, I'm ahead of you. You only think I might not be capable of becoming the director, but I know for sure that you and the yes men you brought to the Pentagon with you are incapable of filling the positions you hold." Jake was angry.

Frieze backed away as if he had been slapped, and left without saying anything more.

Jake's words affected Frieze like he had been scalded, and he reacted as if he was in pain. Always on the alert for slights that could be internalized to spur him to be better than those whom he was sure were against him, he had to do something about the marine general. As someone who had been his student, it was especially important that he put Jake in his place. The marine had been in his seminar, and his independent thought was evident from their early days together.

Frieze hadn't liked Jake then because he questioned most of what was being preached. In the university setting, the dean didn't condone independent thought. It had been awhile, but this was the first time that Frieze had an opportunity to cut Jake down to size.

He rushed up a flight of stairs to his office and without speaking to anyone took the secretary of defense's daily schedule from his assistant's desk.

He looked for a time opening that he might get on the secretary's schedule.

"It looks like SECDEF is going to have a few minutes open at the end of the next hour. Get me in to see him," he ordered his assistant.

The meeting was set, and Frieze cut his own appointments short so that he would be early in the event the secretary had more time. He was lucky. SECDEF entered the office without a coterie of hangers-on.

"Don. What's so important that it can't wait?"

"I'm having a problem with one of the uniforms."

The secretary laughed. "If you have to fire every one of them to get their attention, do it. You have my okay to shape your team with those people who are willing to work with us."

"This one won't be easy. It's General Gregg."

"Shit."

"Yes, sir. I didn't think you'd want to axe him like we have the others."

"That's good thinking. His family and their foundations were major contributors to the president's election campaign, and there is talk about one of his brothers becoming an ambassador. The president wants to throw him a bone for the money he donated." SECDEF paused, trying to think through a situation that could turn into a problem. "This is going to have to be run by the White House political staff," SECDEF mused. "Is there any way we can get him on the team?"

"I don't think so. I had Mr. Chalabi in with the threat-assessment group, and Gregg pretty much deconstructed everything he said."

"Chalabi is a key in developing actionable intelligence on Iraq. We can't let him become sullied by the military," SECDEF was thinking out loud.

"I agree."

"Gregg is a political hot potato. We have to move him out of the way but leave the vice president out of it. Let the political people handle it. We certainly don't want big contributors calling the White House now that we have the president on board. Something like this could cause him to jump ship." SECDEF paused to gather his thoughts, but as he always did, he tried to inject humor. "What the hell is a guy like Gregg doing in the military anyway?" It was a rhetorical question. The secretary wanted no answer.

"One problem," Frieze alerted SECDEF. "Gregg's confirmation hearing is scheduled for tomorrow, and with the glowing recommendations we sent over to the Senate committee with his package, he's a lock to be confirmed. If he is, he'll be the director of operations for the JCS, and that will make him impossible to work around."

"That can't happen. Keep this close hold, but tell the White House Gregg's confirmation has to be torpedoed. Don't speak to anyone but the political staff, definitely, no e-mails referencing this matter. Get rid of him quietly and expeditiously." SECDEF was ready to move on.

Sitting in the commandant of the Marine Corps outer office, Jake was alone, waiting under fluorescent lights that threw off eerily cold light. The commandant, the senior general in the Marine Corps, was hosting the Friday Evening Parade, after which he was supposed to entertain guests until midnight. When Jake got the call to be in the commandant's office on a Friday night and to wait there until his boss arrived, he knew he was in trouble.

With time, he thought back over his career, because after the commandant was through with him, he thought it would be over.

He had regrets, because the life he had escaped by joining the Marine Corps had allowed him to become independent of family. If he was cut loose, their enveloping arms would drag him back in.

Jake Gregg, or as named on his birth certificate Jacob Greggson III, was born into American wealth. Old money, the kind that afforded privilege, was difficult for people to comprehend. That was part of his problem. He had a free pass through life. His great-grandfather and grandfather had amassed a fortune considered to be among the largest in the country, but his father and brothers were content to live off the spoils. They did many good things with their inheritances but accomplished nothing personally. They were the toasts of society and had supplicants fawning over them for donations from various family foundations, and they were content to travel and revel in the acclaim they hadn't earned. Even Jake, when he showed up at parties, was lauded for who he was, not what he had done. He felt oddly like an ingénue on the arm of a rock star. People always made a fuss over him, but he was window dressing.

Educated in private schools, he decided to complete his education in New York at Columbia. His choice was a no-brainer. He didn't have to rough it. He was given a four-thousand-square-foot penthouse on Central Park West. With a playboy lifestyle, Jake didn't have to study to guarantee academic success. The fact that his family endowed the university liberally assured a degree.

Nearing graduation and trying to determine what he wanted to do with his life, he had planned for nothing more than a summer in Europe, and villas across the Mediterranean were lined up for a summer of partying. It sounded like great fun, an interlude before having to settle into whatever his father had planned for his life. Jake dreaded the thought.

Waiting for the limo to take him to a seminar sponsored by Columbia at the UN, Jake stood in the lobby of the Park Towers, an exclusive complex where the wealthy lived and hid. He watched while the doorman made a space in front of the long canopy that ran from the building to the curb. The stooped doorman, drenched by the sheeting rain, directed a car into position. When the door was opened, the doorman held an umbrella so that Jake would not get wet.

Rushing from the building, Jake entered the awaiting limo and when safely inside, the doorman leaned to close the door. In leaning, a small lapel pin on his inner jacket was exposed.

"What's that, Louis?"

"I'm sorry, sir." The doorman was not supposed to wear any adornment on his green and black uniform. "I'll remove it, Mr. Greggson."

"No. No." Jake didn't care about an assumed uniform violation. He wanted to know about the small pin. "What is it?"

"It's a Purple Heart, sir." The doorman quickly closed the door, blocking off further conversation.

The limo eased into traffic, and Jake thought about the doorman. He knew little about the military, but he did know that a Purple Heart was awarded for wounds received in combat. As the car moved through crowded streets, he thought about the man who had been opening doors for him. Jake had looked at him as nothing more than a piece of furniture. In the lobby, there were sofas and chairs and Louis. It was as if a human was an inanimate object. The idea that the doorman had been wounded bothered him. Jake, who had done nothing, was deferred to by a man who had been decorated for his actions in war.

Nearing the UN, Jake decided to miss a seminar.

"Take me back to the Towers."

The driver didn't question and dutifully maneuvered the car in traffic.

Pulling up to the canopy, the door was opened for him.

"Is there something wrong, Mr. Greggson?" the doorman inquired with the inference that he would do what he could to help.

"Louis, what's your last name?"

The question stunned the short, stooped man. In working in the building for nearly twenty years, no one had cared.

"Campanella, sir."

"I didn't know that. I'm sorry." Jake apologized for the entire building of wealthy tenants who had overlooked the bent employee.

Campanella didn't respond.

"Come on up to my apartment."

"Sir, I can't leave the door."

Jake went over to the phone that sat on the concierge desk.

In the uneasy several minutes that he and Campanella waited, neither spoke.

The building manager rushed into the lobby to determine the reason for Jake's call and to correct any problem. When he saw Campanella standing with Jake, he glared at the doorman.

"Is there a problem, Mr. Greggson?"

"No, but it is important that I talk to Louis. So, if you will arrange to get someone to relieve him, I'd appreciate it. When you do, send him to my apartment."

"Sir, is there something I can rectify now." The manager could not think beyond disciplining the employee.

"There's nothing wrong. I need to talk to Louis in regard to a term paper I'm writing. He has information that will help me." Jake lied but knew the explanation would salve the manager's curiosity.

"You could speak to Louis in my office. There is no need to take him to your residence." The manager was trying to prevent a breach of the building protocols.

"Please arrange for his relief and send him up as soon as you can." Jake delivered an order.

Campanella rang the doorbell about an hour later. He was anxious, as he had never been above the lobby level.

"Come on in." Jake was effusive but unsure of what he was trying to do with the doorman. "Take off your coat, and come in and sit down."

A maid stood ready to take Campanella's coat.

Jake led him into an expansive living room with views of the city. "Sit down. Would you like a drink? Can I have anything brought in for you?"

"No, sir." Campanella eased himself into an overstuffed chair.

"Tell me about that." Jake pointed to the lapel pin Campanella wore.

"I'm sorry about that, sir. I'll take it off, and it won't happen again."

"Louis," when Jake used the name, he was for the first time talking to the man, "this isn't about building rules. I don't care about them. I want to know about that." He pointed to the small lapel pin.

The doorman was stunned and unsure whether he should begin.

"Tell me about yourself, and how you came to be wounded, and why you haven't worn the pin before so that I might have known."

"I received this one just yesterday. It came in the mail."

"You received that one. Are there others?"

"Yes, sir."

"Let's start at the beginning. Take as long as you want, but when you are through I'm going to know about you."

After a long hesitation, in which Campanella grappled with memories, he started haltingly. "Six of us joined the Marine Corps after Pearl Harbor. We were all kids from the Bronx, all about the same age. We were all goof-offs and before we knew it, we were on a bus to Parris Island, South Carolina. We had heard about marine boot camp, but we were tough kids. We thought we were tough, but the Marine Corps scared us into growing up. I don't know how they did it, but when we left boot camp we were different people. It's a good thing because we weren't given a chance to go home and tell scary stories of the things we had endured. We were put in cattle cars for the West Coast, and weeks later we were sailing for the South Pacific.

"Three of us were on the second wave at Tarawa." Campanella

paused and took a deep breath. His face changed, and his eyes looked straight ahead, but he was seeing nothing.

Jake sat quietly, thinking that his prying had awakened something in the old man that was better left buried.

"Three of us, Tommy Amico, Joey Pagano, and me hit the beach in the same boat." The old man started as if he was visualizing the events. His deeply lined face contorted as if he was in pain. "When the ramp dropped, all we saw was sand littered with bodies—some dying, most dead. We were assaulting the Japs, but I wasn't prepared for carnage, or the confusion, or the noise. The noise was enough to shut you down to a point where you wanted to sit and wait for it to stop. I remember thinking this is insane. I wanted to go home. I was looking to my buddies for support, and as far away as you are, Joey was hit. One minute he was standing, and with the blink of an eye he was gone. I never knew what kind of a shell hit him, but it must have exploded in him because he disappeared."

Jake was mesmerized, but Campanella was most affected. He wasn't narrating. He was reliving the events.

"The call came down the line for us to hit the deck, and Tommy and I landed in the same hole in the ground with a dead marine that we knew from boot camp. We were trying to move away from the body, and Tommy must have raised up. He took a bullet right through his helmet. I could hear the ping of metal on metal, and when I looked to see what had happened, his face was covered in blood, and bits of his brain were running out. I was shaking so badly I thought I was going to die. I wanted to die. I can't account for what happened, but apparently I went berserk. I charged a pillbox where the fire that killed Tommy was coming from. At least that is what the citation says. They gave me a silver star along with my first Purple Heart for a slug that hit my leg. The wound wasn't that bad, but I can't tell you any more of the war, because I blotted it out. I didn't know that I was wounded a second time until I awoke in a hospital, and some officer gave me a second Purple Heart.

"Of the six of us who joined up, I was the only one who made it home. I went to the old neighborhood, and while the families of my friends were glad to see me, I could feel an underlying resentment. Somehow they faulted me for surviving. That wasn't an odd feeling because I felt the same way. Why had I survived? Did I do something wrong? Did I do something right? The questions tortured me to a point where I wished I had been one of those who died.

"My head was out of whack. I kept reliving the suicidal assaults, but as they played out in my dreams I always awakened in the middle of the night visualizing fragmented bodies flying in space. I tried to fight through headaches that lasted for days and couldn't. I started drinking to forget, but that only made it worse. I became a drunk and would have died on the streets except for Korea. I was called back into the Corps and was assigned to the Seventh Marines. The crazy part is that as soon as I got back into a marine unit, I started feeling normal again. All of us recalls from the war in the Pacific were suffering with almost identical thoughts. An odd calm permeated the veterans. I'm sure being back in war we hoped to die on the battlefield to join friends who were lost. At home, we had all been sitting in bars drinking ourselves numb and reliving what we had gone through, but once we were back together we started talking, letting go of feelings that others who had been to war could understand. It was a big help knowing everyone else was having problems. People who had experienced the same things understood what I was going through, and that helped even though I was being shot at again. It was like we were meant to be there."

Campanella stopped and took a sip of water. He looked at Jake to see if he wanted him to go on. Jake was rapt and indicated that the doorman should continue.

"The Seventh Marines fought their way through Korea up to the Chosin Reservoir before the Chinese entered the war. In a flash, we were surrounded. The Chinese attacked in waves, and we were running out of bullets quicker than they ran out of people.

"Someone said we should retreat, but there was no retreat. We fought in every direction because there were no front lines. The enemy was tough, but nothing like the cold. Growing up in New York, I thought I knew what cold was. Nah. The wind and the cold in Korea were brutalizing and a far greater enemy than the Chinese.

"When we arrived in Korea, we were issued the same gear we had used in fighting on the tropical islands, and the supply system couldn't get us cold-weather gear fast enough. We were losing more marines to frostbite than we were to bullet wounds. We were suffering, but nothing like the Chinese. Some of them were fighting in the snow without shoes or gloves. They were dying where they lay. We'd pass them still in tactical formation frozen solid.

"I came down with frostbite in my hands, and they rushed me to an aid station. The doctor looked at my hands and told me that I didn't have frostbite, but that my hands were frozen. The only thing he could do was stab each of my fingers, put me in a warming hut, and have me come back when my fingers started bleeding. In about an hour, blood appeared. I went back to the medic, and my fingers were padded and taped to protect them from the cold. All my fingers were padded except my trigger finger, because I was sent back to my unit, and I was expected to help them fight their way out of the Chinese trap. I don't think I could have survived much more of the cold, but that became a moot point. I took one in the back and was flown out to a hospital in Japan. The little pin I wore today was the one for the slug in the back."

"It took all this time for the Marine Corps to give you the medal?" Jake tried to determine the number of years that had elapsed.

"Yeah. By the time I got home from Korea, I wanted nothing to do with the military. They wrote me letters, and I just threw them away."

Jake had heard the story, but there was so much more he wanted to hear. The little man sitting before him was a hero. He didn't seek recognition, but he was a man who had accomplished something with his life and didn't want the world to know.

"Louis." He didn't see Campanella as an inanimate object any longer. "I would like to hear more. Could you spare me the time?"

The old man hesitated. He was unsure that he should pick the scab off the memories. "Yeah." He hated to admit it to himself, but talking about it was a relief.

Lunch was brought in and then dinner. The quick conversation lasted into the night, and as it concluded Jake was exhausted. To his dismay, Campanella seemed to get stronger as he unburdened himself.

"You should be more than a doorman for a bunch of ungrateful people." Jake wanted to do something for him. It was merely the matter of a phone call to get him a better job.

"No, sir, Mr. Greggson. I was pretty much busted up after Korea. This was the only job a veteran with only 50 percent usage of his left arm could get. More than that, it allowed me to hide. I didn't want people asking me about the war, either one, and the people here were nice enough, but they didn't care, and that suited me. I hope our talk today doesn't change that." Campanella stopped. He was wise enough to know conversations were two-way.

"What is it you are looking for, Mr. Greggson? I've watched everyone come and go in this building, and I know their quirks. I can tell the real from the phonies."

"What is it that you've decided about me?"

"You have every reason in the world to be happy, but you're not." Jake nodded.

"Have you ever tried to figure out why?"

"I've thought about it." Jake stopped.

"I feel better after getting things off my chest," the doorman informed. "You ought to try it. Sometimes it helps."

"I can have anything I want. I can do anything I want, but no matter what I do or what I accomplish, I will never be sure I did it. It will always have the strings of family money attached, and I don't like the idea." As Jake spoke, he uttered words he had internalized and personalized to a man he really didn't know.

"You can do things on your own. There are opportunities out there for you to make a name for yourself."

"You don't understand. My name can accomplish many things for me. That's not what I want." Campanella couldn't imagine the extent of his wealth.

"Join the Marine Corps as an enlisted man. If you get through Parris Island, you will know you accomplished something on your own, because becoming a marine is something that can't be bought. It is a title that will always describe you as your own man, for better or for worse." Campanella laughed. "You see it in the news all the time. A guy murders someone, and no one cares about the victim. They write about the killer as a marine. Whether you're a murderer or a senator who has done good or bad, somewhere in the story a mention will be made about the person being a marine. It will always be a part of you."

Campanella's suggestion was the furthest thing from Jake's mind. He had never had to tax himself. "I don't think that's for me."

"I told you about me, so I figure I can tell you about you. I've seen all the people in this building walk through the front doors, and you are different." Campanella leaned forward. "I'm not suggesting that our lives are in anyway similar, but I was a seventeen-year-old kid, and the Marine Corps made me my own man. Even now, I'll no longer be Louis the doorman. Every time you see me you will acknowledge me as a marine. You are fighting the Greggson name; add marine to it, and people will look at you differently." Campanella laughed. "They may think you're crazy, but they will look at you differently."

In boot camp, Jake found a world where he wasn't catered to. In watching young men who had nothing, achieve the same things he was struggling to achieve, he realized he had been right in getting away from a life that was handed to him. For the first time, he was yelled at and was frightened while at the same time seeing the humor in it. His platoon sergeant, a wide man shorter than six feet, was in his face, berating him over the cleanliness of his weapon. The words hurt, but the sergeant was right. Jake hadn't taken time to clean every component and tried to get by. As punishment, he was required to break down his rifle and clean it to the sergeant's approval. While he did over what he was supposed to have done correctly the first time, the members of his platoon had to stand at attention and look on. They had earned liberty but could not leave their barracks until Jake got his weapon re-inspected. It was a lesson learned. His actions affected others. He knew that intellectually, but it was the first time that it had been brought home to him on a personal level. He had let down his platoon, and it drove home the point that he had responsibilities to others and to himself.

Jake liked the members of his platoon. Some had come from the inner cities and some from towns with dozens of people. The cultural differences were eye-openers. All his life, he had been around people who had taken their lives for granted. His friends were people who had won the birth lottery. He thought it was a good thing they had because being lumped in with young men from across the spectrum of society, he realized talent wasn't a birthright. He understood that many of the recruits could achieve the things he had if given the opportunity. The marine recruits in many cases were smarter and if given a level playing field would outdo those who were handed life.

Taking on some of their street toughness, his language wasn't as refined as it had been, and he was willing to fight if talking was a waste of time. Standing at attention among the men in his platoon, Jake realized he wasn't the best. Some were smarter, some faster, some stronger, but they were a team. He loved the feeling of belonging to something other than a university club.

Campanella had called it. Jake came out of Parris Island a different person, but serving in the Marine Corps as an enlisted man wasn't in the cards. His history and name caught up with him, and his family moved quickly to have him released from the service. Fighting their efforts, a first in his relationship with his parents, a compromise was reached. Meeting all the educational requirements, he was shipped off to Officer's Candidate School. His family would accept his becoming an officer. That would look better in the society pages.

With his attitude and appetite for work, he became noticed. It didn't hurt that people knew who he was, but he garnered respect for taking on tough jobs. Even as he was on the pinnacle of moving up in the Pentagon, he considered the high point of his career leading a battalion in combat during Desert Storm. He loved being in command because he thought he could lead young men effectively in life-and-death situations. The war experience taught him the value of other peoples' lives and how easy it was to forget that when in the Pentagon planning for war.

A lot had happened in the intervening years. He had good and bad assignments but understood that his talk with the doorman had changed his life. Upon hearing of Campanella's death, he arranged for a burial with full marine honors. He hoped the old man would have approved.

His reverie was broken.

At 2300, he could hear the rushed steps of people heading his way.

The commandant and the Marine Corps Personnel Director Lieutenant General Bob Hickerson entered the room in full dress uniform with the gold braid glimmering. They had apparently left their social duties and had come to the Pentagon without changing.

"Come on inside, Jake." The commandant directed him into the inner office where they could talk out of earshot of the aides who had accompanied them. Turning on a lamp bathed the inlaid wooden desk in light while the three marine generals sat on the periphery in semidarkness.

"What the fuck happened, Jake?" The commandant leaned forward. "I got a call from the White House telling me they wanted you out of the building." The commandant, a grandfatherly looking man with gray hair known for his tact, wasn't displaying any of it. His eyes bored in on Jake, and his lips were pursed as if he was getting ready to strike out.

"I made a mistake. I thought I was assigned here to ask questions about things that might have an effect on national security. That isn't the way it works with the embeds. No questions are tolerated. They are looking for a reason to go to war, and they are listening to anybody who has a story to sell that buttresses their arguments. The Pentagon and the White House are preaching the same thing, and they are marginalizing the rest of the government, especially the military."

"Yeah. All the uniforms understand that." The commandant interrupted him. "But why were you singled out? They usually take time to work a cover story when they dump flag officers so that they can get congressional buy-in. With you, it was get him out of town, now."

"I told Don Frieze that I didn't think he was fit to be in that office because the people he has embedded in the government are spoon-feeding the president with scenarios that are going to lead us to war. They want to refight the Gulf War and are skewing intelligence to make that happen."

"Whew! That would do it," Bob Hickerson, a short gnarly general, interjected. He smiled in an effort to lighten the mood.

"I guess if we had lost fifty thousand troops in Desert Storm they wouldn't be pushing for this. We made it look like war was easy," the commandant mentioned.

"It is always easy for people who have never been shot at," Bob Hickerson, who still carried a shard of shrapnel in his leg from the Gulf War, added.

"Listen, sir. I know I screwed up, and I'll have my resignation letter on your desk Monday morning." Jake was willing to accept the consequences of his actions.

"It's not going to be that easy," Bob Hickerson stopped him. "We have been ordered to get you out of town, but we were told you are not to retire."

"What is that all about?" Jake was surprised.

"You're to be retained on active duty and remain under military regulations about the handling of classified material. All the meetings you have attended are classified. You will be unable to speak to anyone about them. By keeping you on active duty, you will not have the first amendment right of free speech and can be controlled. If you talk about anything you've heard or seen, they can get at you quickly."

"You've got to be shitting me."

"Jake. These people know who you are and the audience you would have if you went public. Your being on active duty prevents that."

"They can't silence me forever."

"If they find a casus belli, your speaking out will not matter. They could get us into war, and your voice would be lost in the noise," the commandant added.

"What will make them happy? Do I get sent to Elba?" Jake was trying to determine his future.

"Quantico has a colonel commanding it. The job calls for a general." Bob Hickerson spoke of the marine base forty miles south of the Capitol. "We don't know yet whether SECDEF wants you farther out of town. So, if it is okay with them, we'll make you the commanding general of the base."

"Will they buy that?" Jake asked.

"It is what we are going to propose. We should know by Monday, but I can't see them vetoing it. There are already people wondering why your confirmation hearing was squashed. When they recommended you to be the director of operations, they sold you as a water walker. Now, they are saying you aren't qualified. Senator Todd has already raised the bullshit flag."

"He would. He's a family friend."

"I know you don't like to play politics, but this is Washington, Jake. Why don't you talk to Todd, and see if he can get you the director's job over DOD opposition." The commandant showed he was willing to use the back channel to ensure that a marine would be in a powerful position. It was difficult for him to suggest, because throughout his career, Jake had fought to avoid any impression that he had gotten ahead because of the influence he could bring to bear in Washington.

"I'd rather not, sir."

"Look, Jake, we've got a bunch of guys running the military who, if given free rein, will get us into war. They are trying to make the case for us to preemptively strike Iraq despite every threat warning we have received that Iraq is well down on the list. The fuckers are dangerous."

"What if I can't get Todd to support me?"

"Press him to have you assigned to Quantico. If you are close to the Capitol, we can continue to feed you intelligence and bring you to the city to speak to the members of Congress that you know."

"If SECDEF or Frieze find out that you're back-channeling me, he's likely to fire you," Jake cautioned the commandant.

"I'll take that risk." The commandant smiled wryly. "I've been to war, as have you, and it isn't a game. Anyone who goes out looking for one is dangerous, and I'll put my stars on the table to prevent it." The commandant had thought out what he was saying. Jake and Hickerson agreed with him. It only took getting shot at once to make them believers.

CHAPTER 5

MARINE CORPS BASE, QUANTICO, VIRGINIA

Jake was ordered to the Quantico assignment after the vice president's office weighed in and told those pleading his case that he would not serve on the JCS or anywhere in the Pentagon.

Quantico was a huge base with military schools, the FBI Academy, the DEA School, the Marine Corps Schools including the Marine Corps University, and it was the home to several major Marine Corps commands. The land area of the base with dozens of firing ranges was problematic, but what made the base unique was that the town of Quantico sat in the middle of the base, and passage of the residents through the military facility made control difficult. The commanding general couldn't rule by decree. It was necessary to bring the mayor into consideration on all decisions because in some way they affected the population of the town.

Jake had thought about what he was going to face and tried to formulate a plan on how to react to the new environment. In the time he spent cleaning out his desk, he looked through personnel files of all the officers and senior enlisted who would make up his staff at Quantico. Without time to form his own team, he culled the records of those who were already in position. He was disappointed by what he saw. Most of the senior officers had taken the base jobs as their transition to retirement. That meant he would be commanding a group that would have a divided attention span. Many would be spending their time writing resumes and interviewing for follow-on jobs, and their attention would be on other things besides the Marine Corps.

He needed motivated officers because Quantico, like most bases, was out of the hard intelligence loop. That information was available, but Jake could not recall ever seeing a general from any base in the Washington area put forth the effort to show up at threat briefings. They were swamped with having to maintain plant, equipment, and personnel, and ignored the larger world outside their gates.

The base staff had been alerted that he would be taking over command, but he purposely stopped any attempt to have a change of command ceremony. His intent was to show up and go to work.

Leaving Washington at 1530, he drove to Quantico in his unmarked personal vehicle and spent time driving around the base. To his dismay, there was no area that he couldn't access. That bothered him. It indicated a laxness in the base's security posture.

Disappointed by things he saw, he didn't want to show up in his new office while he was angry, and he stopped in at the Globe and Laurel Restaurant on Highway One. It was a marine hangout, but since he was in civilian clothes, he sat alone, unrecognized, and picked at a hamburger, trying to determine where he might start in his efforts to change the base's military posture.

At 2200, when the Laurel closed, Jake drove to the main gate and was waved through. The male and female marines in the gatehouse seemed more interested in each other and didn't care about an unmarked car entering the base.

Driving to the headquarters building, he took advantage of a perk and parked in the slot reserved for the commanding general. He entered the headquarters building through the main unlocked entrance and could see light coming out of the duty officer's room and could hear the TV blaring. No one stopped him, so he followed signs that led him to the command suite and entered his new office.

Flipping on the lights, he sat behind the large maple desk and propped his feet on it. Pulling the phone close, he pushed the button marked duty officer and waited for an answer. When a voice responded, he started to change the base culture.

"Officer of the day. Captain Bowling."

"Captain Bowling." His voice was icy. "This is General Gregg. Would you come to my office and explain to me why at 2300 I was allowed to enter the building unchallenged."

After a flurry of excuses, Jake cut him off.

"Come on up to my office and you can explain yourself personally."

In minutes, a worried captain knocked on the door.

""Come on in."

"Captain Bowling reporting, sir." The captain's eyes were wide and looked at Jake as if he was an apparition.

"How about telling me why I'm sitting here and no one on duty knew it?"

"I'm sorry, sir. My bust."

"In fact, I'm out of uniform; I have no ID. How do you know who the hell I am?" Jake scolded.

"I've seen your picture, sir. I recognize you." Bowling shuffled from foot to foot and was grasping for an excuse.

"That's not good enough. I'm going to assume that you were following regulations, but if you were, they are much too soft." In a shift of tone and subject, Jake asked. "What's your job on base?"

"Sir, I'm a fiscal officer, sir."

"Starting tomorrow, you are going to be the rewrite officer. You are going to sit down with the Duty Officer Rules and Regulations and tighten them up. While you're tightening them up, be sure to have a provision that states all buildings will be locked, and that those buildings with duty officers have them placed in positions where they can observe what they are supposed to be guarding. Got it?"

"What will I tell my boss, sir?"

"Tell him you have a new job. And, while you are at it, call every one of the principal staff officers tonight and tell them I want to meet with them at 0730 in the conference room."

"You want me to call them tonight?" Bowling's orders were not to disturb any of the staff unless there was an emergency. He wasn't sure a staff meeting was an emergency, but in looking at Jake, he became convinced that it was.

"Yup." Jake paused, not wanting to cow the junior officer. "That's your second job. Job number one is to get me the keys to my quarters so that I can bag it for a couple of hours. You do have the keys available, don't you?"

"I don't know, sir."

"Goddamn it." Jake wasn't angry, but he spoke purposefully. He didn't expect the duty officer to have the keys, but his effected snit would be carried along with the alert of the staff meeting.

"I'm going to give you something you can handle. Call over to the visiting officer quarters and get me a room. We can figure out how I'll get into my quarters tomorrow." Jake smiled inwardly. The young captain was terrified. "Tell the staff, I'll be showing up at 0730. Anyone not in the room at that time will be locked out. You're excused."

After Bowling rushed out of the office to start waking the staff officers, Jake went to get some rest. He understood that the base job was going to require a lot of minor tweaks and that he wouldn't be dealing with global issues as he had at JCS, but it felt good to be back among marines.

At 0730 Jake stepped into the conference room. Its walls were covered with the plaques of every unit on the base. He sat at the head of a long table and afforded no time for socializing. There were not enough seats for all in attendance, and marines stood along the walls.

"I'm Jake Gregg, the new CG." That was all he said by way of introduction. "Starting with you," he pointed to the officer directly to his right, "we'll go around the table. Introduce yourselves. Tell me who you are. Tell me what you have done in the Marine Corps. Tell me what you do now, and tell me what you have planned to improve what you do now."

All in attendance knew who Jake was. He had served with several of them, but they also knew he had been dumped from becoming the director of operations at the JCS. They wondered if he was angry over his dismissal and was going to take that out on them.

The introductions started but were unneeded. He had looked at the files of each of them. Based on his reading of their histories, he thought he knew those who were keepers. The idea behind having them introduce themselves was to try to find an officer who looked better in the flesh than on paper.

One by one, people lived up to their records.

"I'm Major Fran Matthews." The picture in her file didn't do her justice. Her face was less oval in person, and she was striking. Even with the stark hairstyle required of women marines, there was no disguising her beauty. Sitting down, as she was, it was hard to tell her height. She was tanned, and in looking at her exposed forearms it was easy to determine that she was in shape. Sitting among senior officers that had let their conditioning slip, she stood out.

"I joined the Marine Corps after graduating from the Naval Academy." She was self-assured, and Jake was impressed that she didn't oversell herself. She could have said she graduated in the top ten.

"I'm trained as an intelligence officer, and have worked in that field until my assignment here." She spoke clearly, exhibiting confidence.

Again, she omitted detail. She spoke four languages, and that was why she was assigned to the intelligence field.

"I am currently serving in the base protocol office. Mostly, I plan parties." It was apparent by her tone that she disliked what she was assigned to do. "As for what I'd do to improve my job, I'd cut out the number of parties." She was deadly serious and ignored the chuckles from around the table.

Jake knew she had omitted much more. With her education and intelligence, she should have been serving in a much more responsible position. She had been a rising star destined for better assignments but had abruptly been sidetracked. No definitive reasons were given in her fitness reports as to why she was marked down below her peers, but there were rumors that she had accused a fellow officer of sexual misconduct. Her records had in part been redacted, but the Marine Corps was small enough so that once rumors started to swirl, they took on a life of their own.

Jake couldn't get too interested in her case. The next briefer was already into his pitch before he caught up to what was being said.

The meeting took most of the morning. At about 1000, Jake called an end to it.

"That's it for today. Tomorrow morning, I'll start taking individual section briefs." He stood, and all in the room stood. Looking over the group, he abruptly turned and left. The staff was confused. They didn't know whom he wanted to speak to first, and that was his intent. He wanted them to start figuring things out for themselves.

It took a week of briefings for Jake to realize he was no longer a player on the marine stage. The base staff had been working in offices and sitting behind desks for too long and were reluctant to act on their own initiative. Once they were told what to do, they plunged into the task at hand. Jake let it be known that they could make decisions without his involvement. To show he had faith in their abilities, he started leaving his office so that the staff couldn't come to him for decisions that they were capable of making. Two days a week he braved the morning commute into Washington to receive intelligence briefs.

CHAPTER 6

CENTRAL COMMAND, CENTCOM, TAMPA, FLORIDA

A sleek silver airplane with a powder-blue tail, indicating it was from the presidential squadron, landed at MacDill AFB at 1100. Don Frieze and an entourage of embeds deplaned along with a dozen civilian contractors. They were greeted on the tarmac by General Billy Joe Franklin, the commander of Central Command, the unified command responsible for the Middle East. Up until the new team inhabited the Pentagon, the unified commanders had been called commanders in chief of their areas, but the SECDEF sent a message telling the military that there was only one commander in chief and the generals' titles were downgraded.

In the hot sun, greetings were made all around.

"We didn't receive an itinerary on you." Franklin spoke with a Texas drawl, much of which was affected. "What is it that you want my staff to do for you?" He was taller than Frieze by several inches and had the ruddy looks of a tired cotton farmer. His lower eyelids sagged, exposing bloodshot brown eyes, and a patch of black hair covered the top of his skull. A face that looked worn was in direct contrast to his uniform, which bore creases that hadn't wilted in the Tampa humidity. Despite his trying to act with hominess, Franklin by nature was a gloomy man and was distrusting of anyone in the chain of command above him.

"We are visiting all the unified commands and are looking at their contingency plans. If you'll get us a secure room, I'd like to have my team look over your plans."

"Any specific area?" Franklin knew why the DOD personnel had come to his headquarters.

"No, we'll look at all the plans." Frieze skirted the question.

"I'll make that happen." Franklin was relieved that he didn't have to entertain his Washington guests. "I'll set up some briefings for the civilians who aren't cleared to inspect the war plans."

"For purposes of this visit, everyone has been cleared. They will be in the room with us."

"If you say so." Franklin had never heard of such a breach of regulations, but if the DEPSECDEF said it was okay, he wasn't going to argue. "We've got lunch planned, and while we are eating, I'll have a secure room set up. After lunch, you'll have everything you need."

"Thanks." Frieze wasn't interested in lunch, but he wanted to give the CENTCOM staff an opportunity to get the plans ready.

Once Frieze and his group entered the secure room, classified contingency plans were brought to them. The staff officers charged with helping them noticed behavior that was in opposition to the stated purpose of the visit. CENTCOM had twenty-four countries in its area of responsibility, and each had a contingency plan, some more than one, but the only plan that received attention was that for Iraq. Frieze's team started looking at it at 1500 and worked it into the night and the following day. They made no requests of the people assisting them other than for coffee, sandwiches, and directions to the closest restroom.

When they were finished, Frieze requested a meeting with Franklin and was ushered into the general's expansive office.

"That will be all," the general informed the military personnel who accompanied Frieze, and the two men stood silently until the door was closed, and they were alone.

The office had modern accouterments, but it was more a shrine.

At his rank, Franklin had met most of the world leaders, and the four walls were covered with photos of him shaking hands or standing with them. Missing was any evidence of family photos. In a spot directly behind his desk, his awards and decorations were displayed and protected behind glass. Prominently, a signed picture of the president looked over his shoulder.

"Can I get you something to drink?" The general was hoping Frieze would refuse so that he could get him on his way.

Usually, Franklin's Southern charm worked on Washington bureaucrats, but it was wasted on Frieze. He was comfortable talking to people who were his intellectual contemporaries, and he didn't consider Franklin one of them.

"I'll pass on the drink, and I'll get right to business."

"Suit yourself."

"I've looked over all of your contingency plans, and they all look good, but I have some questions about the plan for Iraq. When was it last updated?"

"It was rewritten just before I got here, so I guess it's about a year old."

"It's out of date."

"How so?" Franklin was curious.

"It mirrors the plan for the invasion of Iraq that was used in the Gulf War."

"That seemed to have worked okay." The general's attempt at humor was lost.

"The world has changed. Weaponry has gotten much better, and we have to rely on it in the event we go to war in Iraq."

"I think you'll find that the latest and greatest weapons are included in the plan."

"Yes," Frieze conceded, "but the plan calls for using the almost same numbers of troops with more lethal weapons available. SECDEF wants the numbers reduced."

Franklin recognized the Washington ploy. By referring to the secretary of defense as the authority wanting the plan changed, there could be no argument.

"And what does the secretary consider a doable number?"

"Cut the current number in half. About 150,000 will be a good starting point. As we rework the plan, the numbers will probably drop, because the contractors have seen many areas where they can substitute civilians for the military."

"Substituting civilians for soldier doesn't mean the numbers will be smaller. All it will do is transfer the responsibility at a greater cost, and my budget won't accommodate the increased expense. Are you going to pay for the civilians out of DOD funds?" Franklin could see problems with what Frieze was proposing, because he was sure money would be taken out of his funding.

Frieze had to be careful. He could run over generals in the Pentagon, but Franklin was a unified commander with the responsibility for Iraq—a war there would be run by him. He had to have a say because there was no way to get rid of him without creating a firestorm on Capitol Hill. It was necessary to get Franklin's buy-in and get him aligned with the neoconservatives.

Frieze had studied the general. He knew his strengths and weaknesses. Franklin was an outsider in the army. He wasn't an infantry officer and had never commanded a combat unit. He had time in Vietnam and Kuwait but was always in the rear. Without real combat under his belt, no one in the army understood how he was given command of CENTCOM. Resented for not possessing the proper credentials within the upper circles of the army, the resentment wasn't one way. Franklin knew how his contemporaries looked at him, and he in turn disliked his fellow generals, many of whom he considered effete.

Frieze was going to play on the resentment and ignore the talk of who would pay for what. If he did it right, he would make Franklin an acceptable commander to the embeds.

"I'm going to be candid with you, General."

"Be my guest."

"We have been receiving intelligence, as I am sure you have, that Saddam Hussein is sponsoring terrorists. He may even be providing them with the ability to strike out at the United States." As he spoke, Frieze watched to see if his words were registering.

Franklin's cold stare didn't change.

"The White House wants to have a quick-strike plan ready to go when it gets proof that Saddam Hussein is an imminent threat. If we decide that we must strike Iraq, it has to be done with as light a footprint as possible. We have to let our technological advantages negate the need for overwhelming force. The SECDEF wants any war to be fought smartly using our entire tool kit of weapons. He doesn't want masses of troops running around in the desert, and he wants to civilianize the war as much as possible."

"I understand his intent, but we will need boots on the ground to defeat Iraq. Technology and civilians won't do the job. Cutting the number of troops required in half isn't a good idea."

"General, I want you to visualize the world after Iraq. If we tie up troops there, we will have none available if we decide to expand our efforts in other parts of the world."

"Yeah," Franklin agreed.

"We made a terrible mistake by not taking down Iraq when we had the chance, and those generals who were involved with that mistake are looked at as having been less than stellar. We may have a chance to rectify that, and when we get through this time, people won't forget the general who ran the war. If we do this right, your name will be mentioned in army lore along with Marshall, Eisenhower, and MacArthur." Frieze bored to the core of Franklin's ego.

The general liked the sound of the words. If he would get on board with the neoconservatives they might make him stand out above all those of his contemporaries who doubted that he could do the job.

"I'll work on bringing the numbers down."

Frieze hooked him, and since he had, he pushed. "There will be further reductions in the size of the force that will be needed, but we can work that out. The main thing is to plan to fight using the latest technology while relying more heavily on contractors to do nonessential tasks, because the SECDEF will insist on it."

Franklin stopped listening. His mind wandered off to all those in the army who were against him. Their snide remarks about his not having had combat time and his lack of command of line units would vanish. He would enter the army pantheon.

In buying into Frieze's vision, both men knew they were tied together. Frieze didn't like the idea, because in any other situation he would have fired the general, whom he considered incompetent. Franklin understood that by tying himself to the DEPSECDEF he might get to fight a war. The general wasn't interested in new weapons. He wanted to bolster the army and take back the gains the special forces were making in the DOD makeover of the military. He would be Frieze's point man, but Franklin had his own ideas on how he wanted to fight wars in his area of responsibility.

CHAPTER 7

WASHINGTON, DC

Jake had been stuck in traffic, and the brief was already under way when he was signed into the secure briefing room in the basement of the Pentagon. It didn't take long for him to catch up with what was being discussed. The same threats that he had dealt with while at the CIA and the JCS were still viable. What made the latest briefs more ominous was the solidifying strength of Al Qaeda and their worldwide reach.

"Dave," one of the generals asked Dave Holt, the briefer from the Defense Intelligence Agency, "is there any specific targeting ever hinted at?"

"We have nothing that says the Washington Monument or the Lincoln Memorial, but DC is the nexus of government, and most of the betting people in the intelligence community would tell you that DC is a target," Holt answered.

"Dave," Jake stood to speak, "the city itself is a target, but it is ringed with military facilities. Do they come under the general recognition as targets?"

"They are soft targets housing areas of specific national security importance. It is felt that any ground-based attack would try for a high-value soft target, hence a base in the DC area."

"Thanks." Jake sat.

Specific intercepts were shared with the marines. Holt did

his job, providing information that would allow those who had heard it to make informed decisions. "Any questions before I wrap this up?"

Jake stood again. "I was a little late, and I missed your opening remarks. In everything I heard, you didn't mention anything about a threat emanating from Iraq. Did I miss something?"

Everyone turned to look at him. They all knew the reason for Jake's being shipped out of the JCS and wondered if he was harboring resentment.

"The reason there was no mention of Iraq is because we have no creditable intelligence that indicates that it is a threat." Holt paused. "The agency presents this brief without reference to Iraq to the military, with the exception of DOD. When we brief them, we give the same brief but do mention Iraq. If we don't, they beat us up over it."

"How about Chalabi and the INC?" Jake pushed.

"Jake, you've worked at the CIA. You know the Chalabi link is bullshit. He's a flake, and every legitimate intelligence agency has blackballed him. Notice, I said legitimate agencies. DOD has a group of embedded whiz kids who are trying to manufacture intelligence that supports their beliefs. They listen to anyone who supports their premise, which is that Iraq is the most evil of the evil. If we at DIA or the CIA don't mention Iraq in our briefs at DOD all hell breaks loose, so we run around town with two briefs—one for the rational world and one for the crazies." Holt paused, and the remark elicited laughs. "We are in dangerous times, and the people running our government are making it a whole lot more dangerous in looking for threats where they ain't."

The meeting ended, and busy officers rushed to get back to their jobs.

Jake waited until Dave Holt had packed up his briefing materials. "Got a minute, Dave?"

"Sure, Jake. How's it going at Quantico?" They had known one another for years, having worked together in their various tours in Washington. "You holding up okay?"

"I'm doing all right. DOD has me where they want me, but I'm worried about you. If the embedded cabal finds out you are undermining them, they'll get rid of you. I guess what I'm saying is to tone down the two-brief explanation. Someone will eventually leak it, and you'll be gone."

"Jake, I've spent a lifetime in the intelligence business. Sometimes I've been mistaken, but not once have I been asked to provide intelligence that I considered bogus. I can't play that game."

"Based on my experience of trying to speak the truth, I wanted you to know they know how to fight the political war, so be careful."

"I will, Jake, and thanks." Holt was leaving, when he turned. "What have you got going today?"

"I'm in the city to escape the tedium of making insignificant decisions. You know when you run a base you are out of the mainstream."

"Let's go to lunch. Then we can go back to my office and I'll show you a couple of threats that could be of concern to the bases in and around Washington."

Jake didn't leave Holt's office until 1930, a half hour after the start of a party that the Quantico staff had put together to welcome him to his new assignment. Wives and girlfriends would all be dressed up to impress him, but the intelligence Dave Holt provided was considered too important to pass up.

"Can I use a phone, Dave? I've got to call ahead with my regrets. I'm supposed to be the guest of honor at a party that has started without me."

"You should have told me. I could have cut off the brief."

"That's all right. The timing will work out."

"Use the phone in my office."

"Thanks."

Jake settled in behind a desk and dialed the Quantico Officers' Club. In waiting for the connection, he thought about how he would apologize to all those who were gathered.

Someone answered, and Jake identified himself and asked to speak to his chief of staff. He explained that he was unexpectedly tied up and apologized. The chief of staff assured Jake that he would smooth over any ruffled feelings.

"Chief, if Major Matthews is still there, put her on the phone."

A minute passed.

"Major Matthews, sir."

"Major, I should be getting into Quantico at 2200. Meet me in the parking lot in back of the headquarters building at that time, give or take fifteen minutes. Be alone."

"I don't have my uniform, sir."

"That's all right. Wear whatever you've got on."

It was dark and several minutes after 2200 when Jake's car pulled into a parking space next to hers.

"Come on," he instructed when they were out of the cars. He led her to his private entrance, a door he could use without the duty officer knowing he was in the building. She followed him to his office.

He flipped on the lights and closed the door. Fran didn't like it. She was alone with him, and it looked as if he had arranged for them to be undisturbed.

"Sit down." Jake led her to a chair that faced his desk and moved behind her, where she couldn't see what he was doing.

"Would you like a drink?"

"No, sir." Fran was wary. She could hear ice cubes dropping into a glass, and her skin began to crawl. It was always the same. A senior officer would get her alone and try to become intimate. Liquor was always involved, so that when she complained, her allegations would be brushed away with the simple explanation that they had been drinking. The drinks were usually the free pass that allowed whatever she claimed to be discredited.

"Mind if I turn on some music?"

She didn't answer and closed her eyes. She was trying to determine how she was going to escape a romantic general without destroying her career.

With the first notes, Fran was stunned. She recognized Vivaldi's *Four Seasons*, and the violin doublets were unexpected. There were no pliant voices or romantic music, only a violin symphony. It was not music conducive to romance.

She wore a cowl-neck black dress exposing the nape of her neck and shoulders, and she felt naked. Jake walked up in back of her, and she was ready to bolt. She was sure he would touch her as his first advance. He didn't. He went around to the front of his desk and poured a soft drink over a glass full of ice. Fran was floundering; she had mentally prepared for a sexual assault, and none came.

He smiled. "I don't drink on duty. Did you think that I was offering booze?"

She was embarrassed and sat frozen.

"Go get yourself a drink." He waited until she returned.

"I'm going to ask you some very personal questions. I expect truthful answers because whatever you tell me will not leave this room." Jake looked at her and could see she was still frightened about what he might do.

"Forget it. I'm going to tell you what I think. If I get something wrong, correct me." He waited. "You have three documented cases of sexual assault in your personnel file. Each time you've reported it, the person you accused was exonerated, and your career was sidetracked because you were considered trouble."

She knew her history. She wanted to tell Jake that she had done nothing wrong and that she was the person punished because once she accused a male officer, the ranks closed around him, and she was damned.

"Am I right?"

"Yes, sir." She was humiliated to be talking about her problems with the commanding general.

"I take it you're so uptight because you expected me to make a pass at you?" Jake smiled.

She dared not make eye contact with him.

"Well, did you expect me to make a pass?"

"Yes, sir." The words were barely audible.

"I won't, but as you are the closest thing I have as an expert on sexual abuse, I'm going to plug into your expertise." He stopped when he saw the look of shock on her face. "Bad choice of words." Jake stopped again. "Look, Fran, nothing is going to happen between us, so relax." He paused. "Since I've been here I've had to institute two investigations into sexual harassment allegations. You can identify with the problem, but I wanted to make sure you still had the fire in your belly to help me stop that crap. You do, don't you?"

"Yes, sir."

"Okay. Here's the deal. I'm going to tell you things tonight that will only be known to two people. If I hear any of it as gossip around the base, I'll assume it was you who talked, and I'll give you a job from which your career will never recover. Is that clear?"

"Yes, sir."

"While I was in Washington this afternoon, I received a call from Colonel Patch, the Fifteenth Marine Expeditionary Unit commander. His MEU is on alert floating in the Indian Ocean. He informed me that one of his best NCOs, a marine I've worked with and liked, had to be put on suicide watch. It turns out that his wife, who is a marine on base, told him she wanted a divorce." Jake paused and shook his head. "She loves her commanding officer and wants to marry him."

Fran knew what she was hearing wasn't good.

"At 0800 on Monday, I'm going to have the CO standing at

attention about where you are sitting. I'm going to ask him if he is or was fraternizing with a female marine in his command. If he confesses, I'm going to fire him for fraternization. If he lies to me and tells me he is or was not, I'm going to fire him for lying. Either way, he's gone."

"Sir, you've got to give him due process," Fran cautioned.

"I'm going to make him an offer he can't refuse. I'm going to let him retire and figure out some way to tell his wife he was screwing around. If he decides he wants to stay, I'll put him under house arrest until a trial date can be set and let his wife figure out what's going on. I'd bust him for fraternization, but with the girl consenting and perhaps pushing the romance, some wiseass lawyer is liable to get him off, and I want him gone. So that brings me to you. On Tuesday morning, you are going to be the new commanding officer of the military police battalion."

"Sir, I don't have a background for that."

"But you know the ins and outs of sexual harassment, and I'm hoping you can sniff it out. The CO that I'm firing has enabled a culture where it was not frowned upon if officers and NCOs hit on young enlisted women. There might be female officers who have been put in awkward or compromising situations, but you know how that game is played. They won't come forward, or they will be marginalized. So you're going to be the CO, and you're going to clean up what I consider a sex ring. As an aside, I've been driving around the base at night, and anytime after 0200 if there are male and female MPs on duty together, they aren't even bothering to get out of their cars. I'm not deluded enough to think that they are just talking."

"I think I know what you want done, but I have no military police experience."

"Major, one of my jobs is to pick out leaders. You are one that I've picked. You may know squat about policing techniques, but you're smart, and your value won't be in being a policewoman. It will be in purging a rotten unit to get it functioning as a marine command.

You have the skill set to do that. I'll surround you with an XO who knows the policing end of the business."

"I'll try."

"You'll do all right, but that is only part of what I want you to do." Jake took a long sip of his drink and looked at her to see if she was overwhelmed. In his opinion, she was holding up. "As you know, I've just been fired from the JCS, but while I was there, we received dozens of threat possibilities for the Capitol. It is expected that any terrorist who wants to blow something up will pick a soft target in the Washington area. They don't get much softer than this base, so here is what I want done. I want a plan for locking down the base. No one moves in or out without some identification process that you'll have to devise. Secondly, all the remote gates to the base are open. I want some plan to lock them down and have guards on them. Thirdly, the most essential building on this base is the water treatment plant. If it is knocked out, the base will be crippled. I say that because Interstate 95 runs right by it. A stone can be thrown from the highway that would hit the building. I don't care how you do it, but figure out some way to protect the building, because if it goes down, we will all be staying home. Finally, in the basement of this building there is a communications suite that some smart young captain took upon himself to start. Work was started on it and was stopped. The reason it was killed was because it was in the comm budget. I'm going to dump a ton of money into the security budget. As the CO of the MPs, that will be your budget, and it will be your responsibility to set up a comm suite capable of talking to the world, and, importantly, in the event of an incident in Washington, a place where the Marine Corps headquarters can relocate."

Jake stopped. "That's the overview. You'll have my backing to get those things I've outlined done. If anyone gets in your way, you have an open channel to me. Use it. I know you are going to have questions, so take the weekend to figure them out. I'm available to answer them." Jake paused and looked at her, trying to determine if she understood what he wanted done. "I know I've dumped a lot on you, but you'll do fine. Do you have anything you want to ask now?"

"Not right now, but I'm sure after I've had a chance to think about things I will have."

"I've got some work to do. Let yourself out." Jake dismissed her.

Fran stood and moved toward the door.

"By the way, you look better in that dress than you do in uniform. You look great."

She went to her car thinking more about the compliment than about the job she was going to take.

CHAPTER 8

SEPTEMBER 11, 2001

"Sir, you might want to turn on CNN." His secretary poked her head in the door to Jake's office.

"What's up?"

"An airliner has just crashed into the World Trade Center."

Jake used a remote to turn on the television sitting on a sideboard near his desk. In his first glance at the smoking tower, he knew it wasn't an accident. Intelligence sources had been reporting that terrorists were considering using airplanes as weapons. With the skies clear in New York, he felt it impossible for the crash to have been an accident.

Unlike the others on the staff who were mesmerized by the television footage, he called the MP battalion.

"This is General Gregg. I want to speak to Major Matthews."

There was a delay before she answered, and Jake didn't hesitate to get his message across.

"Are you watching the news?"

"Yes, sir."

"Lock down the base. No marine leaves. Let the civilian workforce go home, but don't let them back aboard base until we have some clarification of events. And get the communications suite up and running, I've got a feeling we are going to need it."

Entering the adjutant's office, he found two young marines watching the unfolding drama.

"Get your weapons, and come with me." The marines complied with the order.

He led them to the basement of the building where the comm suite had been sitting idly. "This room is going to start filling up with people. Here is a list of their names. Anyone who is not listed will not be allowed to enter. Stay here, and make sure that happens. I'll have the sergeant major relieve you when he can. Got it?" Jake was roiling internally but would not show nerves in front of the young marines.

As he moved through the headquarters building, he wondered if he had overreacted. If he had, the staff would think him crazy, but his senses told him that he was right.

By the time he returned to his office, all the secretaries were standing around, some crying. An airplane had crashed into the Pentagon, and everyone crammed around the TV knew someone who worked there.

Jake drove to the MP battalion. Upon entering, he found the building in turmoil. The MPs from all over the base were being called in and redeployed. Some were running to try to catch up with their assignments. As they passed Jake in the hall, he tried not to get in their way.

"How's it feel, being a commanding officer?" he asked as he entered Fran Matthews's office. "Don't stand up; continue with what you were doing."

She was on the phone issuing orders. After a few minutes she put down the phone, and it rang instantly.

"It's for you, sir."

He listened and was told that as a result of the Pentagon strike, parts of the marine headquarters would need new offices. He assured whomever he was talking to that the base could handle them.

"We did something right," he said as he hung up. "That call wasn't conducted over normal phone lines, The Pentagon is blacked out. That call was through the comm suite you set up. Nice job, Major."

"Thank you, sir."

"How is the rest of the security plan going?"

"If it is not implemented, it is in the process. About two-thirds of the stations have checked in, and they are up and running." She hadn't had time to digest the attacks because she had been too busy making sure what she was supposed to have accomplished was done. In the moment she had to think of something other than putting marines in the right places, the events that had triggered her workload came to mind.

"Sir, how did you know?"

"Know what?"

"That something like this could happen. It is like you prepared for it."

"Lucky guess."

"Everybody in Washington had the same information. Why weren't they prepared?"

"Major. What's done is done. Our job is not to worry about the how and to get to work on ensuring that this base doesn't let a terrorist through the gates."

She looked at him, not satisfied with his answer, but she had no right to question further.

"I'll be out and about looking at the security setup. If you have any questions, you can reach me on the car radio."

Jake left. His answer to her question may have been sufficient to satisfy her, but it bothered him. The information he had based his actions on had been available to everyone in the Pentagon. They knew terrorists were plotting to use airliners as weapons. The intelligence available indicated that there were real threats emanating out of Afghanistan, but they were overlooked. The Frieze embeds in the Pentagon wanted to refight the war with Iraq and discarded any threat that didn't fit into their worldview. Jake wondered how they were going to square the horrific events with their obsession. He didn't know for sure, but he didn't think terrorists came from Iraq.

The DEPSECDEF watched the TV in disbelief. He watched the New York explosions, and when a blast shook the Pentagon and the halls were filled with frantic people trying to escape, his confidence was shattered. Mistakes had been made, but his thoughts weren't centered on his mistakes. His mind raced to damage control. From the information he was receiving, a picture emerged identifying the terrorists. They were Islamic, and all signs indicated that they were directed in their acts from Afghanistan. Not worrying about the people who had died or the damage to buildings, Frieze looked for some way to lay off the blame for missing the signals. He had been in Washington long enough to know that a fall guy was required to take the blame for the attacks on American soil. He would cover himself and the Pentagon by citing poor intelligence. That was a safe bet, because no one ever knew what was good or bad intelligence until it was acted upon. Blaming others would take the spotlight off him and the neoconservatives and their insistence that Afghanistan was not the real threat.

Moving to a secure office, his phone rang constantly, and people rushed into the confined space. Requests for decisions came at him in a torrent of questions. It was as if everyone in the building was paralyzed, with no one willing to make a decision. For the first time, he thought that he had surrounded himself with too many yes men. While others were dealing with the emotional impact of the attacks, Frieze was conceptualizing a strategy to use the fallout of the attacks in facilitating his plans for Iraq. In thinking about the big picture, he knew he would need all the yes men.

Calling a meeting the day after the attacks, he brought together all the people he had brought into the Defense Department. They were subdued and looked only at the immediate consequences of the crashes. The people in decision-making positions were relieved that the secretary and the deputy were implicating the intelligence community. Blaming others would take the heat off them when Congress called for a broader investigation into the facts surrounding the attacks. The more immediate problem was that politicians were calling for a response. After months of ignoring Afghanistan, the Pentagon had no suitable plans ready for an immediate retaliation. There were war plans for Afghanistan, but they weren't streamlined for the type of war that the SECDEF wanted to fight.

In a Pentagon secure conference room, the DEPSECDEF video-conferenced with CENTCOM.

"General," Don Frieze began when the image of Franklin appeared, "we are going to need an immediate retaliation against Afghanistan. What do you and your staff have that we can implement ASAP?"

The weather-beaten general was folksy. "We can dust off the OpPlan for Afghanistan."

"When was it written?"

"In 1992, but it has undergone several major rewrites and updates."

"What is the bottom line troop wise? How many? What types and how long do you estimate it will take you to get troops into theater?" Frieze was blunt. He didn't have time for the general to spin yarns.

"At first blush, it looks like 250,000 troops will be required. It will take about three months to put them in theater."

"That's unsat. What can you put on the ground now?"

"Now?" The word seemed to confuse Franklin.

"Now. Within the next week."

"We can't move that quickly. We have to alert the troops we are going to use and move them into theater so that they are ready for combat. That takes time."

"What about airpower? Can you get that into the theater immediately?"

"That can be done once we get basing and overflight rights in Pakistan. That might take a couple of days."

"How about US-based bombers and naval aircraft off the carriers? Can we get them ready to make a big splash in the next couple of days? We have to do something because there is already a public outcry."

"Sure, once you get me overflight rights we can make some noise, but without troops on the ground, you will not be able to achieve anything. This is going to shape up as an army job." The general displayed a bias toward his service. He wasn't an infantry officer but identified with the core of the army at the expense of the other services.

Frieze listened. In his mind, what he was hearing would be too slow. Politicians would want quicker action. They would want to show constituents that they were on top of things.

"How many special forces can you get on the ground within the next couple of weeks?" Frieze had formulated a plan, and he was going to push it by the general. He didn't need Franklin's buy-in, but it would help if the uniforms and the civilian leadership of the nation's military were on the same page.

"We can get several hundred in within two weeks."

"Does that include the SEALs and Delta Force?"

"Yes, but I think you ought to go light on using special forces. They don't have the firepower or staying power to change the situation on the ground. They can blow things up and make noise, but there are too few of them to hold on to the ground. Besides, they are a pain in the ass to work with. They are always running off on their own, and half the time they don't act like they are military." Franklin felt that the special forces were prima donnas and got all the glory while the real army did the work and was barely recognized.

"General, I need something now, because things are going to start happening fast. I've already had calls from the vice president's office, and he wants action." Frieze paused. "General, the secretary has just come into the room, and he wants to talk to you."

SECDEF showed on Franklin's screen as he moved into camera range. "I want you to scrap any contingency plans you have that entail the introduction of ground troops other than special forces. I don't have numbers for you, but what I envision is introducing special operators and have their efforts supported by air power. Once they have things moving in our direction, we might introduce ground forces but nothing near the numbers called for in any plans I've seen." The secretary put an end to Franklin's idea of launching a major campaign.

"How do you intend to support those troops on the ground?" The general knew that for every trigger puller there were six or seven support personnel required. He thought his question might awaken those in Washington to the fact that there were no ad hoc wars.

"We've lined up civilian companies that will do all the support work. You just worry about getting me a quick-strike package that I can bring to the president."

"Sir." Franklin was not used to being overridden. "I strongly advise against going light on this. You have to have a footprint on the ground so that the commander in chief has options. I'd suggest that we implement the plans already on the books."

"General, you have my instruction."

With the preemptive advice given to the CENTCOM commander, the secretary excused himself and left the room.

Frieze again took over the discussion. "We will work out the details later, but plan on getting special forces and airpower into theater ASAP. I'll expect your plans tomorrow." Frieze was brusque. He wasn't going to listen to further argument. Having cowed the generals in the Pentagon, he wasn't going to let Franklin have a free hand. He smiled inwardly, thinking that the military was thick-headed. With his reputation as one who didn't accept doing things as they had always been done, and his swift removal of those who tried to buck him, he was amused in thinking that there were still generals who thought they had the ability to act independently.

When Franklin's image left the video screen, Frieze spoke candidly to those sitting around the conference table with him.

"Any plan CENTCOM comes up with will be too large for what we intend. I'm sure the general and his staff will bemoan the fact that we don't want them to use the cavalry. So when their plan does arrive, I want it scrubbed. I want a minimal force introduced into Afghanistan."

"Sir," one of Frieze's embeds spoke up, "Congress is thirsting for revenge. They could bring pressure to have a full war plan implemented. Franklin is probably on the phone right now talking to his friends on the hill about SECDEF hampering his ability to conduct the war as he sees fit."

"We came to town with a plan. If we get bogged down in a backwater like Afghanistan we will never get a chance to prove our theories." Frieze stopped and let out a sigh. "Now that the public is hungry for war, we must assure them that the events of the eleventh can be tied to Saddam Hussein. We have to establish a link. Fine-tune that message when you speak before Congress or the press. The thirst for war has to be redirected. In the meantime, we will respond to the pressure to seek revenge in Afghanistan."

No objections were voiced, and most nodded in compliance.

"The vice president will probably need something quickly to present to the president, so get on CENTCOM, and make them meet the short timeline." Frieze's words dismissed the group, and they filed out of the conference room.

DEPSECDEF sat alone and analyzed his course of action. He saw it in two parts. First was getting Afghanistan done and then linking Iraq and the 9/11 attacks. He stood and mused about keeping the war fever going so that no one would look too closely at the neoconservatives as they prepared for war.

A week after the attacks, Washington was still in a state of confusion. Traffic into the city was at a near standstill as security measures in and around government buildings backed up surface traffic that bulged onto the interstate highways. Getting into the Pentagon by car was impossible, so Jake drove only several miles north of Quantico to the Springfield Station and rode the Metro into the Pentagon. From the underground station, he took a long escalator to the working levels of the building. Everyone entering had to have the proper identification. One check wasn't enough. Checkpoints were established in sight of each other, and the final guards, who had seen people checked through a series of gates, insisted on one final check of the same identifications. It was a Pentagon overreaction. No one complained at the time-delaying procedures, as most people still walked around with the glazed look of "what happened?"

Jake made the final checkpoint and had to ask for directions to the marine headquarters. The crashed airplane had taken out a chunk of the marine offices, and they were relocated in a part of the building that was under construction. The refitted offices were usable, but wires were exposed and taped to the floor where the finish work had not yet been completed. The signs on the doors were cardboard and, depending on the penmanship used, legible.

Jake found the operations section and entered the office of the deputy commandant for operations.

"General Gregg to see General Cotton." He spoke to the marine sitting in the outer office.

"Yes, sir, go right in; he's expecting you."

Jake entered.

"How are you doing, Bear?" Jake alerted the senior officer to his presence by using his tactical call sign.

"Come on in, Jake," Cotton responded. He came around his desk and shook Jake's hand. Cotton was a big man. He was well over six six and was massive through the shoulders and chest. Giving him the call sign Bear was a no-brainer, because his brown hair came almost to his eye line and made him look like an angry grizzly. Even when smiling, he was frightening.

It wasn't enough for Cotton to shake hands. If he liked people, and he did Jake, he pulled them in close and hugged them, immobilizing them until he let go. Jake expected it and braced himself.

"Did you lose anyone in the attacks?" Jake asked as he opened space between them.

"Nah. We were just out of the blast area." Cotton sighed in disgust "The navy got hit the hardest. I knew a couple of their guys. What a waste."

"Yeah."

"Let's not talk about it. It's too raw." Cotton paused and reflected on the events before his mood lightened. "The Marine Corps needs your ass, Jake, me boy." He attempted a Scottish accent.

"Does the deputy secretary of defense's office agree that I'm needed?"

"Fuck them. They are so busy trying to cover up their mistakes that they aren't paying attention. Man, they are shoveling blame in so many directions that they don't have time to worry about how the Corps wants to use you."

"How's that?"

"Jake," Cotton ignored the question, "you are not going to believe who is going to run the retaliation efforts against Afghanistan."

"I've heard rumors, but I know nothing for sure."

"Frieze." Cotton paused for effect. "That fucking twit is in way over his head. He's tearing up CENTCOM's plans for Afghanistan and replacing them with his own, which amount to nothing. He is going to try to win Afghanistan with smoke and mirrors without ever reading the history of it. If he had, he'd realize there is no bullshitting your way to victory there."

"What does winning look like to them?"

"They have no idea. No objectives have been stated other than those by the president to kill bad guys."

Jake was harsh. "The last time I read Clausewitz, revenge wasn't considered a military strategy."

"That's what is crazy about this," Cotton added. "We really have no plan for going to war in one of the most difficult places on earth. No one knows what the military is supposed to accomplish."

"Has no guidance come out of the DEPSECDEF's office?" Jake queried.

"Nothing. CENTCOM has sent up four plans, and each has been sent back with the demand for fewer forces." Cotton dismissed the DEPSECDEF's intentions.

"The embeds have never considered Afghanistan a threat, and I'll bet they are worried that we could become tied down there," Jake mentioned.

"Every sane planner in Washington sees a danger in what Frieze wants done. No one is saying anything because he has the White House's buy-in." Cotton paused. "There is a fear that with as many isolated special forces teams as the secretary wants to use, air power will not be able to support them all, and that means there are going to be guys hanging it out."

"Where do you see the marines fitting in?"

Cotton shook his head in disgust. "Somewhere in the Indian Ocean the Fifteenth Marine Expeditionary Unit is floating with a couple of thousand marines and helicopters. They are steaming in a three-ship flotilla. Also in the Indian Ocean but with minimal contact with the MEU is a carrier battle group with five squadrons of fighter attack airplanes, two of which are marine squadrons. In another part of the ocean are four maritime prepositioned ships with enough gear to support an entire division. Each flotilla is going in circles, and they aren't talking to one another. CENTCOM supposedly has control of them. They have control of the MEU, but the carrier battle group is a national asset and can't be used without White House approval. The maritime prepositioned ships are civilian and report to union headquarters in South Carolina. It's a dumb command setup, and we have requested that the carrier battle group and prepositioned shipping join the MEU so that if we have to go to war we won't fall on our faces. CENTCOM has approved putting those pieces together by forming a task force. For planning purposes it is being called Task Force Raptor. It was approved because if things go to shit for the special forces, it will be an option for making a forcible entry and rescuing them."

"I've been watching the intelligence traffic and can see what you are talking about. Why am I here, Bear?"

"Jake, Task Force Raptor will be the only unit anywhere near Afghanistan capable of putting a security force on the ground that could support the special forces."

"It will be in the Arabian Sea. What is that? Seven hundred miles from Afghanistan?"

"Nah. It's about 450." Cotton was unfazed by the question. "You know the MEU's capabilities. With the addition of the carrier's planes and the supplies on the prepositioned shipping, it could get into Afghanistan in an emergency."

"Crossing 450 miles of desert and then making a forcible entry would be a bitch."

"I knew that you'd see the problems, and I told the commandant you were the man for the job." Cotton smiled.

"What?"

"I recommended that you head Task Force Raptor."

"The mention of my name in the deputy secretary's office with a recommendation for any job will get shot down."

"Franklin has approved the task force. He knows that the way Frieze is planning the war it could spin out of control, and he wants options. Frieze has tentatively okayed setting up the task force, because he has to have a backup plan to present to Congress. Having a task force on standby will quiet a lot of politicians. Besides, he is trying to buy time. He knows that it will take awhile to staff any new organization and is sure we will be out of Afghanistan before it would become operational."

"So you're giving me a command, that won't be staffed? That doesn't make sense."

"Before you get all pissed off, think. The units that will make up the task force are in existence and in proximity to where they will be used. Each has a staff that has been operating independently; the task force commander will just have to overlay their efforts and coordinate what they are doing. The reason for putting you in charge is to have you interface with the navy, civilians, the State Department, and the Pakistani government. You know how it is when dealing with the navy and civilians; if you ain't wearing stars, they run right over you. A general gets a seat at the power tables and won't have to back down because of rank. And you, the Marine Corps knows, won't back down."

"Is this your idea?" Jake didn't know how to interpret what he heard.

Cotton started, "We are going to be involved in Afghanistan. Over time, we may fly troops in, but we will have to have some place to land them. Special forces can't clear and hold ground, so right now our only course of action is a forcible entry. Just look at it this way, you may have the opportunity to take amphibious warfare to new heights."

"Spare me the pep talk, Bear. A five-hundred-mile patch of sand between the sea and Afghanistan hardly makes this amphibious. It does make it a bitch."

Cotton pushed a briefcase across his desk toward Jake. "These are your orders, and your plane tickets. You will be met upon your arrival at the Karachi airport the day after tomorrow. From there you will be flown to the MEU. We figure that is the best place to set up your operation. I've already alerted all staffs that they would have to kick in personnel to man the task force. There are maps and some initial planning documents that might help you to hit the ground running."

"I guess I have no rights of refusal."

"Come on, Jake. This is the Corps. We do what we are ordered to do."

"Do I have an open line to CENTCOM?"

"That could be problematic. General Franklin wants to make Afghanistan an army show, so you will have to be careful in what you request of him, or he will cut you off. SECDEF is out, because Afghanistan is not where the neocons want to fight. You are going to have to use back channels to the people you can trust on the JCS, and, of course, you will have an open line to the Marine Corps." Cotton laughed. "The current intel is that the army is way behind on this because Frieze is stopping CENTCOM from putting an army presence on the ground. Franklin is trying his damnedest to gin up missions, but Frieze keeps shooting him down. They are knocking heads, so they won't bother you. Put Raptor together and await a call because everyone knows it will be coming."

"What a cluster fuck."

"Just concentrate on storming the beaches and marching across the desert."

"Thanks, Bear." Jake was sarcastic. "Anything else?

"Yeah. You did a great job at Quantico. It's the only base that was operational from day one. Most of the other bases in the area are still partially operating."

"This is a hell of a reward." Jake was amused. "I guess I'll be talking to you from the Arabian Sea."

Cotton stood and walked around his desk. He shook Jake's hand and pulled him in for the bear hug. "You know, I'd swap positions with you in a heartbeat." He meant it. Marines, no matter the rank, wanted to be in the fight with the troops.

CHAPTER 9

CENTCOM,
TAMPA, FLORIDA

The Tampa weather was hot and muggy, and that didn't help the already oppressive mood at CENTCOM Headquarters. General Franklin had finished his twentieth teleconference with the Pentagon and was angry. As he stormed down the long hallway to his office, he stuck his head in the open door of his operations director and told him that he wanted to meet with the officers on the operations staff. One by one, officers moved toward the general's office. There weren't enough seats, and some remained standing, waiting for him to vent.

"We're getting cut out of the planning for a military strike against Afghanistan. The goddamn eggheads in Washington think they know how to fight wars and not a goddamn one of them has a clue."

The staff listened carefully in the event Franklin put out a "tasker" asking for some specific action to be completed. They were in tune with his feelings, because each had been in contact with counterparts at DOD, and they knew their advice was being discounted. As the command that should have had the lead in planning Afghan operations, they were being ignored. They couldn't be cut out of the loop totally, because they nominally controlled the forces that would be used in Afghanistan, but they were being blunted at every turn. Instead of the combatant commander running the planned war, it was being micromanaged from the Pentagon.

"We're getting snookered by the embeds." Franklin stated the obvious. "The SECDEF has been harping on changing the military since he took office, and now he and Frieze are trying to do it at our expense." Franklin paused, thinking about how far he wanted to go in discrediting his superiors.

"They want everything to take a backseat to airpower. Under their plan, we will control the skies and bomb the Afghanis into submission. As the air force is winning the war from thirty thousand feet, several hundred special operators will rout and control a population of twenty-six million. Frieze and his yes men are going to try to win Afghanistan at minimal cost so that they can push through their agenda on Iraq. The bastards are going to get us into a war in the wrong place."

"Sir, most of the people on the JCS tell me privately that the way you want to fight the war is right, but there isn't one of them with balls enough to contradict the DEPSECDEF." Major General Grady Hatton, the CENTCOM operations director, informed the staff of things they already knew.

"There is no way that this works. All the figures the embeds are showing Congress indicate that the way they want to use the military is less expensive than deploying forces. What they are hiding are the costs of the civilian contractors. They have let out no-bid contracts and haven't put a cap on them. This is going to be the most expensive war we have ever fought, but they will sell it as using the military efficiently. They are trying to make this a pay-to-play nation so that wars will be outsourced and run like business ventures. The only things the army will be around for are parades." Franklin was cynical. "They have already started gutting our operations and maintenance accounts and transferring money to help offset the cost of US contractors, who are outsourcing support roles to Pakistani firms."

Franklin hesitated. "As I see it, there are two imminent wars and one on the horizon that we have to be prepared to fight and win. We have to focus on Afghanistan, even if our advice is not wanted, and a corollary to that is the fight for money surrounding US efforts there. Money will be thrown at the services involved in the hostilities. It will be spent with no accountability, and in that scenario the rich will get richer. Right now, all the services are fighting for a share of that pie, but there is more competition than the other services. The embeds are passing money through the system to contractors without bothering to inform Congress. We can't do anything about that, so we have to concentrate on our direct competition. I don't know how this war will end. I do know it will end, and the army has to have played a part in it, or it will lose out. The air force and the special forces are getting money rained on them, because under the new paradigm, they are the only forces needed. The navy will get their share, and that leaves the army and the marines. Unless the ground forces get a piece of the action in Afghanistan, we are going to shrink. Right now, we are shut out, but Frieze wants to get into Iraq so badly, we may have a bargaining chip. The next time an embed calls and tells us to cut forces in the Iraqi plans, refuse. I don't want any of you cutting troop levels at the behest of any of Frieze's yes men. Troop reductions will be done in negotiation between the DEPSECDEF and me." Franklin made his case. "Now put your heads together and figure ways we can get army troops into Afghanistan. Be smart about it, because if the shit hits the fan, the embeds will be looking for scapegoats. Starting today, I want all conversations and communications with DOD recorded. Record everything—times, dates, subject matter, anything that provides a paper or electronic trail. When the brains in the Pentagon screw this up and start trying to blame us, I want to be able to throw their words back at them. Okay, you are all dismissed. Stick around for a minute, Grady." Franklin instructed the operations director.

"I can understand your wont to get the army positioned in the budget fights ahead, but you mentioned the Marine Corps." Hatton was Franklin's golfing partner and felt confident talking about a sensitive subject with the multiservice staff out of the room. "They are our competition."

"I specifically mentioned them for the benefit of the people who were in the room," Franklin confessed.

"You recently approved establishment of a task force. Does that mean we are giving them a share of the fight?"

"No," Franklin cut him off. "That ain't going to happen. The task force is seaborne and is going to float in circles, because I don't intend to use it. By approving it, Congress and the Marine Corps think I'm a team player. That will stand me in good stead."

Hatton chuckled in agreement with his boss's assessment.

"I don't want to screw the Marine Corps. I want them to succeed in the budget battles. In fact, I want all the services to do well, but I will not sit by and watch the regular army being relegated to guard duty while the special forces take a greater share of the army budget." Franklin spit out the words. "They act like they walk on water while the army is stuck with all the rules and regulations and invariably fights this country's wars and get all the grief." The CG expressed the feeling of most in the army, and he indicated that he wasn't going to let it get any worse on his watch. With the Special Operations Command sharing MacDill Air Force Base with CENTCOM, there was a competition between the commands. It didn't help that SOCOM was putting a $30-million addition onto its headquarters, and Franklin's request to add onto the CENTCOM headquarters was denied."

"Is there anything else?" Hatton was getting ready to leave.

"No, that's it, but make sure everyone on the staff records all conversations with the whiz kids, because when they fuck this up, I want to be able to stick it to them." Franklin spoke with a coolness that hid his anger.

"Yes, sir," Hatton said. "Sir, with all that is going on, do you want me to call off tomorrow's golf game? Everyone knows you're busy, and the regular group will understand your canceling."

"Hell no. We aren't going to be allowed to fight this war. The boys in Washington are, so I'll have plenty of time. See you at the regular time."

Hatton left, thinking that the general should have let him cancel the game because there was a lot going on, and he was sure to be called while they were on the golf course.

CHAPTER 10

KARACHI, PAKISTAN

The Karachi airport was like a bazaar. People were crammed into dirty concourses and moved as a tide. One moved, and they all moved in a like direction and pace. The Pakistani air travelers ran the gamut. Barefooted men swathed in tribal attire moved along with businessmen in thousand-dollar suits. Jake noticed immediately that everyone in the terminal smoked. The high ceiling caught the cigarette smoke, and a purple haze descended onto travelers and peddlers alike.

In deplaning, he didn't know what to expect He was told he would be met but not how or by whom. He wore civilian clothes so that he could blend in with the crowd, and he felt like an invisible man. The thing that set him apart was his beardless face and high and tight marine haircut.

"Mr. General Gregg?" A Pakistani man in a suit and an askew tie came up behind him.

Jake was startled at the closeness but managed not to show his surprise. "I'm Gregg," he snapped.

"I'm Mister Ahmed." He was unshaven and looked as if he had a three-day beard. A misshapen cigarette hung from the corner of his mouth so that he could speak out of one side. "I'm from the Ministry of the Interior, and I've been sent to welcome you to Pakistan." He smiled over a semibow. "If you will come with me, I will take you through customs and bring you to the American representative, who is waiting for you in the VIP lounge."

Jake didn't know that he was going to be welcomed by a foreign national and had no choice but to follow. He was in a strange land, and there were no friendly faces.

Ahmed walked around the line of people waiting to clear immigration and customs and led Jake to a private area where three customs agents waited. His bags had been brought from the airplane to the area, and Jake watched as they prepared to open them. "If you will give them your briefcase, they will finish up quickly," Ahmed suggested.

"It is not a briefcase. It is a diplomatic pouch and contains protected papers. As I am traveling on a diplomatic passport, my baggage is also exempt from search." Jake wasn't sure if what he was saying was true, but he didn't want people going through his bags.

Ahmed and the customs agents didn't know what to do. After a moment of confusion, they decided to call for instructions. Someone in authority made a decision, because nothing further was said, and Jake was passed through to the terminal.

Arriving at the VIP lounge, Ahmed left Jake with a young American.

"General Gregg. I'm David Alexander with the American Consulate in Karachi." A blond young man in his late twenties extended his hand. Alexander wore a blue blazer and a rep tie more appropriate for an Ivy League football game than the Middle East. He had a welcoming smile, and Jake felt relieved to be with him. "Did you have any trouble with customs?"

"They seemed interested in my briefcase. I identified it as a diplomatic pouch or they would have had access to all of my papers."

"That's pretty standard for them. You didn't go through regular customs. The people who wanted to look through your bags were ISI, Pakistani Intelligence. With the world situation being as volatile as it is and with everyone thinking that we are going to level Afghanistan, an American general arriving out of the blue has the Pakistanis running in circles. That's why we wanted you traveling under a diplomatic passport. They shouldn't have touched your personal things, but we didn't complain about it because it makes them feel like they are doing their job." He laughed. "Man, with allies like these, we don't need enemies."

"Do you have an itinerary for me?" Jake asked.

"All arrangements have been made. Would you like to take some time to freshen up? I know you have had a long day."

"No, I feel pretty good." Jake was tired but didn't want to extend his travels.

"Okay. There is an air force cargo plane waiting for you. It is going to fly you to Gwadar in the westernmost port in Pakistan before the sand becomes Iran. From there, a marine helo will fly you out to the USS *Peleliu*, the command ship for the Marine Expeditionary Unit. Our last contact with them indicated that they were about sixty miles off the coast."

"Great."

"Follow me. I'll take you to your aircraft and brief you along the way." Jake picked up one of his bags, and Alexander got the other. They departed the lounge and went down a flight of stairs to the tarmac.

"The Pakis have no idea why you're here. For that matter, neither do we, but the cover story is that there was an accident aboard one of the amphibious ships, and you are here to investigate what happened. There is no way for the Paki Intelligence to know about an accident aboard one of our ships, so they have to buy the story," Alexander informed him. "So far, so good. They have bigger things on their plate. They are running around trying to cover up their ties to Al Qaeda and the Taliban. One general making a stop before going offshore hasn't made too big a blip on their radar."

"Thanks for the info. I'll keep that story going."

"General," Alexander paused, "why are you here?"

Jake laughed. "I'm just going out to a ship to determine how an accident happened. Besides, it will all become clear in a couple of days as I start sending message traffic."

"People I know who know of you said you were a quick study. It appears that they were right."

They reached the airplane, and the crew that had been asleep on air mattresses laid out on the metal floor jumped up to salute their passenger.

"Are we waiting for anyone else?' Jake asked the pilot.

"No, sir. This airplane is yours."

"Are you guys old enough to fly this thing?" he joked with the crew.

"If we're not, you're going to find out at the same time we do." The pilot was not intimidated.

"If that is the case, let's go." Jake shook hands with Alexander. "David, if this assignment materializes as I suspect, I will need immediate clearances for operations in Pakistani airspace. I may be coming to you for clearances after the fact, and I'd appreciate it if you could get them through the wickets."

"That is some hell of a shipboard accident that you are going to investigate." Alexander nodded. "Not to worry. I'll be sure you are covered."

Karachi International was only miles from the coast, and after flying south for several minutes the airplane was over the Arabian Sea. A southerly heading was followed until land was out of sight, and the airplane turned west.

The airplane was noisy and passenger comforts were lacking. It was affectionately called a "trash hauler," and at times the cargo it carried was more important than passengers. People and boxes were afforded the same treatment.

Jake sat against a bulkhead in a strap seat—canvas stretched over aluminum tubing. Prior passengers had sagged the fabric so that it was like sitting in a bowl with metal pushing into the bottom of his thighs. There was no soundproofing, and Jake put on a noise-dampening headset. Even with the ear protection, the high pitch of the engines and the airplane's vibrations made it difficult to concentrate.

He tried to think ahead, but he had been given no guidance other than to put together a task-organized unit that could be employed in combat operations. No specific operations were mentioned. He could only assume how the task force might be employed and knew that there would be no time for second-guessing or refinements. Several ideas ran though his mind, but he was unable to fix on any one. The task force, he determined, would be a come-as-you-are command.

His thoughts were interrupted when the power to the four engines was cut, and the plane started a steep descent that resulted in a hard landing onto the runway at Gwadar. With full reverse thrust applied and with the metering caused by the antilock brakes releasing and grabbing, the airplane shuddered to a stop short of the runway end.

Stopping near a marine helicopter, the back ramp was lowered, and Jake swapped airplanes. As his bags bounced onto the helo floor, the rotors started turning, and he was on his way. They were over water quickly, and the sun was setting when he saw the flotilla that he was going to join.

LHA-5, the USS *Peleliu*, an eight-hundred-foot floating airdrome, was the command ship of the Marine Expeditionary Unit (MEU). It floated with two other troop-carrying ships, but it was the centerpiece of MEU operations. With a flight deck and hangar deck capable of housing and operating twenty helicopters of various sizes, and four vertical take-off and landing Harrier jets, it provided the muscle for forcible entry into hostile lands. Over a thousand marines called the *Peleliu* home and lived in cramped discomfort as they circled in the ocean, waiting for the order to launch. It had its own hospital and a command suite capable of communication anywhere in the world.

As the helicopter carrying Jake landed, the ship's captain welcomed him aboard, but Jake wanted to get to the command center so he could talk to the marines.

"Attention," someone ordered the gathered officers, who stood erect between the radar consoles, screens, plotting tables, and communications gear. A large map of the area of operations was outlined on a Lucite board that could be written on in grease pencil.

"As you were." He had to stoop to enter the hatchway, and his shoulders rubbed on either side of the entrance.

"Welcome aboard, General." Colonel Jerry Patch, the commanding officer of the MEU, greeted him.

"Thanks, Decal." Patch's call sign was a play on his name. "We need to talk." Jake asked the others in the area to give him some time alone with the colonel. "Go get a coffee or something, and come back in about fifteen minutes."

"I'm sure you know the MEU is going to be folded in under a task force I'm supposed to put together?" Jake started when they were alone.

"Yes, sir. We received classified instructions to that effect yesterday," Patch answered. He was Jake's height, and if it were not for the fact he was an African American, he could have been his clone. Both had broad shoulders and trim waists, but it was their hamlike forearms that mirrored the sameness. Patch, like Jake, graduated from college and deferred going into the officer program. He joined the Marine Corps as an enlisted man and went through Parris Island before becoming an officer. With similar experiences, they were comfortable with each other.

"As I see it, nothing will change for you. You'll just be taking orders from me instead of CENTCOM directly." Jake paused. "Since you have been working with these troops for months, you know their strengths and weaknesses. I don't, and there is not going to be enough time for me to learn. I don't know if it is over the wire yet, but we will be starting air operations in Afghanistan tomorrow. That means things are going to happen fast, so I'm going to be leaning on you heavily for advice."

"I appreciate that, sir."

"What I intend to do is strip some people from your staff, grab a couple of marines from the carrier battle group, and task organize a staff. I'll set up a command element that can coordinate all the moving parts floating around out here. I will not be able to set up a staff with all the areas functionally covered, so tell your staff they are dual-hatted. They work for you and me."

"Sir, you tell me what you want, and we'll get it done."

"I'm going to need good people but don't cut essential people out of your staff. I'm going to need a few people who can think." Jake knew how the game was played. When commanders had an opportunity to move people, they usually off-loaded their weakest.

"Some of my strongest officers are lieutenants. They are young, but they are hard-chargers," Patch explained.

"That's fine." Jake showed no concern over working with young officers. "Let's bring everyone back in. I'll introduce myself."

The officers returned to the command center.

"I'm General Gregg. Some of you know me, and those of you who don't soon will." It was all he said in introducing himself. "I bring you news. America will be starting air strikes in conjunction with special operations in Afghanistan tomorrow. We have a foothold in the north against the Taliban and will be working with the Northern Alliance of tribes in taking it to the enemy." A muffled cheer started upon hearing the news. "Notice, that mentioned the north of the country. That is where we have local allies who can carry the fight. The other Taliban stronghold is Kandahar, in the south. There are no local fighters there, because the area is all Taliban. We will have special ops people snooping and pooping, gathering intelligence, but there will be no forces on the ground capable of defeating the

Taliban. Take a look at the map." Jake referenced the map on the wall. "Notice where we are, and notice that there isn't another force in the area with the capability of a forcible entry. We are it. Right now, there are no plans to introduce forces other than special ops, but we are going to have to figure out how we are going to get from here to there if the balloon goes up. That's big picture." Jake looked out over the group of young officers. "Now for the housekeeping. The MEU, the carrier battle group, and the maritime prepositioned ships are folding under Task Force Raptor. I'm here to overlay those units with a command element that will allow me to coordinate with higher commands and keep them off your backs. There are going to be a lot of things coming our way that no one has seen; my job is going to be to cut through the chaff so that you can operate without interference." Jake waited. "Now, since we are all going to be one big happy family, I want each of you to think about how we are going to get seaborne marines across about five hundred miles of desert, and upon setting foot in Afghanistan be prepared to engage and defeat the enemy. Think about it seriously, because if what I expect to happen comes down, you are going to be at the pointy end of the spear."

CHAPTER 11

THE PENTAGON, WASHINGTON, DC

In the days before airpower was introduced into Afghanistan, the twenty-four-hour news cycle had to be fed, and the buzz from reporters was why no retaliatory measures had been taken against the terrorists. Once the bombings started, the Pentagon received a reprieve. They provided photos and gun-camera footage of air strikes that drew attention away from those responsible for the failure to have stopped the attacks on American cities.

It wasn't long after air operations started and the semblance of retaliation commenced that decisions were second-guessed. Some in Congress felt the Pentagon had not gone far enough with the air strikes, others opined that they had gone too far. The use of airpower along with the introduction of special forces was attacked by many elected officials, who thought ground troops should have been introduced into Afghanistan.

Don Frieze had always been able to work in the shadows, but being the Pentagon point man for Afghanistan put him in a visible position. He didn't have the glibness to serve as spokesman for the war and worried that he might misspeak and tarnish his legacy. Annoyed by the constant questioning, he had been in Washington long enough to know in the clamor for news, the quality of answers was unimportant. Long circular answers were best because they allowed direct questions to be eluded.

Seeking an opportunity to solidify his position as the foremost DOD thinker, Frieze sifted through the dozens of requests for interviews that sat on his desk. With his office funneling talking points to FOX News, and with a friendly relationship with their Washington reporters, DEPSECDEF accepted an invitation to be interviewed. Wanting to make the best possible on-air impression, he asked for and received all the questions that he would be asked beforehand. Not liking some of what was proposed, he inserted questions that he could respond to in length. He wanted no surprises.

With the secretary of defense pushing to modernize the American way of war, Frieze inserted several questions about the American strategy in Afghanistan that would bolster the secretary's positions. Only a week into the operation, he was willing to call the tactics being used a success. He could back that claim up with empiric data showing that the Northern Alliance Forces were winning back formerly ceded territory. He would sell what was happening in Afghanistan as proof that the secretary's military modernization efforts were working.

In readying for the interview, he had his staff run the approved questions by him so that he could refine his answers. With days to prepare, DEPSECDEF had a smooth presentation ready for the TV audience. Not considered were the differences in answering questions in familiar surroundings and a television studio. Having makeup artists color his face and lips unnerved him. The people bustling around him broke his concentration. He needed to take a few minutes to gather himself, but the hair stylist was running late, and by the time his hair was blown dry, he was led onto the set. The host was already in his chair looking over the scripted questions and greeted him halfheartedly. Frieze was seated and his suit straightened. The confusion on the set vanished when a countdown began. The lights came up, and the host went into his spiel, introducing the show and the guest. Frieze didn't know what was said about him. His mind was racing, and his temples pounded.

The interview went well for about forty-five minutes. The DEPSECDEF was unaware that the show's producer had edited out similar questions so that the show would not become bogged down. The substitute questions inserted were considered puffballs, thrown Frieze's way so that he could make himself look good. The unscripted questions caught him by surprise, and the change in his demeanor was detected by the cameras. The lines in his face deepened, as if he was fighting off an attack, but the commentator continued.

"Mr. Frieze, there are reports that special forces teams are paying some of the most corrupt warlords to work for us? What are the consequences that you see of hiring these people as allies?"

"Ah. Ah." His head was spinning. He couldn't give an answer that was different than those given by the secretary or the administration, but he couldn't remember what others had said. "The people we are using have Al Qaeda and the Taliban as common enemies with us." He ignored the specific question.

"Does that mean that you see these warlords as viable representatives in any new government we may form in Afghanistan?"

"We are in Afghanistan to rout Al Qaeda and the Taliban, those groups responsible for the attacks on our country. We are not there to build a nation."

"Is that why there have been no ground forces introduced?" The host wasn't trying to trap him. In fact, he didn't think he was asking difficult questions. He was filling time.

Frieze saw every question as a potential trap. "Ground forces haven't been introduced for several reasons. First, the secretary's effort to remake the military into a high-tech and lighter force are on display in Afghanistan. Those efforts are proving effective. Second, we can't allow ourselves to become bogged down in Afghanistan as so many other countries have. Third, we are not going to nation build. That is up to the Afghan people. Lastly, our mission, as stated by the president, is to get rid of the terrorists in Afghanistan and around the world, and we are doing that while husbanding our resources in the event that we have to strike out at other terrorist havens." Frieze looked at the clock on the wall, and time remained with the cameras still on.

"Could I follow up on something you said?" The commentator's pedantic tone annoyed Frieze. "You intimated that a light footprint in Afghanistan provides us with an easy exit, but it appears once the Taliban and Al Qaeda are overthrown, there will be no government and no viable institutions to provide for an orderly Afghanistan. Are you suggesting that we will leave once our enemies are routed and essentially create a void into which the Taliban and Al Qaeda can return?"

"Well, no. We'll provide money and assistance to ensure that any government that comes to power can rule effectively."

"But those we are empowering now, those fighting for us, will most likely come to power, and as I mentioned, they are some of the most corrupt men in Afghanistan. Can we afford to prop up known crooks?"

Frieze didn't know how to answer. He felt nauseous, and there were still airtime.

"One last question, Mr. Frieze. The Powell Doctrine states that wars are entered into with overwhelming force and that there are specific strategic objectives and a definitive exit strategy. Our objective seems to be to kill Al Qaeda operatives, and no one has provided a strategy indicating how that will be accomplished or when we will leave Afghanistan. As you are the person in the Pentagon directing the war, what is our strategy?"

The question almost floored the DEPSECDEF. He wanted to get up and walk out.

"The Powell Doctrine relies on too many troops and too large an investment of national assets." Frieze was dancing around a point of contention in the Pentagon between the military and the civilian leaders. The secretary of defense denigrated the Powell Doctrine. Frieze couldn't say what he was thinking. He reverted to Washington babble. "We have the right mix of special forces and airpower to destroy the terrorists. Their destruction will be accomplished swiftly, and we will not have used up our forces, making them available for other contingencies. We will know when Al Qaeda is defeated, when hostilities in Afghanistan are concluded, and will leave at that time. The American public will see the efficacy of our strategy. Ah."

He was saved when the producer's voice announced, "That's a wrap."

"Nice job," the host said and left the set to conduct another interview. The show business of Washington had to go on.

Frieze was exhausted. The mental strain of having to say all the right things so that no one could take issue with him wore him down. He wandered around trying to get someone to take his makeup off. Finding a restroom, he bent over a sink and washed himself back to recognition.

CHAPTER 12

CENTCOM,
TAMPA, FLORIDA

General Franklin was angry that the DEPSECDEF was cutting him out of the war that he should have been running. He was told what he could and would do, and as he tried to push for a heavier army footprint in Afghanistan, he was rebuffed. His part, he was instructed, was to provide air assets so that the war that the Pentagon was fighting would not become bogged down. Franklin wasn't given a say in the utilization of special ops personnel. Many were coming out of the CIA and those that were supplied by the military were from Special Operations Command, and they were dealing directly with the Pentagon. The two major commands, CENTCOM and SOCOM, on one base resulted in competition, and he thought that under the present system he was losing.

While the general's want to fight the war his way was disregarded by the Pentagon, many elected officials preferred his approach. They wanted overpowering force on the ground to punish Afghanistan. His superiors could keep him under wraps in the chain of command, but they had no control over how he interfaced with politicians, who flocked to get face time with the general running the war. In an effort to suppress what he might tell elected officials, each congressional delegation arriving at CENTCOM had a Defense Department embed in the traveling party to serve as a dampening agent on how the general and his staff interfaced with the Washington crowd.

Sitting at his desk, Franklin looked at the itinerary for the visit by the Senate Armed Services Committee arriving the following morning for a full day of face-to-face briefs. He knew many of the senators on the committee and was surprised that Frieze was traveling with them. He understood that DEPSECDEF's purpose with the group was to silence him, but he wasn't going to let that happen.

"Get Captain Perkins in here," he ordered his chief of staff.

"I'll get her right away." The chief complied with the order.

After a short wait, a knock on the door alerted him.

"Get in here," Franklin ordered.

A female captain entered holding her day planner close to her chest.

"I've got a job for you, and I don't want you to screw it up. Understand?" He intimidated the junior officer.

"What is it that you'd like, sir?"

"Did you make up the itinerary for the Senate Armed Services Committee visit?" His tone was accusatory.

"Yes, sir."

"Well, I want some changes. Write these down."

The protocol officer rushed to comply with his order.

"After tomorrow's briefings, you have me hosting a cocktail party at my residence. Cancel it. I've spoken with Sam Wingate," he referred to a local businessman who was active in supporting CENTCOM social events. "He and his wife Sally have offered to host the senators at their home. As private citizens, they get to determine who goes to their house. Everyone who is with the committee is invited. Since Mr. Frieze is not affiliated with the committee, drop his name from the invite list. Your job is to see that he doesn't show up at the Wingates'. I don't want any foul-ups. Break him away from the politicians so that I can speak to them without his being near."

Franklin waited until the protocol officer understood his intent. "Don't screw this up, or I'll be getting me a new protocol officer. Now get to work on this."

The large black SUVs entered a looping driveway on millionaires' row, a street of oversized homes that exuded wealth. As the cars parked in front of their home, Sally and Sam Wingate stood on a colonnaded porch and greeted the congressional party with the acclaim that the politicians expected. Some had visited previously and were on a first-name basis with the hosts. Others, first-timers, were quickly inducted into the club. The Wingates' home was at their disposal whenever they came to Tampa.

White-coated waiters mingled in the crowd taking drink orders as the people from Washington socialized with the elite of the gulf city. The conversation was sprinkled with references to the bombings in New York and Washington, DC, but there was a self-congratulatory undertone as the politicians told civilians of their efforts to avenge the tragedies. It was accepted that the senators had done a good job in facilitating the US entry into the war and that the military was acquitting itself admirably.

It took a while for people to notice that the general had not yet arrived. His staff called over and informed the Wingates that he had a call from the president and that he would arrive as soon as he was through. It was Franklin's way of setting up his entrance. If the gathered crowd, including the senators, thought he was talking to the president about the war, he would be more eagerly awaited and received.

He stayed in his office, putting golf balls across the flat green rug, before having his aide help him into full-dress uniform. "Make sure my goddamn medals are on straight." His attention to detail over his appearance was in an effort to stage his entrance. The gathered crowd would have had their appetites whetted with the hint of a presidential conversation, and when he entered the party in a uniform that didn't conform to the event, everyone would flock to him.

His car pulled into a reserved spot at the base of the stairs, and his security detail formed a phalanx between the car and the house through which the general strode triumphantly.

Two steps inside the door, spontaneous applause started. He acted embarrassed but didn't raise a hand to stop it until he saw it dying out.

"Sorry to arrive so late. The president needed some data from me, and as you know, he's the boss." Franklin watched the crowd as he spoke. They hung on his words. "But that is over with, so let's everyone enjoy the rest of the evening."

He would have to make himself available to even the most ineffectual in the official delegation, and Franklin accepted that wasting time on them was part of his job. He used his easy Southern drawl to make all who came in contact with him think he was just one of the boys.

"Pleased to meet you, Senator. Some of our best troops come from your state. In fact, when things settle down in Afghanistan, I'd like you to accompany me when I visit the troops." It was the same spiel with different gradations and variations. It was boilerplate party talk. The senators he wanted to speak to were being informed by his staff that the general would like to speak to him away from the crowd.

"General, you seem to be holding up well in these hard times," Stacey Billups, the senior senator from Georgia, mentioned when he was led to Franklin.

"Stace, how they hanging?" Franklin knew the senator and had testified before his committee many times. They both posed as good ole' boys, but that was a façade. They were both hard drivers.

"Would you excuse us?" Franklin spoke to the people he had been talking to. "I have to speak to the senator." With the indicated importance of the conversation, people who had been standing around the general scattered.

"You're all dressed up tonight. Was that for me?" the senator joked. Billups was a short, rotund man with a florid complexion. His face was creased with age lines, but his silver-gray hair, which was trimmed neatly, gave him a senatorial mien. When he spoke he did so in a low voice with a Georgia twang that got people's attention.

"Nah. It was for the new people along with you. I was trying to impress them."

"Mission accomplished. They are in awe." Billups shook his head. "By the way, the president is en route to California. Did he call you from Air Force One?" Billups mentioned this to let the general know that they were equals in playing mind games and that he didn't buy into the stagecraft.

Franklin didn't acknowledge the senator's observation.

"You wanted to talk to me. Anything in particular?"

"Of course." Franklin looked around to ensure that they would not be overheard. "Stace, I think the way this effort in Afghanistan is being run is all wrong. The neoconservative group that has the president captured doesn't know what the fuck they are doing."

"A lot of people on the hill would agree with you." Billups had his own issues with the way the embeds were running the military and was looking for something to buttress his ideas. "What's bugging you specifically?"

"First of all, the JCS has been denutted. There isn't anyone up there who will speak up and contradict the cabal running the Pentagon. It's goddamn embarrassing watching the military being transformed into yes men."

"That doesn't help me, General. Tell me what you think they are doing wrong, the more specific the better. Some of us who have been on the hill for a while don't trust the neoconservatives. We know that they are manipulating the president, but he doesn't have the balls or the brains to stop them. That's his problem. My problem is that they are blowing off the Senate. Why don't you tell me about what's going on in Afghanistan that I can help you with, because we have to get this train back on track."

Franklin's didn't want to discuss how the DOD was running the war. His intent was to try to shake money out of the Pentagon so that the troops under his command were funded at levels sufficient to carry out their missions. With the way the Pentagon was conducting the war, the army was sure to lose budget share and be cut out of any supplemental funding. The supplemental funding was free money, doled out with scant accountability, and he wanted to make a case for the army receiving some of the windfall.

"We are going to get into a mess in Afghanistan unless we get troops on the ground. Airpower and special forces might be able to clean out pockets of the enemy, but I'm worried that with the emphasis SECDEF and that fucking idiot Frieze are putting on keeping the footprint on the ground light, we aren't going to be able to exert enough force to accomplish anything."

"What is it you want to accomplish?"

The question caught Franklin off guard. He had no plan for Afghanistan other than to kill terrorists and get the troops home. His strategy, or lack thereof, was identical to that espoused by the secretary. Franklin groped for an answer that would placate the senator.

"We've got special forces scattered all over hell and back, and there is no way to protect them unless we get some troops on the ground that can provide them the bulk they are going to need for security. We have to put regular army troops on the ground."

"Why haven't you brought this up with the secretary?"

"He and the embeds want to prove their theories of warfare and are using Afghanistan as a proving ground. If they continue, when this war is over the military is going to look a whole lot different. The army is surely going to take a hit."

"The special forces are army, aren't they?"

"Stace, you know goddamn well what I'm talking about. You

have two major army bases in your state. Are you willing to see them downsized or eliminated? If things go on as they are, the regular army is sure to be cut out of the funding, and some of the downsizing will come from the units in your state. That's the way this thing is going to go down if the eggheads running the show aren't reigned in."

"What is it you think I can do?" The idea that bases in his state might be affected if the war wasn't fought in an acceptable way caught Billups's attention.

"I need some help. I want to get some straight-legged infantry into the war, and I want to make sure that they get a fair shake at the money. I think with your position on the Senate Armed Services Committee you might be able to convince SECDEF that we might have security issues if the war is continued to be fought as it is."

"General, I understand you, fully. I'll see what I can do."

Having received assurances, Franklin moved on to another member of the powerful Senate committee. He changed his approach slightly and tailored it for the individual, but he was on a mission and was going to work the room.

CHAPTER 13

THE PENTAGON,
WASHINGTON, DC

Don Frieze entered the secretary's office. It was customary for all of the staff that traveled with congressional delegations to debrief SECDEF. He wanted to be alerted to anything that could turn into a political fight.

"How was the weather in Tampa?' the secretary asked.

"It was fine." They both knew the chitchat wasn't necessary.

"How did our old soldier treat you? I guess I should ask, what kinds of crazy demands did he make of you?" The secretary leaned back in his chair waiting to be amused.

"The good general made no specific requests of me. He went out of his way to snub me."

"That is unlike him. He always has some crazy-assed idea about how we can do our job."

"He may have, but he had his staff split me off from the visiting delegation. They all went to a party at the Wingates'. I think you attended one of their parties."

"You mean you missed all that Southern charm bullshit at the Wingates'." The secretary laughed out loud.

"Yes, sir. I was in some dive with a major and two captains, having to listen to them tell me what a prick Franklin is."

"I knew that the first time I met him. He is another one of those generals who hasn't had an original idea in twenty years. Evidence of that can be seen in his rigidity over Afghanistan. He doesn't understand what he is supposed to be doing there and is perfectly happy to bitch about our efforts. He has the strategic intellect of a slug, so why would a slug want you out of the way?"

"On the flight back, I got to talk with several of the Senate staffers, and they agreed that Franklin cornered all the heavy hitters. From what I was told, he went one on one with them." Frieze explained what he had heard.

"That old piece of leather worked the room?" SECDEF paused before switching subjects. "I received an early-morning call from Senator Billups. After small talk, he got to his point. He thought it would be wise if we introduced army forces other than special forces into the theater. He tried to get me to believe that there were questions of funding that would be brought up before his committee unless army forces were introduced into Afghanistan. So Franklin got to him."

"If that is the case, you are going to receive more phone calls. My information indicates that the general talked to all the power brokers," Frieze confided.

"I expect more calls, and there will be a quid pro quo from all those who call. We are going to go in for a lot more funding, and I want these guys in my pocket, so any future requests we have will slide right on through."

"Do you intend to backtrack on our plan to fight this war with light forces?" Frieze was a true believer and didn't want to see the plan tarnished.

"I'm not going back on a thing. We'll put some army on the ground so that everyone will think they have influenced me."

"But to what end?" Frieze questioned. Nothing in their previous talks indicated the insertion of army forces.

"I don't intend to tie down forces."

Frieze was happy that nothing had changed.

"I kind of expected Franklin to ask for something like this. With the air campaign working so well, he must have panicked thinking that the war would be over before he could call up the foot soldiers. With his love of the army and his heartburn with the special forces, he must have felt compelled to do something."

"Do you think he will keep pushing for more troops?"

"It won't make any difference. In his own way, he is on our team. He's in Tampa, and we don't have our hands on him, but he will do exactly what we say. He's not smart enough to think around us as evidenced by his playing games with you. I guess he believes that there are still secrets in Washington."

"So you're sure that he won't go off the reservation?"

"Yep. He'll keep trying to back door things, thinking this attempt was a success without ever knowing I expected it." SECDEF smiled wryly. "Now what I want you to do is get on the phone with the good general and tell him I've approved his use of rangers in and around Kandahar. Tell him his first job is not engaging the enemy. His first job is to generate some good PR. The president needs some good press, and seeing the army marching across Afghanistan will buy some peace and quiet for him. Tell Franklin it's his choice on how he wants to get the troops on the ground, but make it happen quickly. Don't give him any other instructions. Let's see how he handles working without guidance. Mention that all cost of the operation will come out of supplemental funds. That is what this was all about. That will let him think that his talk with Senator Billups paid off."

Frieze left the secretary's office with a new appreciation for his boss. No one in Washington understood the levers of power and how to use them as he did.

CHAPTER 14

ARABIAN SEA

Jake Gregg surprised everyone when he ignored the perks of power. As a general and being in command of a task force, he put together a bare-bones staff and crammed them into makeshift office spaces. The spaces were roomier than the offices of the ship's company but were primitive. The steel nonskid-coated hangar deck, directly below the *Peleliu*'s flight deck and Combat Operations Center was outlined with masking tape. Cargo containers of various sorts and sizes were placed on the outline to serve as walls. They rose high enough to limit sight but not high enough to stop the noise. Boxes were laid on end to serve as desks, and some were laid over to serve as seats. As the hangar deck had elevators that were open to the sea, there was no way of controlling the temperature, which was hot and muggy, so much so that those working with Jake had to work in T-shirts that were usually sweat-stained by midmorning. Cables and wires ran from the Combat Operations Center down a ship's ladder and were taped to the hangar deck. The wire bundles allowed for a full array of communications, with interruptions and breaks, but for a "Rube Goldberg" setup it worked well enough so that the task force could conduct business.

The troops didn't know what to call the organization he put together. It didn't look like the typical hierarchal organization found in the military. Staff sections had direct contact with him without having to go through layers of control. He took lieutenants and sergeants and gave them the power of his rank. Those that dealt with the junior officers manning the task force called it "the general said" model of organization. It had to work that way. Senior officers would roll over junior officers because they could, but when the general said he wanted things done a certain way, opposition faded.

It was a learning experience. Junior officers were exposed to problems and had to make decisions not normally made at their grade, and Jake learned that young officers were uninhibited by organizational biases that came with years of service. He liked the way they derived answers and courses of action without wondering what looked right within the organization. He also found when he let them take the initiative that they ran with it, and his job boiled down to laying out a plan and stepping back while junior officers made it happen. He joked about his young staff but saw something in them immediately. They were electronically savvy and could assess and process data more quickly than their seniors. If Jake had a question, they knew where to get answers. There was no fumbling with computers like senior officers were prone to do. The lieutenants knew how to tap into sources of information that Jake had no idea existed. The speed with which they could wade through pages of material and the quickness in making decisions based on it was surprising.

He started to rely on Jim Mackey, a newly minted officer out of the Infantry Officers School who had been sent to the MEU without a specific assignment. Upon his arrival aboard ship, all the job slots were filled, and he was designated as a "shitty little jobs" officer. When he was proffered to Jake, Colonel Patch referred him as an officer who had a lot to learn but someone he thought had the potential to make a fine marine officer. With Jake needing a staff so that he could coordinate between elements of his command, he took Mackey. The lanky lieutenant was six feet five and rail-thin. He was all arms and legs and so slender; it looked like a strong wind could blow him over. It became clear as Jake worked with him that despite his freckles, carrot-red hair, horn-rimmed glasses, and scarecrow appearance, Mackey had a will of iron. He was not intimidated by anyone. When Jake wanted something done, Mackey got it done, whether it took walking around people or over them. Jake had never seen an officer so single-minded in accomplishing what he had started out to do. Mackey's questioning mind was an asset, and Jake relied on the gawky lieutenant for unfiltered advice. One thing Jake knew was that when he asked Mackey a question, he would get a well-thought-out answer devoid of the niceties that his rank imposed. Somehow Mackey made it work. He pissed off the wrong people and befriended the right ones, all the time spouting "this is what the general wants." Jake received a lot of complaints about his subordinate, but he was performing just as Jake hoped he would and Jake wouldn't rein him in.

The first question Jake broached in a meeting of young officers was, "What is the end game in Afghanistan?" He wanted the lieutenants to think, not about the tactics, but strategically. He felt that was important because American troops were at war, and no one, not the White House, the Pentagon, or CENTCOM had said anything but that American forces were fighting terrorism. There was no direction of how that was supposed to be accomplished or to what extent. More frightening was that no one in a position of power had defined victory or if victory in Afghanistan was attainable. Those who should have set out a clear direction for the military never went beyond the idea of "killing bad guys." Jake didn't know if, at his level, he could solve the lack of leadership out of Washington and Tampa, but he was not going to put troops under his command in peril without a coherent plan that would conform to his level of operations.

Calling task force elements together, Jake gave his commanders guidance, so that the entire organization would know what he wanted done. The officers sitting on the hangar deck were anxious to find out what their part, if any, was going to be.

There was no more gratifying feeling for a marine officer than to be surrounded by troops that he might lead into battle. There was the legal bond that they would follow their commander, but, more importantly, there was the bond among marines. Everyone listening to Jake would put his life on the line for the person next to him. They all knew it and hoped their commanders would not risk their lives needlessly. Jake felt that his responsibility was to eliminate mistakes that would put marines in unnecessary danger.

"We have a two-part mission," he started. "Of course, it has a good-news-bad-news tag line."

Troops stirred uneasily.

"The good news is that we are a phantom command. CENTCOM knows we are here but has no plans for us. Our immediate orders are to keep floating and be ready to make a forcible entry if called upon to do so. As of right now, that call hasn't come. The war in Afghanistan is being pursued by the air force and special forces, and they are doing a good job. Now for the bad news." Jake waited to be sure all were listening. "My crackerjack staff and I have been looking at the realistic possibilities that we may face." When he mentioned his staff, those assembled laughed.

"What we have seen is that we have had mixed success in knocking the Taliban and Al Qaeda off pieces of ground. In the north, where the Northern Alliance has ethnic armies that have fought against the Taliban and Al Qaeda for years, once they control the ground, they can hold it. In the south, where the Taliban ruled uncontested, we have made little gain. Now if the Taliban is not displaced permanently by our bombings, and special forces can't knock over Kandahar, there is no sense in our being here." Jake shined a laser pointer at a map that all the marines had seen.

"Here's Kandahar." He wiggled the red pinpoint light over the city. "Here we are." The laser shone on a spot in the Arabian Sea. "We are the only force with the size and strength to take Kandahar. My feeling is that we will be getting a call to take the city, because it is the only strategic piece of ground in southern Afghanistan. If we are called upon, it is going to take a forcible entry. We are going to have to fight our way in and then fight to stay there. As we don't have the training to make an aerial assault, we will have to fight for Kandahar the way we know, ship to shore. Only the shore is going to be five hundred miles deep. We will have to carry out the hardest amphibious assault ever attempted. Not in size but in distances involved." Jake paused to see if those listening thought he was crazy.

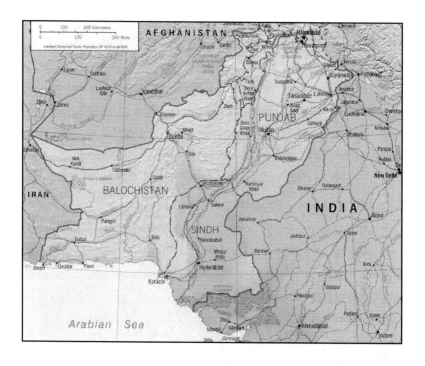

"The only thing amphibious about what we will attempt will be the thirty miles it is going to take to cross the Arabian Sea. The rest of the trip will be over the desert, and after traveling five hundred miles over sand we will have to fight for our objective. Intelligence indicates that Kandahar is fortified, and we could be bloodied in a fight for it, but the forces in and around the city aren't large enough to prevent us from capturing it. However, they will put up a fight and score some victories." Jake looked at the marines and turned to the map and held the pointer on Kandahar. "I've had the staff look at the options, and no matter how the pie is sliced, everything indicates that we will be able to take the objective." Jake paused for what seemed like a minute.

"Then what? No one has an answer. Not me, nor anyone in Washington. I'm thinking that once we get the entire task force on the ground, we are going to be in Afghanistan for the long haul. We have all trained for war, but none of us has an idea of how to provide security or nation build. Before I get out too far ahead of myself, we could be ordered to float out the war, but none of us thinks so. We feel that some way, somehow, we are going to be involved in Afghanistan, and based on history, if we enter, it is going to be a long slog. Despite what is being reported back home that we will be out of here in a couple of months, I don't see that happening. As the people who will likely be on the ground, we are going to have to prepare for a long war." He looked out over the assembled marines and knew they didn't like what he was telling them. They wanted to be home by Christmas. "I see this war as being more like Vietnam than Desert Storm. That said, I have had Lieutenant Mackey set up a link to the archives at the Marine Corps University. I want you all to read about the combined action program that the Marine Corps used in Vietnam. It was working before it was scrapped. I don't know exactly what a combined or a civic action program would look like in Afghanistan or if it is applicable, but look into it and have some idea about how you might interface with the population. It will be a 'learn as you go' project, but we have to have a strategy that will not drive the Afghans into the ranks of the Taliban. I want every one of you to give it thought. I need everyone's best ideas." Jake was getting ready to dismiss the assemblage. "Do your homework on this because you may not only make a historic landing, you could be the people determining the shape of the war."

CHAPTER 15

CENTCOM,
TAMPA, FLORIDA

General Franklin was sure his politicking had closed the deal and had gotten the army a piece of the war. He didn't know what he had specifically said that had moved the senators to push the Pentagon, but he was given a blank check and allowed to function within limits. He would start with the rangers that had been approved by SECDEF, but he had bigger plans. After the rangers settled in, he would work his magic with Congress and expand the role for more army troops. With the narrow opening he had been given, he intended to barge through it and win the scrum for dollars. While money would be tied to the war effort, there would be enough slop in the funding for him to put in place some of the postwar plans that he had. The general started thinking about adding a new wing to his headquarters building. It would be larger and better than the one being built at SOCOM.

The CENTCOM staff sensed that the general was in a good mood. Franklin was smug over the fact that he had outsmarted the brain trust running the Pentagon. It showed. His usual scowl gave way to a slight upturn at the corners of his mouth. It wasn't a smile exactly, but it was progress. Feeling he had won a battle of wills, he wanted the staff to connect him with other army generals so that he could tell them that he, personally, was responsible for getting the army into the war.

Not once after receiving the clearance to use rangers in Afghanistan did he think about how he might employ them. He had a staff that would handle that. In his conversation with Frieze, he ignored any advice the civilian proffered and focused on the importance of making the army's entrance into the war a PR event. He wanted a story that would inform the American people that he was on top of the campaign of retaliation and was punishing those who destroyed American property and lives.

He didn't bother to discuss any employment options or thoughts on how and where the army troops might be used. He farmed out the job to Grady Hatton. He gave the director of operations the responsibility of formulating a plan. His guidance stressed the importance of putting on a good show, something that would elevate the army in the public's eye. After receiving assurances that the operations section had the ball and would run with it, Franklin thought about where else he could leverage the use of the army in the war.

Major General Grady Hatton was the perfect man to fill the CENTCOM director of operations job prior to 9/11. He looked the part. Tall, with a full head of black hair, the only sign of age was his graying sideburns. As an officer who had gotten by on his good looks, quick wit, and golf game, he had been carried along in his career and shielded from having to do any hard work. His claim to fame was that he had arranged General Franklin's change of command, reported to have been the best in CENTCOM history. The praise heaped upon him for that one event didn't provide him with the requisite skills to plan a war. Being three months from retirement, his thoughts had been on his follow-on job in the defense industry. After the 9/11 attacks, he tried to retire immediately because he knew that there would be hard work involved for the director of operations, and he didn't want to take that on. He was in retirement mode, but he was told he could not retire, and remaining on active duty meant having to stay in his office at least sixteen hours a day. It was more work than he wanted to do.

Given no orders on how to plan the army's entry into Afghanistan, he floundered. The staff put forth several plans, and Hatton was overwhelmed. Not wanting to show weaknesses, he made a show of spending time thinking through his decision. Under the weight of a timeline, he settled on what he thought would be the course of action easiest to carry out. Hatton took a plan with glaring holes and staffed it through the CENTCOM headquarters. The ground combat officers on the staff picked the plan apart, but that didn't deter him. The public relations annex to the plan was just what General Franklin wanted, so the tactical deficiencies were accepted. Not only was the PR play acknowledged, it was augmented. The PR staff wanted to put on a show that exceeded anything that was coming out of Afghanistan. They wanted to film at night so that they could get the same eerie effect as that of the airplane-gun-camera photos. They wanted full sound so that the troops could not only be seen sweating but heard grunting.

In order to get the desired effect, what was going to be a difficult daytime operation was changed into a night op. Darkness would increase the difficulty geometrically, but once it was sold as a show, there was no scaling back.

A company of rangers would make a night airborne entry into an area south of Kandahar. The following morning another company would make a daylight helo assault to assist the special forces teams in Kandahar. Once on the ground, the ranger companies would be mutually supportive. With PR stressed, most attention centered on the para drop. It made for a better show.

Once the PR play was briefed, other aspects of the missions were ignored, because it was felt that the Taliban would melt before the sight of American arms. In the time it took Franklin to read the plan, he approved it and told Hatton to put it into effect. He even volunteered to sit for a filmed introduction that would preface the final work.

Alert orders went out to the troops.

CHAPTER 16

USS *PELELIU,*
ARABIAN SEA

"Sir, you'd better look at this." The task force's communications officer handed Jake a message. "It just came in." Jake read and then reread it to be sure he understood how it might affect him.

"Get all the officers together," he ordered the clerk who was bent over a box desk near him.

"Yes, sir." The clerk rushed to alert the officers.

They were still straggling in when Jake started talking to those who sat on the steel hangar deck.

"What we've been talking about has jumped the rails from might happen to gonna happen." He pointed to the message in his hand. "The army is going to insert rangers around Kandahar. I'll bet some of you are thinking, now that the army is in that sector, we just got a free pass. It won't work that way. If I had a guess, I'd say our fate is sealed." Jake paused while officers looked at one another. "According to this alert order, rangers are going to make an airborne drop into an area where special forces have said there is no enemy activity; after they jump in, another company is going to be heloed into Kandahar to assist the special ops people there. In neither location are there going to be enough rangers to make a dent. Both units are going to be on the ground with no supporting arms other than air cover. If they get into a fight, that won't be enough." Jake paused. "Jumping into Afghanistan would be a bitch, but making it harder is that it will be a night jump." Even the most junior officers rolled their eyes in disbelief. They knew the difficulty of night ops and could only imagine how hard it would be jumping into a zone in the blackness.

"Sir," Jim Mackey had worked closely with Jake in formulating amphibious options, and he felt at ease talking up before the gathered officers, "is there any indication as to why the jump will be made at night? If the area of the drop is safe, a night jump seems like an unnecessary risk."

"Nothing I've received explains the whys. I've only got the how, but I'm sure we will be informed when someone feels we have a need to know." Jake didn't want to express his suspicions. "I can guess about the night drop, but it would only be a guess."

"Will that change our planning?" Mackey wanted to know if the plan he and the other lieutenants had been working on would change.

"It shouldn't, but I want every detail checked. Alert carrier air group and put them on a short leash. If anything goes wrong, tactical air will be the only support the rangers will have. That said, even air support might not be enough to cover units in trouble. So, start thinking about how we might play."

"Even at night?" Mackey asked.

Jake was pleased. Mackey was always thinking out ahead of problems. "No, there is no need to risk a night operation. There are too many moving parts in what we will be trying to do to." He gathered his thoughts. "The army operations are scheduled for next week. Anytime after that we are fair game. So keep up your good work and plan how you think we might play to the gnat's ass. We can't be too precise. Now get to work." Jake turned and left.

CHAPTER 17

FORT BRAGG, NORTH CAROLINA

A C-5B, the largest cargo plane in the air force's inventory, lowered its ramp on the tarmac at Pope AFB and awaited the arrival of the A Company, First Ranger Battalion. The airborne-qualified unit was eager to get into the war. Still smarting over the 9/11 attacks, they wanted to play a part in their country's retaliation against "evil-doers."

Before boarding, each soldier checked a partner's gear. Everything had to be ready because once they boarded the aircraft, they were going nonstop to war. The flight would take almost sixteen hours, and the airplane would air-to-air refuel three times. There were two sets of pilots so that a fresh crew would be piloting the aircraft at all times.

In all, 129 soldiers climbed aboard and stacked their gear on the floor in the middle of the cargo bay forward of the mortars, radios, two command vehicles, and three Hummers loaded down with supplies and water. Augmenting the normal load was a pickup truck filled with camera gear and audio equipment. The extra vehicle took up space, but, more importantly, it cut into the weight allowance of the airplane, resulting in ten rangers being left behind.

Those rangers on board were assigned seats resembling an airline seat with not nearly as much padding. The seat backs tilted but not quite enough. If the soldiers got to sleep, it was going to be sitting up. Portable toilets were strapped to the metal floor, and when the rangers entered the airplane they didn't reek, but after sixteen hours, every trooper knew the stink would be eye-watering.

The C-5B was a late replacement for the two smaller C-141s that were supposed to carry the troops. The company commander realized that after such a long flight and being crammed in C-141s, troops wouldn't be able to stand, let alone make an assault jump. Raising his concerns to CENTCOM operations, it was a fateful intersection of the rangers' need for space and the need to get extra cameras to the war. The extra space allowed troops to leave their seats and stretch. A couple of mats were laid on the floor so that those in need of exercise could go through a workout.

As the airplane roared down the runway, the rangers were happy they were going to the fight. After a few hours their enthusiasm waned, lost in the dull routine of trying to sleep, exercising, eating MREs, and repeating. Those who didn't sleep forgot their reason for being on the airplane, and they just wanted to get off.

Night turned into day and then again into night, and they droned on. The company officers looked at maps of their objective area, the Kut airstrip, and tried to pick out terrain features that would be easily identifiable. There were no natural features, as the ground was arid and rolling. The only thing identifiable was a dirt airstrip, the company's objective.

The extent of the instruction the rangers received was that they would be joined by special forces teams already on the ground. Even the young officers who were used to being sent places on short notice with little instruction were surprised at the lack of detail surrounding their first combat mission. They assumed that upon landing the special operators on the ground would outline what was planned for them. The only thing they knew for sure was that they were being sent to fight terrorists. It wasn't much, but it was their ticket to war, and they were excited.

The order was issued for everyone to "suit up." Again, soldiers checked one another. Everything was attached firmly to the body. Emergency chutes were double-checked, and everyone ensured that they had green glo-lites. It would be their way of identifying one another on the ground.

The mission had been too hastily put together, and the late change in planes required a new drop plan, but with lack of coordination between units, none had been developed. The army hadn't calculated the weight increase of the gear designed to photograph the war. The pilots had been given the weight of the load, and with the extra weight a faster drop speed was required. The information wasn't passed to the troops in the belly of the airplane.

The rangers had jumped from the C-141 many times, but few had trained in the C-5B. There was talk of jumping out over the rear ramp, as they would have in a C-141, but the ramp on the C-5 was almost three times as long, and with buffeting air jostling the jumpers, it was felt that many would fall before getting free of the aircraft. The decision was made that the gear would go out the back and the jumpers out the side door. It added minutes to the rangers' exiting the aircraft.

On a calm night, the rangers had a nearly vertical landing, but they were scattered. Worse, special operators reported that the enemy was active in the sector.

Captain Dale Oteen, the company commander, had an easy landing, but he knew something was drastically wrong when he looked around for the glo-lites that each ranger wore and could see only several nearby. There weren't enough troops near him to set up a perimeter. He searched for a defining terrain feature through his night-vision goggles where he might assemble his troops, but the ground was arid and undulating. It all looked the same.

"Sand Bug. Sand Bug." He spoke into his radio trying to make contact with the special operators who were supposed to assist him. "This is Eagle Six." He identified himself as the ranger company commander.

An icy-cold voice responded. "Sand Bug here. You've got guys scattered from here to hell. You are on an east-west axis. I've got a fix on you, and you're about the midpoint. The troops west of you are okay. The troops to the east are going to be in a bag of shit come morning. There are about twenty-four Taliban in the village of Kut, and your outriders are only a half click away from them. If you don't reel them in, they will be in deep doodoo when the bad guys will be able to see you."

Oteen was torn. He had to keep smiling, because the combat photographers who had jumped in with him were filming, and their product was being uploaded to a satellite. What the special operators had told him made him panic. He had spotty radio communication with some of the rangers, but getting them assembled, even with night-vision goggles, was going to be hard. His fears grew when radio contact with those troops most in need of recall proved futile. He didn't know if the terrain was blocking his radio signal or if it was a communications problem, but he couldn't talk to the troops most in peril.

In the middle of a sand pile, Oteen wasn't in a firefight, but if the special operators were right, he would be. He could not think about what he should be doing; he was focused on why things had gone so wrong. His unit had made dozens of jumps and always landed in proximity. He sat on the ground and tried to figure out what he was going to tell the photographers—even worse, what he was going to tell the generals when they watched the uploads.

"Eagle Six, this is Sand Bug."

"This is Eagle Six, go." Oteen was forceful, the picture of a man in charge in front of the cameras.

"Eagle Six. What's your delay? Didn't you understand my communications?"

"Sand Bug. Wait one." Oteen asked for time. "Look, guys," he said to the cameramen hanging on his every word, "we have a situation that is going to require me to move to positions, and that could put you in danger. So turn off the cameras, and when I get back we can start filming again."

At the hint of danger, the cameramen lowered their handheld units.

Without the world witnessing, Oteen moved out of hearing range and spoke into the radio.

"Sand Bug, I'm open to suggestions." In saying the words, Oteen ostensibly gave up command of his unit.

There was a long pause. The special operators hadn't expected a role change. When they came back on the radio, there was no doubt that they accepted the responsibility.

"Okay, Eagle Six. We have eyes on you, and here's the layout. Your heavy gear landed just long of the dirt airstrip and the bulk of your troops are in a line north of the runway. Have all your troops move south until they find the runway. When you get them together, set up a command post and have them bring in the heavy gear. Prepare to defend to the east, but don't overlook any direction. Now the most important part is that we are coming in to join you. Do not, I repeat, do not, shoot us. We will be coming in from the southwest. We are the only people to your southwest, so tell your rangers to be sure they challenge us but that our speaking English should be enough to get a pass into your lines. Got it?"

"Yes." Oteen was relieved to have someone else making the decisions.

"Now recall those troops to the east that you can. When we get to you, have about a dozen troops ready to patrol. We are going to have to find some of your boys one at a time. Capisce?" The voice on the radio used the Italian word for understand.

Oteen knew something was wrong. He could hear firing in the direction from which the special operators were approaching. It took several minutes before two Toyota pickup trucks with antennas sticking up all over neared his position.

A tall bearded man stormed out of the lead truck and headed toward him.

"What the fuck, Captain. I told you to have your guys hold their fire. Jesus Christ, you almost got us killed." The man did not identify himself, but there was no doubt that he was a special forces operator. He wore no uniform, and had bits and pieces of local clothing. He wore no rank.

Oteen didn't like the idea that someone was chastising him, but thankful for help, he kept quiet.

"I'm Angelo. I've got eight guys in my team. We've got a drone up overhead; that's how we spotted your spread on the ground. What the fuck happened?" It wasn't delivered as an accusation. He wanted to know if there had been difficulties with the drop.

Before an answer could be given, Angelo spotted the cameraman getting ready to film him.

"Put that fucking thing in its case. We're not supposed to be here, and pictures might indicate that we are." He waited until he was sure his order had been obeyed.

"Captain, you'd better get your men in a defensive perimeter."

"I've started."

"Sir," it was the first time the special forces operator showed any deference to rank, "you can't just have these guys surround the heavy gear and protect the center of the runway. You have to cover this entire airport in the event you have to be pulled out."

Oteen looked at him blankly. He was tired, and his brown eyes drooped. Adding to his fatigued appearance was the realization that he was in way over his head. The fact that he had graduated third in his class at West Point wasn't helping him, nor was his assignment as a member of the army's Office of Legislative Affairs. He had been assigned to the job as a result of his uncle being an eight-term congressman from the first district of Ohio, and the army hoped to utilize Oteen through his uncle to further their agenda. Knowing he needed a greening tour, a tour commanding troops, he was sent to jump school and assigned as the commanding officer of A Company. He had made several jumps with his troops, including night jumps, but as he stood being instructed by a man he didn't know, he understood that he was woefully unprepared.

"Captain, I'm Master Sergeant Angelo DiBasse from the Fourth Special Forces group." The tall bearded man introduced himself, looking down at the shorter officer. He was older and had been around long enough to be able to smell when a junior officer didn't know what he was doing. "I've got about ten years in the rangers and in that time I trained a lot of lieutenants and captains. If you don't mind, I'd like to suggest a few things?"

Oteen wanted to bite off his head for insubordination, but he needed help, and DiBasse was providing a lifeline.

"If it is okay with you, I'll put a couple of guys with the troops you are going to send out to recover your strays."

Oteen hadn't thought that far ahead.

Without waiting for instruction, DiBasse gathered about a dozen rangers, who were eager to listen to him, and put them with two special operators. He gave them the instructions to stay up on his radio frequency. He intended to use information downloaded from the drone to direct them to the troops in need of being brought in.

With the search party gathering, he didn't seek Oteen's permission before directing troops on where to set up in a defensive perimeter.

CHAPTER 18

ARABIAN SEA

Jake received a call from the commander of the carrier battle group aboard the aircraft carrier the USS *Vinson*. He was informed that a drone would be launched off the carrier to observe the airborne assault on Kut airfield, and an invitation was extended for him to come and see the live-action assault. As the task force commander, he should have known that he had drones available, but there was a CIA detachment aboard the *Vinson* that was so secret, only several members of the ship's crew knew of its existence. It indicated to Jake that the various agencies involved in Afghanistan were running in different directions and that no one was coordinating the American effort. Still, the offer to see the pictures of the attack was one that Jake couldn't refuse.

He appreciated the invitation, because he had his own ideas about the night assault and wanted to learn everything he could about it. He gathered the people who would have an interest in what was going on five hundred miles to their north and heloed to the *Vinson*.

The combat operations center on the aircraft carrier was larger than that on the *Peleliu*, but the consoles were similar with the exception of screens and operators who were controlling the drone. The COC officer greeted the party of marines and explained what they were seeing.

Jake looked at the grainy green images and saw that the rangers' spread across the ground was too great. There was no possibility that fires could be massed in the event of an attack. He didn't know if any of the people he had brought along with him understood what they were seeing, but Jim Mackey, standing next to him, uttered what he was feeling.

"What a disaster."

Jake nodded. "Why do you say that?" He didn't show sarcasm. He tried to make his question bland so that his feeling would not be parroted.

Mackey knew that Jake listened to his subordinates. He took advice from everyone and played it against what he himself was thinking. What he said and did might be his thoughts alone, but most times he blended ideas. He considered a lot of ideas when thinking about a course of action, but once he made a decision he went with it.

"Go ahead, Mack. Tell us what you see."

Mackey squirmed, wanting to get off stage, but Jake's gaze told him that he had the floor.

"I can't criticize these guys because they are on the ground scrambling to stay alive, but from the comfort of this COC, it looks like they screwed up. I guess what I'm saying is this mission was fucked before it took off." He paused to see if he had lost Jake's support. "What could be the possible strategy behind this mission? We barely have enough air ops available to support the current missions in Afghanistan. Now, a company of rangers is dropped south of Kandahar hundreds of miles from the closest air cover. From what we've been able to gather, they have no mission other than to hold an airfield that is incapable of handling anything but small airplanes and helos. These guys are alone. They are more alone than they know. Putting them in the field with no tactical or strategic objective seems crazy."

"What could be their tactical objective?" one of the officers spoke up.

"I don't know," Mackey confessed. "They are about thirty miles outside of Kandahar, but they don't have enough troops to threaten the city. I think these guys are where they are because someone wanted to show the world that we could do it."

The first casualty reports started coming in. It wasn't a clean drop. There were several severe injuries during the landing, and getting them inside the safety of a defensive perimeter was proving difficult. Making matters worse, the rangers that had floated past the landing zone were unaccounted for.

The marines looked at one another, trying to figure out if what they were hearing might affect them. They looked toward Jake. They wanted his views.

"I didn't cue Mack. What he said is right on. This was an attempt to get pictures of soldiers operating in Afghanistan back into the news cycle. It is not good enough for the indigenous troops to fight this war; the public wants pictures of Americans fighting to avenge the attacks of 9/11." He paused. "If I may quote a famous marine, Jim Mackey, this is a disaster. If the rangers they are going to helo lift into Kandahar can't affect a linkage with the rangers at Kut, this is going to boil down to a survival problem. Every casualty the troops at Kut take eats at their strength and makes them more vulnerable." Jake went silent, and every person in the COC waited for him to start again as if he were an oracle. "We are going to be involved in this in some way. I don't know when it will happen, but the task force better be ready. For starters, I want a comm link set up directly with the rangers, because we have to know their situation in real time. Second, I want any calls for air support by the rangers to be given priority over any missions that are assigned by the Joint Forces Air Command Control Center." Jake was bypassing the monolithic control organization that scheduled tactical air as if it were running an airline. Paperwork had to be completed before they would release airplanes for combat ops. "We have to plan on getting airplane wheels up within thirty minutes of a call for help. You don't have to look for me to seek approval to run air operations in support of the rangers. I'm giving it right now," Jake spoke to the Carrier Air Group Commander.

The marines and the civilians who listened to him knew he was taking a risk. In bypassing the Joint Forces Air Command Control Center and assigning airplanes in direct support of the rangers, Jake was sticking his neck out, and those above him in the chain of command would be looking to chop it off if something went wrong. None of those listening to him disagreed with his decision, but none had worked with a commander who did things because they were right. Others always wanted the cover of the organization so that they could diffuse responsibility. They did their damage control prior to making decisions.

CHAPTER 19

CENTCOM,
TAMPA, FLORIDA

The public relations section received the downloaded film and made the first cut to clean it up and put it in a format that General Franklin could look at and hopefully approve. The video section worked for hours, with one shift passing on the project to its relief. Images were edited and spliced, and a movie portraying heroism was produced. No mention was made of the missed landing zone or the confusion on the ground. It was a good movie, telling a story, but not the story.

With the project completed, the PR officer rushed into Grady Hatton's office.

"What have you got for me?"

"Turn your TV on to channel one." The PR officer wanted to get Hatton's set on the CENTCOM Channel.

The film started rolling. Everything had been filmed with night lenses. People and shapes could be made out, but in the grainy footage they looked like war-fighting ninjas. The boarding was filmed as eager troops climbed onto the airplane, smiling and happy to be going to war. There were a lot of pumped fists at the camera. It made for good press. The flight itself had little coverage. There were several shots of troops working out, adding to the story that they were ready, willing, and able. Shots of the troops sleeping on the absurdly long flight had been edited out.

Action picked up, and the troops were shown getting ready to jump. There were shots of the ramp opening, and the heavy gear being pushed out the back. The scene shifted to the jumpers as they exited the side door. The combat photographers jumped with the rangers and filmed the descent. They were able to follow a string of glo-lites to the ground.

One film crew found the rangers' commanding officer and filmed Oteen. He looked good on camera. His all-American boy face was dirty and sweat-smeared, and that fed into the narrative. American boys from the heartland were recapturing America's honor. No explanation was given why the camera was taken off the captain. That part of the story ended abruptly. The scenes shifted to daybreak and the troops arrayed in a perimeter, their weapons facing outward. Sporadic firing could be heard, but the photographers did not get near enough to it to film the soldiers actually engaged.

The film ended with the pulsing of Wagner's "Flight of the Valkyries."

"Perfect." Hatton felt that Franklin would love it. "Have your people set it up again, and come with me. We're going to bring this to the boss."

"What is it now?" Franklin showed his displeasure at the late afternoon interruption.

"You're going to want to see this, sir." Hatton tried to lighten Franklin's mood. "Set up the TV," he instructed the PR officer.

The film rolled, and the general's face softened. By the time the music played the last scene out, he was hooked.

"Run that for me again." The rerun evoked smiles. "That's what I wanted. That tells the army story I wanted to get out."

Franklin paused. "How can I get it to the president?"

"I can get it to his military aide, and he can get it to the president."

"Do it," he commanded the PR officer.

"Sir, shouldn't we run this by Don Frieze?" Hatton didn't understand why the general was ignoring the DEPSECDEF.

"Fuck him. He tried to stick it to me on this. Let the president tell him I was right. In fact, get this to every member of the Senate Armed Services Committee and the House Armed Services Committee. I want a buzz created so that Frieze and his boys will have to call me to find out what the hell is up."

CHAPTER 20

THE PENTAGON, WASHINGTON, DC

The *Washington Post* was on the phone. They wanted details about the ranger raid in Afghanistan. When Frieze had none to give them, they thought he was lying. They had seen the film of the rangers and wanted to know why the Pentagon was holding out. The buzz around the film was such that a press conference was called to dampen the media circus that was developing. The secretary and the chairman of the JCS were out of town, and DEPSECDEF was the next in the hierarchy that would have to go to the pressroom to face reporters. In trying to find answers as to why the Pentagon was in the dark on the ranger raid, the signs indicated that CENTCOM had aired the story without approval being sought. The idea that his office had been bypassed incensed him. Not waiting until he cooled down, he called Franklin to voice his irritation.

"General, we have a bit of a hornets' nest stirred up with the CENTCOM film that is playing all over town. Is there some reason why I didn't receive the first copy?" Frieze didn't try to hide his anger.

"Things kind of got away from us. The film wasn't classified, and copies got out early."

"Is that why everyone on the hill received a copy, and I didn't?"

When he failed to mention the president, Franklin knew that Frieze didn't know about that copy. "Like I said, it was a mistake."

The words belied his amusement. He was happy to be stringing Frieze along.

"I have a press conference this afternoon where the film will be the subject du jour. I need the specifics of how the mission was carried out, if there was enemy contact, and if there were casualties."

Franklin hoped to avoid the question of casualties. There had been more than normally experienced in an airborne assault. That line of questioning had to be stopped because Franklin didn't want Frieze asking him why the jump into a sterile environment was done at night.

"There were just normal cuts and bruises, nothing too serious." He stretched the casualty envelope, classifying broken bones in the cut-and-bruises category. "We have had one wounded due to enemy fire that we know of."

"Reporters have been mentioning more casualties. What do you know about them?" Frieze was digging in.

"We haven't heard anything yet."

"How do the newspapers get out ahead of us on stuff like this? Do you have a tight rein on your staff so that you are sure no one is leaking information to the press?"

"Absolutely. Yes."

"One question we're sure to get is why was this jump made at night?" Frieze wanted an answer.

Franklin paused too long a time for the conversation to remain comfortable.

"My staff presented the plan to me with the assurance it would be the safest way to enter a hostile area. It was done in the best interest of the troops."

"I think your staff screwed up. The JCS have said it was an undue risk." Frieze jabbed the words into the mouthpiece.

Franklin had paid little attention to the details of the mission. His intent was to get the army into the fight. He succeeded on that front, but he should have questioned the night jump. He hadn't because the night filming made the story more impressive and riveting. He was searching for the answer that would turn Frieze off, because he didn't like being taken behind the woodshed by someone he considered as dumb as a bag of hammers. "Listen, Don, before you get too far out on a limb on this, I think you'd better know that the White House has seen the film and is going to use it as a centerpiece in its war on terror PR binge. If you have problems with the time of the jump, talk to the White House. They thought it was great." Referring to the president would stop all discussion.

"How ...?" Frieze didn't finish the question. If the White House was on board, there was nothing more he could do. He hung up and called the operations section of the JCS to find out what more they knew about the operation. He wasn't happy that Franklin had bypassed him, but he knew that if he worked the press properly he would gain acclaim for being the architect of the night raid.

CHAPTER 21

ARABIAN SEA

The task force command element stayed on the *Vinson* longer than expected. Jake wanted to see how the other part of the operation was conducted. An assault on Taliban leader Mullah Omar's compound by special forces was met with light resistance, giving the impression that the Taliban were on the run. Thinking that troops would be entering a sterile environment to conduct a mop-up operation, the helo assault was launched into a soccer field that the special operators assumed to be benign.

The first helo was hit with a rocket-propelled grenade and fell to the ground like a rock, killing several of the rangers on board. As other helos tried to touch down, the enemy fires were so intense the assault was called off. The link that was supposed to have been made with the rangers at Kut didn't materialize. A Company was alone in the war.

Leaving the command center, Jake went out on one of the aircraft elevators off the hangar deck. Away from air-conditioned COC, standing, looking down at the sea rush past, the hot, moist air did not refresh. He thought about the isolated rangers and felt they were screwed. They were in a combat situation with what they had jumped in with, their weapons, about ten days of MREs, and enough water to get them through their food. They were isolated with no means of relief. It was insanity. Jake wasn't sure what CENTCOM had planned for the rangers, but something had better be in the works because the situation on the ground was not tenable. He assumed an air resupply had been part of the package that had committed the rangers, but he had seen nothing of it in the message traffic. A bigger problem, he thought, was that if Kut couldn't be secured properly, there would be no way to get a fixed-wing medevac plane into the area. The only means of medevac would be helicopter. To his knowledge, there were no long-distance medevac helicopters in theater.

He walked back to the command center and grabbed Jim Mackey.

"Get me a comm link to General Hatton. I don't care if you have to wake him. I have to talk to him." Jake had met Hatton a few times but had never dealt with him in a professional capacity.

An angry Hatton got on the line, and his tone indicated that whatever the conversation was going to be about had better be important.

"General, this is Jake Gregg."

"I know who it is. What the hell do you want?" Hatton didn't like being awakened in the middle of the night.

It wasn't the reception that Jake expected.

"General, from what we are seeing and are hearing from the rangers dropped into Kut, they are in trouble. At a minimum, they are going to have to get their wounded out."

"We are aware of that and are working on it." Hatton cut him off.

"Yes. I understand that, but this eventuality should have been planned for when the mission was approved. It doesn't appear that it was."

"General Gregg, I advise you to back off. In the States, the air drop is being played like the war has been won on the backs of those few rangers. At this point in the narrative you are speaking heresy." Hatton paused to let his words gain weight. "Now, you were saying?"

"It may be playing well in the news, but the kids on the ground aren't seeing it that way." Jake ceased with the niceties.

"You don't expect me to run around with my hair on fire and contradict my boss, do you?"

"I'm not asking for that. I want to know if there are assets in theater that can effect a medevac?"

"Not at this time, but it is being worked."

"What's the expected timeline?" Jake was thinking that the rangers wouldn't be so philosophical knowing their fate depended on timing that included building a cover story so that it wouldn't look like mistakes had been made.

"I don't know." Hatton was honest. "General Franklin is weighing the interests of the president along with the needs of the rangers."

Jake wasn't amused. In a tug of war between the president and a few troops in peril, there was a predictable winner.

"The task force has the ability to effect a medevac. All that is required are two marine C-130s." The marine 130s had the capability to aerial refuel the CH-53 helicopters assigned to the task force.

"That's a nonstarter. General Franklin doesn't want marines involved. This is an army show. At best, he'd let the air force get involved in a medevac."

"It would take the air force days to get long-range medevac helos into theater. I don't think we have that kind of time."

"General Gregg. You're trying to get into things that are way above your pay grade. Take a bit of advice from someone who has played in this arena. Let it go. You've got a good gig as a task force commander, or whatever the hell they are calling you. So just relax. Those of us running the war will handle the rest." Hatton had in an indirect way ordered Jake to get the hell out of CENTCOM's business and hoped Jake was smart enough to understand his meaning. "Now is there anything else I can help you with?" It was delivered icily.

"No, sir." Jake hated to show emotion in front of his subordinates, but he slammed the handset into the cradle. "These people are crazy. It is like we don't have troops at war, and the only thing that is important are the photo ops."

"Sir, I couldn't help overhearing your conversation. It was on the overhead speaker." Mackey smiled.

"Great."

"Sir, we have most of the assets on hand to put together a medevac. The piece missing is marine 130s. It doesn't sound like we are going to be able to get them through CENTCOM because they don't want us involved. But supposing we could get 130s and present CENTCOM with a complete medevac package. If they got into a press, they would have to use us."

"I agree, but where can we get refueling airplanes? CENTCOM controls them."

"On the workup for this deployment, the MEU did a lot of training with the Marine Reserve 130s. In fact, we did air refueling with them."

"So?"

"The reserves don't fall under CENTCOM until they are called up. None have been. If we could get them to work with us, CENTCOM might not know or care." Mackey didn't say more. He was getting into force issues that were butting up against legality.

"Are you asking me to disobey orders?" Jake scared Mackey before smiling.

"Get General O'Malley on the hook." Jake instructed Mackey to put him through to the reserve commander. He had met O'Malley socially, but Jake had to approach him as if they were long-lost friends.

"The link is set up, sir." Mackey informed.

"Good. Now make sure it isn't on the overhead speakers because I don't want the world to know what I'm doing."

"Tom, Jake Gregg here." They exchanged pleasantries and talked about the 9/11 attacks before Jake switched gears.

"Tom, I need your help."

"Sure, anything."

"Before you open your wallet, you'd better listen to what I want you to give."

"What do you need that I can do for you?"

"I need 130 refuelers."

"What's going on?"

"I think we have a debacle in the making. You probably know that some rangers were inserted in an area south of Kandahar."

O'Malley interrupted him. "Everybody knows about it. It is all over the news. They are playing it like those guys are winning the war. I take it from your tone that the press has it wrong?"

"They are only reporting what is fed to them."

"So you need airplanes?"

"Yes. Refueling airplanes."

There was a long pause as O'Malley thought over the request. "I can make it happen, but you have to know working with the reserves is different. Unless they are called up, the crews are on a two-week limit, give or take a couple of days. How long will you need them?"

"If possible, I need four aircraft here for maybe four weeks?"

O'Malley delayed. "Off the top of my head, I'm saying we can get you three airplanes, but for that long a time I'm going to have to rotate crews back to the United States unless I can find crews with a lot of extra time. Does that work at all?"

"That will work."

"Where are they going to be located?"

"We are off the port of Gudwar, Pakistan. I have already contacted the embassy in Islamabad and have received clearance for operating fixed-wing aircraft out of the airport. It has a runway that will accommodate the weight of 130s."

"I have an airplane in Bahrain that is off-loading cargo. It was going to turn and come back home, but I can get it to you. I've got another on its way to Bahrain. With luck I can get it to you in about thirty-six hours. The third that I'll send your way is en route to Diego Garcia. It might take a couple of days to get to you. Will that work?"

"Before I end your career, I have to tell you I ran this by

CENTCOM because it is their responsibility, and they shot me down. I hate to have them screw you over this."

"Jake, the beauty of the reserves is that no one on active duty knows how they work. Even better, in instances like this, no one gives a shit. If we're not called up and put into the troop rotations, we can work in your area without having to check in with anybody. No one wants to hear from us unless they can control us, and they can't because we are not called up. It's a perfect catch-22. If this thing goes bad, we'll come up on the wire and say we're training. The worst that will happen is someone on the CENTCOM staff will chew me out and say the damn reserves screwed up again. It's no big deal. It happens all the time."

"Thanks, Tom."

"Remember, Jake, when CENTCOM is trying to knock your head off, keep mentioning you were training with reserves. They might not like it, but they will have to buy it because Congress has mandated that we train with the active forces."

Jake hung up.

"Mack, get the embassy and make arrangements for us to get access to the port at Gudwar. We are going to have to put the MPS tanker in there to off-load fuel."

CHAPTER 22

THE PENTAGON,
WASHINGTON, DC

The latest reports from Kut reached the embeds at the same time they reached CENTCOM, and both staffs realized they had a problem. Both had been pumping out information to any press outlet needing filler about the successes of the rangers. No mention was made of the difficulty they were having, or of the failed helo assault at Kandahar. That part of the two-part mission was ignored. As far as the American public was concerned, it never happened.

Those injured in the jump were being nursed on site, but the ranger medics were saying that the injured needed more care than they could provide. The worst injury was a compound fracture of a leg that was infected, and the injured trooper had to be medevaced out of Kut along with ten others in various states of misery.

CENTCOM was keeping track of the calls for a medevac. With the stories they had been releasing about the successes on the ground, no one wanted to undercut the story line. The public had been presented a rosy picture, with no mention made of anyone being wounded. There was no hint that the Taliban were closing in on Kut. Those details didn't play into the narrative that was being spun, and both staffs knew the danger of changing the story, especially after the president was lionized in the press for his decision to use the rangers.

CENTCOM started making plans to evacuate the injured out of sight of the public. Arrangements were being made to have two jolly green giant rescue helicopters flown to Pakistan, but all the airplanes capable of carrying the helicopters were scheduled, and no one wanted to raise red flags by asking for emergency airlift. It was going to take three days for large cargo haulers capable of transporting the bulky helicopters to become available. The loading, the flight, and the unloading were going to take another two days. With everything falling into place, the earliest the injured rangers would be out of the field was six days. Those in positions of command who were worried about the narrative of Kut thought the timeline acceptable.

The Taliban around Kut threw the recovery plan into disarray. In a night attack they wounded two rangers. The medevac was no longer just another mission; it was a full-blown emergency.

"Don Frieze on the phone for you, sir." General Franklin's secretary informed him. It was a call Franklin didn't want to take.

"How can the military help out its civilian leadership?" Franklin turned on his charm without feeling any of it.

"General, I suppose I don't have to tell you we have a mess on our hands."

"Mess. What are you talking about?"

"You've got at least five dead in an operation that was supposed to be a PR bonanza. I cautioned you about something like this. I didn't want ground troops involved, and you went around me. Your end run with Congress has gotten us in a bind, and I, for one, would like to know what the hell you intend to do about it."

Franklin was unused to being spoken to so harshly, but Frieze wasn't a military man that he could put in his place by ordering respect for his rank.

"We are working on getting the wounded and the injured medevaced. We should have a plan in place soon, and we will brief you on it."

"The White House wants this as your top priority, so I'd advise you to get on it, and stay on it until you come up with something that will make everyone happy, and be sure you stay on message. The story line can't change. Classify everything about the need for a medevac."

"Yes …" Franklin almost said "yes, sir," but he disliked Frieze and wouldn't show overt respect.

"As soon as you find out how you are going to get us out of this mess, call me. I'll make sure it gets through the system cleanly." The phone went dead.

Franklin was humiliated and seething when he called Hatton into his office.

"How about telling me why I was on the phone getting my ass chewed by the three-pound brain?" he started on Hatton. "Who had the responsibility for the insertion of both ranger companies?"

"Several things we hadn't anticipated cropped up."

"Isn't that the purpose of planning, to prevent surprises?"

"Yes, sir."

"So what you're saying is that you gave me a shitty plan?" Franklin had Hatton beaten down. "What kind of a half-assed plan have you devised to get us out of this mess?"

"As soon as we get airlift, we will put jolly green medevac helos in Pakistan and get those needing to be medevaced out."

"As soon as … Just what the fuck does that mean?"

"Airlift is not available unless we put in an emergency request, and your instruction was to keep this low-profile." Hatton gained some space by intimating that the general had been part of the problem.

"I still want to keep this low-profile. That's a must."

"Sir, the only way we are going to be able to get the rangers out more quickly is with an emergency request for airlift. That would probably allow us to get them out in two or three days." Hatton tried to outline the options.

"Christ! What a mess." Franklin stood behind his desk and rubbed his forehead. "Any other options?"

"The Marine Task Force is the closest unit that might have the capability to effect a medevac. I spoke to General Gregg, and he indicated he might be able to put something together."

"I don't want the marines putting a force on the ground."

"Gregg indicated that he could reach the rangers with helos. There would be no marines on the ground."

"How long will that take to put together?"

"He said once he got the call, he could have the helos airborne in four hours." Hatton was angry that Jake had called him twice telling him that he had put a rescue package together and that he was ready to launch. Clueless, Hatton took advantage of Jake's offer.

"Goddamn it." Franklin was disgusted, thinking his efforts to keep the marines out of the war were spinning out of control. "I want you to call Frieze and tell them we are ready to launch a medevac using the marines."

Franklin dismissed the operations deputy.

Hatton walked down the hall to his office. He had been given the responsibility of selling a marine recovery to the Pentagon, and he didn't know if Frieze would get on board with it. He would find out.

He reached DEPSECDEF.

"Don, Grady Hatton. General Franklin wanted me to call you and inform you that we are ready to launch a medevac to pull out the wounded rangers."

"How did he put it together so quickly?" Frieze was surprised. He recognized the severity of the situation at Kut and had the JCS jump in and order emergency airlift. Even with the emergency timelines, the best-case scenario was two days out. He couldn't believe Franklin could put together a mission more quickly.

"We are going to use marine helos from Task Force Raptor."

"Sounds like typical CENTCOM planning." He was sarcastic. "The marine helos don't have that kind of range."

"Marine 130s in the area are capable of aerial refueling helos."

"The marines have no 130s in theater." Frieze wanted Hatton to know that he couldn't be snowed.

"I was told they are reserve 130s. They are training with the task force."

"Reserve?"

"Yes, sir. That's what I'm told."

"How did the goddamn reserves get involved in the war before it's really started?"

"I can't answer that. All I know is that they are training with the task force."

"All right. I'll have the White House approve the medevac, but you'd better pray that a reserve doesn't get killed, because their use has never been mentioned." Frieze thought about what he had consented to. "Jake Gregg is the task force commander. I want him on a tight leash. In no way do I want him to grow a medevac into something that looks like an expanded war effort. I want no marines on the ground."

"We will not let him do anything other than that which we authorize." Hatton wanted to get off the phone.

Frieze didn't want to rehash the past and got back to what had to be done. "You can tell Franklin the medevac will be approved. Tell him he may get some blowback from the White House over it, but if it done properly it will be ignored. Whatever you do about the medevac, make sure that Gregg doesn't get in front of the press."

CHAPTER 23

ARABIAN SEA

The clearance came just before dawn, and the slow-paced morning became frenetic. With everything planned, in the time before launch, a thousand things seemed that they needed to be done.

Jake was in his small cubicle working the phones, giving last-minute instruction when Colonel Patch and Mackey squeezed their way in.

"What's up?" He didn't stand.

"Mack told me that you were planning on riding in the medevac bird." Patch was careful in his wording. He didn't want to sound accusatory.

"I am planning on it."

"It's a bad idea. If something should happen to the helo, and you went down, the task force you're putting together, which isn't written down on paper, would fall apart. You're the glue and horsepower that have made this work. You've gotten it to work so well we are going to get into a war that no one wants us in." Patch made obvious observations.

Jake leaned back. He wanted to be on the helo so that he wouldn't be putting marines in danger that he himself wasn't willing to experience.

"He's right, sir," Mackey spoke. "You are needed here to hold this together. There is another reason you shouldn't go. If you get shot down, it would be a PR bonanza for the enemy."

"I can't let you go." Jake spoke to Patch. "You're running the MEU and the only one who can do that." He thought for a moment. "The reason I was going to ride along was to make an assessment of the condition of the rangers that will be left behind. I need to know that, because it will give me an indication of how soon we are going to have to return in force."

"Mack could do it. He understands what you want and could be your eyes and ears," Patch suggested.

"What about it, Red? Think you can handle this?"

"Yes, sir. Tell me what you want done, and I'll do it."

"You'll have to swing by the maritime positioned ships. They'll have some packages I requested ready for you."

"Is it something I should know about?" Mackey didn't know if he was being kidded.

"I had them package up chocolate bars, cigarettes, water, gasoline, canned juices, and canned fruits. I also asked the civilians to break loose some of their booze and donate it to the rangers. It's not going to be enough to get anyone drunk, but there will be enough for the rangers to mix with the fruit juice and drink something other than warm water. There will also be several boxes of prophylactics."

Patch and Mackey looked at him like he had lost his mind.

"When we were in the sand for six months preparing for Desert Storm, troops were going crazy," Jake explained. "In days of blistering sun and nights of sandstorms, morale was turning to crap. There was no way to motivate troops. One day a box of prophylactics arrived, and as troops do, they saw the humor in it. They railed against the system and made jokes about how they would be ready the next time, if ever, they saw a woman. The important thing was it gave them something to laugh about when their world was turning to shit. My gut feel is that the rangers are feeling that their world has turned to shit, and a couple boxes of rubbers might take their mind off it. They will be able to rail at their fucked-up commanders."

Patch and Mackey knew from working with him that he was smart, but it was his concern for the troops that was his greatest asset. The rangers were suffering, and he wanted to help them get through physically and mentally.

A marine came to his compartment. "Sir, the helos are ready."

"Lieutenant Mackey will be right up." Jake stood. "Mack, you won't have to arrange getting the wounded on board. Three medics will be with you to do that. What I want you to do is look into the eyes of the troops that will remain in Kut. Determine if they are blank or if there is still life in them. Get to Captain Oteen and listen to what he tells you, but watch him. Look at the same things you are looking for in the troops. When you talk to him, check his movements. See if there are any tics, any nervous tendencies. He's under a tremendous amount of stress, and I want you to tell me if he's showing signs of cracking. Find the special ops guy, Dibasse. He's been around and shouldn't show any stress, but check him anyway. Try to determine if he is giving Oteen all the support he can. If you don't think he is, you have my permission to tell him he'd better get on the stick, because if we have to pull those guys out, we'll leave him there. You can use my rank to threaten anybody you think needs coaching up. Got it?"

"Yes, sir."

"Red, don't worry; you'll do fine."

Jake and Patch walked the lieutenant up to the flight deck, where two helos were already turning.

Mackey walked to the helicopter and disappeared inside. The ramp was closed, and he was airborne.

CHAPTER 24

USS *VINSON,*
COMMAND OPERATIONS CENTER (COC)

Jake was deflated. After spending days planning the medevac and thinking that he might ride along, he went to the Combat Operations Center on the aircraft carrier because of its capability to receive the drone downloads. He wanted to see what was happening on the ground. Intellectually, he understood the timelines of the mission, but sitting and waiting gave him the feeling that things weren't going fast enough.

Listening to the communications between the refueling 130s and the helicopters, he was dismayed that on the first attempt at refueling there was a problem. Jake wanted to jump through the screen and be on site to help them fix it but had to sit helplessly.

He stewed as the pilots figured it out. They were flying too low over the desert, and the updrafts caused the helicopters and the fueling baskets to bounce wildly, too wildly to make a connection. They didn't call back to the COC for permission to change the plan. They climbed to smoother air and completed their hookup.

Mackey looked out the helicopter window and saw sand and more sand, and although they were flying higher, he could see the convective waves of heat rising off the arid ground. He watched as the second refueling plug was accomplished and waited for the third. That would mean they were only minutes from their destination. As the helicopter rose to meet the tanker, Mackey twisted in his seat to see what the terrain around Kut was like. He spotted a sliver of green, indicating that there was a water source. If there was one, it ended at Kut, because south and west of the village was barren.

When the aerial tanker broke contact and changed direction, the helicopter maintained heading while descending.

As the noses of the helos rose, and the speed slowed, the rotor downwash lifted a sand cloud. Unable to maintain sight of the ground, the pilots cut power, and the helos dropped to the surface, landing with a thud. In exiting the helo, Mackey couldn't believe the condition of the men greeting him. Their uniforms were the same color as the ground upon which they stood. It would have been acceptable if they had tried to camouflage themselves. They hadn't. Their appearance was the result of living on and in the dirt. They wore protective goggles, and those who lifted them exposed weary eyes.

"Where's your commanding officer?" Mackey asked the first ranger he met.

The soldier said nothing and merely pointed to a Humvee with a tarpaulin over it.

Mackey went in that direction, and three soldiers were on the lee side of the vehicle, using it as a wind block.

"Where is the CO?"

One of the rangers stepped forward reluctantly.

"I'm Captain Oteen."

"I'm Lieutenant Mackey from Task Force Raptor. We brought you some goods we thought you might need." Mackey was spouting words, but he watched Oteen's eyes to see if there was any reaction. The blankness or anger he expected didn't show. The ranger commander's eyes welled with tears. He had thought he was never going to get out of Kut, and the idea that the marines had reached him was a lifeline. In understanding that he wasn't alone in the war, he could not control his emotions.

"Sorry." He wiped his eyes with the back of a dirty hand. "This has been a tough couple of days. Thanks for getting my wounded out."

Mackey overreached. "We're only a plane ride away, and we're there to support you guys." He failed to tell Oteen that Jake had almost lost his job over getting the medevac okayed, and that it was going to be a bitch getting another mission approved. He decided to leave the idea with Oteen that help was on the way.

Mackey watched carefully. The ranger captain's eyes weren't dead. They still had fight, even if Oteen didn't know his purpose for fighting other than that he was holding a worthless piece of ground in the middle of nowhere with the vague notion that his presence there was in some way helping his country's war effort.

The rangers Mackey met had the same confused defiance. They wanted to fight but felt like they were abandoned.

"Where's your special ops guy?" Mackey asked. He was directed to an area in the ranger camp. The special ops people had isolated themselves.

Mackey walked up to a man dressed like an Afghan. "Where's your boss?"

"You got him. I'm Dibasse."

"I need your assessment of the enemy and, more importantly, of the rangers."

"Who the fuck are you?" Dibasse didn't like junior officers questioning him.

"I'm Lieutenant Mackey from Task Force Raptor."

"Like I said, who the fuck are you?"

Mackey straightened to his full height. He was several inches taller than the special operator. His face grew as red as his hair, and he did little to hide his anger.

"Look, dickhead. I was sent here to get answers, and I'm going to get them, or I'm going to get into a fight that I won't lose. Your choice. Now what is the status of the enemy and what is the status of the rangers, in your opinion?"

DiBasse had never seen a junior officer act like Mackey. He thought the marine might have a screw loose, and crazy people did crazy things. He softened his tone. "The Taliban in Kut are about twenty strong. They probe nightly, and we have managed to beat them off. So far, the Taliban appear to be content with their probes. As far as the rangers, they are kids and could have used a lot more training before they jumped in here. They're quick learners and are holding their own after a fucking disastrous night jump." Thinking that Mackey might report up the chain of command, DiBasse used the opening to voice his opinion. "Whoever approved a night jump ought to be in jail, because they know nothing about airborne ops. They were lucky that Oteen didn't lose a lot more. If we hadn't had a drone up, we'd still be looking for guys."

"Anything you need from the task force?"

"We could use relief. We'd sure like to be taken out of here."

"I'll get your request to higher headquarters, but that is a CENTCOM decision."

"That isn't going to work. Just watching how they are running our little piece of the war tells me they are fucked up. They are too busy trying to figure out what to do to worry about us."

"It won't hurt to try." Mackey consoled. He hedged for a minute before asking a question he didn't know if he had the right to ask. "How's Captain Oteen holding up?"

DiBasse understood Mackey's intent. "He's a good kid, but he is in way over his head. It's not his fault. They yanked him from behind a desk and planted him here without the requisite tools." DiBasse didn't want to undermine Oteen. "I'm working with him. He listens and learns. He'll get these guys out of here okay."

Mackey was glad to hear that because he had received mixed signals.

The wounded and injured were loaded. Mackey stopped by the Hummer to see Oteen. Several of the troops were standing around laughing. It was an unexpected sight.

They had found the whiskey and prophylactics in with the resupply. The whiskey was a hit, and various concoctions were being tried, but the prophylactics raised spirits, especially among those who used them to cover their rifle muzzles. It was an easy way to keep them dirt free and also provided evidence to the rangers that the people running the war were screwed up. While they could not grouse about their officers, they could openly insult senior commands for sending rubbers to a place there wasn't a chance in hell they would be used.

As Mackey walked away he could hear the brutally sarcastic jokes being told.

The evacuated landed back aboard the *Vinson* because it had elaborate hospital facilities. Once the helo was tied down, the injured were rushed to medical. It was the consensus among the doctors that one case was just in time; his infection was critical.

Mackey found Jake in the officers' wardroom sipping a coffee that was jet black and had the consistency of paste.

"Mack. Come and sit down." He was at a table covered with heavy gray denim. A silver coffee pot sat in front of him, and he poured Mackey a cup.

"What'd you find?"

"I think if we can get a resupply to them every couple of days they will be able to hold on for a while." Mackey sat down.

"Any thousand-mile stares?"

"There were at first, but when they realized we could get to them, they brightened up. They see us as a security blanket."

"We are." Jake paused. "What was the special ops take on how they are faring."

"The guy running special ops is a cocky bastard, as you'd expect. He started out giving me some shit, before I told him I'd bust his face. After we came to an understanding, he said the rangers will be able to hold on. Before I left, he asked if he could set up a back channel directly to you. He wants to keep you informed of the situation on the ground. He doesn't think the people in his chain of command care what's happening at Kut and was thankful you took on the medevac. I hope it's okay, but I gave him a covered frequency." Mackey didn't know if he had overreached.

"You did good, so good, in fact, I have another job for you."

"Sir?"

"Tomorrow morning same routine. You are taking a helicopter and flying the route we will have to use if we have to go to Kandahar. I had the route surveyed for places where we can set up Forward Area Refueling Points. Only the 53s can air-to-air refuel. All the other helos will have to land to refuel, so we have to pick spots where a 130 with an internal fuel bladder will be able to land, pump gas, and take off. I've got the engineers ready to go with you."

"Yes, sir." Mackey stood. "Sir?"

Jake looked up without speaking.

"The prophylactics were fucking genius." He laughed and left.

CHAPTER 25

THE PENTAGON, WASHINGTON, DC

The offices DEPSECDEF and the embeds working with him that prior to the attack on 9/11 were on different rings and on different levels of the Pentagon, were consolidated because the hole in the building resulted in disjointed staff functioning. By putting his brain trust in proximity, Frieze hoped to improve the group's effectiveness. Taking over several offices, the embeds worked in his immediate vicinity. When they wanted to discuss sensitive matters, all they had to do was walk into the adjoining office and speak face to face and be assured their conversations were private.

"Did you read the reports on the medevac at Kut?" Frieze asked a group gathered in his office.

"It looked like it went off without a hitch. That should make the White House happy," someone offered.

"It should, but I think it is going to lead to a bigger problem. We let Franklin sell the ranger assault, and we hyped its success. We know it was a disaster, but the president doesn't. If the media gets wind of the need for a medevac, they are going to want to know why on a mission that we sold as a cakewalk, we had to evac rangers out. I've talked to the NSC. They have agreed to keep references of the operation out of their daily brief to the president. The danger is that he might get blindsided by a reporter's question." Frieze mentioned his real concern. "Since we have milked every ounce of PR juice out of the story, we have to kill it. We need something to replace it with. Any suggestions?"

"Air operations are going to be expanded. We have enough air assets in theater now to bomb anywhere we want."

"Keep going." Frieze wanted to see what the group was thinking.

"We have intelligence that Mullah Omar is in Kandahar. If we tell CENTCOM to start bombing Kandahar, that might overlay any story that gets out about the rangers at Kut."

"Work the White House on that storyline," Frieze ordered a subordinate. "I think they might be getting tired of hearing from me."

"How many arms did you have to twist to get Franklin to use the marine medevac?"

"I didn't. CENTCOM didn't. The goddamn marines nosed in where they shouldn't have."

"I guess we're lucky they were nearby, because if the medevac had been delayed, the story definitely would have broken, and we'd be up to our asses answering congressional inquiries."

"That's one way to look at it." Frieze didn't think the marines had saved the day. "The marine commander is General Gregg."

"Your old buddy." Someone laughed. "I thought you fired him."

"I did, but the Marine Corps somehow got him out on the Arabian Sea, and he was the one who put this thing together."

"And you don't think that is good?" The questioner didn't have emotions invested in Jake and looked at the mission devoid of personality.

"The reason I got rid of him is that he knows that we want to get into Iraq and are just running a holding operation in Afghanistan. He's not like the generals that we have cowed. If a reporter gets to him and asks a question, he'll answer it. He won't shade his answers."

"I thought you had a gag order on him while he is in the service."

"We do, but with the medevac he pulled off, the Marine Corps may try to get him promoted. If he climbs in the rank structure, he could take apart our Iraqi plans." Frieze was wary of Jake and wanted the others to know his feelings so that they could keep their eyes and ears in his direction.

CHAPTER 26

CENTCOM, TAMPA, FLORIDA

Grady Hatton took the call for the general, who was in a meeting and wouldn't be available until later in the afternoon. He didn't dare say Franklin was playing golf, at least not to Don Frieze. He sat behind his expansive desk covered with papers. Hatton had dozens of things started and none completed.

"The story of the recovery of the rangers is beginning to leak. We are sure the leaks aren't emanating from this end, and I hope you people aren't dumb enough to try to take credit for a successful mission." Frieze was talking down to the CENTCOM director of ops.

"No one here has mentioned it."

"Just to reinforce the point, if you guys start crowing about a successful recovery, the next question is going to be, why was a recovery needed? That would uncover the mess made of the night jump and might expose the failed helo assault. If reporters start nosing around, the wheels are going to come off the story that the ranger insert was a success. I've already checked with the White House, and as of now, the story is dead. No more photos, no more interviews, no mention of rangers being in Afghanistan. For all practical purposes, we are going to play it like this never happened. Neither the jump-in nor the recovery ever happened. Our press people have already started walking back the story, and I'd suggest that your people do likewise. Understand?"

"Got it covered." Hatton had been the one who had put the para drop together and had lived with the accolades when it was news, but he understood the downside.

"We think killing the story will work for a while, but sooner or later it will break free, so I want you, very quietly, and I mean very quietly, to put together a documentary on the medevac. When the story breaks, we want to be able to overlay the ranger story with the story that all combat operations are dangerous and that we had plans in place to recover the rangers. During the narrative, I want shots of the White House staff approving the mission, and the secretary sitting with General Franklin discussing it. You can make yourself the organizing mastermind and take credit for it. Under no circumstances do I want the marines mentioned. Any footage that you have, that you can use, will be army. Black out the marine designation on the helicopters if you have to, but paint the picture with an army brush."

"We have enough stock footage to put a movie together without leaving the building." Hatton was happy. He thought of the places he could insert himself into the script. It was going to work out well. The all-army show would please General Franklin.

"Now that I've given you something that you can accomplish," Frieze was insulting, "I want you to assure me that any further operations in and around the rangers will be accomplished without using the marines. You people wanted to insert the rangers, so you could make a run on the supplemental funding, and I'm going to tell you that if it gets out that the marines cleaned up your mess, you are going to lose out. I'll see to it that the marines get a more than fair share." Frieze had no intention of doing what he said, but it would motivate the CENTCOM staff.

"I've got it." Hatton would omit mentioning the threat to Franklin and would press on with the movie about the recovery.

"When General Franklin is free, have him call me. We are ready to release airplanes for air ops around Kandahar." Frieze didn't say good-bye. Hatton sat holding a dead phone.

CHAPTER 27

Arabian Sea

"For you, Lieutenant," a marine on comm watch alerted Mackey.

"What switch?" Mackey wanted to know the phone he was supposed to pick up.

"Spook one." It was a reference to Jake's covered line. No one used it except Jake, and Mackey worried that the classified frequency had somehow been hacked. He could not think of a reason for someone calling him on that line. In fact, he could think of no way anyone could have discovered the line.

He didn't want to touch the handset, because he didn't know what that might trigger. He could jeopardize all the work the task force had accomplished if he answered and acknowledged the contact. He stood looking at the marine who alerted him. He didn't want to make a mistake.

"Sir?" the marine awaited Mackey's instruction.

"I'll take it." If he was going to make a mistake, it would only be this once, because he would have the line ripped out.

"Lieutenant Mackey." He identified himself with his rank so that if the conversation was being recorded, whoever was listening would realize taping a lieutenant's conversation would be pointless.

"Does your offer still hold?" a voice he didn't recognize asked.

"What? Who is this?"

"This is Dibassie. We talked at Kut."

"You know this is a classified line?" Mackey didn't know what to do.

"Just so that you won't think this is someone playing with you, you were going to kick my ass. Only you and I know that. You gave me this back channel, and I have the ability on my end to talk covered. So no more bullshit! Does your offer still hold?"

Mackey couldn't remember what if anything he had offered. He hemmed.

"You said that your boss was fighting a different war than anyone else and that if push came to shove he'd step over the boundaries to help us. Remember?" DiBasse was specific.

"I remember."

"Now, was that just blowing smoke to keep me happy, or were you serious?"

"I wasn't blowing smoke."

"Good, because we have a situation brewing that could spiral out of control, and we are going to need help."

"Hang on a minute. This is out of my league." Mackey found Jake on the hangar deck.

"Sir, there's a call on the black net that you should take."

"Sure, Mack. What's up?"

"When I was in Kut, I made a promise that I had no idea would be taken seriously." Mackey explained as they were walking back to Jake's box-walled working space.

"What was it?"

"I told the special operator that if he needed help to call us, and we'd help them." Mackey didn't know how Jake would take being committed without his knowledge.

Jake shook his head. "It's all right. We're fighting the same war, and we help where we can. Who will I be talking to?

"Master Sergeant DiBasse."

Jake picked up the handset. "General Gregg."

"Sir, you don't know me, but your bag man said that if we needed help I could call you."

"Since you called, I assume you need help?"

"Not right away, but I want to alert you that the situation on the ground at Kut could get nasty. If it does, I think all of us here are screwed." DiBasse's voice sounded stressed.

"Start from the beginning. What's happening? And how do you see us playing?"

"Yes, sir." DiBasse awoke to the fact that he was getting emotional, a violation of his own code and something trained out of special operators. "General, I've had patrols out well before the rangers jumped in. We thought we had the local Taliban pretty much scoped out, but through a couple of the locals we use, we have received word that the Taliban in Kandahar are going to send about a hundred fighters to Kut. They see it as an easy target, and if they can take it, it will be a great propaganda victory. The influx hasn't started, but we know that Taliban commanders have arrived in the area and are doing their recon. When the bulk of their troops show, they will be able to attack. Ordinarily, I wouldn't worry about it, but the rangers are in an unsustainable position. They are pretty much exposed and spread out over a wide area, making fields of fire reinforcement impossible. Captain Oteen wants to bring the troops in tighter, but the Taliban will have mortars. If the rangers form a tight perimeter, they will be chopped apart because there is no cover. They are dug into the sand."

"I get the picture. Give me a timeline."

"We expect a pickup truck a day to arrive with about five or six fighters. We think their arrival will be staggered because one truck usually can avoid being attacked from the air. If our intel is correct, they will have a force on the ground that could inflict damage on us in about twelve days."

"So we've got a week." Jake cut the timeline short because there was no surety two or three trucks a day wouldn't show up. "Here's what you have to do. Get Oteen on his link to his chain of command and have him request reinforcements. I want him to explain to

CENTCOM what you have told me. At the same time, I want you to use your channels to the Special Operations Command. Tell them what is going on." Jake paused. "I'm not blowing you off, but I've been told to keep my hands off the rangers. So, push as hard as you can through the normal chains of command. The idea is to make enough noise so that you can't be ignored, and if you are, and are attacked, there will be hell to pay. When you talk to SOCOM, you can tell them that we are ready to jump in, and if they can force the issue, we will. Now this is the tricky part. I want to talk to you every day. I want to know the ground situation. If it gets to a point that you think you will lose troops, you get on the line to me. I will not let that happen. When you feel you are out of time, we'll get to you with or without orders. If we're lucky, after the war, we'll be witnesses at each other court-martials."

"Yes, sir, and thank you, sir." The relief in the special operator's voice was evident.

"When you and Oteen uplink your calls for help, punctuate your requests with language that will get action. Say something like, we will have to cede this position. Do not say that the troops will surrender. I think the idea of having to give up anything to the Taliban will get results."

"Thanks, General." Dibasse had something he could tell his troops and the rangers that would ease their minds. "You have no idea what a relief your words are."

"I'd tell you not to sweat it, but I think we all have something to sweat."

Jake signed off and turned to Mackey. "Hell of a mess you've gotten us into."

"Sorry."

"Don't be. They are in the situation that we saw coming, only it's happening faster than we thought."

CHAPTER 28

CENTCOM,
TAMPA, FLORIDA

Grady Hatton came into Franklin's cavernous office with a hastily put together file. He dreaded having to be the bearer of bad news, but he needed a decision and didn't have time to soften the hard edges of his report.

"Something you should see, General." He kept his voice steady, trying not to show emotion. He expected to be abused verbally, because it was a given among the staff that the general was never at fault. It was those who worked for him who didn't fulfill his expectations. As a result, Franklin seldom saw or heard unfiltered information. Reports were massaged and smoothed so that they didn't trigger his temper.

"What do you need?" He looked up over the newspaper he was reading.

"We have a situation that needs your attention," Hatton said as if what he was going to report barely rose to the level of Franklin's attention.

The general put down what he was reading with a sigh of disgust.

"Well, come on. What the hell have you got to say that's so important?"

"General," Hatton shuffled standing in front of his desk. "The rangers we put in Kut have screwed up. They have put themselves in a position that is becoming unsustainable, and they are requesting help."

"Who is the commanding officer?"

"A Captain Oteen."

"He's finished in the army. See that we get rid of him."

Hatton was dumbfounded. Franklin didn't ask about the situation. He wanted to know about the person who he could blame. Hatton knew the blame went at least to his level and probably to Franklin.

"General, I'll take care of Oteen, but this is bigger than him. We have a ranger company and special ops personnel facing a Taliban force that is growing. Estimates on the ground are that in a few days the Taliban will outnumber the rangers and that they may have to surrender."

The word was electric in Franklin's brain. "Get that captain on the line and tell him that no unit under my command will surrender. We'll do what we have to. We will not surrender."

"Our options are limited. We have no way to get support to the rangers unless we use the marines who conducted the medevac." Hatton had looked at the options and realized that the marines were the only realistic choice.

"No, no marines. This has to be an army operation. What units are available that could effect a relief of the rangers?"

"We have nothing nearby. We have units in and around Kabul, but they are required there. We have some staging in Kuwait that we could get into theater, but we have no way to get them close to the rangers because the Taliban control the entire area."

"There has to be some way. This is the most powerful military command the world has ever seen. Are you telling me we can't get army troops into the war?"

"The staff has looked at all the options, and the only way we can get army troops into Kut on the timeline needed is to repeat an airborne operation. We'd have to drop a battalion in, but with the difficulty we have had in supplying those already on the ground, that looks dicey." Hatton wanted to steer the general away from that course of action.

"Get a battalion ready to go. We will not have a unit cede territory or surrender."

"Sir," Hatton almost choked, "the staff feels the best option is the marines."

"Not on my watch." Franklin was rigid. "Can you see the press if the marines rescue an army unit? We could never live it down. Christ, the marines would blow their horns around Washington and cut into the supplemental funding we have started to receive. No, I don't want the marines near this." Franklin paused and softened his tone. "I know a second unit dropping into a bad situation isn't the most ideal military tactic, but there are two parts to any war—one on the battlefield, and the other, the war for money and resources. We have to win both to ensure the army's viability. If we play this right, the army will be in good shape to face the future, because the supplemental money will allow us to reequip the entire army."

Hatton was conflicted. He had sold the idea of the jump into Kut. His hands were all over it, and he thought he should have done more so that the troops on the ground wouldn't be in the position they were in. "Sir," he hated to continue, "the spec ops people with the rangers have been running requests for relief through SOCOM. We don't know for sure, but we think their requests have been forwarded to the DEPSECDEF."

"God damn it." Franklin pounded his desk with his open palm and stood angrily. "You get this fucking staff working on plans for a second para drop immediately. I want to have army troops on their way before we get orders from the Pentagon telling me how to do my job."

"Yes, sir." Hatton turned and left. He was unsure of what he was being asked to do, but he was ordered, and he would comply.

CHAPTER 29

THE PENTAGON, WASHINGTON, DC

Don Frieze received a call that froze him in his seat. The army ranger unit at Kut was indicating that they would have to cede the ground they held. The ramifications of that eventuality made his head ache. He thought about how the press and Congress would handle the news. It wouldn't be pretty. In time, an investigation would be conducted, and his part in allowing the army to jump into Kut would be exposed. Nausea welled in his chest. He had to think. There had to be a way out.

He called the embeds into his office. "Has anyone told you what is afoot?"

"About the situation on the ground at Kut?" one of them asked.

"Yes." The architect of the war was on edge.

"What does the JCS have to say about it?" a prodigy of Frieze's asked. He was a young man willing to seek advice from any quarter.

"The people we installed at the JCS are shrugging their shoulders, and anything done to clean up this situation is going to fall on us."

"I've got a back-channel communication that General Franklin is planning another para drop into the area in support of the rangers already there."

"That idiot." Frieze was acerbic.

"Can we get around him?"

"We will. I'll call the White House, and they'll order him to do what the hell we decide." Frieze knew he could coerce Franklin into line.

"We are going to have to put forces on the ground to prevent a debacle," someone offered.

"We can't let the events on the ground alter our long-term goal." Frieze fidgeted. "We have to manage the situation to get the results we want. As a start, we cannot let General Franklin go ahead as he seems to want to do. If he fouls it up, any ideas we have for an orderly Middle East will vanish in Afghanistan. So tell me, how do we get control of the situation?"

The usually opinionated embeds, known for their spate of ideas, sat silently. They had no answers for getting out of a war they were involved in. They had answers for getting into a new one.

"More rangers in the middle of the desert will not solve anything." Frieze had to take the lead. "It will increase our footprint; eventually it will require a support force that will be larger than anything we want."

"On the other hand, we have to ensure that the rangers don't cede anything, no matter the cost." One of the group realized that if one ranger surrendered, all the high-minded plans for an imperial America would be buried at Kut.

"I don't like the idea of dropping another unsupportable force in the desert," one of Frieze's confidants echoed his boss. "Now that we are bombing around Kandahar, we could provide the rangers with more air support. That might keep the Taliban at bay and allow the rangers to hold out."

"Hold out to what end? Eventually, they are going to have to be saved with either more forces or a recovery." The group was beginning to find its speaking voice as someone else chimed in.

"This could be an embarrassment for the president." The like thinkers saw the ramifications of failure.

"The marines could go in again. They have already been in once, and that shouldn't be too hard," one of the embeds said despite the fact that his boss had shown distaste for using the marines.

"This isn't going to be a two-helo medevac." Frieze was displeased. "We are going to have to extract an entire company, and the spec ops are saying the zone is increasingly hot. It is going to take a major effort well beyond the capability of a few marines." Frieze made arguments both for and against what had been suggested.

"There are troops on the ground, and we have a duty to do something to rescue them." It was spoken by a man from academia who hadn't been in Washington long enough to know moral responsibility played no part in decisions.

Frieze looked into the distance. "If we were to assign marines to this mission, and they succeed, General Gregg will become the go-to guy in Afghanistan. Every reporter would seek him out for his analysis on how the war is going. If he refutes the good news we have been putting out, he will be all over the news."

"Don, when we stopped the PR blitz, we essentially took the ranger company out of the news. We have classified their existence, and for all the press knows or cares, they have been moved to another location in Afghanistan. All the turmoil over them and the problem we are trying to solve concerning them is being generated in military channels, because we are the only ones with information concerning them. We could write off the rangers, and no one would know. Now, I'm not suggesting that, but that's the reality." Most of the group was ready to accept the harsh analysis of one of their own. "If we can classify anything we do that concerns the rangers, we can control Gregg the same way. If he is such a big worry, we can put out a blanket classification for the task force. We can make them our secret weapon under the guise of national security. If we can keep the story quiet for a couple of months, something new will have captured the media's attention, and no one will care about the rangers, the marines, or what happened."

"That works except for Franklin and the Congress." Frieze brought the group back to the realities of Washington. "They would raise hell and start a chain of events that would embarrass the administration."

"Since this is a Franklin-created mess, why not pass the ball back to him? We can explain that the world will be looking at him and grading his performance. If he messes up, let's make it clear that he will be done as a commander. If we tell him we need this done immediately, he will be forced to use a small force, something that we can pull out quickly, negating an ever-enlarging army footprint."

Frieze didn't hesitate. "We'll go for it. We'll let the general play at war but within our time constraints."

CHAPTER 30

ARABIAN SEA

Watching the decision-making process from thousands of miles away, Jake was disappointed. The war being fought wasn't in Afghanistan. The battle between Franklin and the Pentagon was such that they were fighting different wars on the backs of soldiers and marines who wanted to fight because they felt it was their duty to reclaim national honor. CENTCOM wanted a massive presence so that they could carry out the war as a repeat of Desert Storm, without ever considering that they were fighting in a different country and fighting a different war against a different enemy. The Pentagon was trying to fight a war where armies were unimportant. Technology and the privatization of the military would make armies superfluous in their view of warfare.

Observing the message traffic, Jake didn't know the backstory or the players manipulating the war, but it was apparent that confusion reigned. Troops were calling for help, and people in power, away from the war, were cutting the best deals for themselves, using the rangers as pawns. There was no doubt that a recovery was going to take place. The rangers' requests for help were too frequent and too dire to be ignored, and the task force had been alerted with urgency several times, only to be told to back off as army units were being readied.

The situation on the ground at Kut and in Washington weighed on Jake because he had told the rangers he would get them out.

His promise put him on the hook to act, and he would, because he wasn't going to let an American unit be overrun. His fear was that while people in the United States jockeyed for position, he would get a desperate call from the rangers and have to act without the approval of his superiors. The American people would understand a commander rushing to the aid of a trapped unit, but that was not how things worked in Washington.

Floating in the Arabian Sea, the task force was faced with an ad hoc war, and the lack of strategic direction was troubling. Decisions were being made on the fly, and there was no end game. It was insanity but was acceptable in a war being fought to win the news cycle and to give the impression that America was taking it to the enemy. Making matters worse, the Taliban were proving better organized and equipped than the intelligence indicated, and no one tied operations together for their ouster.

The air campaign being waged was making bomb craters. Once the air bombardments stopped, the situation went back to the status quo with maybe one or two Taliban killed in action, and with one or two of the people bombed joining the Taliban. It was a self-defeating attempt to win the war, but it played well in the news. Americans wanted retaliation for the 9/11 attacks.

The call came at 0300.

In looking at what faced him, Jake understood that a war without strategic direction was a lost cause into which young men's blood would irrigate Afghanistan. As he sat alone and thought about his position in the war, he resided in fault lines between CENTCOM and the Pentagon and had an opportunity that few commanders had ever been presented. While the battle went on among higher headquarters, he was told to recover an isolated ranger company, and no one told him what to do or how to do it. It was assumed that he would follow the scenario used for the ranger's medevac.

No one in CENTCOM leadership considered that the recovery of a large unit out of a hot zone could not be run like a medevac. Without enough assets to recover the entire ranger company from sea-based platforms, a land base, where marines could be staged for a sequential recovery, was required.

Kandahar was the center of gravity of the southern part of the country. It was the headquarters of the Taliban and seat of their leader Mullah Omar, making it a strategic objective. Intelligence indicated that the task force had the firepower to take Kandahar. If it did, the balance of power in southern Afghanistan would shift to the Americans. The marines planning to effect the recovery could not understand why those running the war couldn't see that. Without top-down guidance, Jake had to fight the war from the bottom up. Faced with making a decision that no field commander should have had to make, he planned for a fight no one in leadership expected. He didn't do so for selfish reasons; he developed a plan that would provide the marines the best chance of success. With Kandahar close to the rangers and the only city of import in southern Afghanistan, he decided he would achieve two objectives in one mission.

The marines understood that taking the Kandahar airport was the key to controlling the city and by extension the southern part of the country. The airport sat about ten miles southeast of the city, away from the bulk of the population and the Taliban. Sitting in an area of open farm fields astride the Kandahar-Quetta Road, if the marines overtook it and reinforced their position, the Taliban wouldn't have time to get troops into position to knock them off the ground. In the early planning, marines had expected to be directed to take Kandahar, but no guidance came. Everyone involved in planning the recovery breathed a sigh of relief when Jake told them that he would assume the responsibility.

The delay in getting to the rangers was explained to Oteen over a covered network, and he understood what Jake was trying to do. The rangers were on the ground in the middle of the enemy and knew it was going to take a major effort to get them out. Since what Jake was planning was going to be able to support a major effort, the rangers said they could hang on. Oteen understood that taking the Kandahar airport was necessary so that troops could be staged and could in fact make the recovery of the rangers. By building up forces at the airport, the marines would be able to launch a force that could engage those Taliban encircling the rangers. If things got hot at Kut, the marines would be close enough at the airport to lend overwhelming ground and air support.

The first marines to depart the ship were four Cobra helicopter gunships. They didn't have the range to reach Kandahar and would refuel twice at Forward Area Refueling Points on desert roads.

Six CH-53E helicopters that were capable of aerial refueling took off loaded with forty marines in each. They would refuel without landing. AV-8 Harrier VTOL jets were the last to take off. Their speed would get them to the target area more quickly than the helos, and they would provide heavy ordnance if required. F/A 18 fighter attack aircraft would take off from the aircraft carrier *Vinson* fully loaded and be on station as the assault force neared Kandahar. The timing was precise, so that the entire assault package would arrive over target simultaneously.

The assault wave had two jobs: secure the runway and the fuel farm. With airplanes continuing to use the airport, the fuel there would give the marines a wider range of options in how they used their aircraft.

Each unit aboard the helicopters was assigned a sector, and their aim was to keep the runway open, because Jake and another hundred marines would be landing in 130s. As the overall commander, he had a comm suite installed in the airplane carrying him so that he could coordinate with the troops on the ground.

When all the helicopters had departed the *Peleliu*, Jake and the remainder of the marines were ferried to the runway at Gadwar. They boarded 130s in groups of fifty and would serve as the follow-on forces. If the timing held up, they would land thirty minutes after the initial assault wave.

They were airborne before he called CENTCOM to tell them that the recovery was under way. As he expected, he was given instructions, but the advice proffered was of the "cover your ass" kind." Senior staff officers were setting themselves up with alibis in the event his efforts failed. Since he had all the responsibility, he assumed the authority to do things that were in the best interests of the troops.

About ten minutes out of Kandahar, he received the first calls indicating that things wouldn't go as planned. The marines in Kandahar were not in trouble. They had secured their objectives with minor casualties. The problems came from CENTCOM. A team of special operators in Kandahar, thankful for the relief the marine presence provided them, radioed CENTCOM and SOCOM to thank them for finally getting the marines on the airport to take the pressure off them. The marine landing had forced the Taliban to redirect their forces toward the airport, freeing special operators to change their positions and to attack weakened targets. Jake was glad that he had helped, but he didn't need CENTCOM talking to him at that moment asking what he was doing in Kandahar when the rangers at Kut hadn't been reached and were thirty miles away.

He tried to blow off the queries, but they elevated up the chain of command until General Franklin was on the line.

"What the fuck are you doing in Kandahar?" The voice over the radio wanted answers.

"It is the only way we could effect the recovery of the rangers. We didn't have the capability to recover them from the ships. An operating base closer to their location had to be established."

"I think you're talking bullshit. You were supposed to run this just as you did your last mission. I specifically said that I didn't want any marine grandstanding."

"Sir, there is no grandstanding. All I'm trying to do is keep troops, rangers, and marines, alive. I'll take that responsibility."

"You're goddamn right you will. When this is over I'm going to have your ass. You'll never command another unit as long as I'm around."

Jake let Franklin run on. When he had exhausted his threats, Jake said, "We are taking fire. I'm going to have to shut down this link." He didn't give Franklin a chance to continue.

"I don't want to talk to anyone unless they are involved with this operation," he instructed the communications officer. The officers who worked for him smiled. They understood that he had put his career on the line by blowing off the CENTCOM commander.

The airplane carrying the command element was on final approach when Jake received a call from the air element commander. All helos had been refueled on the airport and were asking for clearance to launch to complete the recovery of the rangers.

"Go ahead." The words blurted out of him as the airplane slammed into the runway. Over the noise of the propellers, he could hear sporadic firing coming from the northern side of the airport, the side closest to the city.

He didn't stoop or run after he deplaned. He walked toward the tower, where he found Jerry Patch.

"Any surprises?" Jake asked the commander of the ground forces.

"No, sir. From what is being reported, we are in the process of overcoming the last of the people who were guarding the airport. We caught them unaware, and most of them got out of here quickly. We captured a few, and we're waiting for an interpreter to come in so that we can question them."

"Good job."

"Thank you, sir."

"I'm going to have airplanes go back and start ferrying in the remainder of the marines from Gadwar. Once you have got your full compliment on the ground, I want you to send a force large enough to close the road between Kandahar and Quetta. When we start putting pressure on the city, the Taliban are going to try to flee toward Pakistan. I want to cut them off."

"As soon as I get enough strength to hold the airfield, I'll dispatch others to cut the road."

"Is the tower in operation?" Jake asked.

"As far as I know," Patch answered.

"If it is, keep it lighted 24/7. I want it to be the focal point of any attack the Taliban might launch. Don't house anyone near it. Just use it as a symbol that we are here and aren't going anywhere." Jake paused, "You're in charge; I'm going to take a look around."

"Do you want an armed escort?" Patch expressed concern.

"I'll use Mackey as my guard. You ready to go?" he asked the lieutenant.

"Yes, sir, should we bring along a radioman?"

"That's why I keep you around, Mack. You are always thinking."

They moved in the direction where the ground fire was most intense. Jake wasn't going to interfere with the troops engaged in a firefight, but he wanted to get a feel for the intensity of the battle.

"You'd better take this." Mackey held out the radio handset.

Jake didn't want to talk to higher headquarters and gave Mackey the cut sign, wiping his fingers across his throat.

"Sir, this is important."

"Gregg." He spit the words into the handset.

"Sir, this is Captain Oteen." The words were rushed and panicked.

"What's happening? Is everything all right?"

"Yes, sir. The first wave has just departed, and we expect the helos back in about a half hour to airlift the rest of us out."

Jake was relieved.

"It was a great op," Oteen added.

"Hang on for a while longer, and we'll have you all home free." Jake expected some comment that would express the captain's relief. None came. The handset wasn't dead. There was noise in the background. "What's up?"

"Sir, between the rangers and the spec ops people here with us, we have eight vehicles. With your concurrence, we'd like to drive them out. We feel we can get them to Kandahar."

"Are you fucking nuts?"

"Sir, my troops were set up for failure, because this mission was planned as a PR stunt. I've lost guys for nothing more than putting on a show. Every one of these rangers wanted to fight and was willing to die for a cause they believed in. Now, they are being evacuated. They were bloodied, but they have not been defeated, yet they are being pulled out without their gear. In their minds they are surrendering. If this unit reestablishes itself at Kandahar with the taint of defeat, it will never be able to function as a unit again."

Jake understood what Oteen was saying, but half the rangers were on their way to Kandahar. He couldn't fly them back or leave half the unit in the desert.

"What is it that you want?"

"Sir, those of us who remain here feel we can drive our vehicles to Kandahar. Spec ops has seen trucks of Taliban leaving, to build up forces against you. With the reduced force against us, and with the gunships to follow us along the way, we feel we can do it. If we get our vehicles and the troops back together, I think I can save the unit. There will be no hint of surrender."

"Put DiBasse on the radio, and you stay on," Jake ordered.

"Sand Bug." DiBasse identified himself with his tactical call sign.

"What's going on?"

"Sir, the captain feels we can get these rigs to your location, and I agree with him. I want to get my gear out along with his. I've got some pretty sophisticated and secret electronic gear that I'd hate to have to destroy."

"What's the enemy situation?"

"With you in Kandahar and the Cobras hitting the Taliban from the air, we have seen a lot split. They are unused to being attacked from 'close in' air."

Jake paused and thought over the myriad of things that could go wrong with what was being proposed. Young men, impetuous men, were asking to take on a task that didn't make sense. They had a free ride out and were willing to risk all to save their honor—the unit's honor. Jake could understand their wont to take the chance, but as the overall commander, he had the responsibility to protect them from themselves. He fumbled for an answer. Something Oteen had said about losing the unit even if it was saved stuck with him. If the rangers' spirits were broken, they would never become a unit again. They would never live down the jibes of others as being an American unit that had to be saved.

"Sand Bug, do you have an operator who knows how to control air-to-ground attacks on your team?"

"Roger that, sir."

"Okay. Captain, listen to me carefully. I will have two Cobras and two Harriers overhead your motor column at all times. If things get tight, I'll get you more air cover. Now, here is the tricky part. If one of those pieces of shit you'll be driving breaks down, it is to be abandoned. You will not fight over broken-down tin. Got it? If the gear on one of them is sensitive, burn the rig, and keep going."

"Yes, sir." The glee in Oteen's voice could be distinguished over the scratchy connection.

"Now. When the rangers already evacuated arrive here, I'm not going to let them off the helos. If you get into trouble, call, and I'll get them to you, along with a whole bunch of marines. Once you start this thing, you will not be able to stop. Make one big push to get here day or night. Your mission is to save your unit not destroy it. Got it?"

"Sir, we won't let you down. And thank you, sir. You won't regret it."

"I hope not." Jake murmured as the line went dead.

"What do you have to say?" he asked Mackey, who listened in on the conversation.

"I think you probably saved a unit, but you won't get any medals for it. Once it is discovered what you did, there will be hell to pay." Mackey was grim.

"Yeah. In the big picture, one unit doesn't count for much. It's a good thing there is no big picture for this war." Jake grinned. "Mack, since this is all about saving a unit, I want you on the runway when the inbound helos land. Keep the rangers on board. Tell them that they are the standby force to go out and recover the rest of their unit that is driving in. That ought to raise their morale."

"That's a nice touch, sir."

"Get moving."

Making the decision was easier than living with it. Jake paced as he tracked the location of the rangers. There were no firefights, but their pace was irritatingly slow. The Cobras made several rocket runs at fixed positions, and the enemy disbursed. A Harrier dropped a five-hundred-pound bomb on a roadblock, shattering it, and the column passed through unopposed, but the motor march seemed to be progressing at inches per hour.

It was well after dark when the vehicles reached the airport. Jake was unaware that Jim Mackey had arranged for the vehicles to go right to the helicopters where the other rangers waited. On seeing their comrades and their vehicles, there was a celebration. They hadn't won the war, but they had retained their dignity, and that was important. They could win the war at another time.

A dirt-encrusted ranger Captain Oteen and spec ops operator Angelo DiBasse sought out Jake. He was in one of the buildings the marines had confiscated a good distance from the control tower. He was sitting in a director's chair under the dim light of low-wattage bulbs hanging from chords from the ceiling.

"Sir." Oteen stood at attention and rendered a salute, unconscious of the fact that his quick arm movement raised a cloud of dirt.

"As you were." Jake tried to loosen him up.

"Sir, I want to thank you on behalf of A Company for letting us drive out of the desert."

"No need to. You guys did a great job. I'm sure CENTCOM will be happy to hear that you recovered your equipment."

"General," DiBasse spoke, "you know this wasn't about equipment, and I appreciate your having faith in us. I know this probably won't mean much to you, but I'd serve under you anytime, anywhere, and I think I speak for the rangers."

Jake looked into the special operator's eyes. "It does mean a lot to me. It is what war is all about."

CHAPTER 31

THE PENTAGON, WASHINGTON, DC

Don Frieze replaced the phone into the cradle and closed his eyes to calm himself. He took several deep breaths and thought about the events in Afghanistan. He smiled, thinking that it was just like the military. Once they had a foothold they would continue to grow the size of the force. Having convinced the administration that Iraq was the true enemy and that any diversion of forces into Afghanistan was a mistake, he couldn't let that happen. Even the president saw the historic imperative being presented to him. The White House bought into the idea that if Iraq was toppled they could change the world, whereas a campaign in Afghanistan would be difficult and long with little upside.

The immediate obstacle that DEPSECDEF had to overcome was the CIA. In their morning briefings to the president, they stressed that special operations in combination with the marines could take control of the center of the Taliban government in Kandahar. They cited the marine recovery of the ranger company and the capture of the Kandahar airport as a strategic success and bolstered the CENTCOM argument to commit more forces to Afghanistan. The CIA operators on the ground were happy with the marines' presence in Kandahar because it gave them a base of operations, and their teams had a place where they could rest up and plan their missions.

Frieze understood the CIA's wont to have a fixed base. The British Special Air Services, their elite special operators, working with the CIA, had been calling for just that since their early entry into the war, but he ignored their requests.

With the administration wanting evidence that America was killing bad guys, it could easily lose focus on the real purpose of the neoconservatives, that of shaping the world. Frieze was angry with Jake Gregg. He could think of no other general who would have stretched the bounds of his authority and attacked Kandahar. That hadn't been part of the mission Frieze thought he had authorized. He had been purposely vague in directing Franklin to proceed, thinking that a low-key mission would keep Afghanistan on the back burner. When he told Franklin to go ahead with the evacuation, he assumed that the general would have kept the marine presence small, perhaps three or four more helicopters in a slightly expanded medevac scenario. Neither of them stopped to think that was not realistic. The embeds hadn't asked questions, and Don Frieze didn't want to admit their or his oversights. With the president looking for more positive news from Afghanistan, something that he could sell to the public that showed that the Americans were winning the war, Frieze had to be careful. He didn't care about the reasons the president was on board with the capture of Kandahar, all he cared about was that the president didn't get distracted and think Afghanistan was important.

Frieze pushed his hand through his thick hair. He tried to balance the good Jake achieved against the distraction of a wider war. If Mullah Omar and the senior Taliban leadership could be killed or captured, it would make headlines and show the public that the president was a forceful leader. That would add to the president's creditability as a wartime commander in chief. When and if he pushed for a war in Iraq, it would be an easier sell to the American public. It was a delicate equation for the DEPSECDEF. How far could he let a ground buildup go, and how much was too much? In looking over the variables, he decided that having a president who the public envisioned as a strong leader, one they wouldn't question based on his record in Afghanistan, was the favorable course to take.

With a coalition of tribes under the banner of the Northern Alliance, American air support, and the CIA spec ops rolling up the Taliban in the northern part of Afghanistan, it would be a matter of weeks until they surrendered or were bombed into submission. Al Qaeda and bin Laden were trapped in the mountainous caves at Tora Bora, and the war was within weeks of ending. He saw no role for the military after the Taliban and Al Qaeda were defeated.

He laughed at his initial reluctance to have too many troops in Afghanistan. If he played it right, he could build up forces there for use in Iraq, and he could keep his intent secret.

CHAPTER 32

CENTCOM,
TAMPA, FLORIDA

General Franklin stormed into his office after a night of simmering anger. The staff tried to stay away from him, but there was no escape. A 0900 meeting was called. No agenda was published. None was needed. The staff had been reading reports of the marines' assault on Kandahar and the recovery of the rangers. There had been casualties, a few, and the staff knew that wasn't the reason for the meeting.

Everyone stood.

"Sit down," Franklin ordered. He sat and waited until all motion stopped. "What is the latest from Kandahar?"

Hatton nodded to his subordinate to provide the details. "Sir," a female air force lieutenant colonel started. She was in awe of the general and stumbled through her first words. "The operation you approved for the recovery of A Company has been completed, and the rangers are with the marines at the Kandahar airport."

"Goddamn it," Franklin snapped. His voice echoed off the high ceiling. "I want the marines retrograded out of Kandahar and back to the ships where they belong."

Hatton didn't want to speak up, but he had to. He had information the general needed to know. "Sir, a retrograde may not be possible."

"It is going to be possible. Do you understand? Make it happen."

"Sir," the ops director spoke as if he was walking on hot coals,

"The message traffic that arrived this morning indicates that General Gregg has made contact with the CIA special ops teams and the special forces that have been working in and around Kandahar, and they are moving in concert to drive the Taliban out of their strongholds. The marines have set up a blocking force to capture any Taliban that try to escape into Pakistan."

"Who told Gregg that he could do that? Did anyone on this staff approve such actions?" Franklin was livid.

No one spoke.

"So who approved the marines doing anything other than effecting a recovery?" Franklin was ready to fire the person who had given the marines approval. "Well?'

"General Gregg indicated in his last communications that without guidance, he would assume the responsibility as the on-site commander." Hatton was barely audible.

"Goddamn it." Franklin paused. "Here is what I want done. Start feeding the media the story about the success of this mission. Sell it as being planned here and conducted under our guidance. Do you think that can be done?" He was bitingly sarcastic. "Then I want Gregg relieved of command. Call the Marine Corps and have them get another general to Afghanistan pronto." Franklin made a snap decision, and the staff knew no matter how ill-advised, there would be no talking him out of it. In an embarrassing silence, none of the staff dared to speak. They were saved further embarrassment by the entrance of the general's civilian secretary. Whatever she had to say would be important, because staff meetings were rarely interrupted.

"Sir," she spoke as Franklin glared at her, "Mr. Frieze wants to talk to you. He said it was important. Should I forward the call in here?" She nodded to the phone that was on the table in front of Franklin.

"Yes." Franklin clicked on the speakerphone so that all in the room could overhear. He was going to use the call as a teaching moment to show his staff how he handled anyone who didn't act as he expected.

"Franklin here." He used his most officious voice.

"General, I'm sure you are aware that General Gregg is in control of the Kandahar airport." There was nothing in Frieze's voice to indicate whether he approved or disapproved.

"He got off the reservation, and I intend to bring him back on it and then get rid of him. I'll need your approval because the Marine Corps is going to fight like hell to save him." Franklin was smug.

"What are your reasons?"

"He overstepped his authority, and I'm going to make him pay for it."

"You want me to recommend to the secretary and the president that we remove a commander who rescued a trapped unit, and did so after conducting a historic amphibious assault over five hundred miles of desert? It can't be done. The White House PR machine is preparing a feel-good story about the entire operation. As of this morning, the Pentagon has had over a hundred requests from news agencies that want to go to Afghanistan to debrief Gregg. For the immediate future, he is untouchable."

"You have been pushing me to keep the footprint in Afghanistan down. He has placed over two thousand marines on the ground. That blows the force size that you wanted. Has that changed, and if it has, I'm ready to insert army troops to relieve the marines and take over operations." Forty-eight hours prior, Franklin was being hammered with demands to keep the war one of spec ops and airpower. His requests to put troops on the ground had been shot down. He couldn't figure out why with the marines in place, Frieze wasn't complaining. "Tell me, has something changed that I should know about?"

"We may be asking you to stage more troops in Afghanistan."

"Stage? What in the hell does that mean?"

"The war is drawing to an end, and any troops put into Afghanistan will not engage in a combat role. We are going to warehouse them so that they will be available for future contingencies."

"With all due respect, we are at war. Any troops in theater should be used in bringing the war to a successful conclusion, because from where we sit, we don't see this thing being over quickly. Troops will be in a fight for a while."

"We are in a clearing action that is almost complete. There is no need for combatants."

"Who is going to provide security for the Afghans, who have lost their leadership?" Franklin was angry. "If Afghanistan turns into an insurgency, combatants will be needed."

"We have security firms that can protect the people."

"You can't civilianize war."

"Civilians along with spec ops and airpower will be enough to keep a lid on Afghanistan until we get to a real war." Frieze suspected that their conversation was being overheard by others. "This discussion is top secret. Nothing mentioned here can be discussed other than on a need-to-know basis. General, if you are on speakerphone, shut it off. Our conversation should be private."

"I'm the only one that can hear you now."

"Good." Frieze relaxed. He didn't know how much of his plan he had exposed. "There have been changes that you should be aware of."

"I'm listening." Franklin showed a stern face and used dour tones to impress the staff officers who watched him.

"This nuisance war should be terminated in a month. At that time, there will be little need for troops. We will farm out everything—security, nation building, construction—everything to contractors. However, as far as the press will know, troops will remain in Afghanistan as a stability force. We will continue to build up the size of the force and every once in a while run a mission involving the military to feed the news machine, but the purpose of any further troops in Afghanistan will be to limit speculation about their eventual use. In planning for Iraq, if that war does start, you can use the forces we will have stationed in Afghanistan."

"That's crazy."

"It may be, but it has been approved. If you have any complaints, you can direct them personally to the vice president." Frieze paused. "Now for the immediate problem. I want to get rid of Gregg just as much as you do, but now is not the time. Write him up for a medal of some kind. We'll make him a hero before we cut him down to size."

It was the first thing that Franklin had heard that made him smile.

"Can you do that, General?"

"It'll be done."

After he hung up, Franklin rubbed his eyes. Looking up at the staff, he had to say something. They had heard only his side of the conversation.

"That fucker is the dumbest son of a bitch in Washington, and he has the most power. He's dangerous, and he is heading a cabal that is leading the president around by the nose. But we work for him and his bosses, so we will do their dirty work. While doing it, keep recording everything you discuss with the Pentagon and the White House, because if Mr. Frieze's plans go awry, we want to be able to point fingers, because you know they will try to stick it up the military's ass."

CHAPTER 33

KANDAHAR

Jake called a meeting of all the spec ops teams in and around Kandahar. He wanted to have a workable plan for the removal of the Taliban from the city and environs, a plan in which Americans weren't shooting at one another.

As the teams of special operators straggled into an unused Russian barracks at the airport that had been appropriated as a command center, the common denominator among them was their disdain for authority. They showed it in their dress, which ranged to anything that they wanted to wear. Some went native and tried to fit in with the population; others were just dirty and seemed to like their smell. Most had beards containing various amounts of dirt. In all cases, personal hygiene played a distant second to trying to stay alive.

They had a tough job and knew it, and they wanted everyone who came into contact with them to recognize it. To say they had a superiority complex was an understatement, but the work they did allowed them to display their egos. They looked down on the regular military as unqualified to serve on the same battlefield.

The assembled special operators were sure it was going to be another meeting with a senior officer telling them they had to get in line. They'd listen and blow him off. They had seen the routine before, heard the lectures about being more military, yada, yada, yada.

Jake watched them enter the building and noticed that just as the special operators looked down on the military, there was a pecking order among them. The CIA operators wanted to be recognized as the best. Most had come out of special forces and had years of experience. They were older and not in the shape of the younger military operators, but their covert experiences, where they worked in the shadows and reported to no one, gave them the surety of their actions, because they were never questioned. Delta Force operators tried to act the part like the CIA, but they were under Special Operations Command and subject to oversight, and that subdued them somewhat. They had a combination of age, experience, and physical conditioning, and they worked closely with the elite Navy SEAL Teams, so they paired up and looked down on the army special forces. It was an interesting grouping. Countrymen in the same profession didn't speak to one another.

The CIA had the lead for operations in the area and was led by George Ord, a florid-faced operator who still bore pitted skin from teenage acne. He was older than Jake and an inch or two shorter, and carried an extra thirty pounds around his waist. Even with the stomach bulge, he didn't look soft. He wore a perpetual frown like a uniform. His eyes were nearly squinted closed, and it was hard to read him, but everything about him warned people to stay away.

"Are you in charge of everyone here?" Jake was not put off by Ord's posturing.

"Kinda."

"Look. I haven't got time to play games. Either you are or you are not. If you are not, point in the direction to who is in charge." Jake was setting a tone.

The room, which had been quiet, went still. The special operators were used to being handled with kid gloves. They knew the marine general had exceeded his authority in taking the airport and wondered if he was a loose cannon. They thought he might be, because no one in their right mind talked to them that way.

"I guess you could say I'm in charge," Ord mumbled. "We don't have a formal chain of command. Every team, regardless of their affiliation, works through me, even the British and Australian SAS coordinate through me, but they are on the hook to their own governments."

"I'll take that to mean you are in charge." Every eye was on Jake. "How many of you speak Pashto?" The question caught Ord unaware. He had expected to be told that Jake wanted to take control of the area.

"Maybe four."

"How in the hell can you do your job with so few?"

"It's tough. We have to rely on Pakistani ISI interpreters."

"Can they be trusted?"

"That's hard to say," Ord answered. "We have only caught one fucking with us."

"Mack, get on the horn and scour the Defense Department for Pashto speakers. If there are any, get them here. If they don't have them, search colleges, search the Afghan population in the United States. We have to have people who know the language. Get on it," Jake ordered.

"We're doing all right. We don't need any help." Ord defended what he was doing and how he was doing it.

"This isn't about trying to one up you. I know you are doing the job now, but I see the job changing. Once we get the Taliban routed, we are going to be facing an insurgency, and that is going to require living with the people and trying to keep insurgents, whom I assume will be returning Taliban, at bay. That is going to require people who can communicate with the locals. We may not have enough Pashto speakers in the United States to fulfill our needs, but we'd better find them somewhere."

"General, who are you?" Ord lightened his mood for the first time. "We have been preaching that this is going to become an insurgency from day one, and no one has listened. All we have been authorized to do is clear areas, usually by bombing the shit out of them. We all know that is the best way to make insurgents, but the people running the war don't seem to care."

"I work for the same people, but I've got marines on the ground, and I feel that the best way to get them home is to make friends of the people rather than driving them into the arms of the Taliban, so here is what I would like to propose to you. You can't do a lot of the things you'd like to do because you are light on manpower, so I'd like to put marines with each of your teams. I will chop them to your command, and you can use them as you see fit. The only requirement I have is that you teach them how to snoop and poop like they are going to have to if the Taliban return to this area."

"Did I hear you say that you were going to chop marines to work with us?"

"Yes."

"Does anyone up the chain of command know about this?" Ord laughed.

"These marines are going to be faced with a war none of them has been trained to fight. You guys have, and I want some of them to learn from you. This isn't an exercise where I'm flipping the bird at higher headquarters. This is an attempt to train people so that they will be able to survive in an environment none has thought of. It will be a trade-off. Your teams will get firepower, and the marines will learn how to deal with insurgents."

"You must be the only general who thinks. How did you get promoted?" Ord played to the other special operators.

"I don't have to tell you that we have no plan for Afghanistan. It isn't even considered a war except for those getting shot at. I'd like to say it was an oversight, but this is seen as an inconvenient war that isn't going to require a real effort. I think that is wrong. Afghanistan has never been an easy proposition for any army that has set foot in it. Every power intended to get in and get out. None did. They were all sucked in and bled until they had to leave. I see this little dance we are doing as history repeating. We are going to be here for a while whether we plan to or not, so we'd better learn how to fight the right way."

"I see you've read your history," a British SAS officer spoke up. His thick cockney accent made all the operators look his way. He was senior to most of the Americans and had been telling them many of the same things

"History and the lessons learned from it," Jake responded. "We think that we can accomplish what the Russians couldn't. Smart bombs and gadgetry will not win here. The Russians had smart weapons. They had Spetnaz, special forces, not quite as good as you guys, but they were good, and they had tens of thousands of troops around the country. They also had advantages that we can't replicate. They had Communist Party cells in every major city and were intertwined within the local governments. Afghan communists held several of the prominent national offices. More importantly, they had a long-term strategy. Even with their local political cadres, they had no idea of the xenophobia bred into the Afghanis. They hate one another less than they do foreigners. Now, we are outsiders without a foothold. We have no strategy, and we intend to use the same methodology that didn't work for another world power." Jake hesitated. "Am I painting too bleak a picture of our efforts?"

"Jesus, General, you have got me looking for a way outa here," Ord joked.

"You know more about it than I do. This is your type war. Has anyone laid out a plan or a strategy to any of you?' Jake asked.

The room was silent.

"I'm preparing for an insurgency. I want to try things the Russians didn't. Once we have rounded up the Taliban, I am going to put marines on the streets and in the villages."

"That brings up a good point," Ord informed. "I know you want the escape routes to Pakistan blocked, but you will run into problems with that."

"How?"

"General, there are more Pakistani military and ISI in Kandahar than there are Taliban. The Pakis run the show. They train, supply, and fight alongside the Taliban. Unless you are a miracle worker, there is no way the Pakis will allow you to roll up their personnel. That would lend credence to the fact that they are responsible as much as anyone for the 9/11 attacks. Rolling these guys up ain't going to happen."

"You sure of that?" Jake was trying to determine if Ord was expressing his personal opinion or he had information that Jake didn't.

"Our orders all along have been to engage selected targets. We are told what we can and cannot take on. Assignments come to us from the CIA station in Islamabad, Pakistan. As of yet, we haven't been able to hit a target that has had Pakis involved in it. Your taking over the airport has complicated our relationship with our main ally in this skirmish." Ord shook his head. "Didn't you notice how easily the marines took the airport? It was guarded by Pakistani troops. It was their airport, but they bailed out because none of them wanted to be captured and have to explain taking on Americans. That might be a hard sell in Washington so close to 9/11. To tell you the truth, your taking the airport has fucked up the entire narrative, theirs and ours. Every one of us in this room is wondering why you haven't been canned. There must be a scenario running around in Washington where someone sees a use for exposing the Pakis."

"Our intelligence indicated only several hundred Pakistanis in Kandahar."

"General Gregg. There were over a battalion of Pakis guarding the airport and operating it for the Taliban. There is another battalion in town supplying them with everything they need to stay in power and to teach them how to make war on us. That is a lot more than the hundreds you have been told. And, that doesn't include the ISI. They are running the show politically and providing the intelligence required so that the Taliban can wipe out their enemies, including us."

"You just told me that you were using ISI interpreters. With what you have just described, that makes no sense."

"They are all we have. Our people in Islamabad are trying to vet them, but as of right now we have no way of knowing if they are working for or against us. Our rule is that if we walk into one trap, it was legit. If we walk into a second, the ISI interpreter disappears. We can only hope that makes them a bit more loyal."

"Your point is taken." He spoke to the special operators. "As far as I'm concerned, it doesn't change a thing. I'm going to assign marines to your teams, and I expect them to flush out the enemy and drive them into a trap."

"I'll say one thing, General. You have one set of brass balls."

"When you are in over your head as far as I am, there is no turning back. Now, I've told you what I intend to do. Can you twist your orders a bit to take on targets that might not be assigned?" Jake wanted to know if Ord would help him.

"Sure, why not. It makes no sense giving the Pakistanis a free pass. They created the situation that allowed the Taliban and Al Qaeda to flourish, and even though we are now here, they don't want that to change." Ord looked out at the special operators. "Do you all understand where we are going on this?" He received knowing and accepting nods.

"General." The British SAS operator came up to him. "We have been pressing for a strong military presence in this area. It is the only way the Taliban can be ousted. If it is any consolation, I think you are doing the absolutely right thing."

"Thanks." Jake understood why the American policy makers were resisting establishing a base in Afghanistan. They had another war they wanted to fight. To them, wars were abstract concepts. For the marines and soldiers putting their lives on the line, the abstractions faded into reality. They wanted to survive the fight they were in.

CHAPTER 34

MARINE CORPS BASE, QUANTICO, VIRGINIA

Fran Matthews didn't know how long or how loudly the duty officer had been pounding on her officers' quarters door, and when she stumbled out of bed was unaware of the time. Opening the door a crack, the harsh corridor lights almost blinded her, and she had difficulty grasping what the duty officer was saying.

"There will be a call coming in for you at 0330."

"So have it transferred here. I have a phone, you know." She didn't understand why whoever was calling didn't call her directly.

"Can't. It is going to be coming in over a secure switch, and you are going to have to receipt for it in the communications section. The watch officer is there, waiting for you."

"What's this all about? Has something happened? Has there been an accident?"

"I don't think so." The duty officer knew little but was willing to pass on the scant information he had. "General Gregg is making the call. No one knows the reason. The only instruction we received was to make you available."

"I'll get dressed. You don't have to wait for me. I'll drive over."

Fran rushed to get into her uniform. In the drive to the comm center, she wondered what the call might be about. It was a natural reaction, and she was excited to think she would be talking to Jake again. She had thought about him constantly in his absence, and the thoughts weren't about her job. In the short drive, she fantasized that the call might be personal and that he was calling to tell her that he missed her. She missed him and could think of no other reason for the communication. For two people who had never spent a romantic moment together and who had never spoken of feelings, she knew she was reading a lot into the call, but that was what she wanted it to be about.

She arrived early and had to wait. The marines working the comm suites wondered why a general would be calling her. The idea that she was beautiful and the general was away at war led the marines to think it was going to be a romantic call, and most positioned themselves so that they would be able to overhear. Giddiness was rampant in the room filled with electronics gear. All the personnel were expecting to be able to tell stories about the general and his girlfriend.

Fran waited, and the second hand on the large wall clock seemed stuck. She tried to play down her expectations, but like the others she expected the conversation to be personal.

"You're on deck." The watch officer alerted her that the call was coming in. When the connection was made, he snapped his fingers. "You're up."

Fran didn't know if she was supposed to start or if she should wait for Jake to begin.

"Major Matthews?" The voice came over the receiver, and she tried to interpret the tone, to determine if it conveyed an unspoken message.

"Yes, sir, this is Major Matthews."

"Fran." He used her first name, but that was proper. He was her senior and could become familiar. "I need your help."

"Yes, sir. What is it that I can do?"

"I'm playing with an idea, and I'm going to have the need of six women marines. I'm going to need you to find them for me. Think you can?"

"It would make it easier to recruit them if I could tell them what they would be doing." The conversation had spun away from anything she had expected.

"I have a use for them in Afghanistan, but I can't tell you the specifics now. I have to get them into the country as staff and in noncombatant roles, or I will never get them here." Jake's voice was alive. He was planning to do something that excited him.

"Are there any special qualifications they are going to need?" Fran was wondering if she might sign herself up for the trip.

"Yeah. They have to be in good shape. Living out here isn't easy, and they won't have time to condition themselves to the environment. They have to be able to hit the ground running."

"Are you looking for any occupational subsets?"

"No. Toughness and conditioning are the most important things. I've got about two thousand young marines living in horrible conditions and getting shot at. They are not going to be easy on women in their midst, so tell whoever you pick, they will have to have thick skins, because I'm sure they are going to be teased and chased. Whoever you pick should understand that. It is not going to be easy."

"Sir, Afghanistan has no roles for women. It only has roles for combat forces."

"Thanks for telling me. " His sarcasm was biting. The troops listening in on the conversation tried to hide their smirks. "I want to thank you for the warning, but I'm beyond that, and the women you get for me will be beyond that to. Now, do you think you can find me six to start out?"

Fran didn't know if she could.

"Ma'am." One of the female communicators who had been listening in got Fran's attention. "Ma'am, I'll go."

"Me too," a second indicated.

"Sir, I'll get you the women you need. I already have three."

"Are you one of them?"

"Yes, sir."

"Good. If you don't recruit anyone senior to you, you'll be in charge."

She wanted to ask, in charge of what? She was signing on for a mystery mission, but she wanted to see him and knew from their time working together that he wouldn't let her get in over her head.

"When you get your team together"—he gave her ownership of the assignment—"get their names to the manpower section at Headquarters Marine Corps. I have already made the request for additional staff and told them that it would be heavy with women to cover administrative duties. You won't have a problem getting orders to Afghanistan if people think you are going to push papers. I'll give you the full laydown when you arrive in country, and if it sounds too tough an assignment I'll let anyone who wants to, go home. In making plans to come here, bring only your utilities, and make sure you have a full set of field gear. Right now, everyone is surviving on MREs, but we may have hot chow in a couple of days. I'd suggest bringing air mattresses because the ground gets hard. I'm telling you this because I want you to know that this will not be a picnic. You may want to pass that on to whoever you recruit."

Fran looked up at the women who had raised their hands. They had heard Jake's description of what awaited them. They didn't back away. They seemed to relish the opportunity.

"Yes, sir. I'll do my best to scare them straight."

"Great. One last thing, the sooner you can put the marines together the sooner you'll be here. I've got everything greased for your quick departure."

Fran understood why she respected him. He went beyond calling them women marines to marines. In his mind, they were all green. "I know this was quick and that you have questions, but I have to ask you to trust me. I will answer everything when you arrive. Can you hold off until then?"

"I want to go to Afghanistan, so I guess I don't have a choice."

"That's right." He laughed. "Fran, I'm looking forward to seeing you." With that, the line went dead.

His last words caught her by surprise. What did they mean? Were they a courtesy? Was he expressing his feeling? She tried to gain control of her thoughts.

"You overheard everything, so I know nothing more than you," she said to the two communicators who had volunteered. "I wouldn't blame either of you if you had second thoughts and backed out." She knew Jake and didn't have qualms, but the young marines would buy into him based on her interpretations.

"Ma'am," a young black sergeant who had raised her hand to volunteer spoke, "we have been fighting to be treated as equals since I've been in the Corps. I think General Gregg is offering that chance, and I'm going to take it."

The other volunteer nodded in agreement.

"Are you both in shape?" Fran snapped off the question, happy to have members for her team.

"Yes, ma'am." They spoke in unison.

"You heard the general. Start packing your field gear and be ready to move out quickly, because I don't think it is going to be too hard to find volunteers."

CHAPTER 35

THE PENTAGON, WASHINGTON, DC

With winter approaching, the DEPSECDEF sat in his office looking out over the Potomac River. The trees had changed color, and most of the leaves had fallen. If he stood and went to the window he could see the Capitol, but he had no desire to look at it from a distance. He had testified there two days prior and was angry at the treatment he had received. Senator Billups and other members of the Senate Armed Services Committee had grilled him, trying to get him to lay out the administration's plans for the war in Afghanistan.

Wrapping himself in his academic credentials and speaking down to the politicians, he spoke of how the war played in the larger US strategy. Senators wanted to know about an exit strategy, and Frieze gave no simple answers. His words confused more than they explained. As the point man for military operations in Afghanistan, his references to Iraq were puzzling, and angry senators, feeling rebuffed, failed to make the connection. His mentioning Iraq flew below the radar, but he wanted his words read into the congressional record. The legislators thought he was hiding something and, considering themselves the policy makers for any war, they resented his elusiveness. Not liking his act, they roughed him up him with their words.

He thought about his performance before the committee and decided that he had accomplished what he had set out to do. He described the successes of the American offensive in Afghanistan and took credit for winning the war inexpensively. Under questioning by senators who liked the light shinning only on them, he was forced to mention that there was a growing marine presence in Kandahar, but he assured the committee it was a short-term presence. Once the Taliban were defeated, in a matter of weeks, the marines would be pulled out and the security responsibility would be given to contractors. The mention of privatizing the war was well received, because many members of the Senate panel had close ties to the contracting firms that were lobbying for their use.

The line of questioning that bothered him most concerned Osama bin Laden. Senators wanted to know why more force wasn't being used to effect his capture. DEPSECDEF testified that a trap for bin Laden would soon be sprung, and it would be accomplished with no need for more troops. He dared not say that he didn't care about bin Laden's capture. That wouldn't play well in the existing political environment, but he saw bin Laden as integral to his plans. The effectiveness of the "Wanted Dead or Alive" poster the administration was using to tout its serious intent to capture the terrorist would be invalidated with his demise. If America's greatest single enemy was captured, it would slake the American people's thirst for vengeance. Frieze expected the war he wanted to fight was going to be met with opposition, and having bin Laden on the loose would make the selling of it easier. People would overlook obvious distortions if they were focused on a man living free in a cave. Bin Laden would be neutralized, incapable of launching further attacks, but the idea that he was still out in the world would keep people in a war mentality. With bin Laden a fugitive, Frieze could manipulate the story in highlighting the association between bin Laden and Saddam Hussein. It was a link that would ease America's entrance into a war with Iraq.

The war narrative, the statements of winning Afghanistan in weeks, changed the day after his testimony. The Pakistani ambassador visited the State Department and the White House, making demands that the blockades of Kandahar and Kunduz, a city in northern Afghanistan, be lifted. Air power and the Northern Alliance forces around Kunduz were about to rout the Taliban, and the marines at Kandahar were sweeping the Taliban aside. Both battles were American victories that the Pakistanis could not afford. There were over four thousand Pakistani soldiers and ISI personnel at Kunduz helping the Taliban. They were trapped in an isolated valley, and the noose was tightening so that they would have to surrender. In Kandahar, the Pakistanis had a smaller force of ISI and military but were cut off by the marines from reaching a safe haven in Quetta.

The Pakistani ambassador was allowed to make his case, because the capture of an ally's forces supporting our enemy would be an admission that the American public would not condone. They would demand action of their leaders to rectify such an abysmal situation.

Frieze wasn't in the meetings, but he was told that the ambassador broke down and confessed that there were in fact Pakistani troops aiding the Taliban. Then he discussed the situation in both Afghan cities in terms of realpolitik. If the Pakistani troops were captured, it would destabilize the sitting government that was supporting the United States, and it would plunge Pakistan into chaos. No one knew what faction might rise to power. It might be a group that would stop the United States from using Pakistani ports and roads. If that happened, American efforts in Afghanistan would be starved. The ambassador couldn't say for sure if the nuclear weapons in Pakistan would remain secured. He intimated that if the government fell, nuclear war might be unleashed.

It was a scary thought for the administration. They had to let the Taliban and their enablers escape or lose Pakistan. The duplicitous Pakistani government in power, working with the Americans, was better than any conceivable alternative.

The administration quietly called off the Northern Alliance and the marines. A halt in the fighting was arranged so that the Taliban and the Pakis could cross the border. The free pass wasn't about saving American troops' lives. It was about saving the Pakistani government. Letting the Pakistanis escape was an odious decision, a decision that had to be kept from the American public, so it was classified.

Don Frieze didn't like the idea of giving the Pakistanis an exit pass. His plans called for destroying the Taliban in the battles in the two cities, declaring victory, and leaving Afghanistan in the hands of civilians. Having the Taliban reestablish their forces in Pakistan threatening Afghanistan meant that America would have to use a more sizable force to provide security. As far as he was concerned, the fighting in Afghanistan was over even without victories in the north and south, because it was unimportant in the big picture.

CHAPTER 36

KANDAHAR

Kandahar was crumpling under the pressure brought by the marines, special operators, and air power. The Americans could go into any part of the city and establish bases, limiting the Taliban access to the population. There were sporadic firefights, but all indications were that the Taliban political and military structure was crumpling. The Americans on the ground could sense the victory at hand, and when Jake was ordered to lift the blockade of the Quetta-Kandahar road he was stunned. With the strategic center of the war ready to fall, he was directed to give the gains away. It didn't make sense, nor did the explanations he received out of Tampa and Washington. No one could tell him why he was being ordered to make an unwise battlefield decision. They could only tell him that the orders came out of the White House.

Jake needed to vent and thought George Ord, who received direction through CIA channels, might lend some insight into the senselessness of throwing a victory away. He found the CIA operator in a stone-walled hut that served as his operations center. The floor was dirt, and no attempt had been made to cover it. There were no windows, and the only natural light provided was through the doorway and cracks in the ceiling that allowed for peeks of the sky. Any wind that blew, and it always blew, raised dust within the walls so that Jake looked like he was talking to Ord through a fog.

Supplies lined the floor between cots and air mattresses that were pressed against the walls. The living conditions were similar to those endured by the marines. The centerpiece of the room was a radio suite that was more sophisticated than anything Jake had ever seen. The high-tech gear allowed Ord to talk to anyone in the world in real time.

"What brings you to my humble part of the world?" Ord asked.

"I want to talk to you about my orders to back off blocking the road to Quetta."

"Pretty fucked up, huh? My sources indicated that the Pakis were scared shitless and pleaded around Washington for relief. They got it, but no one knows how high up the chain of command it was given." Ord paused. "I don't know how good your comm is, or if you have been following the radio traffic, but relieving the blockade of Kandahar amounts to small potatoes. In the Kunduz area, the Pakis had to evacuate almost four thousand army troops and hundreds of ISI personnel. The Northern Alliance wanted to continue their assault to wipe out the bunch of them, but we threatened to stop providing air support to get them to back off. Even at that, we have only bought twenty-four hours, before they are going to restart their attacks."

"So, we bought the Pakis a day?" Jake asked.

"Yeah, but the trouble is Kunduz doesn't have a connecting road to Pakistan that can handle the amount of traffic that will be required to evacuate that many people." Ord laughed. "I'll give the Pakis credit for balls. They wanted us to fly them out. Thank god someone in Washington figured out that might blow apart our arrangement with the Northern Alliance, so we did not provide airlift. Pakistan went to plan B. They are using aircraft we gave them to fly any evidence that they were in Kunduz out. Of course, all the markings are painted out so the airplanes can't be traced to us."

"How did we get the Northern Alliance forces to hold off finishing the job?" Jake was curious.

"They rely on our air cover, so if we hold it off, and they continue attacking, it will be a tough fight. And, of course, we threatened to hold off paying the warlords carrying out the battle. They really don't need the airpower now, because they have the Taliban and the Pakis beaten, but money, they always need that, so they bought into a uniquely insane American solution to this war." Ord shook his head in disgust. "When you've been doing this shit as long as I have, you get to see some crazy stuff, but I can tell you this ranks right up there with the weirdest shit ever."

"Did you get any feedback as to why?" Having received orders without explanation, Jake was interested.

"When the Russians left, the Pakis started supporting and training the Afghan Taliban in Pakistan, and when they were trained, sending them back into Afghanistan. They kept the Taliban going until they toppled the Afghan government. The Paki plan is to control the Taliban and thereby become the de facto rulers of the country."

"So, our being here has ruined their plan?" Jake uttered.

"Big time. The Pakistani government barely governs Pakistan. Those in power have remained so because they have been able to export their crazies." Ord looked at Jake to determine if he was being believed. "Supporting the Taliban keeps the religious fanatics focused externally. If we capture Pakistani troops working with the Taliban and destroy the Afghan Taliban, the Pakistani domestic lunatics will have to focus on their own government. That would mean those in power would be replaced by a group that might be more radical. I assume we are backing off because we have to keep the existing government propped up, even though we know they are lying to us and working against us. There has to be the shell of a government that lets us support our war effort, whatever that is."

"If the Taliban reorganize and are allowed to gain strength across the border, this is going to be a long war," Jake mused.

"Sure it is, but we can only carry out the war with the aid of Pakistan, so we made a Faustian bargain in order to do so."

"It won't work." Jake was sure.

"Maybe. But there is no turning back. We are here and have decided that we need Pakistan. You and I are on the ground getting shot at and are thinking, wow, this is fucked up. People back home are being fed a steady diet of gun-camera footage and told stories about the successes of the ranger company that you had to save. The average guy thinks our leaders are doing things correctly. When they are told that Pakistan is a good and reliable ally, they believe it. Unfortunately, most of Congress believes the same thing."

"Where do you think that leaves us?" Jake had had enough background and wanted to see how the changed situation on the ground was going to affect the marines.

"As soon as you backed off in blockading the road to Quetta, most of the Taliban and Pakis pulled out. Aerial photos make it look like the gold rush in the Old West. They fled on motor scooters, bikes, in cars, in buses, and in trucks. In places the road was so congested that traffic came to a stop. While the city is now, mostly clear, several small groups are remaining. They will serve as the nucleus for any returning Taliban. That will give us a window of opportunity to do some one-on-one stuff with the local population. The key to that will be getting to Abdul Dawad. Any success we will have in getting the locals to work with us can only be accomplished if we can get to him."

"Money?" Jake questioned.

"We've tried that. To tell the truth, we have no idea what moves him. He is a sheik in the Barakzai tribe, the largest and most powerful subtribe among the Pashtuns, who ruled Afghanistan for the last couple of hundred years until the last king, who was from their tribe, was ousted. The Pakistanis distrust him, as do the Pakistani Taliban because the Pashtuns and the Barakzai live in both countries. In fact, they don't recognize a border, meaning Dawad has influence in Pakistan as well. He was not executed because all parties trying to control Afghanistan need the Barakzai. If they executed him, they would lose the tribe and would have had a fight on their hands because even deeper than religious sentiment runs the affinity to the tribe." Ord took a sip of coffee from a foam cup that looked like it had been sitting around for a week.

"What moves him? There must be something we can offer him." Jake was fumbling for a solution.

"Dawad is Indian-educated and speaks fluent English and is not a fanatic. He's a moneyman."

"With the Taliban underground, what role do you see him playing?"

"Hard to say, but if we could approach him, it would make getting to the locals easier."

"What have you tried?" Jake wanted to know what he could do.

"You name it, but he has blown us off. You are going to have to make contact."

"Me?"

"Yes. He's …"

Two special operators entered the hut, looking dirty and tired.

"What's up?" Ord asked, trying to determine why they were interrupting his conversation with the marine.

"Snipers. We had no idea they were out there. They caught us in the open, and took out Ali One." They referred to an Afghani interpreter.

"Son of a bitch," Ord mused. "Well at least we know Ali One was on our side." Ord turned to Jake. "We can tell which interpreters are working with us, because the Taliban take them out before they bother to shoot at our guys." Ord shook his head at having lost another interpreter. "How'd it happen?" He turned his attention to the special operators.

"The warehouse." It was all they said. It was taken for granted that Ord knew what that meant. "The number of shots indicated that there were probably three. Our team took them under fire, and they split, but this is the third time they have used the building."

"Okay. See that we get Ali One back to his family, and then sack out. You're done for the day."

When the operators left, Ord turned to Jake. "Where were we?"

"You were telling me about Abdul Dawad."

"Yeah; he has his fingers in everything. A case in point is the warehouse the snipers used. He owns it, and he could stop these guys from using it. He doesn't, because like everyone in this part of the world he is playing both sides and won't commit to one unless he's sure there will be a clear-cut winner."

"Let's present him with a clear winner," Jake mentioned as if that would be easy.

"He needs nothing from us."

"There has to be some way to get to him."

"I've got a complete file on him." Ord rummaged through a cardboard box filled with papers. "Here," he blew the dirt and dust off a folder and handed it to Jake. "It's yours. See if you can see something about him that I didn't."

"Thanks. Can I take this with me?"

"Be my guest." Ord had no use for the file. "Assuming you can't get to Dawad, what is your plan now that the enemy has fled to Pakistan?"

"I'm going to work the problem as one of civic action. Marines will provide local security based on the intelligence your teams provide. When we establish security, I'm going to try to rebuild all the Taliban has torn down, one brick at a time if I have to. It will give the people a contrast of the two systems—theirs and ours."

"I guess you aren't privy to the master plan for Afghanistan?" Ord thought Jake was not going to be able to do what he wanted to do.

"What's that?'

"The military is not going to be able to engage in nation building. The defense contractors that suck around DOD are."

"Rebuilding this place is going to take lots of security. Corporations aren't going to be able to do that."

"That's what we argued, but the plan is to make this a mostly civilian operation to save troops in the event of another contingency," Ord said coolly.

"Is that the story line going through the CIA?" Jake asked.

"Nah. That is a George Ord quick look at international relations."

"Are you pretty sure?"

"Shit, yes," Ord averred. "We were attacked on 9/11, and we were pretty sure who attacked us, but on 9/12 our leaders started talking about a war with Iraq, who we know had nothing to do with the bombings. On October 7, we went to war here to repay those who attacked us. Only, it's a half-assed war. We are not using the number of troops required to fix this place. Every war plan I've seen calls for hundreds of thousands, and we are now fighting it with thousands because we may need troops for other unnamed but identified contingencies. The fuckers in Washington are going to get us into a war that doesn't need to be fought." Ord shook his head in disgust.

"I worked with the people running the Pentagon. I think you've read them correctly."

"I don't want to speak heresy, but one of our teams is sure they have bin Laden cornered. They don't have the strength to get to him and have called for rangers to augment them. They were told there were none available. Since the company of rangers you rescued is sitting at the airport doing nothing but waiting for a ride home, I find it odd that they are not being used to take down the biggest target of the war. I don't want to scare you, General, but I think your friends who are trying to get us into Iraq are making it possible for bin Laden to escape. It'll keep him in the public's mind. If they tie him to Iraq, and I'm sure they will, they will have a reason to go to war." Ord paused. "Sometimes I think I've been doing this too long. I'm becoming cynical." Ord apologized for his rant.

"I know the neocons in the Pentagon want to change the world, but I can't figure out their obsession with Iraq. They have been trying to get at Iraq since the Gulf War. What's that, ten years?"

"It goes further back than that," Ord corrected. "My first posting was in Baghdad in 1980. Several of the big thinkers populating the administration now were going to change the Middle East, but by using Saddam Hussein because the Reagan administration wanted to slap down the Iranians and their Islamic Republic. We provided military assistance and intelligence along with lots and lots of cash to prod Hussein into taking on the Iranians. At that time he was considered a moderate leader, and our forward thinkers thought they could manipulate him.

"The unwritten plan was for Iraq to overrun Iran so that we could install a surrogate. If that could be accomplished, America would gain control of the combined oil reserves of Iraq and Iran. With both countries in the bag, we could have controlled both the supply and demand side of the oil trade. The whiz kids, several of whom currently advise the vice president, looked down on Hussein and thought he was going to be a puppet. They never once thought that he was the winner in a political system where those who failed were killed. He had more street smarts than any of the people who thought they were using him.

"At our coaxing, he invaded Iran, but Iranians braced, and the war stalemated into a war of skirmishes that lasted eight years. At the height of the war, the Israelis leveled the Iraqi nuclear reactor at Osirak, and Hussein started shying away from us, knowing the Osirak attack wouldn't have taken place without our support. The same guys who are howling today that he is a savage, didn't say boo when he was gassing Iranians. They didn't say a word when one of his airplanes almost sank the USS *Stark*, killing thirty-seven sailors. After eight years of back-and-forth trench warfare, a cease-fire was negotiated between the Iraqis and Iranians, and Hussein got off the leash.

"The neocons responded like jilted lovers when he decided to sell oil on the open market without knuckling under to American influence. The final insult, to all those who sang his praises for a decade, was when he invaded Kuwait. The neocons still want to get control of Iraqi oil and will use Iraq to change the world, but without Hussein." Ord paused. "That, General, is the back story on the boys running our government."

"I saw their fixation in person, but that explains a lot." Jake was not surprised by the story.

On the helo flight back to the marine encampment, Jake looked over the Dawad dossier. He saw nothing that stood out that would serve as an entrée to the Afghani, but he would let others look at the paper files to see if they could find something.

Entering the building used as his office and staff living quarters, he threw the folder on the cot Mackey used as a bed and desk.

"When you get through reading, take a look at this. I need fresh eyes on this file."

Mackey was sitting on the edge of his rack reading and stood lethargically.

"What are you reading?" Jake asked.

"Rousseau."

"The philosopher?"

"Yes, sir."

"That seems like a rather odd selection in the middle of Afghanistan. Shouldn't you be reading something that could help you save your ass when all this goes south?"

"I'm not worried about that."

"Does anything you are reading have application here?"

"Not really. There aren't many parallels between the European enlightened model and Afghanistan."

"Keep reading; something might pop up."

"I think the best we will be able to do is to organize the Afghans under a system of laws that fit this society. They may not be laws that we would buy, but it may take hundreds of years to get democracy to work here."

"Since we have hundreds of years, look over the file. It is on Abdul Dawad, who I'm told we will need to get on our side if we are to get anything done. See if there is anything that indicates that we can get to him." Jake was frustrated.

"Did you know that the last king of Afghanistan was from his tribe?"

"Red, you surprise me more every day," Jake complimented him. "I learned that today. The question is how did you know that?"

"I started reading Afghan history when it looked as if we might get into the fight here."

"Did you see anything that would lead us to Dawad?"

"His family shows up throughout Afghan history, and he shows up in current events."

"In what you've read, have you been able to figure him out?"

"He's not an ideologue. He bends with the wind, usually for a profit. I think that if we can make ourselves the new wind with a money tree attached, we could get to him."

"Money is easy. Finding the wind is what I'm looking for. Look over his file, and pass it around to others on the staff. I want a lot of eyes on this." Jake was searching for a solution.

"Yes, sir."

When Jake left, Mackey sat on the cot and opened the Dawad file. He had never seen such a comprehensive file on one person. Everything that the intelligence community could find was in the folder, including search results of members of his family. In the thousands of words written, nothing was indicated other than that he was well connected in the Islamic world and, more importantly, he worked for every sect and faction in Afghanistan and Pakistan, some in direct opposition. He was an international banker, who invested, laundered, and made money for his investors/sponsors, who left him alone as long as the money kept rolling in.

After hours of reading, Mackey thought he had picked up a thread. The Afghan noble was allowed to operate in a tough neighborhood because he paid extortion money to a lot of people who had the ability to shut him down or, worse, kill him. He could not miss a payment or declare bankruptcy. He paid, and on time, or else. In Afghanistan, there were no shareholders only tribal leaders, warlords, thieves, bandits, and the Taliban to be bought off. Being allowed to operate in a war zone had its risks, but the profits made were mind-boggling.

Mackey didn't know if he was reading too much into Dawad, and he passed the file to others while he slept on what he had learned.

Rolling off his cot, he walked into a part of the building where Jake had staked out an office. The only thing identifying it as an office was a large wooden desk of Russian manufacture. It had bullet holes in it, but it was a usable spoil of war.

"What's up?

"I've an idea on how we may be able to get to Dawad."

"What have you got?"

"General, this might be crazy."

"This entire operation is crazy. What's a little more?"

"I think I've found a chink in Dawad."

"Keep going."

"In order to continue operating as he has under various regimes, he has to pay extortion money to the people who carry guns."

"That means he's paying everyone," Jake interrupted.

Mackey got back on track. "I counted the number of people he relies on to stay in business. He funnels money or supplies or goods or perks to fourteen people or groups. He's been able to keep up with the demand of his pay-offs because he skims money off every transaction, so he always has cash. All transactions go through multiple shell companies that he owns. Nothing goes from A to B.

Case in point; he buys the Taliban opium crop at a price that he rigs. The cheap opium goes to his processing plant in Pakistan. There are four transfers before it gets to Pakistan, and at each of those transfers the price goes up. Once the opium is processed, it is sold on the open market. No one knows how much it sells for. A reverse of the opium scheme works for weapons. He buys trash weapons from the Pakistani ISI and sells them to the insurgents at ridiculous prices. Everyone knows that he is screwing them, but they need his network to keep money flowing."

"How does all that help us get to him?" Jake liked the narrative. It showed that Mackey had done his homework, but he didn't care about the Afghan's personal finances. He wanted a means so that he could become one of those Dawad worked for.

"Mr. Dawad works in parallel economies. Once he pays off his extorters, all monies are shipped out of the country. He can't use normal banking channels, so his relatives carry suitcases of money out of Afghanistan and Pakistan. The file shows that three shifts of the money are made before it is adequately laundered and banked in Dubai. When not in Afghanistan, he lives like a king. He has mansions in Switzerland, Dubai, and Bermuda." Mackey took a long breath and slowed himself. "His first priority is to pay off his protectors, which he does with the profits made off his everyday transactions, but once the money leaves the country it doesn't come back, or it can't come back in time to meet his near-term needs. I think if we can do something to disrupt his immediate cash-generating operation, he would be in a world of hurt and may have to look to us for protection."

"Are you telling me to close him down?" Jake didn't know where Mackey was going.

"No, sir. We have to interrupt his business."

"How?"

"The warehouse to the northeast on the airport generates a lot of money for him."

"The one that the Taliban use to fire on us?"

"Yes, sir."

"What of it?" Jake wanted answers not riddles.

"How about if the next time we come under fire, we take the building out? Losing it would put a hurt on his immediate cash flow."

"You mean take the Taliban out?"

"No, sir. Dawad doesn't give a shit about the Taliban. He cares for the warehouse because it is a moneymaker. If it goes away, he has to make up the money from other sources. He may not have the ability to react quickly enough to cover a shortfall. He won't sleep easily if he misses paying those he has to pay."

"So, if I understand you, the next time the Taliban occupy the warehouse and fire on us, we beat them off and occupy it?"

"That's one way."

"Where are we going with this, Red?"

"General, occupying the warehouse would result in Dawad running to the Pakistani and Afghan governments, and they would complain to the US Embassy. Accommodations would be made, and some excuse would be found as to why we had to return it. That wouldn't get his attention. It would only make him feel that he had won." Mackey paused, knowing what he was going to say might be too radical an idea. "We have to send a message. The next time the Taliban fire on us, let's do our normal clearing. When we are done, we could isolate the building behind some visible barrier. It would drive the locals crazy, and they would wonder why we are keeping them away. In the middle of the night, with the warehouse unoccupied, we can light it with lasers and have fast movers take it out with two thousand-pound bombs. That will make the warehouse disappear. It won't take too long before Dawad puts the sequence together. A marked building means something is going to disappear."

"Have you lost it?" Jake wasn't angry. He was amused.

"Think about the psychology of it, sir. The next time we are fired upon, we could isolate another of Dawad's buildings. I'm betting before it disappears, he will want to talk to you."

"Mack, that is either the most stupid thing I've ever heard or genius. I wish I knew." Jake rubbed his chin, thinking. "Nothing we have done to date has gotten him to talk to us; maybe playing with his head will. Since we are going to play head games, why not go one step further. Paint a huge red triangle on the buildings. Red is indicative of blood and passion and is an important visual stimulus in this society. It will make a greater psychological imprint. What do you think?"

"That sounds even better," Mackey agreed.

A spec ops team took fire from the Dawad warehouse and cleared the Taliban from it. Like every other sniper attack, the enemy slipped away before they could be trapped. Upon receiving the report, Mackey led two marine squads to the site. The movement didn't look like a military operation. It had the appearance of a painting contractor's truck going out on a job. With fanfare, the marines jumped off the trucks, cleared everyone away from the building, and circled the area with a single strand of barbed wire, from which they hung small red pennants. It wasn't enough to keep anyone out who wanted to cross the line, but it was a symbol that people should avoid approaching. The marines placed ladders against the building's bullet-pocked walls, and cans of red paint were carried upward to try to outline a triangle. Relieved of normal duties, the marines were playful. It was the first time in months they could act as young men, and paintbrushes substituted for water pistols. In trying to paint the building, they also tried to paint one another. While something akin to a triangle was sketched, paint splatters made their work look like a Pollock mural. Taking a minute to admire their work, the marines loaded their ladders and, with as much paint on themselves as there was on the building, disappeared.

The locals didn't know what to make of the behavior. They could only assume that they had finally driven the marines mad.

There had been a lot of conversation about the choice of using laser-guided dumb bombs over the newer sophisticated smart weaponry available, but Mackey argued that the smart weapons were too clean. A missile could be put in a window-sized space, but because of the weight of telemetry involved in the guidance systems, they sacrificed explosive power. A muffled surgical strike was not what he wanted. He wanted two thousand-pound bombs that would be fairly accurate and that would generate a lot of damage and, more importantly, a lot of noise and shock to make the ground rumble. As the warehouse sat in the open, the frag pattern wouldn't damage any of the local housing, so the louder and more destructive the explosion the better.

At midnight, Mackey rendezvoused with a forward air control team that had been schooled in laser designation of targets. As the team was moving into position, two F-18s were readied for launch off the USS *Vinson*. The carrier turned into a twenty-mile-an-hour wind and with its thirty-knot speed the wind across the deck was considered adequate for launching the heavily loaded fighter/attack airplanes.

The first jet was catapulted off the deck with full afterburner engaged and descended perilously close to the water before a combination of airspeed and power allowed it to begin a gradual climb. The second jet followed, and the flight of two headed north to rendezvous with a tanker.

At 0350, the ground team and the air team were in position and communicating.

The target was lased and the pilots could hear a low hum indicating that the bombs were locked onto the signal. With an easy push over, the planes started a shallow dive and steadied up on the laser-designated target. They pickled simultaneously, and pulled away. The bombs, succumbing to gravity, stayed locked on the laser with minute corrections provided by their fins.

Mackey wanted an explosion to wake the people, and he got his wish. Even in his safe position, a shock wave rolled over him. Through a night-vision scope, he could see the warehouse had not only been damaged, it was gone. All that remained were fires as the petroleum products stored in the building exploded.

The marines had no way of knowing how the destruction affected Dawad. What was apparent was that the locals had been affected. They had lived through the Russian occupation and the Taliban brutality, and no occupying force had ever acted so crazily. They had seen destruction before and could live with it. The thing that troubled them was the red triangle. They tried to figure out its meaning and how it might affect their lives. The Taliban hid until they figured out how to counter the American tactic. In a new twist, they started using farmer's houses, especially those farmers who hadn't and didn't support them. Spec ops and the marines starting taking fire from houses that had previously been considered friendly, and Jake marveled at how quickly the enemy had adapted.

"I thought it would work." Mackey apologized. He had been sure that the bombing would bring Dawad to the table.

"It has only been what, ten days?" Jake explained. He wasn't ready to give up. "Dawad hasn't responded, but the locals have changed their attitudes. Spec ops are getting more intelligence hits. People are walking in and telling them where the Taliban are. So, we did some good."

"But we haven't gotten to Dawad, and the fight is moving outside of the city, away from his prime assets." Mackey was trying to describe why his plan might fail.

"We linked enemy action from his property as the reason for the marking. Let's decouple them. The next enemy action anywhere will be reason enough to paint one of his buildings. It is the psychological stigma of being painted that will get him to come to us, not the fact that a building will be destroyed. If there is enemy action on the south side of Kandahar, I want his distribution center, where the trucking to and from Quetta assembles, painted."

"Are you really going to destroy it?" Mackey was unsure of Jake's intent.

"It is the crown jewel in his trading empire in this part of Afghanistan. I'm betting that he won't risk losing it. If he calls my bluff, then the painting game is over. We'll have to figure out some other way to get to him." Jake indicated he had no further ideas on how to get to the Afghan.

The marines at the Kandahar airport had been there long enough to become experts on the weather. When the sun came up with no particulate in the air to refract its brightness, the marines knew that at about midmorning the wind would start blowing. The warning breezes would be gentle and last for about an hour. Then they would intensify, picking up the sand and creating a layer of dust that rose to a hundred feet. In the dust cloud, visibility would be limited, and goggles would be required. On the bad days, the natives hunkered down and didn't move about. When they did, they looked thorough eye slits in the scarves wrapping their heads.

Those marines standing guard closest to the runway heard the approaching plane before they could see it, and as it roared overhead they couldn't believe anyone was flying on such a rotten day. The airplane was buffeted by the wind, and as it closed toward the runway, it seemed unable to land. The strong winds were keeping it airborne. That changed in an instant. The bottom dropped out, and the airplane fell as if was being sucked into the ground. It hit so hard that it went airborne a second and then a third time. It was a controlled crash, but the marines had seen many and weren't concerned.

Fran Matthews and five other women marines endured the landing. The serial impacts with the ground forced them into their seats, and they weren't sure what had happened. When they were given clearance to stand and exit the aircraft, they did so tenuously, not sure their legs would work.

Exiting using air stairs that extended from the aircraft's side, their first steps in Afghanistan were not greeted. They stood outside the airplane wondering what they should do next. Fran could hear what sounded like firecrackers and could see marines running for cover.

"Let's get out of here," she ordered, and six women marines ran for the closest building. She could see her gear and the gear of all the women being tossed out onto the tarmac as the airplane scrambled to get airborne and out of Kandahar.

The group pressed against a building, realizing that they were in the middle of a war.

Two Humvees came screeching to a halt by them, throwing up a dust cloud that was lost in the more ubiquitous one the wind was generating.

"Ma'am," the sergeant driving the lead Hummer greeted her, "the general sends his regards. I'll take you to your building, and he'll see you when he gets a chance." Fran was glad they had been found but was unsure of her saviors. The young marines had been living in the field and, seeing women who were still fresh in clean utilities, didn't hide their lustful looks. None said anything, but their eyes told the story. All the women marines at one time or another had been exposed to overtestosteroned men, but this was different. These marines were at war, deprived of the normal expectations of life, and their expressions were resonant with sexual innuendo uninhibited by the consequences of punishable acts.

The women were driven to an old barracks building that had been used by the Russians over a decade earlier, and it looked it. No attempt had been made to clean up the spaces to make them livable.

They retained the harshness of Russian military life. Latrines were at the end of the living quarters with no wall to hide them. They sat exposed so there was no privacy afforded during moments that required privacy. Even worse, they were open holes running to a slit trench besotted with the stench of past usage.

Fran saw cots with folded blankets laid out. She didn't know what to do. She had expected rough conditions, but what she saw was beyond anything she dared imagine.

"I guess we'd better start unpacking and setting up house." She spoke to the women, who were in an equivalent state of shock.

No one complained, but their disillusionment as a group was felt.

They picked out cots and stored their gear next to them. With nothing to do, they sat on the edges of the cots and individually wondered what they had gotten themselves into.

A vehicle stopped outside but none of the women had the curiosity to see who it was.

Jake entered accompanied by Jim Mackey. He stopped and looked over the living conditions.

"Who set this up?" he quizzed Mackey.

"The battalion supply officer."

"Did you tell him the reasons for setting it up."

"Yes, sir."

"It sucks." Jake made the comment and turned to find Fran.

She wanted to rush up to him as if he was going to save her, but she stood and hid her delight at seeing him. "It's good to see you, General," she said professionally.

"And you; it's good to see you all, but first things first," he said. "I want to welcome all of you to Kandahar. After I get you settled, I'll tell you what I have in mind for you. At that time, you may wish you hadn't volunteered, but I will thank you for taking a chance on me in advance. This is Lieutenant Jim Mackey. If you have any questions or need anything, speak to him. You can see from your elegant accommodations that he's a crackerjack in the logistics field."

Jake joked, and it broke the tension that the women and Mackey were feeling. "This building is unsat, and I guess it is somebody's way of telling you you're not wanted here. That means squat. I want you here, and I'll get you into some place that is livable."

"Sir?"

"Yeah, Fran?"

"Every one of us expected hardships, and we have all at one time or another had to suffer through somebody's idea of a joke. If you move us out of here, I think you will be playing into preconceived notions that women marines can't cut it. We don't necessarily want to be pioneers, but we all want a chance to prove ourselves. If it takes living in filth to gain the respect of the other marines, so be it."

Jake looked over the women, and they were intense, buying into Fran's words.

"Okay." When he said it, Jake saw them relax. "I will let you stay here, but I'm going to provide you with the materials to make this place livable. I don't want you going to the communal shower. That would create problems I'm not ready to face." When he said it, the women nodded. They understood there would be riots. "Mack, locate a couple of fifty-five-gallon drums and some tubing so that a cold-water shower can be set up indoors, and get some burn barrels so that the heads can be scraped and burned. Get some wood so that walls can be built. Fran, I'm not going to have anyone help you. Fix this place up any way you want. It is going to be your project, and it will send the right message. I'll give you the rest of today and tomorrow to get your feet on the ground. When you're up and running, I'll brief you on what I have in mind for you. Deal?"

"Yes, sir." She had told the other women marines that Jake was decisive and charming, and they saw those attributes in person.

"Mack, get them what they need."

"Yes, sir."

Jake left, but Mackey stayed to help them figure out what was needed. The logistical questions were settled quickly. The queries after that were about Jake. The women wanted to know what was planned for them.

Mackey could tell them little. He didn't hide anything. He didn't know.

A firefight not near any of Dawad's buildings was the trigger Jake needed. Marines with their paint cans marked Afghanistan's largest distribution center. A double cordon of barbed wire and an especially large red triangle left little doubt that the building was slated for destruction. The marking was a hollow threat. The marines needed the supplies that came through the center as badly as the Afghans. Knowing that Dawad was in Kandahar, Jake hoped he would bite on the inference of the previous bombing.

George Ord was in Jake's small barebones office. There were no constructed walls. Blankets hanging from ropes served as room dividers. The CIA operator had just handed over a packet of photos of Dawad properties outside of Afghanistan.

"This is what I've managed to get for you, but if you aren't going to bomb them, I think you are out of leverage." Ord liked the idea of playing head games with the Afghans, whom he considered essential in any counterinsurgency effort.

"After the last bombing, I was told to knock it off," Jake confessed. "The Pakis threatened to shut down their ports if we bombed another building. They want Dawad to stay in business. He seems to be the only one with the ability to move things in this part of the world."

"That and the fact that they are all crooks and they don't want to see their money train sidetracked."

"Yeah, that too." Jake smiled.

"What are you going to do if Dawad changes his mind and doesn't show up?" Ord was curious.

"I've been prohibited from hitting him militarily, so I've thought about slowing down his operation by erecting checkpoints that all trucking will have to go through."

"That ain't going to fly." Ord was sure. "You will have the Pakis calling Washington, and they'd bring pressure to close that down."

"What would you do? Give me some ideas."

"I'm out of ideas. You better hope he bites."

'That is kind of a fine filament upon which to hang our war effort."

"At least you have a filament. Nobody else running this operation has a clue as to what they are doing." Ord finished about the time two black Mercedes limousines drove slowly up to the building. The Americans looked at the scene unfolding.

The car doors flew open, and four bodyguards took positions at the corners of the automobiles. It was for show, because they had been stripped of their weapons by the marines before they were allowed to enter the airport. They were big and looked fit as they eyed the surroundings to see if they could find a threat. When the lead guard nodded, Dawad and another man stepped out along with a marine who had been assigned to escort them through the American camp.

The marine led the visitors across a dusty patch of weed-infested dirt toward Jake's office.

"This is big time," Ord informed Jake. "The second guy is the police chief of Kandahar. He doesn't usually show up with Dawad. They like to keep their connection secret. The fact that he is here kinda says that you got the big man's attention."

"You can stay for this, or you can slip out the back. Your choice." Jake gave Ord the option.

"If it's okay with you I'll stay. I may learn something."

"Sir," the marine escort poked his head into the office, "Mister Dawad is here to see you."

"Give me a minute. I'm on a call to Washington and can't stop right now." Dawad's presence indicated that Jake had the upper hand and by keeping him waiting he hoped to increase his psychological advantage. He waited for a couple of minutes before shouting so that he could be heard throughout the building. "I don't care what the general says, I want more artillery in Kandahar, and I want it now." He slammed his hand on the desk, and shrugged playfully at Ord.

In a mellow voice that was a sharp contrast to the shouting, Jake said, "Please bring Mr. Dawad in."

One of the bodyguards held back a blanket, and the Afghan tribal leader entered not knowing what to expect. The two voices he had heard left him wondering if the marine commander was erratic, a man he might not be able to deal with.

Dawad, unlike the police chief, wore the trappings of his power. Over a silk sports jacket and an open-necked white shirt, he wore his tribal cape of red, green, and black vertical stripes. He was hatless, and his full black hair covered his sloping forehead, which maintained its angle into his nose. It looked like his hair had been razor cut, definitely not the look of someone living in the squalor of Kandahar. He was clean-shaven, and his skin looked as if it had been recently oiled. It was hard for Jake not to look at Dawad's hands. A diamond ring as big as his knuckle caught and refracted light, but Jake was more interested in Dawad's fingernails. They were manicured and polished, causing him to wonder where Dawad had that done in Kandahar. The Taliban had only been routed for several weeks, and Jake wondered if a manicurist had been recently imported or if Dawad had a deal with the Taliban when they controlled the city.

The two leaders of differing tribes eyed one another warily, each trying to figure out the other from external appearances. Jake thought he had a hint of the man.

The Afghan stepped forward, and having been educated in India under the British system, extended his hand. Jake didn't take it. In the Afghan tradition, he bowed slightly, lowering his head and shoulders in a gesture of respect for his visitor. Dawad tried to make up for his misstep in front of the police chief by copying Jake's greeting.

"I'm General Gregg, Mr. Dawad. It is an honor having you come to my humble surroundings. And who is your friend?" Jake bowed to the police chief. An interpreter translated the words. Dawad spoke English, but was hiding behind the interpreter's words in trying to gain an advantage.

"Sorry." Dawad apologized in English for not introducing his companion. It was a slip that was going to make it impossible for him to retreat behind language. The apology told Jake that Dawad was still moved by his education and the polite Indian ways he had been taught.

"This is Akbar Gul. He is our police chief in Kandahar District."

Gul was not nearly as polished as his boss. He wore a black suit and black shoes that were covered with dust. His black beard was a dust collector and was tinged gray, but it was hard to tell if it was hair color or dirt.

"Welcome," Jake said. "You know Mr. Ord?" he asked Gul directly. Following Jake's lead, Ord ignored the proffered handshake and bowed in a sign of respect to the Afghans.

"Yes." The response told Jake that Gul too spoke English.

"As you can see, we Americans are living humbly in your country, but anything I have is yours." Jake offered what was his in the Afghan tradition of welcoming guests, but as the Afghanis looked around they saw nothing that they would take.

"We should have met sooner," Jake apologized. "But I have been trying to organize the marines in the event of a new Taliban offensive."

Gul was the one who reacted to the comment. The arrival of the Americans had allowed him to resume his position as police chief, and the thought of the Taliban returning was not well accepted. Jake noted the response. Gul was easy to read and would be amenable to American overtures. It was nice to know, but unless Dawad bought in, nothing could be accomplished.

"I assume this isn't a social visit? Since we are guests in your country, how can we work together?" The phrasing indicated cooperation in solving common problems. It wasn't what the Afghans expected.

Dawad looked at Gul, indicating that they had different agendas, but Dawad would go first.

"General," he started. "A building in Kandahar has been defaced by your marines. I would like to know the meaning of their actions and what you intend to do about it?"

"So that we don't waste time," Jake changed his tone. "The building has not been defaced. It has been marked." He paused to let the words sink in. "It will disappear tonight."

"You can't." Dawad wasn't panicky, but he looked to Gul for support, even flicking his head, indicating that Gul should get involved.

"General. The buildings are Afghan property posing no military threat. Their destruction is outside your authority. The Geneva Convention prevents you from targeting civilians and civilian properties." Gul strung words together that he thought might make an impression on the marine.

"Our intelligence indicates that the Taliban use the building as a staging area, and that makes it a military target."

"General, what could we Afghans do that would have you call off destroying the building?" Dawad saw that neither he nor Gul was going to be able to intimidate Jake. He had to strike a bargain.

Ord tried not to smile, but he was amused by the way Jake had positioned his adversary.

"I come to you for help." Jake switched tone, intimating that he was the supplicant. He had to bring the Afghans on board voluntarily and leave them with the impression that they were in control. "Since the Taliban have been displaced, I have noticed the police you are recruiting are not equipped to maintain order in Kandahar District and would like to lend support in training them and arming them so that the district will remain peaceful." Nothing he said was disputed. Gul was in control of the city, but barely, and an updated police force would enable him to maintain order. The Afghans were incredulous that the American wanted so little in return for saving a building. Gul spoke to Dawad in Pashto, so the Americans were ignorant of what was said.

"Mr. Gul. Don't do that again. All of us in this room have to understand what is being said. Your talking in Pashto indicates you might not be able to be trusted, and I won't work with a man I can't trust," Jake scolded the police chief.

"I am sorry," Gul intoned.

"Here is what I want from you." Jake spoke directly to Dawad, taking advantage of the police chief's error. "I want buildings in and around Kandahar made available to the marines and the special operations personnel. In these spaces, I will house marines who will help train your police, repair schools, and rebuild other local government projects that the Taliban destroyed. My feeling is that unless you can show the people that you can provide security and services, the Taliban will return and displace you." The argument made a bigger impression on Gul, who had been displaced under the Taliban and had barely survived.

"For this, you will not destroy our building?" Dawad made clear his priority.

Jake looked at him. He wasn't angry but wanted to let the uncomfortable silence indicate his displeasure. "Of course, I want all the sniping on the marines stopped." He threw down the gauntlet.

"That is impossible," Dawad argued.

"Mr. Dawad, nothing happens here that you don't know about. Your dealing with many groups enables you to stay in business, but the deal I will make with you is this. I want to know whenever an attack is being planned. You will not be able to inform us of every attack, but I don't want to be surprised too often." Jake stared at the Afghan.

"I could try, but there are no guarantees."

"That's good enough. There is one more thing that I would like your help with."

Dawad didn't say a word. He felt he was already committed to too much.

"We are increasing the amount of matériel that will come into Kandahar over the road from Quetta. The American Embassy has hired American companies, who have in turn subcontracted their jobs to Pakistani truckers to ferry goods into Afghanistan. As the matériel passes through Pakistan, America pays people in every district and municipality for safe passage. At the border, Pakistani drivers continue to bring the goods to Kandahar. I want to change that. I want you to replace Pakistanis with Afghans. It is my feeling that we have to employ Afghans so that some of the money being made will remain in Afghanistan. At the border, I will have the supplies inventoried as they enter Afghanistan, and I will give you 5 percent of everything that arrives minus the discrepancies between the initial inventory and the actual goods that get to Kandahar." Jake stopped. "If you can control the pilferage along the road to Kandahar, you will make more money in a legitimate enterprise than you could steal."

Dawad liked the idea. "I'll see what I can do to stop any further attacks on the marines."

"Good. One last thing," Jake could have asked for anything for the amount of money the Afghan saw he could make. "When the schools start up again, I want girls educated."

"That can't be done." Dawad protested. "It is against Islam."

Jake corrected. "The prophet ordained women as coequal partners to men. The positions taken in different Islamic cultures are a matter of interpretation of the Quran. The Taliban take the position that women are slaves. Other Islamic cultures have given women rights, including education. The Pakistanis at one time had a woman prime minister, and they share your faith." Jake paused, leaving Dawad to wonder just how much he knew about Islam. "You understand that Afghanistan can't move ahead with half the population ignorant. It is going to require everyone's skills."

"Women in all societies should remain subservient." Dawad wasn't about to budge.

Jake opened the folder of photos Ord had provided and motioned Dawad over to his desk. Flipping to the last photo, taken from the sea of Dawad's palatial waterfront home in Dubai, it showed Dawad with a naked blonde girl. His arm was around her, and they were drinking something that could not be identified, but the shape of the bottle indicated it was champagne. Dawad's mouth flapped open in amazement.

"Some women are not subservient," Jake said.

Dawad's worry was that Gul had seen the photograph, but Jake had shielded it from his view.

"Can women and girls be educated?" Jake asked softly.

Dawad nodded reluctantly.

"Then we have an agreement?" Jake asked both of them. Gul looked at his chief before nodding.

The Afghans left. When their cars drove away, Ord smiled. "You are one slick mother fucker. I've been trying to get those guys to work with me, and they've shot me down. Nice work. I've only got one question. Do you have the authority to give them 5 percent off the top?"

"I don't know. I do know that we are losing almost 30 percent of all goods between the border and Kandahar, so if this deal holds, we'll improve our supply posture by 25 percent."

The rehab would have been a lot easier if the woman marines had accepted the help offered by sex-starved men. Not allowed in what became known as the "pussy palace," the male marines hovered outside a wire barrier erected to provide a buffer zone.

Fran had chosen her team well. All the women were intent on doing the job and weren't distracted by amorous leers. Without knowing what was in store, they kept themselves busy, and their quarters reached a point where they became livable in a fourth-world kind of way. Fran's worry was that they would run out of building projects, and questions as to why they were there would begin.

As the last nails were being pounded, a truck arrived at their compound, and Jim Mackey jumped out. He ignored the string of barbed wire that was supposed to keep people out and proceeded to the door. Pounding it with his fist, he waited.

"Major," he greeted Fran, who opened the door. "You're up. The general wants to talk to all of you."

"Thank you, Lieutenant. How much time do we have?" Fran was thinking that the women were dirty, and their T-shirts were sweat-stained. They were not dressed to meet with a general.

"None, ma'am." Mackey was matter of fact but sensitive to the major's concerns. "The general doesn't care about stuff like this." He pointed to the women, who were wiping themselves off.

"Are you sure, we can't have a few minutes?"

"I'm sure." Mackey shut off further discussion.

They walked to the idling truck and sat in the open back. In the first hundred yards traveled, the women were glad that they hadn't changed. Dust billowed up from the dirt roads and covered them.

Jake was waiting. The first impression the women marines had was not of Jake. They looked at his office space. It was no better than the building they had fixed up for themselves. It surprised them and made him seem on a par with those who worked for him.

"You can stay, Mack. We aren't going to be sharing secrets."

Jake had folding chairs for his guests, and when they were seated, he went around and shook their hands and asked them a little about themselves.

"Thanks, Fran. You did a good job picking your team." Jake didn't bother to ask her about herself.

"I'm sorry for the secrecy, but if I had come up on the wire and said how I wanted to use you, you'd still be stateside," he confessed with a sly grin. "I was able to work the system by saying that you were needed as administrators. The world took that to mean secretaries." He took notice of the disappointing effect his words had on the women. "I don't intend to use you that way. So if when I'm done outlining my plans, any of you want out, say so. All I ask is that when you get home you keep what I'm going to tell you quiet so those who stay will have a chance to prove or disprove my ideas."

The talk of allowing people to back out got the women's attention. Fran was unconcerned. She knew he wouldn't take risks with a marine's life.

Jake gathered his thoughts. "We are in Afghanistan without any clear direction. Our charter is to kill bad guys. It is a rather ill-defined mission. Nowhere has winning been outlined, and if we get to a point where the politicians think we have gone far enough, what our exit strategy will be. I feel that if we manage to capture bin Laden we'll declare victory. Trouble is, we are doing everything wrong in trying to capture him. So how long will we be here? What is our job here? Those are the million-dollar questions." Jake took a deep breath. "I'm betting that we will be here for a while. I know that the Taliban will be here, and I expect a full-blown insurgency. The only way we can counter it, if we can at all, is to start using counterinsurgency techniques before the Taliban have a chance to figure out how they want to take us on. I have marines working with spec ops teams trying to make inroads to the local population. We have had some successes, and I've come to an agreement with the police chief to be able to enter his police stations and help his force in any way we can. That is progress, but this country is never going to break the strangle hold the religious fanatics have over it unless women are educated and see role models capable of working alongside men. That's where you come in." He looked at the women, who were hanging onto his every word. "I'm going to place you in units that are working with the local police. "I want you out front so that you can engage women whom you will undoubtedly meet. Eventually, after the local women are used to seeing you, I intend to extend your responsibility so that you can go on patrols in remote areas in an effort to bring Afghan women out of the dark ages."

"Sir, we have no training for working with police." A female staff sergeant voiced her concerns.

"You won't need it. Your training as marines will be sufficient. You will be carrying weapons, and the local women will respect you for knowing how to use them." Jake wanted to sum up his remarks and to give them an opportunity to question him. It was through their questions that he hoped to find out if his plan was a step too far. "You have all been the brunt of resentment from male marines, but that was kiddy stuff. The Afghan men are going to feel threatened, and they are going to viscerally hate you. Some whacky bastard is liable to try to kill you, so be vigilant. The men here have total power over women, but if they push you, I want you to push back while remaining in control. Let them see no fear, only disgust. By your actions you are going to be showing the women how to raise themselves out of years of being told they are dirt. This might not be what you expected, and, as you can see, I'm winging it. We are going to learn from our mistakes. I'm open for your questions."

A young lieutenant raised her hand. "Sir, I want to thank you for bringing us here. These women have a long way to go, but we have prejudices in the Marine Corps that have to be overcome, and this challenge will help in the fabric women are knitting."

"Let's worry about one thing at a time," Fran interrupted. She felt it was an opportunity to prove women could operate in combat, but she and the others would have to survive before that point could be made.

The marines in Kandahar sat by quietly and waited for the lid to come off the "women experiment," as it was sarcastically called. The pessimism was palpable, but Jake didn't back off. He made his opening gambit and assigned Fran Matthews to George Ord and a group of mixed spec ops and marines. Ord had been to the main police station with his team and could walk into Gul's office without being stopped. The routine was always the same. Trucks pulled up to the police headquarters, and the team got off to enter the building. None of the local constabulary raised an eye. Few even noticed the fair-skinned marine they hadn't seen before.

Ord went in to see Gul, and the team waited in what was the police assembly area. Knowing it would be awhile, they sat on the floor and took off their helmets. There was no hiding Fran. The Americans saw the horror-stricken look of the policeman sitting at a desk as he rushed into Gul's office.

The police chief came out followed by Ord, who had expected just what had happened.

Gul stood in front of Fran and couldn't bring himself to speak to her. He turned to Ord.

"We can't have this." He was upset.

"This is Major Matthews. She is one of the foremost military police experts and is here to help you organize your force." Ord exaggerated and was enjoying himself.

"That cannot be. Afghans can't work with a woman. She is unveiled, and that is a sin under our law. I won't have this. Leave. Leave." He shouted at all the Americans.

"It is a sin under Taliban law. You have to remember that they displaced you. Is that the kind of law you want now?" Ord placed his hand up under Gul's arm. "Let's talk." He directed the police chief back to his office.

"This cannot happen." Gul laid down his marker.

"Mr. Dawad and the general agreed on this. You can't back out on that agreement. What you have to understand is that the general wants this to happen. What is it going to take?"

"Are you trying to bribe me?" Gul lived in a system where kickbacks and a piece of the action were a part of life, and he wasn't insulted by Ord's question. He asked it to determine if Ord was serious.

"What is it going to take?"

Gul rubbed his dirty beard. "I can't take any portion of Dawad's profits other than that which he gives me, but I would like to receive some more of the supplies that the Americans are getting."

"How much? We'll take it out of Dawad's cut?" Ord played with him.

"No. No. You must not do that. You cannot reduce what Dawad is receiving."

"There is not too much to skim off after Dawad gets his cut, but I think I can get you 1 percent. That doesn't sound like much, but you have seen the quantities of American supplies that are arriving. One percent is going to equate to a fortune. You can either receive it in goods so that you can help your people, or we can change it into American dollars and place them in your Swiss account."

Gul was surprised that Ord knew of his secret account.

"It's my job to know," Ord explained. "What is it going to be?"

Gul pondered the question as if he was struggling for an answer. In reality it was an easy choice. "Place it in my account. I would like it done secretly so that Dawad does not find out."

"Done." Ord had him hooked. "Now the general would like the women that he sends to the police to receive the same treatment as the men. He wants them to be able to patrol with the police. Understand?"

"It won't be easy, but I will do it for the general." Jake suddenly became Gul's new best friend as he was counting money in his head.

"I'm going to bring in Major Matthews. You should meet her and tell her when she can start out with the police."

Before Gul could object, Ord called Fran into the office.

"Police Chief Gul, this is Major Matthews."

Fran was as tall as Gul and looked at him eye to eye.

"It is my honor, Mr. Gul." She bowed slightly in a sign of respect. The gesture put Gul at ease, as he realized that he would not have to shake her hand or touch her.

The Afghan didn't know what to do. Fran was the type of blonde woman that he usually bought for sex when he traveled outside of Afghanistan. He would like to have her around, but not in Afghanistan, where he had to keep up pretenses.

"I'd like to get the marines with your police on foot patrols through the city." Fran got right to business.

"Yes, yes," Gul agreed. "I will go out and talk to my assistant." He left the office.

When they were alone, Ord spoke. "I've got you in the door, but watch this guy. He'd sell his mother. Don't believe a thing he says, and always, always have your weapon with you. Gul was an easy sellout, but there are crazies who would kill you in the name of Allah. Shit, there are plenty who would kill you for the fun of it."

"Thanks for the advice."

"You know, when the general first broached this idea with me, I told him he was out of his mind. The more I thought about it, I was even more convinced."

"Have you changed your mind?"

"Yes and no. When we were driving here, I saw the way the women who dared raise their eyes looked at you. Jake was right there. And he's right about thinking this backwater will never evolve unless the women are brought out of the shadows. He's also right that no invader of this country tried to empower women. They all left the status quo and failed." Ord paused.

"So what's the part bothering you?" Fran was direct.

"While I've begun to buy into the experiment, I fear it may fail. If it does, Jake is going to get hammered. My worry is that he is the best military commander I have ever been around, and America can't afford to lose him."

"I don't intend to get the general fired, Mr. Ord."

CHAPTER 37

THE PENTAGON,
WASHINGTON, DC

Don Frieze was frantic. The news broke that the request for more troops in the hunt for Osama bin Laden had been denied and that the terrorist had most likely escaped. Questions swirled throughout the government and in the media as to where in the chain of command the request for extra troops had been denied. Pundits were hinting that the Defense Department had made a mistake. In Washington fashion, systemic errors were overlooked in the hunt for a fall guy, and the indicators pointed to the DEPSECDEF. He had worked in government long enough to know that news cycles sustained themselves until the next big story, but the news storm that was growing around bin Laden intensified daily. Any idea that he could lie low came apart when the political staff at the White House called, telling him that he had to go on the Sunday morning news shows to deflect questions of incompetence that were swirling around the president. A report surfaced that the administration wasn't focusing on Afghanistan and that was the reason for bin Laden's escape. The White house didn't care how he did it. Frieze's job was to take the spotlight off the president.

As he sat in his office preparing for his next-day series of television interviews, he thought of ways in which to spin the narrative. With the administration's concurrence, he had CENTCOM essentially starve the spec ops teams that indicated they had bin Laden trapped. The gaps in the ground coverage were known, and nothing was done to block them, because bin Laden was of value seen as a perceived threat. The administration agreed that he had been neutralized and was of no danger, but free, he had propaganda value.

Since the administration had requested that the interviews be conducted to clear the air, Frieze couldn't feed the media questions he wanted to answer. He had to respond to what they wanted to ask. Knowing there was always a danger in unscripted interviews, he developed statistic-laden answers for what he considered the most likely questions. His intent was to be as boring as possible.

He had been sent to the shows to answer questions on current events, but his secondary purpose was to plant the seeds that Iraq might have played a part in the 9/11 attacks. He would not provide intelligence or facts. He would let the media have a field day with speculation.

Sitting in the makeup chair, two women colored his cheeks and combed his hair. He didn't have to move; once the cosmeticians were done, audio personnel clipped microphones on him and went through sound tests. When he was ready, cameras rolled in before the host, Chris O'Dell, the face of a friendly network, occupied a chair across from him.

They made small talk, but O'Dell paid little attention. He listened to his producer giving him instruction through his earpiece.

"Are you ready for this?" O'Dell asked nonchalantly. Having conducted hundreds of interviews, he didn't get excited about them.

"Yes." Frieze smiled to show confidence, but it was forced.

"Five, four, three, two, you're on." The countdown came from an unseen control room.

"Welcome to the *Truth in News*." O'Dell looked directly at the camera. "The only news show where we cut to the chase and don't give you biased opinions."

Frieze smiled to himself. His job for the day was to spin, spin, and spin and to bury the truth.

O'Dell gave his guest's biography.

"After 9/11 we set out to dismantle Afghanistan, a failed state, from which the terrorist attack emanated. I feel, as I'm sure the American public feels, that we had a moral obligation to invade Afghanistan. Now that we have troops there, give the people your assessment of our actions to date."

It was a nothing question designed to make the host look like he had a grasp of the situation.

Frieze answered with a long rambling statement containing data points that only an insider could understand. He did well. His first answer went through the commercial break and had to be picked up on the other side of it.

O'Dell was used to doing most of the talking. It was his show, and he wanted the camera time, so he tried to make his questions specific and hoped for concise answers. Frieze wasn't buying. Even with time running out, he rambled.

"There are reports that bin Laden might have escaped into Pakistan." O'Dell had gotten nothing from his guest and hoped a provocative question would evoke an answer that might help his ratings.

Frieze couldn't evade the question.

"We have no indication that bin Laden is anywhere but in the caves of the Tora Bora Mountains. Our forces are tightening the noose around him."

The short answer left time for a quick follow-on question.

"Mr. Frieze, the New York Times is going to run a story stating that you have not supported the spec ops teams that have bin Laden trapped. To cite sources, the story will detail requests for more troops they say you pointedly denied."

"I can't respond to an unsubstantiated story, but I can tell you that we are using all available force to bring bin Laden to justice."

Driving across town to a second interview, the feeds of the O'Dell interview preceded Frieze. The consensus among newspeople was that the interview with O'Dell had been a disaster from a television standpoint. Frieze had been too long-winded and had said nothing. Interviewers had their staffs scramble to come up with questions that didn't require lengthy answers. Producers assisted by changing the ad schedule, and the talking heads were given permission to cut into answers to keep the programming lively.

In a game of news manipulation chess, Frieze suspected what was coming and in the backseat of his limo started thinking about how he would answer more direct questions.

It had been a long morning, in which the DEPSECDEF answered similar questions over and over. Each interviewer wanted breaking news, and in a form of word-trench warfare neither side gave an inch.

Somewhere in the fourth interview, when he was off air, Frieze thought he was clear of the nuisance of having to inform the public. The host had unhooked his microphone and asked if bin Laden couldn't be dislodged from his mountain redoubt, what plans the Defense Department had. Frieze went unscripted. "We'll put a force in the area that he won't be able to fight against. We'll wipe out his entire complex."

"We've bombed and bombed it, and he's still there. Overwhelming force doesn't seem to have worked."

"We'll use ground forces, but we'll get him out of the caves."

It was a throwaway line. It should have been conversation between friends except the microphone that had been detached from Frieze was still hot. Before he left the studio, his words were transcribed and were ready for the evening news shows and the Monday-morning newspapers.

The White House staff saw only the recorded shows and were happy with Frieze's performance. He received a congratulatory call from the vice president. He had adequately covered the president, and he could get back to winning the war.

CHAPTER 38

CENTCOM,
TAMPA, FLORIDA

Sitting in the commanding general's quarters on MacDill Air Force Base, General Franklin was sipping bourbon on the rocks. Watching the news before dinner, he didn't know what to make of the report that Frieze had mentioned using ground forces in an effort to dislodge bin Laden. It had never been mentioned. His last instructions were to keep the pressure on in the air campaign and not to commit any further troops.

He got on the phone to each of his staff officers who might have been recipients of the information and who might not have passed it along. One after another, each denied any knowledge and noted that in their last conversations with the Pentagon they had been told that no further troops would be needed. Nowhere in the conversations between CENTCOM and the Pentagon was the use of ground forces in Afghanistan hinted. They had, in fact, been told to put a cap on the forces already in country.

Franklin recorded it as another Frieze "fuck up," and he worried that the press would start hounding him to respond to the remarks made by DEPSECDEF for which he had no answers. Reluctantly, he called Frieze. They had to have a game plan so that it would look like they were talking with one voice, and Franklin didn't want to say anything that would get him crosswise with the White House. He wanted it on the record that he had talked to the DEPSECDEF and had been told how to respond.

CHAPTER 39

KANDAHAR

Jake sat behind his desk doing something that was far afield from his normal duties. He reflected on what had been accomplished and what needed to be done in his area of responsibility. He was at war, and those pursuing it had abdicated their responsibilities to the troops fighting it. Seven- and eight-man teams and platoons with no connectivity to the national command authority were making decisions on the fly, decisions that were locking America into Afghanistan. In pushing off the responsibility for the war onto the shoulders of nineteen- and twenty-year-olds, he felt that America was going to be the next power that had temporary aims in Afghanistan and that stayed because Afghanistan had a way of sucking nations in. The egotism of occupiers made them think they could remake the people and the country in their image. History proved the reverse was true. In order to stay in control, those who came to do good lowered themselves to the baseness of the population they were trying to elevate. High-minded armies and their surrogates killed as brutally as those people they were trying to raise to meet their higher standard.

Jake leaned back in his chair and looked at the dirty latticework that served as a ceiling. He knew the history of Afghanistan and understood that Western thought injected over a short time was not going to make a long-lasting impression. At its core, Afghanistan was tribal—a culture based on loyalty to the clan overlaid with Islam that allowed the tribal leaders to inject mysticism in order to retain control.

If Americans thought that by ridding the people of the Taliban grateful masses would rush to support them, it was a misguided dream thought up by men who dealt with abstract concepts and believed that they could be applied to the real world. Too many layers of the Afghan society had to be chipped away, and each level had a vested interest in the status quo. The Afghan beliefs were a reverse of Western thought. When the West emerged from the dark ages into an enlightened period, the Islamic world went from the forefront of scientific questioning into the dark ages of radical Islam. Planting the seeds of freedom in arid minds would not be successful.

Jake thought about the Afghan people and the invaders and wondered why neither had made an impression on the other. He knew he couldn't change history but hoped that by exposing Afghan women to new ideas he could make inroads in moving the society away from its past. Education might be the key to breaking the cycle of ignorance and suppression. He felt that was the one thing he could affect. Dictating freedom and justice was beyond the scope of an invading power, but with education, freedom and justice would follow, maybe.

Those were problems for another day. His concerns were that the marines were on the frontlines. The American venture would succeed or fail with them. He hoped that exposing the Afghan people to new and better ways would pay off in fewer casualties.

The police experiment seemed to be getting the results he wanted, but that was only one level of education. He wanted schools built, so that he could inject ideas, good and bad, but ideas, into the lowest levels of society.

"You wanted to see me, General?" Fran Matthews poked her head around the cloth drape serving as a door.

"Come on in, and sit down."

She moved into the room and took the only chair.

"Is this a bad time?"

"No. I was just sitting here trying to find the key to unlock this place," Jake said, rubbing his temples.

"Any luck?"

"Nah." He stood and arched his back, trying to stretch his muscles.

"You look tired, sir." She didn't know if she had overstepped the bounds of protocol, but she was concerned and wanted him to know it.

"I'll be okay." He craned his neck before sitting.

"I wanted to talk to you about an idea I've been playing with." He hesitated. "First, let me say the women you picked to come to Afghanistan are great. They are making an impression on the local women."

"I hope so."

"They are. I know because I get complaints about them every day. The Afghan men don't like seeing them doing things on their own. They are afraid that their women are going to stand up to them."

"That was the idea, wasn't it?"

Jake looked directly at her, making Fran feel uncomfortable. "It's a good start, but I want to stretch the envelope."

"I'm sure everyone would be agreeable to that."

"So far, you have been used in Kandahar. Prior to the city being overrun by the Taliban and the imposition of their harsh rules, it was a crossroads, a trading center. Women had exposure to outside ideas. They may have only been the ideas of Pakistani traders, but they saw a bit of the outside world. I guess what I'm saying is the women in Kandahar are as cosmopolitan as any women in Afghanistan. That will give you a base line on how far they are behind."

"How does that affect us?"

"I want to use you outside the city in areas that haven't been exposed to the little that Kandahar has. I've talked to Gul, and he will send a liaison out with you to identify any of what remains of a policing force in the area around Garz."

"That sounds pretty much like what we are doing here."

"It is exactly, but the society you'll be exposed to there will be different. Women will wear the full burqa, not because the Taliban forced them to do so but because their men have controlled them in that fashion for hundreds of years. I almost hesitate to send you or any woman there, because you will confront resistance. At best, you could be rejected. At worst, they could kill you."

"Some of the men we have confronted in Kandahar had the same attitudes." Fran tried to allay his fears.

"Maybe, but the women you'll be trying to interact with in Garz haven't been out of their village. They know nothing other than what some holy man or their husband tells them." Jake was mulling over the difficulties.

"Obviously, you think there is something to be gained by doing this?" Fran wasn't shying away from the talk of hardship.

"I think there is. We are not going to make changes from the top down that will succeed our leaving Afghanistan. The only change that will stick will be from the bottom up, and that means we have to get out into villages, where the resistance to change will be the greatest."

"I agree with you." She indicated that she trusted his judgment.

He paused for an uncomfortable moment. "Okay, here's the deal. I'm going to use you as a test case and send you out to Garz. You'll have, as I indicated, a couple of Gul's operatives, and for your personal protection I'm going to assign two squads of marines. I'll put one of the best gunnery sergeants in charge."

"Why so many troops? It might send the wrong message."

"A couple of reasons. First, I don't want you getting hurt." When he said it Fran blushed. She was flattered that he was thinking of her safety. "Second, this isn't going to be an assignment where you will be coming back to base every night. Dawad has arranged for several buildings that will serve as your base of operations and living quarters. Your contact with this headquarter will be by radio, so if you get into trouble, you will be at least an hour away. That is why I want you with a bulked-up force." Jake continued to spell out how he saw the assignment unfolding, but Fran was wrapped around the words that he didn't want her to get hurt. They conveyed a lot to her.

Garz was forty miles northwest of Kandahar, and it didn't take Fran long to realize that while she was moving across the landscape she was moving back in time. The passable roads of the city gave way to dirt tracks that were rutted so deeply that the four trucks transporting her and the marines and their gear moved along at a crawl. The slow pace left them vulnerable, and the troops riding in the open-bed trucks were on full alert.

The country they crossed was arid and a light wind picked up dirt, covering everything with a sheen that obliterated color and presented a mono-hued landscape. Those houses rising above the dirt were difficult to pick out unless the sun was at an angle that allowed them to cast shadows, indicating that something was rising above the ground.

The groupings of population that they passed were nothing more than clusters of huts constructed of a crude adobe slathered with mud that had long since dried. The windward sides caught the brunt of the flying dirt, and Fran tried to imagine what they might be like inside. The construction was square, and she thought there could only be one room. Everything a family did took place in view of others behind the one closed door.

Garz was listed as a village on her map, but on arriving she understood it was a small village, possibly forty houses spread across the flat ground. There were no straight passageways between the homes that could be considered a street or an alley, and she wondered how the people kept track of their property lines. There were no fences, and none of the houses rose above one level, although one or two had several extra courses of adobe bricks making them stand out. Like the countryside, the homes of Garz looked like the dirt.

All the houses sat in the open away from the hillocks that overlooked them. The low hills were outcroppings rising above the flat ground and somehow supported plant life. Scrubby and gnarled trees covered them. Away from the hills and east of the village, cultivated fields ran for about a quarter of a mile. The fields were bisected by irrigation canals that carried water diverted from the Helmund River. Hand-dug canals wended through the fields and water was distributed through a series of manually operated gates. Gates were opened, fields flooded, and gates were closed. Knowing how water rights in the United States were fought over, she wondered how the sharing took place among the Afghans.

The two policemen from Kandahar who rode along with the marines guided them through the patchwork of buildings. People looked up from their work but didn't seem alarmed. They had seen soldiers and other armed men come and go and were sure they would outlast these new arrivals. They could not stop and think what the Americans might bring. They were too busy scratching out a living. The Garz inhabitants were Barakzai Pashtun and were allied with the Dawad family.

The buildings that the marines were to occupy were the former administrative building and the mosque of a sect that had not been accepted by the Taliban. Both buildings were in disrepair, left standing as monuments to the impotence of all things not Taliban. They sat on the edge of the collection of homes that had obviously received the wrath of the Taliban, who were intent on destroying the old order and things associated with it. From the exterior appearance and the number of bullet holes, it was evident that the Taliban had driven off the former occupants. The roofs, or the better parts of them, were gone, looking like they had been torn off. Neither building had doors, and stone floors were contoured according to the thickness of the stones used.

Fran noticed that there was no plumbing. She wasn't worried about washing, but she knew that relieving herself would be more difficult than for the male marines. She saw "honey pots" in the corners, but there was no privacy.

Being a staff officer, she had no control over the marines. They reported to and responded to the gunnery sergeant. He was the operational commander, and she was an observer. Jake had handpicked Gunnery Sergeant Moreno because he had the flexibility to adapt to a convoluted officer-enlisted relationship. Moreno, a short swarthy young man in his early thirties, knew the limits of his authority and was smart enough to bring Fran in on his decisions. He was in charge and was the final authority, but he always listened to her and measured her input.

He broke up the squads and assigned them to a building, and each was responsible for fixing up their area. He didn't tell anyone what he wanted done; he let the marines figure out how well or how badly they wanted to live.

Fran was assigned to the larger admin building, and after looking at the situation, Moreno asked her what kind of privacy she would require in the all-male unit. She didn't require a lot and was given help in installing a barrier wall that she could live behind.

As an officer and a woman, the marines didn't expect her to work and appreciated that she pulled her load. While they were working, Fran took off her utility blouse and worked in her khaki T-shirt, exposing herself as a woman. The locals, who couldn't be bothered to look up when the marines arrived, gathered to observe. No women were in the group that came forward, and Fran couldn't tell their mood. She didn't care. She would try to educate them at another time. At that moment, she had to get a place to sleep ready before it got dark.

As the sun dropped below the horizon, several of the homes

showed light, and from its yellow hue, the marines assumed that the locals were using kerosene lamps. With fuel a precious commodity, the lamps went out quickly, leaving the village unseen.

The marines kept their generators running and left their lights on for only a short while so that they wouldn't annoy the population. As Fran lay in the dark she tried to figure out how she might accomplish her job of trying to reach out to women. If the men she had observed were an indication, that might be an insurmountable task. In a sleeping bag that wrapped her in cocoon-like warmth, she found no answers.

Young boys were allowed to move about freely, and in the early morning one was curious about the Americans and came near. The marines were outside sitting with their backs against walls eating MREs, and the boy didn't run away. When Fran came outside, he froze. He had never been alone in the presence of a woman other than those in his family. He had never seen blonde hair and was transfixed. As his eyes followed her, he was both fascinated and scared.

Smiling at his curiosity, she went inside to retrieve her computer. Fran had used cartoons in Kandahar's more sophisticated society as a way to break the ice with young people, and placing her laptop on a fuel drum, she turned it toward the boy and inserted a disc.

In seconds, the roadrunner and Wiley coyote appeared. The boy stood rapt. When the cartoon finished, she stepped forward and selected replay. After the second time through, the boy ran away to return with every boy too young to work in the fields. They all rushed to the barrel, and Fran obliged them with another showing. The young minds hadn't yet been soured with the prejudices of their elders and were inquisitive enough to laugh in the presence of the strange woman. As they awaited a replay, Fran borrowed a boom box from one of the marines, who had brought the large black box to Garz to entertain and annoy his comrades, who were tied to their personal music through earphones. She inserted a cassette tape she had brought from Kandahar of Copland's *Fanfare for the Common Man*. The strident melodies enthralled the boys even though the audio system didn't do the music justice.

She replayed the music before she stepped forward and ended the entertainment. The boys' eyes were wide in amazement. Fran had seen the reaction in Kandahar where she had used the same tactic. Finding the policeman Gul had sent along, she told him to tell the boys that she would give them a show at the same time the following day.

Before the sun rose, she could hear the commotion outside the building. In the gray before dawn, she saw boys eagerly waiting, but, surprisingly, their fathers were with them. She waited for daylight and emerged with the laptop. Using the same barrel, she set up the cartoon. The boys, having seen it previously, were ready to laugh while their fathers stood back and tried to figure out what was happening. She gave them a replay before inserting the music into the boom box. She inserted a cassette borrowed from one of the marines and didn't know what to expect. She couldn't identify the music, but it had a loud and strong beat with unintelligible lyrics. It didn't seem to matter; heads bobbed up and down rhythmically. Some of the Garz men had been to Kandahar and had heard music other than that which they could sing or play on rustic instruments, and the pulsing noise gripped them. In a brazen move, Fran had the police interpreter tell the men to bring their women, and she would provide more music. The suggestion didn't go over well. Men talked among themselves and left.

The children continued to come to the morning show, and she provided the full array of the cartoon library that she could borrow from the marines at Kandahar. When she had the men and boys hooked, she started weaning them off the full showing, cutting it down to one cartoon and one song. During the day men would come by the building to see if there was entertainment. She didn't oblige them, and made it clear that if they wanted more, they had to bring women. She sweetened the pot by having the interpreter tell the men that she had music that had been approved by the imam in Kandahar.

The standoff was broken after three days, when burqa-clad women dressed in black from head to toe were herded by their husbands and fathers into an area near the barrel. The women looked like monuments of death. They had to stand behind the men, but they were there with their heads bowed as if ashamed to be in daylight. She played Islamic music, with its atonal wails, but it captivated the women. She watched and saw heads rise surreptitiously. She couldn't see eyes behind the mesh serving as faceplates, but the holes looked at her. Hoping not to alienate the men, she stepped forward inserted the musical score from the movie *Titanic*. She wanted the women to hear the voice of Celine Dion singing "My Heart Will Go On." The Afghan women would not understand the words, but they would identify the beautiful voice as that of a woman. It might give them pause to think that women could achieve things. There was no denying the impact. Faceplates rose to look at Fran. The moment of freedom didn't last long. Male relatives, thinking that they might lose control, led their women away with their heads bowed.

A squad of marines worked helping the police officers Gul had sent along repair buildings, mostly Dawad properties, while Fran served as an observer with the squad that patrolled around Garz. Where she could, Fran made contact with the locals. Her advances were not always rebuffed, especially when she and the marines provided muscle power in helping the Afghans repair dikes and levees. After years of Taliban neglect, the ancient watercourses needed repair, and the marines had the manpower and equipment to help, but the thing the marines provided that was more welcomed than their labor was entertainment. Every two days trucks would arrive with resupply, and the trucks carried discs of anything that Fran could scrounge up. She let the morning crowd hear rock and roll, country western, classical, and rap. It made no difference what she played; the audiences continued to return.

Other than being a master of ceremonies, Fran was making only minor inroads to the women. With time on her hands, she started looking for things to do, and she roamed with the squad searching the countryside. She was trying to figure out why the Taliban had so tightly controlled the area. From all outward appearances Garz had nothing of value that should have made it a place of Taliban interest. The water irrigating the fields was of value, but the agriculture around Garz was subsistence.

As days passed, the patrols ranged farther afield. Cutting through a gap in a range of hills miles north of the outcroppings west of Garz, the marines found an agricultural economy in full bloom. Poppy fields spread out in a colorful panorama across an irrigated valley. In the panoply of color, it was apparent that the land was too valuable to grow food on, and the little extra that Graz produced was needed to feed the poppy farmers. The puzzle of the Taliban hanging onto Garz was solved. Its people hadn't been beaten down for their religious beliefs. The people fared badly under the Taliban because their crops were required to feed the opium growers. As the poppies were the Taliban cash crop, they did everything they could to ensure that nothing interfered with the orderly flow of money. It explained why in Garz, where young men were required to work in the fields, there were none. The young men were cheap labor, slave labor, for the Taliban overlords who were addicted to the money opium could bring.

"Major," the sergeant squad leader said, "I think we'd better get out of here."

The squad quickened its pace to get away from the valley. They had stumbled onto something they all knew meant trouble and thought that by moving quickly they could outrun the discovery. In a loose scouting formation they passed isolated structures that made Garz look cosmopolitan. The bleakness was startling.

Moving close to one of the lonely homes, the marines stumbled on a scene that they couldn't ignore. A bearded man in a black robe and turban, the dress of the Taliban, was beating a woman lying on the ground with a wooden staff. None of the marines could understand her cries for mercy, but they were appalled at the brutality. The idea that the man still wore the garb of a Taliban made their decision to act easy. "I'm going to cold cock that mother fucker." One of the marines started to move forward.

"Wait a minute, corporal. Let me try." Fran walked directly to the man and stood within his striking plane. She didn't say anything but got in the way. He looked at the stick in his hand and thought about striking out, but she stood legs apart daring him. She caught his eyes, and he turned away. He was going to kick the woman on the ground, but Fran closed in on him. She was taller and menacing with the marines standing off to the side with their weapons ready. The man shouted something that sounded threatening and rushed off. Fran looked at the woman splayed on the ground. Her burqa was filthy. Dirt was ground into the fabric, and the faceplate was covered with fresh and dried blood. The woman was saved further beating, but the marines wondered what would happen to her when they left. She was out without her husband or whoever the man was who was beating her. It was a sin that couldn't be atoned. The woman would go back to her assailant and hope that he didn't kill her.

A young marine understood the dilemma. "Major, what are we going to do with her?" It was the question on everyone's mind. "That guy was probably a Taliban. We should have whacked him."

"He wasn't armed. We can't assume that he was Taliban." She gave them justification for not killing the assailant.

"We'd better get back to Garz before that guy gets his gun and comes back," one of the marines cautioned.

The plight of the woman hadn't been solved, and Fran didn't

know what to do other than help her to her feet. She didn't know how far her responsibility stretched, but she couldn't kidnap an Afghani, even if it was for her safety.

"Does anyone know what he was yelling?" she asked.

"He vows your death," one guessed.

"Great." Fran was sarcastic, but it was prudent to get away from the situation, and the marines started moving out. The woman stumbled along after them. The pace was rushed, but the woman, hunched over in pain, only fell back a short way. By following the marines, she was gambling with her life. To return after such a breach of custom was a sure death sentence. The woman was hurt, and her moans could be heard, but she continued to follow Fran like she was a lodestar.

"That's it." Fran stopped the marines. "We have to help her."

The decision was met with mixed emotions. It was the right thing to do, but some wondered if it was legal in Afghanistan.

As the marines tried to help, the woman cowered.

"She won't let men help her." The medic stated the obvious.

The job was defaulted to Fran.

The marines were moved away so that they would not see her uncovered. Fran had her sit on the ground and raised the burqa. The sight was repulsive, causing her to recoil. The woman or girl, there was no way to tell under the extreme swelling, must have suffered through many beatings. Among the newly opened sores there were black-and-blue streaks indicating old punishments. One eye looked as if would never be usable, and the mouth was unrecognizable as such. The lacerated, pulpy flesh was beyond Fran's expertise to handle.

"Doc," she called for the medic. "I can't do anything for her. See what you can do."

The woman tried to sidle away, and Fran stopped her. The medic was reluctant, but in seeing the woman's face, he relented. He spoke softly in his best bedside manner, and whatever he said seemed to soothe her enough for him to clean the wounds and put antiseptic salve on them. Fran suspected that the woman's body might be in the same shape and decided to get her to Garz and have her medevaced to Kandahar, where doctors could treat her.

In debriefing Gunny Moreno, Fran discussed the poppy fields and the idea that they would be something the Taliban would protect.

In the sunrise of a new day, something had changed. No local could be observed. Even children shunned the Americans, and the tension in Garz was palpable. The marines thought bringing the Afghan woman into the village might have been a mistake. She had been in Garz for no more than fifteen minutes before a helo arrived to take her out, but it was enough.

A tense day passed, and it was hoped with the night and some time away from the incident, the new day would be better. At dark, changes were noted. Not one lamp in any house was lighted.

"Something screwy is happening," Gunny Moreno confided to Fran. "We had better stay dark. We don't want to be the only lights that can be targeted."

The first mortar rounds hit after 0400 and indicated that those firing had good targeting information. A round hit close to the admin building, spewing dirt and rocks against its walls. Fran couldn't see anything but heard the marines grabbing their gear and rushing to fighting holes that girded the building. The overhead fire made that a bad choice, but no one seemed to care.

"We have to get out of here. Rendezvous at the point where the main aqueduct and the stem canal meet." She identified a landmark that all could find and could hear the marines scrambling to follow her instructions. In seconds after the marines had cleared their fighting holes, the mosque holding the other marines came under attack. The fuel drums used by the generators close against the walls took a direct hit. Flames and metal fragments sprayed in all directions, igniting the building. The fire flares provided light, and

Fran saw no marines exiting. In a moment of concern for those who might be trapped, she ran toward the burning building and had no trouble entering through a hole blown in the front wall. Finding dazed and wounded marines, she tried to coax them to move, but her words weren't getting through. Knowing they were conditioned to obey orders, she yelled at them, and they began to stir.

"Where's gunny?"

A marine pointed. Moreno was under a pile of rubble. In freeing him, his damaged leg and shoulder became evident. Another mortar round exploded, and debris flew through the house.

"Doc," she called to the medic, "take a quick look and tell me if we can move him." It was a wasted request. She was going to move him and the marines regardless.

"He's okay, but I'm going to have to get him someplace to work on him."

"You, you," she identified two marines. "Grab the gunny. Let's get out of here."

With all the marines assembled away from the targeted positions, Moreno was the only one who was out of service. There were several deep cuts and bruises among the others, but only the gunny had to be medevaced. The shelling continued and was shifted to seek out other targets. A generator and a truck were destroyed and in flames as mortar rounds continued to land in the open areas away from the buildings where the marine vehicles were parked. A mortar found a second truck, and it exploded skyward. It was apparent that the attackers didn't know or care that the marines had moved.

"Major, I had to knock the gunny out. He was in big-time pain." When the medic spoke, all the marines within earshot knew they were leaderless. Most of them were nineteen- and twenty-year-olds who had training in small unit tactics and knew how to fight. Falling back on their training, they wanted to assault the mortar positions. Fran listened to a plan being made at the direction of a twenty-year-old sergeant with the help of young boys.

When all was set, and the assault routes were laid out, Fran interrupted. "You can't attack. Whoever it is on the outcroppings will be shooting downhill. You can't stumble into their lines of fire at night. It would be suicide."

The young marines stopped, a pause that dampened their blood lust and allowed them to slow their thinking. They all looked at her, and, without a word, command was shifted. They would do as she instructed.

"Is anyone a forward air controller?" She asked, knowing the answer. She broke the silence. "Get me a radio."

When the radio operator got the gear operating, she called Kandahar and requested air cover.

The request calmed the marines. There were always two Cobra helicopter gunships on airstrip alert in Kandahar for contingencies such as the one the marines at Garz were facing.

"The people firing on us have been firing on the buildings and shooting up our equipment for almost an hour." She got a muffled concurrence. "I haven't heard any rifle fire, so I'm guessing that they are in position to harass us and destroy what we have come to represent in the village. I don't think they want a face to face." Again she received muffled acknowledgement.

Two Cobras called in and reported that they were about ten miles out and wanted targeting information.

Fran explained the ground situation. She gave the pilots the Taliban position based on directions from the burning equipment and requested that they take in specific run-in headings. She wanted the Cobras to keep the enemy tied down. The pilots were surprised to be receiving targeting information from a woman, but their job was to shoot things up, and they complied with her instruction.

With the gunships overhead, they could not find the target. That changed when a rocket-propelled grenade was launched at the lead helicopter. The smoke trail led the helicopters directly to the Taliban position. After the first aerial attack, Fran requested a longer interval between strafing runs. She wanted the helos on station for as long as possible and requested that the pilots call for another section of two helos to relieve them after they expended their ammunition.

"Doc, what's the gunny's status? Can we keep him here through the night? I'd hate to bring in a medevac with the Taliban able to shoot down on us." She spoke quickly and wanted answers in the same way.

"He's good to go until daylight, but those guys will be able to shoot down on us in the morning."

"They'll be gone before daylight." She paused and set her jaw.

Every marine looked at her.

"This attack is harassment. They don't want a fight, or we'd be engaged by now. Before daylight, they are going to have to get back to their safe haven." She composed her thoughts while faces looked toward her. "There is only one route they can take with the helicopters overhead. They will have to get to the vegetation and trees along the canals so that they will have cover. The closest point to the outcropping where they can make a run for it is in the low area where the canal seepage has allowed reeds to grow. If they can get there, they will have cover until they can get to the denser vegetation. We are going to have to beat them to that point and try to block their escape."

"Gunny can't be moved that far," the medic informed her.

"I'm leaving a squad here with the gunny, and I'll leave the radio so you can communicate with the helos. If these guys attack, the helos will be overhead to beat them back."

"What group do you want me with?" the medic asked.

"Doc, I want you with the gunny."

"Yes, ma'am."

"Does anyone have NVGs?" All marines had carried them to Garz, but in their want to escape the shelling, she didn't expect them to carry them out of the chaos.

One pair of NVGs was all that showed up.

"Okay. The ambient light is enough to let us walk over the flat ground. When we get to the reeds, you," she spoke to the marine with the NVGs, "will take the lead and guide us. Lead us to the edge of the growth closest to the outcropping. Do it slowly and quietly. Corporal," She spoke to the marine who would be in charge of the stay-behind group. "Do not expend your ammunition firing at the hills, because it will highlight your position, and I don't think they know where we are. If I'm wrong, you may need it."

It took over a half hour for the marines to reach a position in the reeds that Fran expected the Taliban to transit. The tall grass was interspersed with willowy bamboo that was difficult to push through. With no marine carrying chopping tools, it required making an opening in the growth and holding it open until the person in trail passed.

Reaching the forward edge of the vegetation, the marines lay abreast on the moist ground. Their bodies were in the grass, but their rifle muzzles were in the open, providing fields of fire.

The marines were eager. They had been in firefights in Kandahar and had always been at the disadvantage of not being able to see their enemies. With the odds in their favor, they relished the chance to fight. Fran had mixed emotions. Planning the trap had been exhilarating; springing it came with moral conflict. While planning the ambush, she had not thought ahead to the end result. People were going to die.

As the sun came up, she was going to be able to see the men she was going to kill. Nothing in her training provided her an ethos to be a killer and she didn't know if she was capable of telling young boys to pull the trigger.

Hulks of men could be seen scurrying toward her. They were slowed because they were transporting their mortar tubes. It looked as if they had expended all their ammunition because the ammunition bags they carried were empty. As they neared, she could pick out their features as human beings. The targets drew closer, and the marines fidgeted, waiting for her command. Fran's fingers danced over the safety on her M16 rifle. She didn't want to take it off because that meant she would have to use the weapon. Having only fired the M16 twice, both times in the sterile environment of the rifle range, where she was given commands to fire, she now had to make a decision. She held off, and with each step, the Taliban became more human. Her mind raced, seeking options. Thinking she might provide some warning and give the Taliban a chance to surrender, she understood that would put the marines in unnecessary danger. If the Taliban didn't heed her warning, they would know where the marines were located and could engage them. Some of them might be killed. She thought of some reason to hate the men in her sights so that she could act. In an indecisive moment, she dug deep for the image of the damaged woman's face. At that moment she nodded, and the firing erupted.

It was a quick fight—three enemy dead and six wounded. Fran was surprised that she didn't quaver. She didn't have time to worry about what she had done, only what remained to be done.

CHAPTER 40

THE PENTAGON, WASHINGTON, DC

Don Frieze was furious. The *New York Times* ran a story that had been tamped down for over a week at the Secretary of Defense's request, indicating that bin Laden had escaped. The story, based on information provided by unnamed sources, would be discredited, but it was sure to start members of Congress calling the Pentagon and asking questions. Frieze didn't want that because the questioning would be kicked up to the White House, and they would scramble to piece a story together that would placate the public. While he didn't consider the escape a bad thing, admitting that would be political suicide.

Spec ops reports he had been receiving for weeks indicated that the Americans didn't have enough assets on the ground to prevent bin Laden's walk across the Pakistani border. That would be a difficult story to spin, so the DEPSECDEF would have to deny any escape. He wouldn't address anything about bin Laden's location because everything about him was classified. Citing secret material would get him a free pass, but that would only provide cover for so long, and he needed a creditable story, something that looked like all efforts were being taken to capture the fugitive.

Having stopped General Franklin from planning a military operation in the area believed to be hiding bin Laden, Frieze didn't like the thought of having to change course. He did not want troops in the area, but he had to show that he was doing something. Thinking over his options, he decided that a military incursion, with the story line that the search was being expanded, would sell well with the public. An assault by a few extra troops would serve as a preemptive assault on the media's bin Laden story. He would further sweeten the pot by giving reporters first time access to the troops that would be involved in the operation. The freedom to talk to the troops engaged in combat would slake reporters' appetites for news from the war. Cameras would be allowed to follow Americans as they hunted the world's most hated man. None of the media allowed to go to Afghanistan would know for sure that bin Laden was gone, but they would buy into the stagecraft. Frieze thought that the reports of American forces failing to capture bin Laden after making what he would describe as a herculean effort would be an easy sell to the public. They would understand that the military had tried and failed.

He called Franklin to address the change in plans and didn't know what to expect. The general knew bin Laden was gone, and a futile assault wouldn't help the narrative he was trying to develop as a military commander.

"General," Frieze started when he had him on the phone, "we have to kill the reports coming out that bin Laden has escaped."

Silence greeted the opening gambit, but it was too important a matter to the DEPSECDEF to let the military man rebuff him.

"General Franklin, the White House is requesting that you run a sweep in the Tora Bora Mountains." Frieze put the full authority of the president behind his order.

"What has changed that makes a sweep so important now?" Franklin doubted that the president knew what Frieze was asking to be done, but he had no way of challenging him other than to call the White House directly, and he wasn't going to do that. He assumed that somewhere in the decision-making process the White House had approved a sweep but was distancing itself from it.

"The bin Laden story is breaking, and we need to be able to say that it isn't true, because even now we are planning an assault of Tora Bora to get rid of him."

"The CIA reports indicate that he is already gone." Franklin tweaked the civilian.

"That is debatable, but if we run a mission, that will prove or disprove it once and for all."

"I don't like it," Franklin cut in.

"Your likes and dislikes are of no importance. If you don't run this mission at my request, you will receive an order from the president, and I will personally recommend that you are relieved." Frieze wasn't going to play games. He was tired of the generals dragging their feet when it came to taking necessary actions. Franklin was the worst. He was in charge of a unified command and a geographic area in which a small and obscure war was being fought, and he wanted to make it into something much larger.

"We've got plans ready, but I want more troops involved."

Frieze shook his head in disgust. He knew all that was needed was the show of an attack, but he couldn't say that. He had to pretend that the sweep had importance so that it would play in the political-military circles in Washington. "How many?" He hoped the concession would appease the general.

"I want the about six hundred marines assigned to an army commander for the extent of the mission." Franklin was tired of the marines getting all the press in Afghanistan. He intended to split up the marines in Kandahar and place half of them under an army commander, so that in the big picture the army would be the senior command and would receive the credit.

The DEPSECDEF had shot down the request several times in previous discussions. The marines were getting accolades because they were accomplishing things. Jake Gregg was proving to be an outstanding commander. They had their differences, but Frieze could work with Jake on an intellectual level. He couldn't with Franklin, who barged ahead on intuition.

"Okay. You can have the marines," DEPSECDEF conceded. "Now, this has to be put together quickly. Here's what I want from you. Once this operation is completed, pull most of the forces out of combat operations and base them around the country in an alert status. The SECDEF wants troops there only for as long as it is going to take to set up a new government. So keep your numbers down. Work with me on this."

"I'll have my staff look at the numbers again." Franklin was willing to concede the point because he had won the battle for the marines.

The fog of war overtook the bin Laden story. The spec ops team that had located bin Laden and that had been asking for support in capturing him reported that he had fled to Pakistan. The report was leaked, so the administration had to suffer through the embarrassment of having abetted the escape. It was a PR defeat that had its roots in the failure to consider Afghanistan a battleground. Before the press had a chance to uncover the full extent of the failure, an upbeat military story was required to overlay and bury the report. Chasing the news cycle that the administration was falling behind, the mission to capture bin Laden was changed to a mission to kill and capture high-value Taliban targets in the Shahi Valley, an area where the border was indistinct and where people crossed from country to country with impunity. The story to capture high-value Taliban was rolled out with a lot of noise and publicity, so much so that it made the bin Laden escape seem insignificant.

When the CENTCOM staff was given the change in plans, they were on a short timeline and scrambled to put something together. In his brusque manner, Franklin told the staff that he wanted the revised plan on his desk the following day. The staff shook their heads. It was no small job, and there was little time to think about the refinements that would be required with a different objective. Trying to keep the general happy, they cut and pasted the names and the locations from Tora Bora to the Shahi Valley. The name bin Laden was exorcised and replaced with HVT, high-value Taliban. The troop lists weren't changed, but a scheme of maneuver had to be developed quickly. The officers at sea level in Tampa assumed a sweep of one mountainous enemy redoubt would be like any other. They accepted that there would be holes in their plan, but it would be on Franklin's desk in the morning.

CHAPTER 41

KANDAHAR

"Can I come in?" Fran looked into Jake's bunker.

"Sure. I've been meaning to talk to you." He smiled as he looked up. "You did a great job. Gunny Moreno made it a point to debrief me before they medevaced him. He paid you the highest compliment possible among grunts. He said he would serve with you anytime."

The words didn't affect her. She stood in front of his desk.

He saw the tension in her eyes. "Sit down." He assumed a dual role of commander and friend. "Is everything all right?"

"I've had a couple of bad days. I haven't slept."

"The doc will give you pills. They'll put you to sleep."

"It's not that." She stared straight ahead.

"Let me guess? You're having problems with your actions at Garz?"

She nodded, without looking at him.

"It helps to talk these things through."

She didn't speak, and Jake wasn't about to rush her.

Fran didn't know where or if to begin. She couldn't imagine any of the male commanders coming in and looking for advice after a firefight. She had acted like a marine but had thoughts that were internalized, and she couldn't put them out of her mind.

Jake tried to ease her into conversation.

"I've read the after-action reports, and I put you in for a Bronze

Star. I've got a feeling this isn't about awards. It's about the aftershock of killing at close range."

"I don't know why it's affecting me this way," she confided.

"This isn't a Fran Matthews thing. Every rational person who experiences what you have has similar doubts. Did I do right? Was there another way? Was there a moral justification? There are a thousand nagging questions you ask yourself, because until that point you haven't had to make the decision to kill someone. It is even worse when the killing takes place at close range, where you can see the faces of those who are going to die." Jake spoke softly, hoping to break through her remorse. "Am I getting warm?"

"Yes, sir."

"Look. Everyone who has done what you did feels guilty, and the guilt that haunts most is the idea that when you were going through it you felt exhilarated. It is an emotional rush you feel you shouldn't have had, and now you are having a hard time understanding it. How can I, me, a person who dislikes violence, have felt so juiced when it was happening? At the time, you probably thought yourself so powerful you felt as if you were going to explode. But you didn't. Your head did as the moral and ethical ramifications of your actions returned and replaced the high. You wondered if there is a core of evil within."

Fran was stony. Her emotional roller coaster was exactly as he described, but she didn't want to admit it.

"Your feelings are no different than anyone in combat who has pulled the trigger. You learned that this isn't a game, and you also learned from the mortar attack that those you killed might not have felt remorse over your death." Jake stopped and watched her to see if his words were getting through. "What you felt is inherent in mankind, because we are only an eighth of a genetic strand from dragging our knuckles. No matter how sophisticated we kid ourselves that we have become, warfare, especially close-in combat, lets prehistoric emotions bubble. So you felt a spike. What differentiates good commanders from killers is that the good ones know when to call it off. Your stopping the marines from killing the people you took as prisoners indicates that you did what you had to do in entering the fight and then in winding it down, because one of the most difficult things to do when young marines get on a killing jag is to control them. They don't want to let go of the adrenaline high." Jake looked at her. "Fran, you acted as I would expect one of my commanders to act. I'm proud of you. The troops are proud of you, and they know by your cool handling of the situation both in Garz and during the attack that you saved their lives. As a marine commander, you could do no more."

"Thank you, sir." She looked at him.

"Did any of that help you?"

"Yes, sir."

"Now are you ready for a laugh?"

She nodded affirmatively.

"I put you in for a Bronze Star and a Combat Action Ribbon. The Bronze Star is still in the works, but the awards board wants me to soften the language and just mention the heroic things you did in organizing the marines while you were under fire. They don't want the fact that you engaged in a firefight mentioned. The Combat Action Ribbon is being denied, because women aren't allowed in combat, and if you get the CAR, it will indicate that you were. I told higher headquarters you led our most successful military operations to date, and they said that you couldn't have, because women aren't allowed in combat. Does that help wipe a bit of the remorse away?"

"Yes." A smile appeared at the corners of her mouth.

"I'm not through with this. I'm going to keep submitting you for the recognition you deserve. If I become too big a pain in the ass, the worst they can do is fire me."

"Don't do that. We need you here." She almost slipped and spoke in the first person singular. Fearing to show her feelings, she stopped talking.

"Your stumbling into the poppy fields has had other beneficial effects. I've reset my dealings with Dawad, because he is obviously involved in the poppy cultivation in some way. I have already pressed him for concessions to allow marines in areas farther out from Kandahar. Since he has agreed, I can assume he is neck-deep in the poppy operation." Jake could see that the chatter was bringing her around, and he didn't know whether to broach a subject that she would be interested in, fearing it might cause her to become morose.

"The woman you rescued was hospitalized, and the reports I have received indicate that she is going to make it. The doctors said she had internal bruises but no organs were damaged. I don't know how she managed to follow you out of her husband's house, but she did."

"What will happen to her when she is released from the hospital?" Fran didn't want to admit it to herself, but the abused woman was part of her reason for taking on the Taliban. "She can't be allowed to go back to her people."

"With no facilities for women in her situation, I've put pressure on Dawad to open a school for girls to teach them skills that will enable them to survive on their own. He's addicted to our cash, so when I upped his take of what we bring into the country, he agreed."

"Is that legal?" She was concerned that he had overstepped his bounds.

"This isn't about legality. There are imperatives that in my mind exceed what we consider right and wrong at a particular point in time. The women here have neither justice nor dignity, and if by paying Dawad with goods and money that are slipping through the cracks allows that to change, I'm willing to take the chance." Jake stood and walked to her side. He placed his hand on her shoulder. "Feeling better?"

She reached up and laid her hand on his. They said nothing but knew they had experienced more than a counseling session between a commander and subordinate.

CHAPTER 42

CENTCOM,
TAMPA, FLORIDA

The plan for the raid in the Shahi Valley, Operation Conda, was the CENTCOM staff's handiwork, but it had Franklin's fingerprints all over it. He wanted a grand sweep through the valley that would be an epic show. He wanted it so badly no one on the staff dared question the plan's deficiencies. All staff members agreed with his ideas because doing so made their lives easier. The size of the force was directed out of the deputy secretary's office, where the numbers of troops used was tightly controlled. The Pentagon was intent on preventing the raid from developing into an elaborate spectacle, and the regiment that Franklin wanted to use was downsized. Essentially, two unsupported light battalions would enter the valley and conduct a sweep that would either capture high-value Taliban or allow the Pentagon to say the area was cleared.

The back and forth between Washington and Tampa slowed the planning, but it moved forward under its own bureaucratic inertia. Finally, in an effort to develop good news, the plan was rolled out, and the staffs in both cities were in self-congratulatory moods. Each had given something but got some of what they wanted, and no obstacles were encountered until the plan reached Kandahar.

In seeing the final product, Jake called Grady Hatton and informed him that he was not going assign marines to an operation that had all the earmarks of a second Charge of the Light Brigade. He unequivocally told Hatton that he wasn't going to allow six hundred marines to be sacrificed carrying out a flawed plan. The discussion between Jake and the director of operations wasn't heated. Hatton had no emotions vested in the planning, but he informed Jake that General Franklin and DEPSECDEF had approved the placement of the marines in the troop lists. Hatton thought that by telling Jake that he was receiving a direct order, the marine might soften his tone, but Jake didn't budge. Hatton had been through ethics classes where disobeying suicidal orders on moral grounds had been discussed, but he had never heard of a commander who stood up to the system.

Hatton was stuck. Not wanting to face Franklin's wrath, he called Don Frieze in for a "work-around" to the marines' obstruction.

The DEPSECDEF took his call because he was receiving blowback on using marines, as called for in the plan, from the marine headquarters in Washington.

"We can't delay Conda," Frieze informed Hatton. "We have rolled this out with the president's approval, so it has to happen. He'd get crucified if we canceled the mission after letting bin Laden escape."

"I understand that, but Gregg has flatly said he will not chop troops to the mission."

"Keep pressuring him, and I'll try to work with the marine commandant again." Frieze had spoken to the commandant, who had backed Jake, and he was grasping for a solution. "I don't think that we will be able to move the marines off their objections, but we have to try. As a fallback, I am going to go directly to the Special Operations Command and have them hire indigenous Afghan troops that can replace the marines. Whatever you do, do not make a fuss over the marines being dropped out. We can't have this blow up into an interservice fight and have Congress get involved. I know General Franklin wanted the marines, but we have to get Conda operational; a lot is riding on it."

Hatton knew the only thing riding on Conda was the storyline that the administration was being forceful in hunting down the Taliban. "I'll work Gregg again from my end, and I hope you have luck with the Marine Corps." Hatton signed off.

In three days of hasty and heated communication between CENTCOM and Kandahar, no solution was found, but SOCOM identified Afghan forces that could be used in the battle. They were from a tribe that had been used during the offensive against the Taliban, and were willing to commit to further combat for a price. With the army battalion and a battalion's strength of Afghanis, Hatton had the strength on the ground that Franklin and the Pentagon agreed would be involved at Shahi.

During the final planning sessions for Operation Conda, Franklin was out of Tampa on the speaking circuit, giving after-dinner talks, and he wasn't involved with the details of the operation. In his absence, it was easy for the staff to work in the changes that would allow the plan to move forward with the Pentagon's approval.

Scheduling the final briefing in the CENTCOM conference room just before Franklin's golf game, a time when his attention would be on other things, Hatton hoped to get the plan approved so that it could be implemented. The director of operations briefed the scheme of maneuver without ever identifying the units that would be involved.

It worked for a while, but Franklin had a keen interest in the marines.

"What unit is Gregg going to chop to us?"

Hatton squirmed in his seat, and the entire staff had something to read on the table before them.

"What the fuck is going on?"

"Sir," Hatton spoke in a calm voice, "the marines are not in the final troop list and DEPSECDEF's staff has approved the change." Hatton identified the Pentagon as having approved the plan in an attempt to mollify his boss.

"I specifically said I wanted marines. What the hell are you telling me?"

"I spoke to General Gregg about chopping some of his forces to General Atkins for the raid, and he said to do so would jeopardize the operations at Kandahar. He said taking that many troops from his area of responsibility would leave him with too few to defend his area."

"I'm the over-all commander for Afghanistan. I say what troops are supposed to be in which area."

"I mentioned that to him, but he refused to make any marines available."

"Everybody out." Franklin cleared the staff from the room. "You get me that mother fucker on the line right now. I'm going to tell that bastard how CENTCOM works."

Franklin didn't leave the conference room, and he paced angrily while the call was placed.

"General Gregg on the line, sir." Hatton gave his boss a heads-up. Franklin indicated with his thumb that Hatton should leave him alone.

"General," Franklin started with a friendliness that was acted, "what's this I hear about you wanting to take the marines out of Operation Conda. When my staff told me that, I assumed they had made a mistake." He stopped and left it up to Jake to explain.

"When marines fight they do so as a combined arms force. The Conda Plan has them fighting as unsupported infantry. There are no provisions made for air cover or artillery support, and placing unsupported infantry in the Shahi Valley would be suicidal. I can't put marines' lives on the line in a flawed plan." Thinking that Franklin would have known all that he was talking about, Jake was calm in refusing to accept his superior's lead-in.

"That's all well and good, General, but it is not what's going to happen. I'm tired of sitting back and watching the air force and spec ops get all the glory in Afghanistan. This is a war in which the infantry should be calling the shots, and we are going to do that. The marines and the army are going to make that sweep and take control of the battle space." Franklin stopped to see if he had convinced Jake.

"It won't work. Putting a ground force in the Shahi Valley without a full package of combined arms is a recipe for disaster. I can't buy into that."

"Who in the hell do you think you are talking to? You work for me, asshole. You'll goddamn do as I order, and I'm ordering you to cut the marines loose to an army command."

Jake was stuck. If he didn't do as Franklin threatened, he was done in the military. He thought over the Conda OpPlan and saw no way in which anything could be achieved without unwarranted casualties. In good conscience, he couldn't commit marines to a suicide mission. "General, I understand that I work for you, but part of my job is to give my advice. The advice I would offer is that Conda is a disaster waiting to happen. Troops committed in the valley will be cut apart unless they have supporting arms with them."

"I looked over the plan, and I say it is what infantrymen do. They fight."

"The other part of my job is to refuse to accept orders that are ill founded, and the plans for Conda are insane." Jake was unemotional. He wasn't fighting for his job; he was fighting to keep a lot of marines alive. "Conda risks the slaughter of American troops for no gain. The strongholds you want to capture have no strategic importance. Every intelligence report from spec ops personnel serving there indicates that the high-value Taliban have flown the coop. Conda is merely attacking an unimportant position because we can. I don't have the marines to waste on that." Jake exhaled. As the words blew out, he knew he had taken a stand from which there was no retreat.

"You son of a bitch. You're through as a commander. I'm going to fire you, and see that the Marine Corps dumps you. How's that for your righteous bullshit? You're done." Franklin slammed down the phone, and Jake sat stunned "That went well," he said sarcastically to Jim Mackey, who was sitting with him and heard only one end of the conversation.

"You are going to get hammered." Mackey stated the obvious.

"You have to wonder what went on in the planning sessions for Conda. No one thought it out. I've got a feeling it is a bone the staff is throwing to Franklin because he sees the army getting shut out. He's pissed because spec ops are doing all the work, and the Special Operations Command is blowing him off and is getting all of the credit."

"And now you've blown him off, but you don't have a command structure to protect you." Mackey was worried about his boss.

"Mack, I don't have a command structure, but somewhere in this cesspool common sense has got to count for something." Jake didn't seem concerned.

CHAPTER 43

THE PENTAGON, WASHINGTON, DC

General Franklin rarely flew to Washington to see Don Frieze, but he needed DEPSECDEF's horsepower behind him in his efforts to get rid of the marine. In a building where people fretted over how people acted toward them, Franklin was told to wait in Frieze's outer office. A four-star general, used to people opening doors and currying to his every whim, waited and stewed. Sitting in his crisp uniform with ribbons streaming down his chest, he knew Frieze was playing games, and he resented it.

When he was told he could enter, Franklin rose to his full height and puffed himself up so that he would tower over Frieze.

"Come on in, General Franklin. Have a seat. I'm sorry I had to keep you waiting, but I was on the phone with the president. It was a call I had to take." The inference was supposed to impress.

"Your staff told my people that there are problems with the marine participation in Conda and that you want to change the command structure." Frieze was being diplomatic.

"You're goddamn right I want changes; I want Gregg fired. He disobeyed a direct order, and that bullshit doesn't cut it. He has to go." Franklin was not in the mood for soft selling.

"Suspecting that you wanted Gregg gone, I did a little background checking. I spoke to the commandant of the Marine Corps and told

302

him that you wanted marines involved in Conda, and he agrees with Gregg that if the marines are used they will go as a combined arms team. He prefers marine combined arms but said any combination of air support and artillery would be acceptable. He said that is the way marines train and that is the way they fight. He pretty much echoed Gregg's position."

"Fucking marines." Franklin was stymied but only for a minute. "This is the military, and the last time I looked, Gregg was under my operational control. The Marine Corps doesn't have a say in this. I gave Gregg an order. He refused. Disobeying a lawful order is a court-martial offense. If I can't get him relieved, I will bring him up on charges. Tell that to the goddamn commandant. See if he wants his fair-haired boy dragged before a court?"

Everything Franklin said was correct, but the DEPSECDEF couldn't have an interservice fight breaking out over Conda. It was a mission designed to divert media attention and to keep them busy and hopefully happy. A fight between the services would make his stewardship of Afghanistan look bad and might focus attention on that country.

"Cool down, General. Think this thing out." Frieze hoped to talk Franklin from the brink of doing something that he considered stupid.

"He disobeyed my order."

"And I agree that is a breach that has to be addressed. I will fly to Afghanistan and speak with Gregg and try to get him to go along with your plans for Conda. Whether he does or not, I will get rid of him. I don't need him interfering with future plans."

"Why don't you just give me the okay to fire him now?" Franklin wanted the immediate satisfaction of destroying Jake.

"That won't be easy. He is the star of the American efforts in Afghanistan." Frieze mentioned Jake as the star to irritate Franklin. "We can't relieve our best general. Let me set him up, and then I will pull the rug from under him."

"What are you going to do if you can't talk him into giving me the troops I need?"

"Even if he does provide the troops, I intend to get rid of him. However, knowing him, getting him to agree may prove difficult, so conduct Conda with the Afghan partisans SOCOM hired." Frieze hoped he had given Franklin enough to make him back away from his request for an immediate dismissal.

"I'm going to hold you to that. If we can't get rid of him for disobeying orders, we will get rid of him for incompetence or something. I do not want to see his name as one of the commanders I have to work with if we enter Iraq."

"We are going into Iraq, and you won't have to worry about having Gregg around." Frieze's confidence on both issues was enough to make Franklin think he had accomplished what he had come to Washington to do.

CHAPTER 44

KANDAHAR

The party from Washington landed at Kandahar in the middle of the night, and, as was custom, the senior member of the party deplaned first. DEPSECDEF stepped to the tarmac and was greeted by Jake and several marines.

"Welcome to Kandahar," Jake greeted Don Frieze with an extended hand.

DEPSECDEF obliged and shook it.

Standing at the base of the jet stairs, Jake had an opportunity to look at other members of the party who were deplaning. He hoped to see familiar faces, people with whom he had worked, but military personnel were missing from the entourage. Frieze traveled with representatives of the major defense contractors. He was going to expose them to the war and let them determine which parts of it they wanted.

"We don't have great quarters for you, but they are adequate for sleeping. We have briefs set up for you in the morning."

"I don't need sleep. This is going to be a refueling stop, because I want to be out of here before daylight. We've got meetings in Pakistan tomorrow." Frieze spoke of meetings as his reason for a quick departure, when, in fact, he wanted out of the war zone.

"Suit yourself. What do you need from us while you are here?" Jake suspected why Frieze had made the unnecessary stop and was not surprised when DEPSECDEF didn't want to know the situation on the ground.

"I need a place to talk to you privately."

"Sure. Mack, keep the people here and give them what they need. Mr. Frieze and I are going back to my bunker." Jake led the civilian to a Hummer.

Entering the bunker, Frieze couldn't believe how primitive it was. It was called the bunker because it had a dirt floor, but the building was in the same poor shape it was in when the Taliban left it, bullet holes and all.

"This is a pig sty." Frieze wanted to put the marine on the defensive.

"We are at war, you know."

"That is what I wanted to talk to you about. You refused to chop some of your forces to Operation Conda in direct violation of an order you received from your superior. Now, Franklin wants you fired, and I agree with him, but knowing you and liking you, I wanted to give you a second chance to comply."

"Don," Jake got familiar, "I didn't refuse to chop forces to Conda. I have told CENTCOM repeatedly that I would assign marines but only with adequate air and artillery support."

"Franklin doesn't think that is necessary and wants only ground troops."

"Therein lies the rub. Have you studied Conda?"

"I've read it and approved it."

"That's not like you," Jake looked directly at him. "You are usually quick to get on the winning side of things. We will not win if Conda is run the way it is planned. In fact, deploying troops into the valley without suppressive fires from both artillery and air is a recipe for catastrophe. I can't risk marines' lives in an operation that is doomed to fail."

Frieze was startled at Jake's bluntness. "Conda may have problems, but it is going to be run with or without you. I'm afraid that if it is run without you, you're done in the Marine Corps."

"My disobeying a legal order is not the issue. I am disobeying an ill-conceived order. I say that knowing what is in store for me, but that doesn't change my mind; I have the lives of marines in my hands."

DEPSECDEF realized he had no leverage. Jake wasn't a general who needed money and the follow-on job his rank would gain him in the defense industry when he retired. Jake Gregg didn't need the Marine Corps. The fact that he was serving his country at all was a conundrum. In the military, he only had influence commensurate with his rank. In the civilian world, he would have much more influence if he chose to use it.

In the times they had butted heads previously, Jake didn't move off positions that he thought correct. DEPSECDEF had to conclude that the marine believed in what he was doing, so he had to go. He would have to be careful in how he replaced him. It would take some finessing in Washington to separate him from the service, but he would do it. "Well, Jake I admire you for your conviction, but the only people you are going to impress are a bunch of kids who won't remember your name two days after you are gone."

"That's the way it should be." The comment surprised Frieze. Jake paused. "Before you rush head-first into Conda, take a look at this." He led Frieze to a wall where two map overlays of Operation Conda were stapled to keep them flat and readable. Troop dispositions and the order of battle, using the international symbols for different-sized units, were displayed along with arrows showing the axis of advance. "Have you seen these?"

"Of course."

"Do you know what they are?"

Frieze exhaled his disgust. "Yes, the map overlays for Conda."

"Take a good look at the one on the left," Jake instructed.

Frieze reluctantly complied. "They look the same to me." He showed his disgust at playing Jake's game.

"Read the instructions at the base of the left overlay."

On seeing the detail on the overlay written in Russian, Frieze balked and backed away.

"That is the Russian overlay for the OpPlan they used in Shahi, and it is eerily similar to Conda. They had air cover and were defeated. Do you think it is a good idea to repeat history?" Jake asked.

Frieze was speechless. He understood the looming disaster, and his mind raced with thoughts of how he might distance himself from it. He thought about having convinced the White House to approve the mission.

"Conda has been cleared by the president. It has to go as scheduled."

"You do know the Russians were routed in Shahi and suffered heavy casualties?"

"It is too late to change plans now. The White House has already leaked its intent to the press."

"You and Franklin may be right." Jake shook his head in revulsion. "It is time to relieve me of command, because I can't sit idly and watch this go down range."

"All the information you have on Conda is classified. You will speak to no one about it. Do you understand that? Conda is classified." Frieze was going to silence Jake.

"The Russian order of battle is in the public domain. Don't let this plan go forward," Jake cautioned.

"You will speak to no one about it." Frieze ended his visit.

The start of Conda was days away, and there was no time to relieve Jake before it went operational. Marines were replaced on the troop lists by hired guns, native soldiers offered up by Yousef Dhani, a warlord who had worked for the Americans in the war against the Russians. In previous battles in the American effort in Afghanistan, Dhani was paid, defeated in battle, retreated, and paid a second time to reengage the enemy that had driven him off his lands. Defeated a second time, he was paid a third time to hold his position and pledge not to join the Taliban.

George Ord provided Jake with the background information on the replacement troops.

"Who throws money at these people?" Jake was incredulous.

"We do." Ord referred to the CIA. "We were so unprepared for this war we bought anyone who said they would carry guns for us. A couple of the bigger crooks have had us bomb their competition under the guise that they were Taliban so that they could expand their fiefdoms. Dhani, we know, is one of the leaders of the Afghan mafia. They are crooks who make our guys look petty. Our deal is that he will help us drive out the Taliban for the small price of our looking the other way and not interfering in his operations." Ord was amused and repulsed at the same time.

"Is there any chance Conda can succeed with these troops?" Jake was concerned.

"Conda couldn't succeed if you put every marine you have at your disposal in Shahi." Ord shook his head. "There are two Australian SAS teams that have been playing cat and mouse with the Taliban entrenched in the mountains surrounding the valley, and they have been reporting that the Taliban are dug in, as they should be, with the twenty years they have had to prepare. The SAS boys have also reported that the Taliban have mortars registered on every potential target. Now, get this." Ord paused for emphasis. "The SAS teams have called for aerial bombardment of known Taliban positions in advance of any attack. CENTCOM has blown them off. Franklin wants to make this infantry only and feels that with a suppression bombing, the air force will get credit for cleansing the valley. The army and the Afghan hires are going to go in cold."

"It doesn't make sense. What the hell is Franklin trying to prove?"

"He has control over the army, the marines, and even the navy ships floating off the coast, but the majority of the war is being fought by spec ops and the air force. The general has a long-seated dislike of special forces. They are army, but they act independently. He wants to bring them back in under his wing, but they aren't having any of it. The air force, while being under his command, is flying long-range missions that they haven't given him control over. This Conda thing is all about reestablishing control." Ord stopped.

Jake needed a sanity check, and he called in Jim Mackey. He relied on the lieutenant's advice, because he always got an opinion that wasn't clouded with big-picture considerations. Mackey was close enough in age to the troops to be able to provide the gut feelings of people who were called upon to die at the whims of leaders who were removed from the action. War to the bureaucrats and their generals was a conceptual exercise, moving big blue arrows across plotting boards. They would watch the advances across hostile ground with no awareness of the severity of the ground or the fights going on for it. None of them would ever get dirt under their fingernails or be so scared they pissed in their pants. They made decisions and forgot about those left to die.

"Come on in, Mack." Jake invited the lieutenant in after he poked his head into the bunker.

"I'd offer you a drink, but you forgot to stock my ice chest." It was a joke. Jake had told Mackey from the very first that he was not to act in any capacity that hinted that he was an aide. He was to do none of the menial work of primping the general's uniform and keeping his schedule. Jake used him as a fixer. Got a problem with Dawad, send Mackey. Got a problem with spec ops, send Mackey. He was a lieutenant but in reality was acting as a chief of staff for an operational commander. It caused resentment with some senior officers, but Mackey didn't care. He considered that many of them could not see what Jake was trying to do, so he used the general's name to blow right by them. The other quirk in Mackey's personality that was considered an asset was his blind loyalty. That coupled with a hair-trigger temper made him effective in pushing through Jake's agenda.

"I come to the oracle, seeking advice," Jake said and pointed to a chair for Mackey to sit.

"The oracle is batting zero for today." Mackey laughed. "I just got off the phone with CENTCOM, and I think I told some general I never heard of to go fuck himself."

"You think?"

"Yeah. There were a couple of guys on the line; it might have been a colonel." Mackey shrugged.

"You are going to have a short career."

"I knew what I was doing. They were raising hell over your decision to blow off Conda. I went ballistic so that they would think your staff was so confused you were led into making a bad decision."

"I appreciate the effort to shield me, but I'm a big boy."

"Yes, sir, but when I listen to people who don't have an idea of what's going on over here bad-mouth you, I can't let it pass. You're the only general who knows the situation on the ground. Those serving under you know it, and those you serve don't."

"That's what I wanted to talk to you about. I want your opinion on Conda. You've seen all the planning, and I want to know if you think I've overstepped my bounds."

"You haven't had time yet to read the latest reports from the Aussie SAS teams in Shahi. They flat-out say, if Conda goes forward as planned, the troops are going to get whacked, and they suggested that the operation be delayed until air can prep the battle space. They used more diplomatic language, but reading between the lines it spells big trouble." Mackey stopped. "I'll get you the messages if you want to read them."

"I've seen variations of them for weeks, but you didn't answer my question."

"Don't ask me. Every marine here knows what is going on. Go

and grab any one of them, and they will give you an answer after they kiss you for having the balls to stand up in the face of idiocy."

"Thanks, Mack. I knew I could count on you to clear things up."

"Can I speak to the general?" Fran Matthews looked in.

"Yes, ma'am, sure." Turning to Jake, Mackey asked, "Did I answer your question?"

"Yup."

Jake didn't speak until Mackey was out of earshot. "What's up?"

"The rumor mill is churning and saying that you are going to be fired."

"That is a distinct possibility."

"They can't fire you." She was intense. "You are doing too many good things here."

"You know how that goes; one 'aw shit' erases a hundred 'atta boys.'"

"Don't joke. I don't want to see you get hurt."

He sensed that the conversation was veering to the personal, and he looked at her not knowing how to respond.

"The worst that can happen is that they will make me retire."

"Isn't there something you can do to stop the process?"

"Not unless I send marines on a suicide mission."

"There has to be some other way."

"Fran, I'll be all right. Being dumped doesn't bother me, because I will have done my job as I saw fit. I will—"

"Stop talking about yourself. The marines here need you. I need you." She didn't back away from her comment. "Yes, I need you. I love you."

"Where did that come from?" He knew there were star fuckers throughout the military, women that bedded generals just to say they had. It was like hanging a pelt on the wall, but Fran wasn't one of them.

"That first night, in your office at Quantico, I was sure you were going to try to bed me; when you didn't, I knew you were different.

It played with my mind until I couldn't stop thinking of you. Since I've been here, seeing you without ever getting a chance to tell you, it has driven me crazy. I knew you were busy and my feelings in all of this were unimportant, but you've become an obsession, one that I don't want to lose over a dust up with CENTCOM. I'm afraid that if you leave, I won't ever see you again."

"Fran, I really like you—"

"I just bared my soul to you." She cut him off. She had expected a more emphatic response, something that indicated her feelings were reciprocated.

"Sit down. Take a deep breath." He waited. She wasn't hysterical and looked at him.

"Since you brought it up, let's talk about that first night. It was the first time I had seen you out of uniform. You were stunning, and I wanted to jump your bones, but I couldn't. I wanted to use you to stop the harassment of women and the fraternization within the MPs, so I couldn't very well fraternize with you. I brought you to Afghanistan to do a specific job, but part of my requesting you here was that I wanted to be around you. I don't know if that is love, but it doesn't matter. As long as we are in the Corps, I will not consummate any feelings I have for you."

"Why not? I'm an officer, and I'm a consenting adult."

"I've got several thousand marines here, and if they even smelled that I bagged you, I would get a one-day burst of macho applause that would erode when they realized that I would hammer them for doing the same thing. Sure, fraternization happens; the rules are easily twisted to fit individual situations, but in each and every instance, the values that make the military an organization steeped in honor are eroded. When I order marines to risk their lives, I want them to comply with orders not because I have legal authority over them but because they respect me for complying with the same dumb rules of behavior that I ask them to follow." Jake looked at her to see if she understood. She didn't respond. "Look, you should know what

I'm talking about. When you were at Garz and the troops followed you, you had no legal authority over them, because women aren't supposed to be in combat. They could have blown you off, but they followed you, because they respected you. Does that make sense?"

She nodded. "Now that my feelings and our limitations have been exposed, what's next?"

"I'm going to be booted out of the Marine Corps, so I'll be free to hook up with you wherever you are. Then we can see if we can stand one another."

She smiled. "I'm sorry. I've been able to control this, but it all erupted when I heard what they were going to do to you."

"It's good that the air was cleared. I wanted to say something, but I was afraid if I told you what I was thinking, I would unlock feelings that I would not have been able to control. Now, we can plan to see if we can live miserably ever after." Jake helped her from her chair. "Come on; clearing the air before I get booted has made me feel better." He shook his head.

CHAPTER 45

SHAHI

Shahi Valley was a sandy expanse, forming a natural bowl about two miles in diameter between four mountain ranges. Its military value was that once through the eastern mountains, there was a pathway into Pakistan. That was the reason the Taliban held it. It was a place from which they could continue their fight and, if the situation on the ground got hot, escape.

The valley floor was over seven thousand feet above sea level, and the mountains surrounding it rose in places to fourteen thousand feet. A road crossed the valley on an east-west axis. It was as straight as a road could be across open terrain. The only irregularities in the straight line were sharp jags where the dirt roadbed gave way to natural depressions that had to be avoided.

Entering the valley from the west, the road descended about five hundred feet to the midpoint and climbed to leave the valley. Aerial photos gave the valley a flat appearance, but for the Aussie special ops personnel on the ground, it was more like a sink, and they cautioned the Conda planners that the most vulnerable point was at the base of the sink. They were sure that the plug would be pulled on any troops at that point. Issuing warnings through the spec ops chain of command, their message was blunted by CENTCOM. Men on the spot were told their advice wasn't needed because the planners were sure that the presence of a large American force would cause the Taliban to run.

One person who heeded the warnings was Don Frieze. After Jake's warning, he became more interested in the battle plan and, in reading the elevated warnings from the SAS teams, recognized there was a high probability of failure. He used the information to minimize embarrassment to the administration by calling off the media coverage. He didn't try to stop Franklin from making a blunder; the plan was too public to be scuttled. He felt a military setback halfway around the world would go unnoticed, especially with the media out of the way, and the blowback for a failed mission would stop at the military.

The assault troops massed outside of the western end of the valley were loaded onto trucks while the blocking forces moved into position. The assault force's intent was to drive into and across the valley at such a speed that they would be at the base of the Taliban strongholds quickly. So quickly, that the enemy would not have a chance to register their mortars. It was determined that the road was stable enough for the trucks to move out at about thirty miles an hour. A rapidly moving assault force of American and Afghan troops would be at the base of the Taliban lair, in close enough to fight their way into the mountain redoubt before the enemy awoke to the fact that they were under siege. As troops were engaged, a helo assault would swoop in from the east, trapping the Taliban between the two forces. With blocking forces north and south, the Taliban would be crushed.

The first trucks entering the valley were loaded with Afghan fighters, and they raced down to the base of the sink at the speed intended. Reaching the drain, they started climbing toward the Taliban before trucks carrying the Americans followed.

As the lead trucks slowed in the uphill climb, a remotely controlled land mine exploded and shattered one of them. The column stopped, and mortar rounds smashed into the road. The Taliban had their mortar fires registered. They knew precisely where the rounds would hit and started walking their fires back over the convoy. With no air cover or artillery to suppress it, the Taliban mortar fire continued unimpeded. The Taliban remembered the Russian assault, and when the helos started to land, mortar fire ripped the landing zone, destroying helicopters and men. Even the blocking forces came under fire, but it was the troops on the trucks that were doomed.

The Afghans jumped off the trucks, but on the barren valley floor, there was little vegetation to hide behind. Hired Afghan soldiers were hunted in the open by overhead fires. Their lines broke, and they started moving in disorganized groups back toward their entry point. The Americans loaded in the backs of trucks looked at the chaos they were nearing, and before they could pass judgment on the fleeing native soldiers, mortars started falling near them. In the first salvo, a dozen were dead or wounded. Confusion reigned, and like the Afghans, the Americans bunched and moved in clusters to get out of the valley.

The Australian SAS operatives that had been working in the valley expected the disaster they saw unfolding and were quick to get on their radios to call for air cover. It didn't come. Since CENTCOM had balked at using air assets, none were on hand. The most available aircraft were marine Harriers at Kandahar. Jake had expected the calls from the Aussie SAS and had the aircraft loaded and on standby on the runway, but even with their quick response, it was too late.

Panic gripped the American soldiers, who had weeks before been operating in the United States and weren't mentally conditioned to the brutality of war. In the chaos of battle, their officers exhorted them to maintain unit integrity. The orders went unheeded, and junior officers took the hint of the troops in seeking cover. When the commander of Conda informed CENTCOM that he was pulling back, his comments were met with disbelief. The staff in Tampa didn't want to hear excuses, and finally Franklin ordered General Atkins, the on-site commander, to get his ass back into the valley.

Atkins understood that if he went back into the valley, he would be going alone, because the troops, once safe, hunkered down.

Jake didn't receive all the reports, but he heard enough to know that he had been right to keep the marines out of the fight. He had been right, but he didn't feel good about it. The idea that such an assault was attempted spoke ill of the military and civilian leadership running the war.

"What a mess," Jim Mackey, who was standing next to Jake, said. He wasn't gloating. He was in a state of shock. He, like Jake, could not believe that military leadership had been in such short supply in planning the assault.

The mission that was supposed to be the cover for letting bin Laden escape wasn't mentioned in the press. Some reporters got snippets of Operation Conda, but they could not piece a story together because they were denied access to Afghanistan. The media were swamped with Pentagon and CENTCOM press releases about how successful the mission had been, and were told they would be allowed to visit the battlefield once all remnants of the Taliban were cleared out. It would be a couple of weeks before the massive aerial attacks ordered by CENTCOM destroyed the Taliban enough so that they left the area. The switch in tactics was not for public consumption. For all the press knew, the aerial bombardments were a continuation of the ground assault at Shahi.

In the Pentagon, Don Frieze couldn't blame Franklin because if he was discredited and the American public saw how nasty another war might be, they might not be able to be talked into going into Iraq. Bypassing Franklin, those within the Pentagon went after General Atkins, a general the public didn't know. He had been unable to carry out a simple plan and was retired quietly. Franklin was all for it. Making the field commander the scapegoat protected his reputation.

In the fallout from Conda, both Frieze and Franklin knew they couldn't relieve Jake. Two commanders relieved over the same operation would start an inquiry that would blow up the cover story.

If the press got to Jake, he might mention that his relief was over a disastrous mission that he warned against. The fear was that there had been enough back-and-forth communications that would back the marine's story. That might result in reliefs that reached into the Pentagon, so orders were dispatched "for his eyes only," in which Jake was informed in writing that all events surrounding Conda were classified. Included in the classification was the overlay of the Russian battle plan. The classification was compartmentalized so Conda could only be mentioned on a need-to-know basis.

With no one officially telling him that he could continue as commander in Kandahar, Jake went about his duties. He continued to engage remnants of the Taliban without specific guidance, and he pushed Dawad for more access to the people.

CHAPTER 46

KANDAHAR

George Ord came into the bunker unannounced.

"Well how does it feel to have dodged the biggest bullet in the war?"

Jake looked up, confused by Ord's words.

"What are you talking about?"

"You are not going to get relieved for disobeying orders. You are going to get promoted and kicked upstairs."

"What are you smoking?" Jake laughed. "That's never going to happen."

"Yeah, it is. Mind if I sit down?"

"Be my guest." Jake waited. "Now, was all the talk you just spewed to wake me up?"

"You know I get info out of Washington a lot quicker than you do, and the intelligence channel says you are going to be the new military assistant to the secretary of defense. They are even going to promote you to three stars."

"I don't believe it." Jake tried to put an end to what he considered crazy talk.

"Look, Jake, I have never led you astray. This is going to happen."

"It can't. I'm against everything the people running the Pentagon are setting out to do."

"You're one hell of a war fighter, but you know squat about fighting wars in Washington. Did you ever hear the old Eastern adage about keeping your enemies close? Well, they see you as an enemy, and they are going to get their arms around you. They are going to hold you so close they will suffocate you. You will have a title and will be shut out of everything, and they will have full control of you. You won't be able to speak to anyone about what happened here, and especially about Shahi. They don't intend to let you become a hindrance. You are going to become a three-star potted plant. You'll look good, but your input will count for zip." Ord painted a bleak picture.

"Are you sure of your sources on this?"

"Yes. You should be getting confirmation in a couple of hours."

"I can't do it. After what I've seen here, I can't pretend that things are being done with a purpose. I surely can't sit by as they plan for a war that doesn't have to be fought, because if this war is an indication, we will not have our shit together for a larger fight in Iraq." Jake's head was roiling. The military, the last institution in America that valued duty and honor, was selling out to the neoconservatives by remaining silent as they planned to change the world. He kept thinking about the young men and women who would die in an effort to prove the embeds' schemes right.

The substantiation of Jake's promotion came from an unexpected source. Abdul Dawad arrived at the bunker in his convoy of black limousines. Dawad was familiar with the layout and made his way right to Jake.

"Congratulations." Dawad swept into the small enclosure.

"Why am I being congratulated?"

"I am told that you will be filling one of the most important positions in your government." The Afghan was gushing, wanting to share in Jake's elevation, thinking that he himself might have played a part.

"Thank you." No word had arrived officially. Jake shook his head. If the intelligence community and an Afghan nabob had the same news, it had to be true.

"I don't think this would have happened without your helping me in Kandahar." Jake flattered Dawad.

The Afghan beamed. He had helped an American who was going to hold a high position in government. It would be a great business contact.

"You will be leaving soon, and I would like to have you open the new school for girls."

Jake thought about how his world was changing. Dawad had fought him in trying to prevent girls from becoming educated. The sudden change of heart was welcomed, but Jake suspected after opening the school, once he left, it would be closed. Still, the tokenism of opening a girls' school was important.

"It would be my distinct honor to open your school. I think since you were instrumental in starting it, it should bear your name." Jake hoped that if the school was named after Dawad, it might survive his leaving.

The idea was a hit.

The Mursal Dawad School, named after Dawad's mother, was not an impressive structure but was upgraded when it was determined it would memorialize the family matriarch. It resided in a formerly abandoned building that American labor and material had restored with mixed results. Bullet holes had been patched and doors replaced. Tarpaulins covered the dirt floor that retained the unevenness of the ground. The roof had been patched, and there were no light leaks, but the windows made it an impressive structure by Kandahar standards. The Americans did their best to supply the school with desks, and there were enough for each girl, but they were all different shapes, colors, and sizes. Someone found a blackboard and a rag hung over it, as no erasers could be located. The layout wasn't much to look at, and no one could tell if it was going to be able to help, but there it was, sitting off a side street displaying the Afghan flag.

With the dedication ceremony taking on the air of Afghan pageantry at the expense of American contributions, Jake, in his final act before he left for his new job, decided to put the Americans in the forefront. The women marines brought into country and who had served as role models would stand directly behind the official party. In his remarks, Jake intended to praise their work with the Afghani women. He talked with Fran about it, and she agreed, but she wanted to know about her situation personally. Even with Jake leaving, they would not consummate their relationship, but they agreed that once they got home and one of them left the service, they would. It was an unsatisfying solution that had to satisfy.

A procession of cars, of various manufacture, supplied by Dawad, carried persons to be honored to the schoolhouse. Dawad and his family exited the first vehicle, and Jake, Fran, Jim Mackey, and George Ord exited the second. A third carried all the women marines, and trucks full of marines followed as security for the ceremony.

The vehicles parked across the street from the school, where girls ranging in age from the teens downward stood to greet them. They wore powder-blue dresses with no leg showing, and each wore a white scarf covering her head. All exposed their faces in public, to the dismay of some of the local men. It wasn't going to be a popular ceremony, and the threat warnings that the spec ops teams had received in the days prior to it were cause for concern. The fact that Dawad didn't back down in face of the threats was seen as a good sign.

Five people playing sitars tried to add pomp to the ceremony, but to the American ears, the music was discordant. Jake marveled that Dawad had learned his lessons from the Americans well. TV cameras and reporters from Kabul and Kandahar, along with the Pakistani press, took enough pictures to lend an air of importance to the ceremony.

While the sitars serenaded the honorees, Dawad, Jake, and Fran stood facing the assembled girls. They were in line, and each would get a chance to go to the lectern, fashioned out of two-by-fours, that was to the side of the girls. A portable sound system sat on the ground under the lectern, but no one knew whether it would work, because the sound checks were a series of modulated squeals.

Standing and listening to music that seemed interminable, Jake became antsy.

He heard nothing above the musical noise, but Dawad, who was standing to his right, crumbled. Jake could see blood spray from his shoulder as he fell. Chaos overtook the crowd. All Jake could think of was getting Fran out of harm's way, and he spun in her direction, tackling her. As they were falling to the ground, he raised his right arm to shield her face. It was too late. The bullet meant for her was already in flight and entered his body under the armpit. The slug twisted its way through soft flesh and cut through his lung on the way to his heart, where it detoured and exited his back.

Fran understood what had happened and was glad that he had protected her. It was an act of love greater than any words he could have spoken. Her bliss lasted until she felt the warm wetness of his blood seeping onto her. She didn't know what to do. She couldn't force herself to push him aside. That seemed cold, and that wasn't the feeling she had for him. She felt another body pile onto Jake, trying to protect him. It was Jim Mackey, but he quickly realized the futility of his act and stood. He carefully lifted Jake off her.

The young girls had seen death, brutal death, all their lives and didn't run away. They watched Fran. Having seen the look of distress and despair on their mothers' faces over the loss of a husband or son, they could identify with what Fran was feeling. The anguish in her eyes was evident, but unlike their mothers, she didn't clutch the body of her loved one and wail, letting out her feeling in one cathartic act. She looked at Jake and fought back tears. It took a long minute before she realized she was the senior marine present and started directing marines, men and women, to enhance the security along the street.

One young girl watched Fran and how she functioned when her world was shattered and decided that she wanted to be like the American woman.

Fran had done the job Jake had asked her to do. She had opened the eyes of one young Afghan woman. It was a small victory, but if Afghanistan was ever going to move from its medieval roots, it would be a long, slow process of winning one small victory, one person at a time.

THE END OF THE BEGINNING